I0629713

SON OF A SAILOR

A COZY PIRATE TALE

MARSHALL J. MOORE

ATOLL PRESS

ATOLL PRESS, LLC

For the best sailor, storyteller, and man I have ever known.

I miss you, Dad.

1

Like most pirates, the crew of the *Bloody Angel* were not famed for their emotional intelligence.

So when Captain Redbeard emerged from his cabin for the first time in hours after receiving the black letter, their reaction was to "get 'im too drunk to remember he's sad," as the boatswain had so eloquently put it.

"On Me Life I Never," declared Ophelia, the *Angel*'s first mate, a rangy blonde with more tattoos than half the rest of the crew combined, "stole an Imperial Commodore's hat right off his head."

Of the other three players, only one drank. Quint Thatch, better known across the Eight Seas as Captain Redbeard, tipped back his bottle, the coconut rum so sweet he could hardly taste the faint sting of alcohol. They sat in a loose circle on the *Angel*'s deck, the cool night breeze blowing the ship over calm waters beneath a moonlit sky. Aside from those who had the watch, they were alone, the rest of their crewmates either sleeping soundly belowdecks or passed out in a loose semicircle around those who persisted in the game.

"My turn?" Quint asked, staring hard at the space between him and Ophelia as if he expected another player to have materialized there. True, there had been more players at the game's start, many hours past—a few lay scattered about the deck in various states of repose, whether it be cuddled up against one another like Darby and Vigo or leaning precariously against the rail like Bonnie Kate.

"Aye, Cap'n," said the player to his left. True to his name, Fillbrick the boatswain was an enormous rectangular block of a man, with a granite-deep voice to match. "Your go."

"Right." Quint nodded, then instantly regretted doing so as the ship rolled in a way that had nothing to do with the waveless sea beneath them. "On Me Life I Never, uh...fought a duel and lost."

"Liar." The fourth player pointed the neck of his own nearly empty bottle like an accusing finger at the captain. Rusty "Rustbucket" Russell was a short, scowling man whose bald dome reflected the moonlight with startling clarity. "What about that time you went ten rounds with the middleweight champion of Citrine, eh?"

"I'm not sure that boxing counts as a duel," Quint said, pressing a hand to his side in memory of the bruised ribs that match had earned him.

"Rustbucket's right," Ophelia agreed. Of the three, she'd been with Quint the longest; they'd deserted from the Imperial Navy together, once upon a time. "Any one-on-one fight with rules is a duel, in my book."

"Fine." Quint lifted both hands in acquiescence, tipped the bottle, and drank from it. "Right, then. On Me Life I Never tried to kiss my sister."

Ophelia and Fillbrick both turned to Rustbucket, whose face had turned almost as red as Quint's hair. "That was *one* time. And I didn't know...I mean, it was dark—"

"Drink, drink, drink," the others chanted in chorus. Grumbling, Rustbucket did.

"My turn," Fillbrick declared, his great square brows drawing together as he thought. Upon first meeting the boatswain, many thought him stupid, but they missed the mark. The wheels of Fillbrick's mind turned slowly but surely.

"*Turn!*" a harsh voice squawked. There was a flutter of wings, followed by the arrival of a parrot with vivid crimson-and-green plumage upon Quint's outstretched arm. "*Turn!*"

"Evenin', Jimmy," the captain said, grinning down at his pet as she waddled up his arm and onto his shoulder. "How're the skies?"

Jimmy nibbled his ear affectionately. "*Clear skies, nobody dies!*"

"I'll never understand why you keep that bird around, Cap'n," Rusty said, glaring at the parrot. The two had a long history of mutual dislike.

"Jimmy?" Quint blinked, as if there were some other parrot the crewman might have been referring to. "She was a gift when I first went to sea, given to me by my—"

"On Me Life," Fillbrick intoned, perhaps because he had finally selected a topic, or perhaps because he sensed the conversation veering toward the very reason they'd conspired to drink their captain into a stupor, "I Never dressed meself up in a Callinist nun's habit."

Ophelia raised her bottle, then frowned upon seeing that her captain hadn't done the same.

"What?" he asked her, tugging idly at his namesake beard. As far as he could recall (admittedly, not terribly far back at the moment), he had never been a novice to any monastic order, regardless of gender.

"You did do that," Ophelia reminded him. "At Blacksand, remember? That time you were hiding out in the convent—"

"Right, right." The captain combed two fingers through his beard, then took a swig from the bottle. Depending on where you stood, rum's ability to make you forget was either an annoyance or a blessing.

Tonight Quint counted it as the latter. The game had been going on since before sundown, and the watch-bells had last tolled ten—or was it twelve? That too was hard to recall.

He'd stopped counting bottles after the first half-dozen, embracing the rum's twin properties of numbness and amnesia. He'd drunk enough for the tips of his fingers to have grown pleasantly tingly and—as the game evidenced—enough to forget certain episodes of his highly checkered past.

Almost enough to forget the crumpled-up letter lying on his desk back in his cabin, and the black envelope it had arrived in, which in Her Majesty's Empire meant only one thing. Almost drunk enough to forget the message it contained.

His initial reaction upon reading it had been one of disbelief; that it must be some sort of deeply unfunny prank. His second response, almost as unreasonable, was that it was a mistake—that surely the message had been meant for some *other* Quentin Thatch, addressed to him by a mother who *also* happened to live on Ember Bay, whose father too was—

No, Quint chided himself. The truth loomed behind him like the edge of some fathomless cliffside, one he might slip and fall from at any moment. But so long as he kept his back to it, it could not hurt him.

"My turn," Rustbucket said, flinching a little as Jimmy flapped her wings while Quint swayed beneath her. "On Me Life, I Never held the Governor of Tellego's daughter for ransom."

"These are starting to feel very pointed," Quint objected, though the bottle was already to his lips. "And you helped with that one, as I recall."

"All I did was blow a hole in the wall." Rustbucket tugged on his own beard, a single long orange braid like a bomb's fuse. "You're the one who actually ransomed her."

"That's not all he did," Ophelia muttered, raising her bottle to her captain in salute. "Cap'n Redbeard, scoundrel of the seas, ravisher of—"

"Hey now!" Quint frowned at his first mate, though his eyes were beginning to have trouble focusing, especially since there now appeared to be three of her. "I ain't never ravished anyone who didn't explicitly ask to be ravished."

"Wait your turn," Ophelia said. "And speaking of ravishing: On Me Life I Never courted a commander in Her Majesty's Imperial Navy—"

"I didn't know she was in the Navy!" he protested, but upended his bottle regardless. Considering the state he was in, the amount that actually made it into his mouth was impressive. His beard caught most of the rest.

Jimmy flew off with an irritated screech, bombarding Rustbucket with a spray of droppings as she passed.

"Vanessa didn't know you were a pirate, neither," Fillbrick pointed out, his deep voice uninflected as ever.

"Don't remind me," Quint muttered darkly. The dissolution of a relationship was never easy, but that one had been particularly painful, in more ways than one.

He opened another bottle of coconut rum, or at least tried to. For some reason the thing was damnably resistant to his efforts. Maybe if the boat stopped rocking so much it would be easier.

"Cursed thing's stuck," he grunted.

"You sure it ain't you?" Rustbucket asked, smirking a little. "You've drunk enough to drown Captain Wolf and all his Sea Dogs."

"Wolf never drowned," Fillbrick objected. "I heard he almost did, once, but the Seagod wouldn't let him. Didn't want Wolf's bones profaning his waters, I heard."

"It was an allusion, Brick," Ophelia said, glancing over the rail at the smooth, calm waters all around.

The boatswain's frown deepened. "Like when you think you see land, but it's just the sun playing tricks?"

"That's an—" Ophelia shook her head, then grimaced, looking as though she regretted it. Watered down or not, rum was still rum, and they'd been playing the game for hours. "Sure."

"There!" Quint grinned at last, triumphant. The cork rocketed from the bottle like a tiny cannonball, narrowly missing Rustbucket's head.

"Now," their captain continued, raising the bottle. His struggle with it had unlocked some kind of madness within him. No more was he standing with his back to the great abyss; now he was fully facing it, taking a last deep breath before the plunge.

Ophelia must have seen some hint of this in his eyes, for she started to say something, hoping no doubt to divert him. Silly of her, really. She had sailed with him long enough to know there was no dissuading Captain Redbeard of his course once he had set his heart on it.

"My turn again," he said, raising his bottle as if in salute. "On Me Life I Never loved anyone more than I love my old man."

Silence greeted this pronouncement. The others exchanged glances, then lifted their bottles to their lips in unison.

"To my pop," Quint proclaimed, climbing unsteadily to his feet, legs swaying beneath him as the *Angel* cruised calmly onward. The madness had fully taken him; he could almost feel the whistling of wind past his ears as he took the final, fatal plunge into the abyss he'd kept his back to ever since the letter's arrival.

He held out his bottle toward the sea, to the distant dark shapes of islands passing silently by. "He may not have been a pirate, but he was a sailor, and a damned fine one. A great tale-spinner, a better angler. The best—"

His voice broke.

"Cap'n," Ophelia murmured, coming to her feet beside him. Quint turned to look at her, his eyes wide and wild and bloodshot.

There were still three of her, and each of those had grown blurry besides. Quint swallowed, trying to say something to one of the Ophelias, only for his body to lose its long battle for balance. He pitched forward like a masthead felled by a typhoon, the bottle dropping from his numb fingers.

Fillbrick caught it, one of his massive hands shooting out with alarming quickness to snatch the rum before it could smash against the deck. Ophelia did the same for her captain, easing him down, folding her legs beneath her so that when he slumped to the deck it was with his head pillowed on her thigh rather than crashing to the unforgiving timbers.

"Finally," the three Ophelias said, looking down at their captain's head in their collective lap. Quint gazed past her, to where the stars wheeled overhead, dizzyingly fast and wholly out of sync with the rocking of the ship beneath him. He closed his eyes, just for a moment, hoping that when he opened them the heavens would have resumed their customary stillness.

"Thought he'd never pass out," Rustbucket's voice said from somewhere nearby, his tone equal parts admiring and resentful. It was deep, deep into the night, and their game hadn't excluded any of them from watch duty. "Especially with how watered down that rum was."

"His wasn't," Ophelia said, easing Quint's head out of her lap.

What? Quint wanted to say, but speech had grown difficult.

"Let's get this over with before he wakes," Ophelia said, in the briskly commanding tone that was a first mate's most invaluable tool.

"Hold him down."

The strong arms of Fillbrick and Rustbucket suddenly seized Quint's arms and legs, holding him firmly against the deck. With an effort of his fading will, Quint forced his eyes open, just in time to see Ophelia straddling him, a straight razor in her hand and a determined look in her eyes.

"Keep him still, lads," she said as Quint's vision turned black at the edges, too dulled to feel fear or alarm. She pressed a cool hand against his forehead, touched the cold steel of the razor to Quint's throat, at the place where the first ruddy hairs began to sprout. "I've never done this before."

2

Captain Redbeard had never been happy to awaken with a hangover.

Nor was he glad of it the following morning. He did not awaken so much as find himself forcibly dragged into painful, merciless consciousness, fighting the entire way to claw himself back into the blessed oblivion of sleep. It was a battle he was doomed to lose.

The first sensation his addled mind became aware of was that someone seemed to be stabbing his eyes, no matter how resolutely he kept them squeezed shut. Stabbing him with a blade made of light, which struck him as particularly unfair. It wasn't like you could parry *light*.

He endured this relentless torture for as long as his willpower permitted. It felt like hours but was probably only minutes. Finally, with a titanic effort, he opened his eyes.

The source of the stabbing, Quint was only mildly surprised to discover, was the sun, its blinding rays piercing through his cabin window directly into his brain.

"Good thing I didn't try an' swordfight it," he muttered to himself, or tried to. His tongue felt too big for his mouth, his throat like someone had poured sand down it. So what he actually said was something more like "goothing din tryan sorfyit."

He tried to pull himself into something resembling a sitting position, motivated by some vague ambition to pull shut the cabin's curtains, but the accursed sun retaliated by redoubling its assault on his brain. Even the *Angel* itself betrayed him, the cabin tilting at an angle that seemed improbable given the vessel's construction.

Seeing that the fight was lost before it had begun, Quint surrendered to the pull of gravity and let his head fall back to the pillow. The headache did not abate, but at least the ship ceased its spinning beneath him.

Lying flat upon the bed, a thousand tiny pirates beating on his skull with hammers, Quint let his mind drift back to the night before. He had been drinking; that much was obvious. There was a vague memory of sitting cross-legged on the *Angel*'s deck, some of his crew in a circle alongside him, more of them scattered and sprawled about the deck. Ophelia, Fillbrick, Rustbucket, each entry in their game of On Me Life I Never a pointed exploit from Quint's own history. Stumbling to his swaying feet, raising his bottle in toast—

Quint groaned.

As miserable as he felt, the hangover had been good for one thing, and one thing only. For the briefest span of time between his first stirring and the slow, resistant climb back into something resembling consciousness, Quint had not thought of his father once.

All that came crashing down now. The black envelope still lay crumpled on his desk, the message within written in his mother's neat, even hand. Short and to the point, as was her wont.

Darling Quentin, it read, *I'm sorry you should find out this way, but your Pop has gone on to the Heavenly Waters. I'm sure you're busy with work, but if you have any time to take leave I would dearly love to have you home for as long as you're able.*

All my love,

Your affectionate Ma

Were this one of the melodramas Ophelia dragged him to whenever they were ashore in a major port, the letter would have been so tearstained as to hardly be legible. But that had never been Ma Thatch's way. By the time she'd sat down to pen the letter, Quint knew, her tears would have all run dry. It was not that her mourning would be over; she was simply the sort of woman who saw little point in sitting about feeling sad when there were things that needed doing.

"Thingsh," Quint said to the empty cabin, pleased to hear that it came out as an actual word, even if a little slurred, "need doing."

After all, he was his mother's son. No point mourning horizontally, not while there was a ship to run, a crew to lead. He was the famed pirate Captain Redbeard, Scourge of the Eight Seas, Terror of the Archipelago, Bane of the Empire. There were ships to capture, ports to plunder, aristocrats to ransom—

I would dearly love to have you home...

He closed his eyes, feeling the suffocating weight of grief press down against his chest. There were all those things, yes; but there was also a father to mourn. A mother grieving alone.

She should not be alone.

The thought pierced Quint with the keen, somewhat guilty conviction common to all children whose adult lives took them far from their parents. Pillage and plunder could wait; they'd just come off an *extremely* successful raid on Fort Amell, after all. The crew had more than earned a break, and so had their captain.

They'd be fine without him, he decided, at least for a few weeks. Long enough to return home to see his ma and lay his pop to rest. Maybe see a few of the old gang; childhood friends he'd drifted apart from. His best friend growing up, Hari Anand, had departed Ember Bay for the Jewel Isles not long after Quint had enlisted in the Navy, but others like Chuck Chambers and Lex Presley would still be there. Hopefully those others included the beautiful and wicked-tongued Amara Salazar. Idly he wondered whether Amara still thought about him from time to time. Angels above knew he certainly still thought of her.

Right, then. A course of action was decided on. He'd inform the crew of his decision to take a few weeks off for travel, commit the *Angel* to Ophelia's capable hands. As of last night, they were half a day's sail from Port Solace; he'd book passage on some local ship for Ember Bay from there.

"First thingsh first," he said, and was again pleased to hear the words were mostly intelligible. "Geddoutta bed."

He pressed the heel of his palm against his brow, hoping the added pressure might ease the worst of his headache. No luck.

Idly, his hand traveled down his forehead, past his temple, to his cheek.

Something was different.

He ran his hand slowly down his face a second time, trying to place exactly what the difference was. His cheek was rough with stubble, but his beard felt...

His beard.

He patted his face with both hands, fingers roving for the familiar thatch of rusty hair that was the source of his famous sobriquet. But all he found were uneven patches of stubble, evidently left behind by a barber who was either an amateur, incompetent, or both.

The captain formerly known as Redbeard stumbled to his feet, pure rage driving him forward as headache, hangover, and even grief were pushed aside. He stumbled across the floor (still tilting), steadied himself on the doorframe, and turned the knob. A blast of morning light assaulted him as he threw the door open, but the sun was the least hated of his enemies now.

Filling his lungs with warm salt air, he bellowed in a voice that must have been heard from Port Solace:

"WHO IN THE NINE HELLS STOLE MY BLOODY *BEARD*?!"

⚓

The culprit owned up to her crime readily enough.

If anything, Ophelia seemed almost smug about having carried out such an audacious assault upon his person, idly toying with the straight razor the way she did her vast collection of blades.

"Point that somewhere else," the beardless captain ordered, wincing as the reflected sunlight off its blade stabbed his eyes. At least he'd regained the ability to speak in full sentences. "Or better yet, put it away. Don't need the crew to see you flaunting the evidence of your mutiny."

"Pretty unsuccessful mutiny, I'd say," she said, smirking. The two of them leaned against the ship's rail, the captain taking particular care to keep beneath the shade of the topsail. "You're still captain."

"But I'm not Captain *Redbeard*," he protested, running a hand along the scruffy edge of his chin, feeling the unfamiliar bristles there. "You think Captain Nobeard is a name that'll strike fear into the hearts of the Empire?"

"Imperials don't have hearts, Cap'n."

"Stop avoiding the issue," he snapped, glaring at her through bleary eyes. "Shaving a man's beard is an unpardonable sin."

Ophelia snorted and brushed the long strip of blonde hair from her eyes. Somewhere in the Nine Heavens there was an angel keeping careful record of her sins, and she was confident that shaving her captain's facial hair was very, *very* far down the list.

"Write that sin down in your own ledgers, then," she said, handing him a waterskin. He took it grudgingly, but drank anyway. "It was your idea."

The captain choked, water sputtering from his mouth onto the deck. "*What?*"

"You don't remember?" Ophelia asked, then shook her head. "Of course you don't." In twenty years of comradeship, she'd only seen her friend and captain that drunk on two other occasions. One had been the night they'd infiltrated the High Governor's birthday party disguised as an obscure noblewoman and her husband. Having successfully passed themselves off as the idle rich, they'd availed themselves of the lavish food and drink on offer without restraint and competed to see who could seduce the Dauphiness of Montonne first (a competition Ophelia won). Those parts of the night they could both recall had been memorable indeed.

The other had been after he and Vanessa had parted ways. That night did *not* bear remembrance.

"Remind me," the captain said, trying another sip of the waterskin. This time most of it made it into his mouth.

"Right." Realizing she hadn't yet complied with her captain's earlier order, Ophelia snapped the straight razor shut. It disappeared into one of the innumerable sheaths hidden about her person. "Yesterday, after you got the, ah...the black letter."

"Sure." Again the dark tide of grief threatened to rise up and swallow him, but with an effort of will he forced it back down. "What'd I do?"

He was genuinely curious. Truth be told, he didn't remember much at all between his initial reading and that morning's hangover.

"Locked yourself in your cabin," Ophelia said, nodding toward the aftcastle as if he had possibly also forgotten the location of his quarters. "For hours. Caused quite a stir amongst the crew, I can tell you."

"I expect it did," he allowed. The *Angel*'s captain was not a man given to extended solitude. Doubtless his sequestering had caused as much scuttlebutt aboard as the black letter's arrival had.

"You called me in around sunset," Ophelia continued, her voice softening. "Told me about your pop. I said I was sorry, by the way."

"Thank you." His voice was oddly hoarse. *Probably the hangover drying out my throat,* he told himself, but didn't believe it. Ophelia was not fooled either.

"Seeing as you don't remember, I'll say it again." She clapped her hand on her friend's shoulder. "You've my sympathies, mate. I ain't never met your pop, but it's clear he did a passable job raising you."

"Thanks, mate." The captain snorted, then raised the waterskin in silent salute. He tipped it back, let the lukewarm contents wash down his parched throat.

For a few moments they stood leaning against the rail in companionable silence.

"Alright," he said, once he was reasonably certain his voice would not crack or tremble. "So, I called you into my cabin, told you about my pop. Let's take as given that there was lots of wailing and gnashing of teeth. How'd we get from there to shearing me like a thrice-damned sheep?"

"Again, your idea." The razor made a reappearance, conjured as if by magic. Ophelia tossed it idly into the air, end over end, unerringly catching it by the handle as the blade flashed in the morning light. "You told me you were planning on heading back home to see your ma."

"Oh." He felt foolish for having so triumphantly arrived at that same decision this morning. "Right. And the beard?"

Ophelia caught the falling razor, used that same hand to shade her eyes as she peered over the rail, toward the stern. Somewhere in that direction lay the site of their latest triumph, where a fleet of Imperial

vessels were likely still swarming about like wasps around their dis-
turbed nest.

"Considering that we just robbed the vaults of Fort Amell and made
off with half the Empress's crown jewels, we both decided it was probably better if Ember Bay isn't suddenly visited by a fellow who matches
one Captain Redbeard's description exactly."

"Oh." He felt foolish for not realizing the soundness of that log-
ic sooner. One more thing to blame on the hangover, he supposed.
"That...makes sense."

"Yeah." Ophelia ran a finger down his scruffy cheek, and he batted
it away in mock annoyance. "Figured the last thing you'd want to deal
with while settling your pop's affairs is for some Imperial pirate catcher
to get wind that Captain Redbeard had turned up in some nowhere
backwater. No offense, Cap'n."

"None taken," he said, shaking his head and immediately regretting
it as his stomach roiled in protest. Ember Bay *was* a nowhere backwater;
a sleepy little island where nothing happened, save for the intermittent
explosions of the volcano the island was formed from. It was a testa-
ment to how dull his hometown was that even volcanic eruptions there
were somehow boring.

Like most children of such sleepy villages, he'd hungered for a life beyond the confines of the world he knew, which was why he had signed
on with the local Navy recruiter as soon as he'd come of age—much
to his parents' disapproval. The Navy hadn't stuck, obviously, but it
had given him his sea legs and (perhaps more importantly) Ophelia.
Most days he never regretted leaving home for the wider world beyond
Ember Bay's shores.

But most days didn't see the arrival of the black letter, or the loss of
a father.

"You still going to do it?" Ophelia asked, guessing the direction his thoughts had turned. "Go home, I mean."

"I think so." The captain turned, squinting against the sunlight as he looked forward down the length of the *Angel*. A dark splotch had broken the boundless horizon, the shape of its lonely mountain peaks identifying it even from this distance as the island of Solace. "After the mess we stirred up back at Fort Amell it'll be best for you to take the crew and lie low for a few weeks while I'm away."

Ophelia nodded, secretly glad to hear the strength returning to his voice as he issued commands, charting the course of their immediate future. Her captain was back.

"Load up on provisions in Solace," he continued. "Spend the next three or four weeks skirting the outlying islands. Find some hidden cove to lay anchor in, maybe. Angels know there are enough of them on this end of the Archipelago."

"Aye," Ophelia agreed. "For how long?"

Her captain rubbed at his chin, feeling the unfamiliar stubble where his beard had lately been while he silently calculated how long it would take for him to journey to Ember Bay, put his pop's affairs in order, then make his way back to something resembling civilization.

"Two months," he said at last. "By then the search will have died down a bit, and I'll have done what I needed to. You alright with being left in command that long?"

"'Course," Ophelia said breezily. "Fillbrick's dependable as stone; I can rely on him to keep the deckhands in line."

"Naturally," Redbeard said, looking sternwards toward the *Angel*'s helm. "What about Vigo and Darby? Are they honeymooning or fighting these days?"

Atop the aftcastle, Darby, the *Angel*'s second mate, was peering down the length of his beaky nose through his spectacles at a battered oilcloth map. At his elbow Vigo, the *Angel*'s third mate and Darby's only mate, kept a steady hand on the ship's wheel.

"The former," Ophelia answered, following her captain's gaze. Darby was jabbing an emphatic finger at the map, which Vigo gave a perfunctory glance before giving a dismissive wave of his broad hand. "For now, anyway."

"Hopefully it'll last the next couple of months," Redbeard said, scratching at his cheek. He wondered how long it would take to adjust to the absence of beard. "How're we on supplies?"

"Bonnie Kate says six weeks' comfortable rations. Ten if we stretch it."

That was good enough for him. Bonnie Kate was seldom seen without a ledger in hand, and her record-keeping was meticulous. Doubtless she'd taken careful account of every last drop of grog and morsel of food aboard the vessel.

"Make it twelve," he decided. "Take a little of what we've saved—not the recent plunder, what we've got in our stores—and resupply at the next port of call after Solace."

Ophelia quirked an eyebrow. "Which is?"

The captain took a deep breath. "Before I tell you, you're going to have to promise me something."

Ophelia frowned. "For the last time, Cap'n, I'm not spending any of my hard-earned coin on investing in our own rum distillery—"

"Not that," he said, waving an impatient hand. "Rustbucket. You're going to have to keep a close eye on him."

"Ah." The amusement faded from Ophelia's voice. Rustbucket was a man of volatile passions, with a fuse shorter than his braided beard. Worse, once he was in his cups, no secret was safe with him, as last night's game had demonstrated multiple times over.

"The Navy knows it was the *Angel* that raided Fort Amell," the captain continued. "But they don't know our heading, nor whether we plan on trying to pawn the booty or squirrel it away."

They had flown the black flag proudly as they made their escape, the crimson-winged angel stitched upon it taunting their pursuers. The theft of the Empress's jewels was quite literally the *Angel*'s crowning achievement. Soon the story of their daring raid would be sung throughout the Archipelago—but not if the Navy caught up to them before they did away with the plunder.

"I intend that the Navy remain uninformed as to our whereabouts." He fixed on Ophelia through bloodshot eyes, his expression uncharacteristically intent. "Mine, the *Angel*'s, the treasure's. Understood?"

Ophelia answered with a full salute, something she'd seldom done since their long-ago Navy days. "Aye, Cap'n. I'll keep Rustbucket on as short a leash as I can manage."

"Drag him around by that stupid little beard of his if you have to," the captain advised. "Once we part ways, set a heading for the outer islands and lay low for a few weeks, until the hunt dies down. In two months' time I'll meet you at Sweetharbor."

"Don't take too long, Cap'n," Ophelia said, grinning. Sweetharbor was a notorious den of vice, where every pleasure imaginable could be purchased for the right price. "You let the crew spend too long in that port o' call, there won't be any of the Amell booty left to spend."

He winced. Even Ophelia, loyal mate that she was, wasn't going to take kindly to what he was about to propose.

"Right," he said, taking a deep breath. "About the treasure..."

3

So it was that the captain formerly known as Redbeard departed the *Bloody Angel* with not one but two sea chests. One contained a few changes of clothes, a waterproof book of matches in case he wound up shipwrecked, an emergency bottle of rum (for the same reason), and other various and sundry personal items.

The other contained Her Imperial Majesty's crown jewels, and a wealth of other treasures besides.

Both chests were fastened tight with sturdy iron locks, but that was all the security he permitted himself. Anything more would seem excessive and would inevitably arouse curiosity. A chest with more than one lock was a chest with something valuable inside, and though the Archipelago was not quite as lawless a region as it had been in Captain Wolf's time, there were still plenty of ne'er-do-wells upon the waves willing to rob anyone who seemed like easy prey.

He should know, being one of the ne'er-do-wells himself.

⚓

It was easy to find a ship heading west from Port Solace, and easier still to book passage in exchange for a handful of silvers. He traveled under his birth name, which he'd used only seldom since deserting the

Navy. Doubtless the Empire was even now scouring the Archipelago for Captain Redbeard, but with one exception, not a single soul in the employ of Her Majesty's Navy knew the name Quint Thatch.

A week's travel brought him to the Reach, the broad western arm of the Archipelago that had been the Empire's frontier scarcely a century earlier. Unlike the scattered and low-lying isles to the east, the Reach's islands were a mountainous chain, each one rising from the ocean depths like the broad back of some titanic sea turtle. An actively volcanic range, it was a rare night that passed without a distant spray of fire leaping into the starry sky, lighting like sudden candle flames above the water.

For Quint, growing up on Ember Bay, the nightfires had been a fixture as regular and familiar as the slow turning of the seasons from dry to wet. It was only once he'd sailed away at the age of fifteen that Quint had realized their uniqueness. And although after nearly twenty years in the wider Archipelago he'd grown accustomed to the darkness of sea and sky, it sometimes still struck him as strange not to see the sky broken by the occasional gout of flame reaching heavenward.

That was the thing about home, he mused to himself as he leaned over the rail of the fishing boat he'd chartered for this last leg of the voyage. You took for granted the things that made it special, unaware that what was normal in one place was extraordinary in another. And every place had something of the extraordinary about it, if one cared to look.

It was hard to believe he had ever so easily dismissed the nightfires, Quint thought, watching as a distant volcano blossomed into a flower with flaming petals. That once he had thought them no more remarkable than the rhythm of the tides, or the coarse feel of sand between his toes. As if those things themselves were not small miracles in their own right.

I've been away too long. The thought came to him unprompted, at once guilty and wistful. When was the last time he had visited? Ten years back? That had been the last time he'd seen his parents; the very last time he'd seen his pop, though neither had known it then. Quint wondered if he would have done things differently had either of them known.

There were things a son needed to hear from his father; things fathers needed to be told by their sons. Wise words, vulnerable words, about life and love and honor and pride. They had both spoken of these things to each other, but only ever piecemeal; an offhand comment here, a vague allusion there. Both had assumed they would find the right words in time. That they would have time.

The captain who could no longer rightly call himself Redbeard closed his eyes. As with the nightfires, he had taken their time for granted.

Fitting, then, that now they should guide him home, like torches held aloft to light his way back to the place he'd run from so long ago.

"Rest easy, Pop," he whispered to the sea and sky, the distant volcano painting both a fiery orange. "I'll be home soon."

Home appeared above the horizon on a bright clear morning, exactly two weeks after he'd departed the *Bloody Angel* with a pair of sea chests.

No fires belched from the great crater of the volcano that gave Ember Bay its name, only a faint wisp of smoke curling up from its peak. This too was one of the peculiarities of the place that had not struck him as unusual until he'd left. The volcanic peak was naked gray rock, but three hundred feet down it gave way to a lush tropical forest, its slopes steadily giving way to the gently rolling hills of the island.

Ember Bay was the name of both town and island, though the village itself was only one modest-sized harbor on the island's northwestern coast. A stirring Quint could not name tugged at his pirate's heart as the fishing boat rounded the northern peninsula, revealing the long spit of promontory rock upon which the village lighthouse sat. It had been a game amongst the island children for time out of mind to clamber over the rocks to the lighthouse, whose keeper was a famously reclusive and bad-tempered old coot by the name of Tom Brittle. The game was to knock on his door, then try to flee back over the rocks before he caught you and gave you a thrashing.

He wondered who had the job now, and if they were any more personable. Likely not; the solitude of the lighthouse keeper's trade seemed to attract cantankerous personalities.

They rounded the lighthouse point, revealing the broad, shallow harbor of Ember Bay. And beyond that, the town itself: a collection of wooden houses, each painted in bright pastels that contrasted vividly with the lush greenery of the forest behind them. There had been a time when Quint had hated those bright pinks and cheerful oranges; had thought them a vain attempt to plaster over the dull reality of the sleepy village. Funny that now the sight of them sparked a feeling of contentment instead.

The fisherman docked just long enough for his sole passenger to disembark. Quint had barely set his sea chests on the pier before his ride had unfurled sails and set off back across the harbor. He could hardly blame him for being eager to return; it had taken a generous amount of silver to convince the man to take a break from his trade for the few days required to sail to and from Ember Bay on a vessel that size.

"Could have at least stayed to help me with the luggage," Quint muttered to himself.

"Luggage!" Jimmy squawked from her perch on his shoulder, then fluttered off without another word. This was her custom whenever they made landfall; she would return to him when she felt like it, and not before.

Sighing, he stacked the lighter of the two chests on top of the heavier one, then hauled them both slowly over the uneven planks of the dock. Though he was far from the praying sort, Quint silently implored whichever poor angel the Heavens had assigned him to keep the dock from giving way beneath him. It would be mighty embarrassing to drop the Empress's crown jewels into the waters of Ember Bay.

By the time Quint reached the harbormaster's office, sweat was streaming down his neck and brow. Treasure, as any pirate who'd experienced a measure of success knew, was *heavy*.

The harbormaster's office was little more than a wooden shack with a thatched roof of palms sitting at the end of the dock. The woman peered at Quint from behind a pair of spectacles, a fine chain trailing from each of the thick lenses.

"Master Thatch," she said, and though her voice was nearly as dry and creaky as the dock's timbers, the lilt of the familiar Ember accent was like hearing a half-forgotten song again. "Good to see you."

Quint stared. The deep-lined face, the skin like weathered parchment draped over bony limbs, the bright eyes half-hidden by glass lenses: all were unchanged as the day he'd last seen them.

"Mrs. Cavendish," he said, his voice sounding strange in his ears. "You..."

Haven't aged a day, he was going to say. But what came out instead was: "You're still alive."

"Obviously." Mrs. Cavendish, harbormaster of Ember Bay for angels knew how many decades, adjusted her glasses. "You missed the funeral, you know."

The words were not accusatory, just a statement of fact. But they stung all the same.

"I know," Quint said, nodding. "I came as soon as I received the letter."

Mrs. Cavendish pursed her lips, swiftly performed some mental calculations. On an island as sparsely populated as Ember Bay, the position of harbormaster was by necessity also that of postmaster. The black letter had probably gone directly from Quint's mother's hands to hers.

"I suppose you did at that," she admitted, having worked out the timing. "It was a nice ceremony."

Quint blinked. "You went?"

"Of course I did." The look she leveled at him through those thick-framed glasses was pitying, as if it were obvious. "There's five hundred people on this island, Master Thatch. I go to all of the funerals."

I knew that, Quint recalled. Something his pop had said to him once, as they made their way home from a memorial service for old Mayor Broadbent. *Old Mrs. Cavendish likes funerals,* the old man had said. *I think she thinks it's a competition, seeing who can stay alive the longest. So far she's winning.*

As with most things, Pop had been right about that. Now that he had recovered from the shock of seeing her again, Quint realized that his initial assessment of Mrs. Cavendish had been an understatement. Of course the old harbormaster was unchanged; she was practically mummified.

"Ma still at the Arms?" he asked, hoping to steer the conversation into more comfortable waters.

He was rewarded with that pitying look reserved for those who asked stupid questions. "Where else would she be?"

"Right." Quint looked up the slope of the village high street. Behind a grove of trees he could just make out the old inn and tavern at the top of the hill. *Right where I left it,* he thought.

He looked back down at the chests beside him, stacked one atop the other. Then back at the hill, and again to Mrs. Cavendish, who'd lost interest and was now paging through a yellowed newspaper at least a month out of date.

Quint cleared his throat. "Mrs. Cavendish?"

She peered up from her newspaper, brows rising as though surprised to see him still standing there. "Yes, Master Thatch?"

He fixed her with his most winning smile, one that he'd used to charm maidens beyond counting, and patted the topmost sea chest. "I don't suppose you'd loan me a cart?"

If Mrs. Cavendish had been a few decades younger, Quint told himself, the smile would have worked.

"Or maybe centuries," he muttered to himself, dragging the chests along behind him up the high street. If it had been only the one containing his personal items, he could have shouldered it easily. If it had only been the one containing the Fort Amell plunder he would have been able to carry it with some difficulty. It was their combined weight that was making the process so arduous.

He supposed he could have left one of the chests at the harbor office with Mrs. Cavendish, but he'd wanted to keep them both in sight at all times. Theft was next to nonexistent in a community as small and sleepy as Ember Bay, but experience had taught Quint that misfortune usually chose to strike at the moments one least expected it.

Grunting and cursing, he hauled both chests—still stacked one atop the other—along behind him up the street, pausing every few minutes to wipe his brow. His shirt was already soaked through with sweat. He'd need a wash and a change once he got home.

Home. One of those curious words that was too small for what it meant. Like love, or fear, or want.

Curious, too, was how little the place had changed. Quint had expected to return to Ember Bay a stranger. To see the buildings along the high street and not recognize them. For the people he had not seen in decades to be made more from memory than flesh and blood.

Yet the town was almost identical to how it appeared in his memories. Each building he passed bore the same lettering above its doors as he remembered, carefully maintained against the relentless weathering of the tropical sun. Delman's Barbershop, Helo's Bait & Tackle, Avon's Grocery. There on his left: the cheerful red storefront of Rosa's Mercantile, Rosa herself sitting in her rocking chair with her rainbow shawl draped about her shoulders, contemplatively puffing on her long-stemmed pipe. As he passed her by she raised a weathered hand to him.

"Morning, Quentin!" she called, as if she saw him every morning.

Quint was so surprised he could not muster a reply, only wave back as he strained to haul the chests uphill. He was nearly halfway now—not so very much further. He could see the orange shingles of the tavern roof at the top of the hill, the wooden signboard hanging outside the door flapping in the breeze—

His hand slipped.

The chests began to slide downhill.

An inarticulate cry of distress tore its way free from Quint's lips, so high and undignified that his crew might have mutinied on the spot if they'd heard their captain make such a sound. He reached for the handle of the nearer chest, but his palms were so sweat-slicked that it slipped from his grasp.

Still stacked together, the chests slid further downhill, picking up speed. Abandoning any pretense of dignity, Quint bent his knees, preparing to dive headfirst after them. He sprang—

—only to find his motion arrested by a brawny arm clasped around his waist, a steadying hand clapped on his shoulder.

"Whoa there, young Thatch!" a voice bellowed in his ear, distantly familiar. "You nearly took a tumble!"

"My chests," Quint panted, struggling ineffectually against the massive arms restraining him. "My things, they're—"

"Not to worry!" the voice half-roared, half-laughed. "The girls are on it!"

A breeze tickled Quint's cheeks as two blurred figures went bounding past, one on either side of him. He had an impression of black hair, broad shoulders, sun-bronzed skin.

Quick as thought, the two women seized the chests, grabbing onto the handles and halting their backslide down the street with surprisingly little effort.

"There!" the roaring, jovial voice said, its owner releasing Quentin from his hold with a final pat on the shoulder. "No harm done. You all right, lad?"

Quint turned to see the giant of a man who'd seized hold of him. He found himself peering up into a face he knew, though the laugh lines around the eyes had deepened, and the fine wispy mustache had turned from black to white.

"Uncle Jun?" Quint asked, as though trying to convince himself of the truth of it. The unaltered appearance of both Mrs. Cavendish and the town had half-convinced him that time truly didn't move in Ember

Bay the way it did for the outside world, but the reappearance of an old family friend had shattered that illusion.

"You seen any other Aiwi giants on this end of the Archipelago?" Jun asked, his grin broadening. "Aside from the twins, of course."

Quint turned to see the girls who had stopped his chests from sliding into the bay—chests each balanced on her broad shoulders so easily Quint couldn't say for certain which one was laden with treasure and which contained his personal effects.

"Ling, Tai," Jun said, waving a huge hand at his daughters. "You remember your cousin Quint?"

"Of course," said one of the two, peering down at Quint. "Sorry about your pop."

"We both miss him," the other said.

"Ling," Quint realized aloud. She had a birthmark on her neck her sister didn't share; he remembered that. But he also remembered a pair of gawky young girls, not these towering giantesses who could lift better than a hundredweight of treasure like it was nothing. Now they stood before him as living reminders that time had proceeded apace on Ember Bay as it did everywhere else while he had been gone.

He nodded to Ling, then to her twin. "Tai. Thank you both for your help."

"See?" Tai nudged her sister with an elbow. "Told you he'd remember!"

"Of course," Quint said, glancing back at his beaming uncle. "I just…"

Jun's smile was knowing. "Didn't expect them to have grown so much, eh?"

"Clearly I should have," Quint said, rubbing ruefully at his chin.

Jun bore no blood relation to either side of Quint's family, as his Aiwi heritage indicated, yet he had been a fixture in Quint's early life in Ember Bay. To a child, all adults were giants. Yet Quint had been surprised to discover that as he grew older and the rest of the adults in his life shrank, Jun retained his towering stature. Small wonder that his daughters had inherited his prodigious size.

"We were shorter than you last time you came to visit," Ling said, holding her hand palm down to indicate how tall she'd been then, somewhere in the vicinity of Quint's chest.

"And Baba's hair was still dark," Tai chimed in, grinning fondly at her father.

"Gloat while you can, young'n." Jun winked at his daughter. "One day you'll wake up to find someone's stolen the black outta your hair, same as mine. But enough standing around in the street!"

He clapped Quint on the shoulder, nearly sending him sprawling. "We've taken enough of your time, lad. Let's get you home to your mother."

A lump rose in Quint's throat. The surprise and joy of this reunion had almost eclipsed the reason for his return to Ember Bay.

Something of that must have shown in his face, for Jun's own expression softened. He said no words of comfort, only squeezed Quint's shoulder.

Somehow that said all that needed to be said.

4

They parted at the hilltop, the twins ducking around the corner of the tavern to take Quint's chests to his room (how they knew which was his, he resolved not to dwell upon). Jun left him at the doorstep, but not without extracting a bone-crushing handshake and a solemn promise for Quint to call on him if he should need anything whatsoever during his time on Ember Bay.

Thus, Quint suddenly found himself standing alone outside his family home, the only sound the gentle creaking of the wooden signboard over the door as it swayed in the wind. The sound drew Quint's gaze.

He stared, dumbfounded.

THE QUEEN'S ARMS, the sign read, in the familiar blocky lettering his pop had carved. He remembered staring up at that signboard as a child, trying to puzzle out the meaning behind the chipped and faded symbols of the coat of arms Pop had painted there. He never had, and now it was too late to ask.

The signboard had been painted over. In place of the indecipherable heraldry stood a woman wearing a crown, the sleeves of her dress torn away to reveal a truly impressive set of biceps.

"That's new," Quint heard himself say.

He lowered his gaze to the door. *His* door, with the brass mermaid knocker, the faded green paint that Pop had always meant to repaint but never quite gotten around to. Never would, now.

The mermaid knocker was cool beneath his hand as he opened the door. Cooler still was the inviting dark of the tavern, a respite from the already-sweltering heat of the tropical morning.

As his eyes adjusted to the dimness, he inhaled deeply, breathing in the smell of the place. The faint tang of varnished wood, the earthy smell of spilled beer that permeated every surface, the whiff of oil from the lanterns hanging from the rafters—and over everything the briny taste of the salty sea air.

His eyes having grown accustomed to the lower light, Quint looked about the common room. Save for the repainted signboard, the Queen's Arms was unchanged from how it appeared in his memories. The same stuffed sailfish was still mounted above the bar, a rusty old harpoon mounted opposite it. The walls were festooned with the same nautical knickknacks his parents had accumulated over the years: spare bits of netting, brass portholes, even a broken ship's wheel. A dartboard hung in one corner, and unless Quint's eyes were deceiving him the constellation of darts upon it was identical to when he'd last been here. The tables too were in the same configuration as he remembered; he could have navigated through them blindfolded.

Even the patronage was unchanged. A withered skeleton of a man in the tattered remnants of what once might have been a seaman's jacket sat slouched in a corner booth, both hands clasped around a frothy mug despite the early hour.

"Hawkins," Quint greeted him as he made his way to the bar. Old Hawkins was as much a fixture of the Queen's Arms as any of the decorations adorning the wall. On an island with as little to do as Ember Bay, the position of town drunk was a hotly contested one, but Hawkins was the undisputed reigning champion.

"Young Thatch," Hawkins answered, raising his mug in salute, as if they'd last seen each other only ten minutes ago rather than ten years.

Quint picked his way through the maze of tables to the bar, pausing for a moment to run his hand over the brass figure of a snarling dog that jutted proudly up from the counter. Pop had always claimed that it had once been the figurehead of a famous explorer's ship, though exactly whose ship and which sailor changed with each telling. Quint no more believed it than he believed any of Pop's tall tales, but he rubbed his hand on the dog's nose all the same.

Behind the bar sat countless bottles upon their shelves, the mirror behind them doubling the tavern's lighting. Of everything in the Arms, only the bottles were different from how he'd remembered. During the last few years Pop had looked to expand their offerings, and now a surprising range of wines and spirits sat alongside the more traditional bottles of beer, grog, and rum.

He leaned against the bar, tracing a finger along its scratches and stains, as familiar to him as the lines on his own palm. "Ma?"

"Be with you in a minute," a voice called from the swinging half-doors that led to the kitchen. A familiar voice, but not his ma's.

A grin spread over Quint's face. He tugged at his shirt, hoping to dry off any remaining traces of sweat, then ran his fingers through his hair. A quick glance at his reflection between bottles of rum confirmed that his locks were artfully tousled in just the roguish way he liked.

He had just a moment to wistfully regret not having a beard to complete the look when the kitchen doors swung open, revealing a willowy woman carrying a tray stacked high with dishes in front of her. A few curling strands of hair trailed from her sensible bun, which Quint was surprised to see now bore some slight streaks of gray.

These only added a certain dignity to her beauty, which had not faded in the intervening years, nor been exaggerated by the rosy tint of Quint's memories. Her full lips parted in surprise as she registered who it was leaning casually against the bar, her dark eyes widening. "Quint?"

"Morning, Amara," he said, quirking a devilish smile at her, confident it would work better on her than it had on Mrs. Cavendish. "It's been a while."

"It has," she agreed, not returning his smile. Amara set the tray of dishes down atop the bar, revealing what they had hidden from view. Quint stared.

"You're pregnant," he said, his mouth dry. *That* was certainly a change from the young, wickedly grinning Amara from his memories.

"What?" Amara's tawny features paled as she looked down, eyes widening in mock horror as she clasped her swelling belly with both hands. "Angels above! When did this happen?"

"Very funny," Quint said, swallowing to wet his abruptly parched throat. "I didn't know you were, ah..."

"Spoken for?" Amara quirked a dark brow and waggled her left hand at him. The tavern's dim light sparkled off the glittering gemstone on her third finger. "What, you thought I'd been spending my days pining away for my lost love, like the heroine of one of those dreadful pirate adventure novels you were always reading when we were kids?"

"'Course not," Quint said, shifting uncomfortably. Certain nighttime fantasies of their reunion had started out precisely like that, in fact, but he would let Ophelia shave his beard *again* before he ever admitted to that. "Congratulations, I suppose. Ah, when...?"

"Did I get married?" she finished, resting a hand atop her belly and staring hard at him. "Oh, some three, four months after you left me for the last time."

Quint stared back, a horrified realization dawning. "You don't mean..." His gaze dropped to her middle. "There's not...not another...?"

"There is," Amara said solemnly, holding his gaze and refusing to let it go.

It was ten years since they'd last parted. A vision rose in Quint's mind of a young boy, nine years old, with curling red hair and dark eyes. "Amara, I..."

She burst out laughing. "I'm screwing with you, Quint. There's no kid. I mean, there is, but he's certainly not yours."

"Thank the angels," Quint blurted, before the full impact of what she'd said hit him. "Really? Then whose—"

Still laughing, Amara shook her head, wiping a tear from her eye. "Never you mind. Heavens, you really thought I would've raised up your bastard, and in ten years no one would've told you?"

"I suppose not," he admitted, feeling more foolish than ever. Attempting to steer the conversation into safer waters, he asked, "What're you doing at the Arms, though? Last we...er, last I heard you were still apprenticing at Anand & Sons."

"I'm still there." Amara nodded. "Graduated my apprenticeship with old Manish a few years back, but Mr. Anand and I have a lot more help these days, so I lend your ma a hand here in the mornings."

"Speaking of Ma," Quint said, "where is she?"

"Here."

He turned around, his mother's entrance preceded by the creaking of stairs as she made her way down to the common room.

It startled Quint, as it did at every homecoming, just how much older his ma looked. The vision of her that lived in his memory was a robust, matronly woman with wide shoulders and an easy smile, her wavy hair cut to a practical, short length. There was a comforting solidity to her presence, as immovable as the mountain in whose shadow the town stood.

Strange, then, how in her age and his manhood he stood more than a head taller than her, his own shoulders broader than hers. When he took her into his arms the fragility of her bones was new and almost frightening, as was the wrinkled texture of the skin that brushed his cheek, or the brittleness of her gray hair.

But the smell of her was just as it had ever been—coconut oil and pine, the same as the forest that sprouted up above and around Ember Bay. And the arms that pulled him close and held him tight were as strong as they had ever been.

"Welcome home, son," she murmured in his ear. Quint felt a tear slide down his cheek, hot and wet. Whether it was hers or his own, he neither knew nor cared.

They stood like that for a long while, finally breaking apart.

"Let me look at you," Ma said, clasping both hands about his cheeks, turning his head this way and that as if he were a horse she was inspecting before purchase. "You've shaved your beard, I see."

Despite her skill with blades, Ophelia was no barber, and had left him with uneven patches of stubble. He'd finished the job himself and had diligently applied his own razor each morning since. He was gradually growing accustomed to his new appearance, though he was still startled at his reflection sometimes.

Captain Redbeard was gone, for the time being. And perhaps that was not such a bad thing.

"Yeah," Quint admitted, neglecting to mention the circumstances. "It was time for a change."

"Can't say I'm sad to see it gone, I'll admit," Ma Thatch said, patting his now-smooth cheek. "Never understood why you insisted on hiding your face behind that thing. You were always such a handsome boy, Quentin."

Amara snickered from somewhere behind him.

"It's Quint, Ma," he corrected her for the millionth time.

She sniffed. "Quentin is a dignified, respectable name, dear. Quint is vulgar."

"I'll say he is," Amara chimed in.

"Careful, dear," Ma Thatch chided without looking. "You'll turn his face as red as his hair."

Quint cleared his throat. "If we're *quite* done emasculating me..."

"Never," Amara said, coming out from behind the bar. "Kitchen's clean and the counter's all stocked, Lola. You need anything else from me this morning?"

"Nah," Quint's ma said, shaking her head. "Hawkins'll be the only customer until at least noon, and he knows where everything is. He'll help himself if he ever gets done nursing that pint like it's his child."

"So long as he remembers to put it on his tab," Amara said, putting her hand over the child she would be nursing before too long. "I'll be off, then."

"Give my love to the boys," Ma said, blowing Amara a kiss.

But Amara did not take her leave immediately.

"It was good to see you again, Quint," she said. "You should stop by the shop later. I'm sure Mr. Anand would love to catch up with you."

"It'll be good to see Manish again," Quint said. Mr. Anand had been one of his pop's close friends for years, as well as the father of Quint's own childhood companion, Hari. Though like Quint, Hari and his brothers had departed Ember Bay soon after they came of age, setting off to seek their fortunes in the wider Archipelago.

"And..." Amara's tone grew softer and less teasing than it had been. "And...I haven't said. I'm sorry about your pop."

Quint's throat went dry again. Before he could muster a response Amara took a darting step forward, gave him a quick hug, then turned and slipped from the Queen's Arms without another word.

"Come on, love," Ma said, throwing an arm about his waist and leading him to the stairs. "Let's show you to your room."

5

"Where's Jimmy?" Ma Thatch asked as they climbed the stairs to the tavern's upper story.

"Out and about," Quint said. "Poor girl wanted to stretch her wings as soon as we made landfall. Think she missed home as much as I have."

"Dratted bird," Ma said affectionately. "Work's going well, then?"

Quint nearly missed a step.

"Passably," he said, recovering as they reached the upstairs landing. "You know how it is. Always busy."

"They work you too hard on that ship," she sniffed, striding briskly down the long corridor, the doors at either hand leading to the inn's bedrooms. "You still on the same one, then? What was it called?"

"The *Waterhouse,*" Quint said, glad her back was to him. Deception had never come easily to him, and lying to his mother still felt especially wrong, even after almost twenty years.

"And you're still ship's clerk?" she said, trying only a little to disguise her tone of disappointment. "No promotions in the last, what? Five years?"

"It's a competitive field." Even to his own ears, it sounded like a lame excuse. Quint made a mental note to update his cover story before the next time he visited. Half a decade of static employment did not align well with the adventurous, ambitious young man he'd been when he'd first left Ember Bay for the wider world.

"Must be," Ma said, shrugging her broad shoulders. "At least the pay is good. They've given you enough shore leave for this visit, I hope?"

"Plenty."

"That's good, at least." She stopped before the last door on the left, pushed it open. "Here we are."

Quint stepped through the door, and into a memory.

More than anywhere else on Ember Bay, his room was frozen in time. It looked precisely the way it had when he was a teenager. A woodblock print framed above the bed depicted the legendary Battle of Zelda Strait, two fleets exchanging volleys of broadsides as the looming cliffs towered above their sails. A collection of nautical paraphernalia lay scattered about his dressers: ships in bottles, lengths of cord he'd used to practice knots, even a heavy brass sextant. All exactly as he'd left them the last time he'd slept here, save for the two sea chests the twins had stacked beneath the window.

Beside his bed sat a stack of leather-bound books with yellowing pages, the most tattered and dog-eared of which bore titles like *The Buried Plunder of Ebony Cove* and *Captain Storm and the Cursed Skull*. A mingled feeling of embarrassment and nostalgia crept through him as he recalled the late nights he'd stayed up reading them by moonlight, unwilling to risk his parents seeing lamplight streaming into the hall beneath his door.

So much has changed, he thought, and yet this room at least was the same. A memorial, almost, to the person he had been. So long ago, and so young.

The Quentin Thatch who had left this room behind at fifteen was, officially, dead. A shipboard accident involving a loose cannonball, a birdcage, and a cask of rum had resulted in an unexpected explosion aboard the Navy vessel *Reign of Peace*, seemingly resulting in the deaths of two young midshipmen while leaving the rest of the crew miraculously unharmed. Now safely deceased, Quint and Ophelia had slipped away in the commotion their scheme had caused, setting out to begin their new life of piracy.

But where Ophelia had no family worth the name, Quint still had his ma and pop, and Ember Bay itself. Fortunately, the glacial pace of the mail service to the remote isle had worked to their advantage, and one of Captain Redbeard's first piratical successes had been intercepting the postal vessel carrying news of Quint Thatch's demise. So for eighteen of the last twenty years, Quint's parents had labored under the carefully crafted delusion that their son had given up his dreams of a Navy commission for an unremarkable career in nautical accountancy.

He'd thought about telling them the truth on more than one occasion, but had always balked at the last minute. It was safer this way, he'd told himself, for both of them. No one in the wider Archipelago knew that the dreaded Captain Redbeard called this lonely island home, and no one from Ember Bay had ever made the connection between the wayward Quentin Thatch and the famous pirate.

One day, Quint had told himself, he'd tell them the truth. But he hadn't.

"I thought you'd have gotten rid of all this by now," he said, picking up one of his old favorites, a ship in a bottle. "Cleared it out so the Arms would have another room for rent."

"Don't think I haven't considered doing just that," Ma said, mock-fearsome. "But your father wouldn't hear of it. Said it's your room, and unless you decide it should be something else, your room it'll stay."

This last was followed by a pointed look.

"Maybe one day," Quint allowed. That was too far into the future to even contemplate. "I..." A lump in his throat. "I missed the funeral. I'm sorry."

"Of course you did." Ma Thatch waved a dismissive hand, but the words held no sting. "Quentin, love, your pop died a month ago. We weren't going to keep him lying around waiting for you to come back. Imagine the smell."

It wasn't funny, not really, but sometimes laughter was the only alternative to tears, so Quint chuckled. "I'd rather not."

"It'd drive the customers away, for one thing." She smiled sadly at him. "It was a nice enough service, you'll be glad to hear. And if you want to do something to remember him, we can host a shindig in his memory. If you want."

"I might," Quint admitted, pacing across the room. The creaking of the floorboards was as familiar as the chorus to a favorite song. He sat, the bed groaning softly beneath his weight. "Is there...are there any other things that need doing? About Pop, I mean."

Ma frowned. "How so?"

"Taxes," he said. "Or the law, I guess? I don't know. I haven't..."

Quint gave his hand an inarticulate wave, as if that could complete the sentiment. That he hadn't lost a father before. He supposed most people were amateurs in such an area, until they were suddenly forced to become experts.

Ma Thatch seemed to glean his meaning. She came over to the bed and sat down beside her son, pulling him into her gravity as the bed-frame groaned beneath the added weight.

"My sweet boy," she murmured, pulling Quint's head onto her shoulder. He didn't resist, just closed his eyes and breathed in the smell of coconut and pine. "Don't you worry about that. I talked to old Madam Stede right after the funeral. She got her solicitor's license some seven, eight years back, did you know?"

If he had ever known that tidbit of information, it'd been buried in the pile of other meaningless town gossip that arrived in his letters from home, but Quint nodded anyway.

"She took a look at Pop's documents," Ma continued. "His affairs were all in order. No loans, no outstanding contracts or anything like that. Everything's settled."

Quint exhaled, and felt a little of the pressure that had wrapped itself around his heart ease, just a bit.

"Well." There was enough hesitation in his ma's voice that he lifted his head from her shoulder, scooted away so that he could look at her full on. "Except for one thing."

"And that is?" Quint asked, the tightening around his heart returning as a thousand terrible scenarios chased themselves through his mind, each worse than the last. Pop had contracted some terrible disease. Pop had been attacked by a gang of cutthroats. A gang of cutthroats had attacked Pop *and* given him some terrible disease—

"It's that damned boat," Ma said.

The morbid fantasies vanished.

"The *Wisherman*?" Quint asked, frowning. "What about it?"

"It's the one thing in his will he left entirely to you," Ma Thatch said, heedless of how her words tightened her son's throat. "Everything else goes to me, since he knew you weren't interested in staying on Ember Bay and running the Arms."

"He left me the *Wisherman*," Quint repeated, his mind drifting back, back, back in time.

To long days spent trimming the sheets and hauling the lines of the little sailboat, Pop bellowing out one of his endless repertoire of sea shanties in a horribly off-key voice as he steered them around Ember Bay's coast. To diving from the deck into the crystalline waters of the southern lagoons, spear in hand, cutting through the waves as sleek and nimble as any fish.

To him and Pop sitting with their legs dangling over the rail, fishing poles in hand, lures bobbing up and down with the tide. To lying stretched out along the *Wisherman*'s deck while a million stars wheeled through night sky, Pop pointing out each of the constellations, his deep voice reciting the myths that had given each of them their names while the distant nightfires lit his craggy face orange and gold.

"It was a shrewd move, I'll admit," Ma was saying, jolting Quint from his reverie. "Suppose he knew that if he'd left it to me it would've just ended up as so much kindling."

Though she had been a capable mariner herself once upon a time, Lola Thatch had not shared her husband's obsession with the sea. And while she had not begrudged him the *Wisherman*, she'd complained often and loudly that taking the sailboat out upon the waters would be the death of him someday, whether by shark or storm.

Angels, Quint thought suddenly. *I hope neither of those were what got him in the end.*

He still didn't know what had, he realized.

"Ma," he asked, and was surprised to find his heart racing like it did before a raid, "how *did* Pop die?"

"Ah, love." Lola Thatch looked down at her hands in her lap, as though unsure what to do with them. "It were his heart."

"Oh." The words fell on Quint like a hammer. Strange that the best part of his father should be the part that killed him.

"Don't worry yourself over it too much," Ma said, in that tone of exaggerated calm folk used when they were trying to speak easily on a hard subject. "It all happened very fast. Doc Peake said he probably didn't feel any pain at all."

Small mercy, Quint thought. He rested his head against his ma's shoulder, and for a while they just sat like that: not crying, not speaking, just taking comfort in one another's presence.

"I'm sorry I wasn't here," he said at last.

"It's alright." She reached down and squeezed his hand. "You're here now."

Quint nodded, not trusting himself to speak further.

"And we've got what he left us," Ma continued, looking around Quint's childhood room. "Our memories, and this place, and that damned boat."

Quint barked out a startled laugh.

"Don't suppose you *would* sell me the boat, would you?" she asked hopefully. "I've talked to Ms. Jacques—not Francesca, she retired a few years back, I mean her daughter Antoinette—and she said she'd get us a good price—"

"Absolutely not." Quint stood, the bed creaking its protest at the sudden shift in weight. "Where is she?"

Her brow furrowed. "Antoinette Jacques? The lumberyard, of course—"

"No," Quint said, shaking his head. Excitement was growing from his grief, like a flower from waste. "The *Wisherman.* Is she still seaworthy?"

"I'm not sure she was *ever* seaworthy," Ma said, but raised a palm in acquiescence. "She got pretty battered by a typhoon last wet season. Your pop beached her at Cinder Cove, well past the high tide line."

Quint whistled. Cinder Cove was a secluded beach an hour's hike south through some of the island's thickest jungle. But after so long aboard ships, maybe it was time for him to stretch his legs.

"I'll head there now," he said, going to the door, then paused, hand on the knob. "Unless...if you need help around the tavern..."

Ma Thatch rose from the bed, waving a dismissive hand. "Your pop and I have run this joint for almost forty years, love. I'll be alright for the morning, and we employ some of the village youth for the afternoon and evening shifts."

Quint nodded. He had been one of those youths, and had learned how to properly pour a pint well before he'd been old enough to drink the stuff.

"And Amara?" he asked, trying to sound casual.

"Just helping me out with the morning duties," Ma said, with a look that told him she knew exactly why he'd asked. "She likes having a break from a houseful of young boys."

Boys? Quint wondered how many children she must have at this point. Wondered too whether some of them might have had red hair, if things had turned out differently for them both.

"Go on," Ma said, opening the door for him. "Go take a gander at Pop's boat. Your boat now, I should say." She pursed her lips. "Don't suppose I could at least convince you to rename her?"

"Not a chance," Quint said, kissing his ma on the top of her head. Then he ducked out of his childhood bedroom, heading toward his inheritance.

"Oh," Ma Thatch called after him. "And watch out for the mermaid!"

6

Quint made two brief detours before heading to Cinder Cove. The first was a stop at Rosa's Mercantile, from which he emerged carrying a rod and tacklebox under one arm and a picnic basket in the other. Cinder Cove was known across the island as a good fishing spot, and he expected he'd work up an appetite on the hike there.

Though if a mermaid had taken up residence at the cove, it might not be as popular as it had once been.

It was a short walk down the high street from Rosa's to the local carpenter's shop, which still bore the hand-carved lettering ANAND & SONS over the doorway. The *blam-blam-blam* rhythm of hammering echoed from within, along with the softer sighs of wood being sanded.

"Mr. Anand?" Quint called as he stepped inside, his eyes once more taking a moment to adjust to the sudden change in light. "It's Quint Thatch, Clarent's son—"

"Hey, Quint." The figure that had been bent over a half-finished table straightened, rubbing sawdust from his hands on his apron. Not the venerable Mr. Anand, but his son, a handsome man with dusky skin, calloused hands, and a neatly trimmed black beard.

"Hari?" Quint felt his brows lift in surprise. Of all the other islanders his own age, only Hari had been able to match Quint's enthusiasm for getting off Ember Bay and seeing the wider Archipelago. To find him here, in his father's shop, struck Quint with an odd sense of guilt. "I...wasn't expecting to see you here."

"Why not?" Hari said, stepping in and wrapping Quint into a friendly hug, which he returned. "It's my name above the door."

"Yours and both your brothers'," Quint replied, falling almost unconsciously into the rhythm of their long-ago banter as they separated. "I thought Chander or Lalit would've been the ones to take up the family business."

All three of the Anand sons had departed Ember Bay once they'd come of age, seeking apprenticeships with master carpenters in the cosmopolitan Jewel Isles rather than with their father. Quint hadn't seen either of Hari's older brothers since he himself had left for the Navy, and when he'd last visited home a decade ago Hari had still been abroad.

"Nah." Hari stroked his beard, peering at the beam above Quint's head as if he could see through it to the sign on the other side. "Chander opened his own shop on Opal, and Lalit got married to a nice boy from Sapphire, so Papa left me the place when he retired."

"Congratulations," Quint said, wondering whether he would have taken over the Arms if he'd stayed. Probably not; his parents didn't believe in retirement. "Guess you'll have to change the sign."

"Says who?" Hari quirked a smile, glancing over his shoulder.

Now that Quint's eyes had adjusted, he saw several young boys laboring in the back of the shop, sanding down the edges of chairs or measuring lengths of wood for sawing. Quint counted four of them, all under the age of ten.

"Quite a crew you've got there," Quint said, trying to recall whether Hari's younger self had dreamed of fatherhood, or if this was just one more example of the apparently inevitable transformation into one's parents that seemed to strike all of Ember Bay's residents. "Must be nice to have the extra help."

"Gotta keep them out of trouble somehow," Hari smirked. He looked about to say something else, but was interrupted by another *blam-blam-blam* round of hammering.

"Mani!" he called, turning around. The eldest of the four boys froze in place, hammer raised with both hands over his head, guiltily awaiting his father's judgment as Hari strode over to examine the wooden cart he'd been working on.

"You're supposed to hit the *nails*, kiddo," Hari said in a voice of long-suffering patience as he surveyed the round indentations the hammerhead had left in the wood. "Now I'm gonna have to replace these planks before we get this back to Mrs. Cavendish."

So she really *hadn't* had a cart to loan him this morning, Quint noted, relieved that his charm hadn't failed him after all.

"Sorry, Papa," Mani said, lowering his hammer and running a hand through his curling mop. His expression brightened. "You want me to saw the new planks?"

"No," Hari said, a little too quickly. "No, kiddo, I'll do it myself. Just...how about you measure them instead, okay? You're good with measurements."

The boy's eyes widened, as if his father had just promised him an unimaginable treat. "Can I use the straightedge?"

"Sure," Hari said, mussing his son's already-mussy hair. "But no sawing them yourself, no matter how confident you are in the measurements. Not until I've had a look, understand?"

Mani grinned and sped off toward the back of the shop, nearly toppling a pile of wooden beams as he sprinted past.

"Absolutely hopeless," Hari said fondly, turning back to Quint. "Let me guess. You're here to see if I can fix up the boat."

Quint's jaw dropped. "How'd you know?"

"Lucky guess." Hari shrugged and looked around at the tools hanging from the walls, the half-finished projects scattered about the shop floor. "Fathers have a way of leaving the things they love most to their sons."

"I suppose they do." Quint nodded, a fresh wave of pain rising up inside him.

Grief, he'd learned, was like the tide. It ebbed and flowed, sometimes deep enough to drown in, other times low enough that he scarcely noticed it. He wondered whether it would ever fully leave him, or if he simply needed to learn how to live with this new rhythm.

He suspected it was the latter.

"Right." Hari looked around at the shop, gave a pensive frown. "Afraid you're out of luck, though. I've got a full backlog right now."

"I can see that," Quint said, looking around at the various tables, armoires, carts, and crates in varying stages of construction. "Don't suppose I could convince you to bump me up the queue at all?"

Hari snorted. "The Anand family's immune to bribes, Quint. No matter how good the salary of a ship's clerk might be."

Quint opened his mouth to protest, but suddenly Mani was at his elbow, a straightedge ruler in one hand and a hammer in the other.

"You're a ship's clerk?" the boy asked, staring up at him with bright, inquisitive eyes. "Really?"

"Aye." Quint nodded, a little taken aback. "Aboard the merchantman *Waterhouse*."

"What's her tonnage?" Mani asked, eyes growing wide. "Which routes does she take? What percentage is your upcharge after accounting for shipping fees and import tax?"

"Uh..." Quint shifted his weight, feeling suddenly as if he were treading on uneven ground. No one had ever shown *interest* in his cover identity's job before. Hells, he had chosen it specifically for that reason. Whenever he mentioned being a ship's clerk to someone from Ember Bay their eyes immediately glossed over, followed by a hasty change in the subject of conversation.

"It's not fixed," he said finally, avoiding the boy's gaze. "My cap'n likes to haggle for the best price, you see."

But Mani was not to be deterred. "But there's got to be a minimum percent—"

"Mani," Hari said, settling a calloused hand on his son's shoulder. "Mr. Thatch is a customer."

"Oh!" Mani raised the hammer and gave Quint a gap-toothed grin. Quint fervently hoped the two were unrelated. "What needs fixin', Mr. Thatch?"

"Nothing," Quint lied.

"Then why're you in our shop?" a familiar voice said from behind him.

Quint turned in a slow circle. Amara stood in the doorway, a laundry basket balanced against her hip.

"Amara," he said, connecting the dots in his brain. "I...you and Hari?"

"No need to sound so surprised," Hari smirked, as Amara set the laundry down on the shop counter and kissed her husband's cheek. "After I came back from the Jewels you were out of the picture, so I didn't have any competition for the title of Handsomest Man on the Island."

"You never did, dear," Amara said, winking at Quint. "What's he here for?"

"I..." Quint looked between the two of them, happily leaning against one another. Two of his oldest friends, together. It felt right.

"You and Hari," he repeated, grinning like an idiot.

"We heard you the first time," Amara said, smiling. "Besides, I told you that you should stop by and see Mr. Anand."

Hari snorted. "As you can see, motherhood has only improved our dear Amara's sense of humor."

"Actually," Quint admitted, "I came here looking for help fixing up my pop's boat. But seeing as you're all booked up—"

"Can I help?" Mani asked, waving the hammer. Quint neatly side-stepped it, and it passed through the space where his ribs had been a moment before. "He's a *ship's clerk*, Mama!"

The mundane title was half-whispered in a tone of utmost reverence.

"He is," Amara agreed, looking appraisingly at Quint. "And he needs help repairing his ship."

Mani's eyes grew so wide that Quint was afraid they might take leave of his skull. "You have a *ship*?"

"Yes," Quint said automatically, before remembering that he wasn't Captain Redbeard here, nor captain of anything else, as far as the good folk of Ember Bay knew. "I mean, no. It's a boat."

"A *boat*," Mani whispered in that same reverent tone, as if he did not live on an island where he saw them every day. He turned an imploring gaze to his parents. "Can I help Mr. Thatch fix his boat, Mama? Please?"

"I think that's a good idea," Amara said, a familiar mischievous glint in her eyes. "Don't you, Mr. Thatch?"

Quint opened his mouth to say no, but Amara wasn't finished. "And while you're working together, you can tell Mani everything you know about being a ship's clerk. It's his dream job, you know."

She held his gaze, as though daring him to disagree. Hari looked on, amusement dancing in his eyes.

"Of course," Quint heard himself saying. Amara had always had a knack for getting him to agree to things he'd had no intention of. "I'd love to have his help."

Mani gave a whoop of delight, swinging both hands into the air. The hammer passed inches from Quint's elbow.

"Finish measuring those planks for me first, kiddo," Hari said, seizing his son's wrist and gently prying the hammer from his grasp.

Undeterred, Mani ran off to the back of the shop, narrowly avoiding knocking over a pair of sawhorses.

"He'll be useless at repairs," Hari confided, leaning in so that neither Mani nor his younger sons could hear him. "But he'll do great on the boat once you get her seaworthy. He's almost as obsessed with ships and boats as he is with record-keeping."

"I'll be glad to have him," Quint said, and halfway meant it. The boy's exuberance had to count for *something*, even if his skills were not nearly the equal of his parents'. Besides, Quint had captained a vessel long enough to know that an extra pair of hands was always useful, no matter the task.

He just had to keep Mani away from any hammers, saws, shears...all tools, really.

Maybe I'll let him hold the nail bucket, Quint thought, but was immediately assailed by a dozen distressing visions of how even *that* simple task could go horrifically wrong.

"The boat's beached at Cinder Cove," he said, returning to the task at hand. "I'll head down there myself, see what condition it's in. Then Mani can come lend a hand tomorrow afternoon."

"Watch out for the mermaid," the Anands said in unison.

"She tried drowning Horatio Clarke last month," Amara added, by way of explanation. "Poor bloke turned tail and ran before she could get too close, but it was still a near thing."

Great, Quint thought. He smiled at them. "I'll be careful. And keep an eye on Mani while I'm at it."

"Thank you," Hari said with a grateful nod. But his wife was not as quick to let Quint off the hook.

"*And* teach him everything you know about being a ship's clerk," she reminded him. "Don't break a promise to a little boy, Quint."

"I won't," he said, ignoring the sting in those words. He placed one hand over his heart, raised the other to the heavens. "On my honor, I'll teach your son every last thing I can about figures, sums, taxes and fees, and all the rest. Every single thing I've learned my whole life about being a ship's clerk."

It would be the easiest promise he'd ever kept, since he knew absolutely nothing on the subject.

7

B linking in the bright morning sun, Quint emerged from Anand & Sons to the sound of a familiar scratchy voice.

"*Cap'n on deck!*" Jimmy squawked, landing with a fluttering of wings on Quint's shoulder. "*Look alive, Cap'n on deck!*"

"Pipe down, you," Quint growled, glancing quickly up and down the main street to see if anyone had overheard. Thankfully the only other souls in sight were Rosa, sitting in front of Rosa's Mercantile, and her longtime suitor Beauregard Devereaux, who appeared to be performing a sonnet for her. Neither was paying any attention to Quint.

Reassured that he was in no danger of being found out, Quint set out into the lush tropical forest of the island, Jimmy flapping along above him.

The town of Ember Bay had been founded a little over a century ago, but the island itself had been used as a stopover point by the nomadic Ikai, one of the Archipelago's indigenous peoples, since time immemorial. It was they who had first trodden the well-worn hiking path through the tropical jungle Quint now followed, and a few of their distinctive stonework monuments still marked the trail.

Growing up, Quint had never devoted a great deal of thought to the island's original inhabitants, merely assuming that they had decided at some distant point in history that Ember Bay was no longer to their liking and sailed their catamarans and outriggers to other shores instead. It was not until he'd enlisted in the Navy that the possibility had occurred to him that the Ikai may not have ceased their visits to Ember Bay voluntarily. It took him longer still to come to grips with the brutal truth that the Navy he'd grown up hero-worshipping had played a direct hand in ousting the Archipelago's native peoples from their ancestral lands.

These were not the sole reasons for his eventual desertion and subsequent life of piracy; just one link in the chain of events that led to that irrevocable choice. But his conscience was lighter once he had ditched the purple jacket at last, all the same.

Now, as he hiked the well-worn trail beneath palms and pandanus and pines, he felt a faint stirring of guilt whenever he caught sight of the ancient stone figures, with their stylized faces and intricately detailed hands. He wanted to apologize to the long-departed stone carvers, to make amends, somehow, for the wrong that had been done them.

But—as Quint felt more keenly now than ever—there was no undoing the past. All he could do was utter a silent prayer to whichever angel had provenance of the Ikai people, and hope that the small part he'd played in their oppression would not count too strongly against him in the heavenly ledger.

The ancient waystones were few and far between, however, and Quint found it impossible to maintain his melancholy mood. The sun had climbed high into the morning sky by now, but beneath the shade of the jungle canopy the air was cool and still. Vines draped over the branches of the trees, their flowers filling the air with their perfumed scents as hummingbirds and bees flitted between them. There was no sound save the faint whistling of the wind through the leaves above, punctuated occasionally by the chatter of birdsong or the croak of some tropical frog.

Quint inhaled deeply through his nose, breathing in the rich loam of the soil beneath him and the sweet petals of the flowers above.

It was good to be home.

$$\text{⚓}$$

Quint smelled the cove before he saw it.

Until his trek through the jungle, Quint had become so accustomed to the sting of salt air in his nostrils that he'd hardly noticed it. Now, after only a brief respite, the briny scent of waves and sand drew him onward, until he could see the faint gleam of golden sunlight glittering off blue waves.

"*Safe harbor!*" Jimmy squawked, flapping away to glide down the beach as Quint emerged from the trees.

True to its name, Cinder Cove was a black sand beach, its dark coloration due to the volcano that dominated the island's skyline. It was shaped like a south-facing crescent, its tranquil waters protected by a pair of rocky jetties to the east and west. A long wooden dock extended from the northern jetty, and though it looked battered and splintered by the wet season typhoons, Quint could easily picture his pop fishing off the end of it.

Despite the shade of the jungle, his hike had left him hot and sweaty. He stripped off his shirt and tied it about his waist, exposing his various tattoos to the sun for the first time that day, then set off down the beach in search of his boat.

The air thrummed with a distant rumble, one that might almost be mistaken for thunder, were it not for the way it shook the very ground beneath Quint's feet. Above the tree line a thick plume of black smoke rose from the volcano's crater.

"*Thar she blows!*" Jimmy called, skimming low over the sand. She landed beside Quint, little bird legs strutting as she struggled to keep pace, her head cocked toward him. "*Thar she blows, all hands on deck!*"

"She's just letting off some steam," Quint assured her, glancing up at the volcano. Already the plume of smoke and ash was tapering off, as he'd known it would. There hadn't been a major explosion on Ember Bay since shortly after the village's founding, and though periodic tremors and small lava flows were a constant fact of life on the island, most villagers gave the volcano no more thought than they did any other feature of the landscape. The likelihood of a major eruption occurring during the month or so Quint intended to stay here was vanishingly small.

"*All hands on deck,*" Jimmy repeated, sounding as dubious as a parrot could. She flapped up to Quint's shoulder, and he tickled the spot beneath her chin that she liked. He was rewarded with the high-pitched chirping sound Jimmy made whenever she was happy.

The *Wisherman* lay just ahead, her prow sticking out of the jungle as if it were a wave made of trees. He could just make out her peeling and faded paint, white above the waterline and red below, save for the barnacles still clinging to her hull.

The swell of grief rose in Quint once more, but this time it was mingled with another feeling he could not immediately name. It was as if he'd awoken one morning to find that his lover had left him, only for a long-lost and much-beloved family pet to return that same day. It did not negate the loss, but it lessened the sting of it, just a little.

He dropped the lure, tacklebox, and picnic basket onto the sand. Jimmy fluttered up to the bowsprit, the end of which had been snapped off by whatever storm had prompted Quint's pop to beach the *Wisherman* until he could find time to repair her. Time he hadn't had, but Quint did.

"Hey, old girl," Quint murmured, reaching out and running his hand gently along the hull. The paint beneath his fingers was chipped and faded, the bare wood showing beneath in more places than not.

There was a small hole in her starboard hull, just below the waterline. Quint was relieved to discover, upon closer inspection, that this was the result of damage rather than a rot in the wood. The former was fixable, while the latter would have required far more drastic repairs.

"Pop must've run her aground," he told Jimmy, who was strutting along the boat's rail above him.

"Better run aground than in the ground!" she squawked, eliciting a sad smile from Quint. It was one phrase among many she'd picked up from Pop.

As Quint traced the outline of the jagged hole, a memory rose: Pop's voice speaking to him from across the vast distances of time and mortality.

"You might think a ship's hull is like her skeleton," he'd said, while he and a much-younger Quint had examined a smaller puncture near the stern, which Quint could no longer recall the source of. "But you've got to think of her as the ship's soul. Hull, soul. Aye?"

The younger Quint had frowned, his hands behind his back. "I don't understand."

"Well." Pop Thatch had rubbed at his beard, which even then had been more gray than brown. "Sorry to say, lad, but you're going to experience some hurt in this life. Show me your hand."

Startled into compliance, Quint had extended his hand, revealing the half-inch splinter that had sunk into the tender flesh of his palm.

"Like that," Pop had said, taking Quint's slender hand in both of his larger ones. "Hurts, don't it?"

Quint had tried to keep his tone manfully stoic, but his adolescence betrayed him with a cracking voice. "Y-es, sir."

"Trying to hide it from me, eh?"

No longer trusting his voice, Quint had nodded.

"There's times to hide your pain," Pop had said, "and times to let another help you with it. Here."

His big hands had moved with surprising speed, and suddenly the splinter was gone.

"Ow!" Quint had yelped, more from surprise than actual hurt.

"Pain's like that," Pop had said, rubbing the spot around where the splinter had sunk in with his thumbs. "It hurts—can hurt a quite lot, in fact—but it's just pain. You'll heal from it in time, so long as you take care not to let it fester."

Quint's brow had furrowed. "Fester how?"

"Let it change you." A distant look had come into Pop's eye. "Make you sick, bitter. Pain passes, lad, but bitterness can rot you from the inside, if you let it."

The metaphor had been lost on young Quint. "What does this have to do with the *Wisherman*?"

"This is just damage," Pop had said by way of answer, slapping his palm against the hull beside the hole. "It'll mend, with care and attention. But if it were rot, it'd be a lot harder to fix. Y'see?"

Quint hadn't been sure if he did, but he'd nodded anyway. "I think. But...Pop?"

"Eh?"

"If you're...if there's rot"—he'd wet his lips, swallowed—"can it still be fixed? Or are you always going to be sick?"

Pop Thatch had clapped both hands on his son's shoulders and looked him in the eye, his green gaze so intent Quint had felt the urge to squirm away, though he'd resisted it.

"There's a cure for every sickness of the soul," Pop had said at last. "Folk can change, lad, no matter how far gone they might be. But they've got to recognize the need for themselves to change first. You understand?"

This time Quint thought he had. "If that's the first thing, what else do people need to change themselves? For the better, I mean."

"The same thing any mending needs," Pop had said, grinning as he'd handed Quint a hammer. "Time and hard work, and folks you trust to help you. Today, lad, that's you."

⚓

Quint made a slow circuit of the boat, assessing the damage with a seaman's experienced eye. Ma hadn't been exaggerating; the *Wisherman* had been badly battered by the typhoon, and she would need a good deal of care and attention before she was seaworthy again. Quint fervently wished he'd been able to procure more skilled assistance than that offered by Hari and Amara's eldest son.

In addition to the punctured hull and the broken bowsprit, several of the stanchions connected the rail to the deck had been snapped off, leaving the rail uneven. The keel and rudder were both intact, to Quint's immense relief, but the wheel was jammed, meaning he'd have to check the pulleys that connected it to the rudder to see if one of them had gotten stuck on something. The mainsail had been folded and placed in an oilcloth tarp, and the rigging stowed in a watertight container inside the *Wisherman*'s cramped cabin.

After an hour's careful assessment, Quint came to the relieved conclusion that the damage was fixable. It would take a few weeks, perhaps a month—but that was the time he'd allotted himself for this homecoming visit anyway. And what more fitting way to spend his time ashore, lying low from Imperial attention, than to fix up his pop's beloved boat?

He circled the *Wisherman* again, his hand trailing lightly along the hull, wary not to catch a splinter. The old wood with its chipped paint was familiar beneath his hand. Here and there he traced older dents and deep gouges; the scars not of the recent typhoon, but of countless nautical misadventures.

Some he had taken part in, like the time he and Pop had gone swimming with a pod of dolphins, only for the pod to scatter as a juvenile (but still massive) sea serpent had cruised through their midst. Pop had practically hurled Quint back into the *Wisherman*. Hauling himself up after his son, he'd landed against the deck so heavily that the point of his elbow had driven a divot into the planks, which remained to this day.

Other damage Quint had not been present for but had heard the stories repeated so many times that he could close his eyes and see the events unfold as if he'd been there himself. The long, shallow dent in the portside rail, for instance; a souvenir of the time Pop and Uncle Jun had gotten so drunk that they'd attempted to race their boats all the way around the island, only to collide and nearly sink each other before either could make it out of the harbor. To hear Ma tell it, that incident was the closest the two had ever come to blows in all their long friendship, but Jun and Pop had never been able to finish the tale without one or the other laughing to the point of tears.

For every scar, a story.

Pop, at the center of all those stories. Now gone from them, as empty and sharp and jagged as the hole in the *Wisherman*, or the one in Quint's heart. Strange, how absence stabbed deeper than any blade.

Quint pressed his hand flat against the hull, heedless of any splinters doing so might incur, and rested his head against the rail. Jimmy fluttered down to perch on his shoulder, nibbling his ear affectionately.

"*If wishes were fishes,*" she cackled. "*Hey-ho, ho-hey!*"

Startled by the old song Pop had named his boat for, Quint choked out a surprised laugh. Teardrops shook free of his abruptly stinging eyes, watering the black sand.

"We'd all swim in riches," he said, picking up the second half of the verse. "All live-long day."

He would have continued on to the next line, but a splash drew his attention, sending Jimmy squawking up to the *Wisherman*'s mainmast.

A long, sinuous shape had drawn itself up the beach, past the breaking waves and onto the damp black sand. Quint's first impression was that of a green-gray serpent, its tail flattened into a vertical paddle not unlike those of the tropical reef snakes he'd seen while diving in the Jewels. But where those were small and shy, this creature's body was bigger around than those of the great anacondas that lurked in the Ziltar waterways.

But the creature that surveyed Quint through wide, almost entirely black eyes was no more a snake than Quint himself was a monkey.

As he stared at it, the last of his unshed tears rolled down his cheek. The black eyes followed its trail with alert, curious interest, until it slipped from Quint's chin onto the sand. Then the creature's gaze jerked sharply upward, back to Quint's own eyes.

"You're leaking," the mermaid said.

8

Startled by the appearance of the creature gliding up the beach, Jimmy squawked and flapped into the trees, leaving a trail of parroted curses in her wake as she abandoned her master to the mermaid.

Quint's first instinct was to reach for the cutlass at his side, only to belatedly remember that the only blade he'd brought with him to this lonely cove was a kitchen knife, safely stored in the picnic basket lying in the sand at his feet. That had been an intentional choice, as most mermaids reacted even more poorly to armed humans than they did to those unarmed. Yet now, as those huge dark eyes stared unblinkingly up the beach at him, he found himself wishing for the comfort of a weapon all the same.

Another one of Pop's witticisms rose to mind, no doubt prompted by his other recollections.

"It ain't the gun you need to fear," he'd said while teaching Quint to shoot. "Gun's just a weapon, and a weapon's nothing more than a tool with a very specific purpose. It's the hand that holds it that makes it dangerous."

The hand, Quint thought, looking down at his own empty ones. *Or the man.*

He looked back up, just in time. The mermaid had begun to slither up the beach, but froze when it saw him looking. Its head swiveled around slowly as it took in its surroundings, pointedly avoiding looking at Quint, as if it hadn't noticed him yet.

"Hello," Quint said.

The mermaid gave a guilty start, then lowered its huge black eyes to him.

"You've stopped leaking." The voice was surprisingly high, with a mournful, haunting melodic quality to it. It sounded like whalesong rendered into plain human speech.

It also sounded disappointed.

"Just a thing we do sometimes," Quint said, fighting down the urge to wipe at his face, still splotchy from tears. For all he knew, the creature's apparent fascination with his crying was all that was keeping it from seizing him and dragging him down into a briny grave.

The mermaid's head tilted to one side, eyes narrowing as if in deep concentration—a gesture that was alarmingly human. The long dorsal fin that ran all the way to its tail began at the point where a human's hairline would, giving the impression that it had a single narrow stripe of hair, not unlike the style Ophelia sported. This dorsal fin was more pronounced on males, Quint recalled; the specimen on the beach before him must be female.

"Do you often do that?" she asked. "Leak, I mean."

"Not if I can help it."

"Hmm." Her tail lashed idly across the sand, leaving shallow furrows in its wake. Quint hoped it was a sign of boredom and not agitation. "Sometimes when I am below I release bubbles and watch them rise. Is it like that?"

"Sort of." Given the life he'd led thus far, this was not the strangest conversation Quint had ever participated in. But it was certainly edging its way up in the rankings. "Are you going to drown me?"

"Who said I was going to drown you?" the mermaid asked, placing one webbed hand against her chest in such an exaggerated posture of wounded pride that Quint would have wagered the *Angel* that she'd picked it up from observing humans.

"You're a mermaid," Quint said. "It's what you do."

"That's a rude assumption," she said. "I'm not drowning you *now*, am I?"

"Not yet."

She folded her arms across her chest. Contrary to the fancies of homesick sailors everywhere, she had not the slightest suggestion of breasts; mermaids were aquatic reptiles and did not nurse. "Exactly."

"Hmm." Quint turned slowly back to the *Wisherman*, then turned suddenly back toward the mermaid. To his utter lack of surprise, she'd slithered a few feet closer.

"See?" He leveled an accusatory finger at her. Just as before, she'd frozen when she'd caught him looking. Distantly, Quint wondered whether this was something they did with smaller prey, or if she just assumed his relatively smaller eyes were worse at tracking movement. "You're doing it again!"

"Alright, *fine*," the mermaid said, throwing up her webbed hands. "I'm trying to drown you. Happy?"

"You're not doing a very good job of it," Quint said, his voice calm even as his palms had begun to sweat. She was about ten feet away now, but that serpentine body could move almost as quickly over sand as it could through the water. If she came after him his best recourse was to turn and hightail it through the jungle, where the dense foliage would slow her down enough for him to escape.

He hoped. But then, he also hoped it wouldn't come to that.

"Now you're just being impolite," the mermaid said, her humanish torso swaying a little atop her tail—a posture that communicated indecision across species barriers.

"Not impolite," Quint shook his head, "just honest. And since we're being honest with each other, I have a question for you."

"Oh?" Her tone was coquettish, but the O shape her too-wide mouth made revealed sharklike teeth behind her thin lips.

"Where's the best fishing in this cove?"

Mermaids were territorial by nature. Her voice turned flat, suspicious. "Why do you want to know?"

"Just asking," Quint said. Careful to keep his eyes on her, he bent and picked up his fishing rod from where he'd stuck it in the sand, then pointed it at the battered pier extending over the northern edge of the cove. "It's there, right?"

Her hairless brows lifted in surprise. "How'd you—I mean, what makes you think so?"

"I grew up here," Quint said amicably. "That spot was my...was an island favorite for years. And you know what *this* does, right?"

He shook the rod for emphasis. The mermaid gave it a distasteful look, one webbed hand rising to her lip. "Might be I do."

"So," Quint pressed on, "if you *really* were set on drowning me, why not wait until I'd set myself up on the pier? You could've just dragged me into the water without so much fuss."

"I could have," the mermaid said slowly, as if working up the courage to admit to some embarrassing personal fault. "But I didn't."

"Why not?"

"Because I wanted a closer look at your patterning." She leaned demonstratively closer, and Quint had to fight down the urge to retreat a step. Up close her face was human enough, save the eyes: just slightly too large to sit comfortably within a human skull, and almost entirely occupied by the enormous pupils. Only a thin ring of cyan around them gave any indication of the iris.

"My patterning?" Quint blinked, then realized that her gaze was fixed not on his face, but upon his bare chest—and what was inked upon it. "You mean my tattoos?"

"Those," she confirmed, pointing a webbed finger. "Can I have a closer look?"

Quint suppressed the urge to smile. True, this wasn't quite how he'd expected this encounter to play out, but he'd be lying if it hadn't worked in his favor regardless. "Only if you promise not to drown me."

The mermaid froze, save for the agitated lashing of her tail back and forth across the sand. The inhabitants of the Archipelago knew little of the elusive mermaids' culture, which like any people's was not a monolith but varied between their pods and tribal groups that roamed the islands and the open seas. But of what little was known, one thing was held in common between them: to a mermaid, a promise was an inviolate thing. It was not that they were incapable of breaking their word—they were conscious beings possessed of free will, after all—but the cultural taboo amongst them for breaking a spoken promise was as strong as that of cannibalism in most human societies.

"But I *want* to drown you," the mermaid protested. "Like you said, it's what mermaids *do*. Especially to humans who intrude on our territory."

Quint made a show of looking about the cove where his late father had stowed his boat. "And Cinder Cove has been your territory for...how long, exactly?"

"That's not the point," she said, a ripple running down the length of her dorsal fin. Quint guessed this was a sign of embarrassment. "The point is that it's mine, and you're intruding."

"Uh-huh," Quint said, hooking his thumbs through his belt and leaning with feigned nonchalance against the *Wisherman*. "Look. I don't want to intrude on your territory, *and* I don't want to be drowned. Supposing we can cut a deal?"

The mermaid lowered herself so that she lay nearly flat against the sand, propping herself up on her elbows. "What kind of deal?"

"You don't drown me, for starters," Quint said, counting the points off on his fingers. "Or anyone else who comes here with me, for that matter."

"So far this doesn't sound very appealing," the mermaid complained. "What's in it for me?"

"You're allowed to ask me any question you like," Quint said, gambling that her initial curiosity about his tattoos was indicative of a broader inquisitive spirit. "About my tattoos, human society, or anything else you like."

She smiled, showing her pointed teeth.

"If I want a closer look at your *tatus*," she said, sounding out the unfamiliar word, "I could just drag you under and observe them at my leisure."

"You could," Quint allowed. "But that won't tell you the stories behind them."

She cocked her head in undisguised interest. "What stories?"

"All kinds." He tapped the pair of frigatebird silhouettes, identifiable by their outstretched wings and distinctively forked tails, soaring between his heart and his collarbone. "My best friend and I got these after we deserted the Navy together. To remind ourselves that we were going to fly free through fair weather and foul, and that we were going to do it together."

The mermaid slithered a bit closer for a better look, but Quint held out his hand. "Promise?"

Her tail lashed across the sand. "You don't expect me to spare you for stories alone, do you?"

"Of course not," Quint said. He nudged the picnic basket with his foot. "Can I open this?"

The mermaid nodded her assent. Quint crouched, not taking his eyes from her, and drew out a pair of roundish fruits, their green skin just beginning to turn red. "Ever had a mango before?"

"Is it food?" There was definitely a hopeful cast to the mermaid's singsong voice. "It looks a little like an egg."

"It's a fruit," Quint said, tossing one to her. "Here."

She caught it between her webbed fingers and held it up to her huge black eyes, inspecting it closely. Quint reached into the basket and pulled out his kitchen knife, intending to show her how to peel the skin with the pointed nails of her webbed fingers. "Here—"

He needn't have bothered. The mermaid opened her mouth wider than any human could, revealing a front row of perfectly triangular teeth. Quint just had time to note with some surprise that behind them lay flat molars before the mango disappeared whole into the mermaid's mouth.

Her jaw worked with a terrifying, mechanical violence. Quint was deeply thankful that her initial curiosity had won out over her desire to drown him.

"There's a pit—" he tried to warn her, but the pulped remains of the mango were already disappearing down her throat, pit and all. A thin trail of juice dribbled from one side of her mouth.

"It's good!" she exclaimed, her eyes so wide that the whites around the narrow rings of blue were revealed. "It's—it has a taste I can't describe. A little like halibut, or scallop, but the texture's closer to sea-grass."

"It's sweet," Quint said, using the knife to cut a slice of his own mango. "That's the other half of my offer. I can't promise I'll stop by here every day, but I will most days. And every time I do, I'll bring you something to eat."

It was a bargain he could reliably keep. Ma Thatch kept the kitchen of the Queen's Arms well-stocked, and a few extra lunches was a small price to pay for keeping the mermaid pacified.

Said mermaid licked her lips with her disturbingly long tongue. "More mangoes?"

"If you like," said Quint, grinning as he popped another slice of his own mango into his mouth. *Just wait until she discovers cake.* "Do we have a deal?"

She considered for only a moment longer, then gave a vigorous nod, rising up so that she was nearly eye level with Quint.

"We do," she said, crossing her arms in a deliberate gesture of nonaggression.

"By sea and sky, I"—she made a long, musical sound no human throat could possibly replicate—"do agree to your terms, so long as you uphold your end of the pledge."

"I, Quentin Thatch, so swear," Quint said, falling back on the phrasing of his oath of loyalty to the Imperial Navy. This promise would be easier to keep, at least, and trouble his conscience less.

He stuck out his hand. "You can call me Quint, though."

"Quint," she said, sounding it out. "You can call me   "

Another long, echoing whalesong sound.

"Right." Quint coughed, cleared his throat, and made an attempt at replicating the sound.

"Stop!" The mermaid waved both her webbed hands frantically. "Your pronunciation is *highly* offensive."

"Sorry," Quint apologized. He opened his mouth to try again, but the mermaid shook her head.

"Don't," she said, frowning. "Your voice is not strong enough, is it?"

"I don't think it is," he admitted, rubbing his chin. "Does it...mean something? Something in human words?"

"Hmm." Her huge eyes blinked slowly, evidently in concentration. "I suppose the closest meaning in your tongue would be She Who Glides Through the Current to Lurk Unseen Amongst the Seaweed Groves."

This time it was Quint's turn to blink.

"She Who Glides Through the Current...er. That's a bit of a mouthful."

She smiled her shark's smile. "Lurk will do."

"Lurk," Quint said, trying it out. It suited her, somehow, with her snakelike body and its wavy stripes, which no doubt were a great aid in keeping her hidden amongst the drifting strands of seaweed. "Pleased to meet you."

She nodded, then slithered forward with such alarming speed that Quint had to restrain himself from fleeing into the jungle. *She promised,* he reminded himself, and a mermaid was no more likely to betray her given word than he was to eat a baby.

But then, if cannibals existed, surely lying mermaids did as well.

He needn't have feared. Lurk halted just in front of him, drawing herself up so that her eyes were level with his chest. Her huge dark eyes peered at the frigatebird tattoos he and Ophelia had gotten together, what felt like a lifetime ago.

"I've seen birds like this," Lurk said after a moment's consideration. "With the split tails. They flock whenever there's a school of a fish in frenzy, out in the Deep."

Quint nodded. "They're good luck. One more reason for the tattoo."

"Tattoo," she repeated, pronouncing it correctly this time, then reached out and touched one of the inked birds. Her fingers were scaly and smooth, but not unpleasant. "It doesn't come off?"

"Some do," Quint said, thinking of the elaborate henna patterns Hari and his family adorned themselves with on festival days. "But not mine."

Lurk sank lower, her tail slithering backwards to allow for the decrease in height. "What about this one?" Quint looked down, realized she was peering at the chain of flowers adorning his left bicep. "And these?"

"Got a scar in a knife fight," he said, wincing at the memory. "Still there if you look close, but for a while it was pretty ugly. I got these to cover it up."

"I guess that means you won the fight," Lurk said. Quint thought it might have been a joke.

She rose with that same alarming serpentine swiftness, looking closely at a tattoo on Quint's shoulder. The only tattoo, he realized with some alarm, that he'd hoped she wouldn't notice.

"What is *that*?" Lurk asked, looking closely at the half-naked female form on Quint's shoulder, her hair draped artfully to protect her modesty.

Nothing, Quint almost said, but realized in time that denial would negate their agreement. Embarrassment was preferable to being drowned, if only just. "A mistake."

Lurk's gaze drifted to the lower half of the offending tattoo, to the sensuous fishtail the woman's torso sprouted from. Her eyes widened. "Is that—by the Deep. Is this what you people really think we look like?"

"Only those of us who are young and stupid," Quint answered, feeling a flush rising in his cheeks.

"Oh," she said brightly. "So you're both?"

"I used to be," Quint admitted, rubbing at the back of his neck. "Less of either as time goes by, I hope."

Her laugh was high, musical, and startlingly human. Quint's flush deepened.

"You change color, too?" she said, slithering around him for a better look at his neck, which had turned nearly as red as his hair. "I've seen octopus do it for camouflage, but had no idea humans could too."

She returned to in front of him, looking up and down the beach at their surroundings: green jungle, black sand, blue water. "Can't imagine turning red would help you hide much, though."

"That's not why we do it," Quint said, putting a hand over the offending mermaid tattoo. "It's…we can't do it on purpose—hey!"

Lurk had darted forward, the motion one of her more unnervingly snakelike ones, bringing her face mere inches from his. Quint had a panicked recollection of the boy's adventure stories he'd devoured growing up, their pages filled with beautiful mermaids falling in love with brave sailors, and found himself fervently hoping such accounts were wholly fictional.

He needn't have worried.

"What do these ones mean?" Lurk asked, her sharp nail poking him just below his right eye. Quint winced. "They're a different color than the others."

"Those aren't tattoos," Quint said. "They're freckles."

"I've never seen a human with them," Lurk said, leaning away. Quint was glad for the breathing space. "Then again, I've never been this close to a human before either. At least not a live one."

Quint decided not to ponder the implications of that statement. "Most don't have them. Mostly those of us whose skin is…"

"Fishbelly colored?" Lurk suggested.

"Pale," Quint corrected. Mermaid values were not human values, and a creature whose name included elements like "lurk" and "seaweed" might see nothing objectionable in the comparison. "Freckles are more common in those of us with lighter skin."

"Is that why you turn red?" Lurk pressed. "So people can't see these freckles?"

"I suppose," Quint said, eager to move on from this topic of discussion. "Are you still hungry?"

Lurk smiled, revealing her pointed teeth. "Always."

"Lucky for you, then," Quint said, bending to reach into the picnic basket, "I brought enough for two."

He unfolded a small tablecloth he'd borrowed from Rosa's Mercantile, spreading it across the sand between them, then put a pair of plates on it. These he piled high with the contents of the picnic basket: sliced pineapple, sweet bread rolls stuffed with shredded pork, and mounds of rice liberally sprinkled with dried strips of coconut.

"I hope you like it," he said as he scooped the last of the rice from the ceramic pot it had come in. "I'm not sure what mermaids eat."

"Everything," Lurk said, busily stuffing slices of pineapple into her mouth. Quint wondered whether he should teach her how to use silverware, then wrote it off as a waste of time.

Instead, he reached into the picnic basket and produced a bottle. "I forgot glasses. You don't mind sharing?"

Lurk shook her head. "What is it?"

Quint uncorked the bottle and offered it to the mermaid, grinning. "Have you ever tried lemonade?"

9

T he sun was just sinking toward dusk when Quint returned to the Queen's Arms, the lantern hanging above the smiling, improbably muscular monarch already lit. He put his hand on the brass doorknob with its mermaid knocker and stepped into the cool dimness of the Arms, already calling out. "I'm back, Ma, sorry it's so—"

"WELCOME HOME!" came a chorus of bellowing voices, loud as cannon fire in the tavern's small space.

Quint blinked, looking around as his eyes adjusted to the lower light. Half the island, it seemed, had packed themselves into the Arms. Every stool at the bar was full, every table and booth occupied. A sea of faces grinned at him, some with froth still on their lips from their raised tankards.

A pop echoed in the wake of the chorused voices, gunshot-loud but merrier in character. Ma stood behind the bar, foam spewing from the champagne bottle she'd just popped as she poured it into a set of glass flutes.

"What is all this?" Quint asked, unable to contain the grin spreading across his face.

"Ain't they teached you to read, boy?" Old Hawkins, unmoved from his habitual booth, jabbed a finger into the air. Quint followed it to see a banner stretched out across the tavern's rafters, proclaiming WEL-

COME HOME QUENTIN in an elaborate, flowing script that was nearly the precise opposite of Pop's blocky lettering.

"You shouldn't have—" he started, but already a champagne flute was being pressed into his hand. Quint was pulled into the crowd of beaming townsfolk. Many of their faces were familiar, though the passing of years had driven the names of most from Quint's memory. Those whom he didn't know were mostly younger, but their faces bore clues of their relation to his childhood friends and acquaintances. Nearly all greeted him by name, and he did the same where he could.

More than a few had kind words to say about his pop. Quint thanked them, finding himself at a loss to find a better way to express his gratitude. Not for the first time he wondered at the inadequacy of mere words, set against the whole of a person's vibrant, teeming life.

"He was a right rascal, your old man," Mr. Anand was saying. Save for his thick silver mustache and balding crown, Ember Bay's retired carpenter was the mirror image of his son Hari. "Did he ever tell you about the time we threaded the Ziltar Needle?"

Pop had, in fact, but Quint saw no reason to dampen Mr. Anand's spirits. "Remind me."

"This was a long time back, mind," Mr. Anand said, extending the hand not holding a glass of lassi for emphasis, as if that span of years could be encompassed by the length of his arm. "Back when I had a full head of hair, and your ma and pop had barely started courting. We were taking some shore leave on South Ziltar at the time: me, your folks, and your Uncle Jun, all holed up together after—"

"After the typhoon," Ma Thatch interrupted, deftly elbowing her way between Quint and Mr. Anand on her way to one of the booths, a tray full of drinks balanced expertly in one hand. "Remember, Manish? We had to stay in that dreadful tavern near a week while it blew through."

"Right." Mr. Anand nodded as Ma continued past, toward a booth full of young fishermen who had to have been teens the last time Quint had visited. "Like your ma said, we'd holed up in a South Ziltar tavern, and after a week we were desperate for some fresh air and a chance to stretch our legs. While we'd been cooped up your pop had struck up a wager with one o' the other folk stuck there on who was the better sailor. Now, what was his name..."

Quint sipped his champagne politely while he waited for Mr. Anand to recall the name of the other sailor.

"Cap'n Montcrief!" Mr. Anand said, snapping his fingers. "That was his name."

"The pirate?" Quint felt his eyebrows lift. Pop's retelling of the story had only ever referred to his rival as "Monty." That the elder Thatch had raced one of the most fearsome pirates of the last half-century in a friendly competition strained credulity.

"Of course not," Uncle Jun's voice boomed, the man himself appearing a moment later to throw a massive arm about Mr. Anand's shoulders. "Manish is just mixing up stories. Happens to the best of us once we've had a bit too much to drink."

Frowning, Quint was about to ask what story *had* involved the infamous Captain Montcrief but was cut off by Mr. Anand's vigorous nodding.

"Of course," he said, taking another sip of his lassi, leaving a drop trailing from his mustache. "I misspoke. Anyhow, the four of us took this other fellow up on his challenge to see who could thread the Ziltar Needle fastest."

"Damned fool notion," Uncle Jun said, but he was smiling at the recollection. "I told your pop not to a half-dozen times at the least."

"You were there?" one of the twins asked Jun, appearing beside Quint so unexpectedly despite her size that he nearly dropped his champagne.

The other was suddenly flanking him, her eyes equally bright with interest. "How come we've never heard this story?"

"Never you mind," their father scowled, but Mr. Anand grinned.

"Not surprising he never told you this one," he said, clearly enjoying having fresh ears to share the tale with—nearly as much as he was enjoying Jun's evident discomfort, Quint noticed. "Your baba's part in it is...ah, unglamorous."

Jun's scowl deepened. The twin to Quint's left—Ling, he remembered, noting the birthmark on her neck—giggled, but to his right Tai made an impatient "get on with it" gesture.

"The Ziltar Needle," Mr. Anand continued, "is a narrow channel between North and South Ziltar, where the two islands come together. A few thousand years ago they were a land bridge between the two, or so the scholars say..."

"More to the point," Uncle Jun chimed in, his embarrassment over his unspecified part in the story giving way to the sailor's compulsion not to leave a tale unfinished once started, "the Needle runs a full mile between the two islands. To either side, steep cliffs of crumbling rock, some like as not to come crashing down on the heads of the unwary. The currents runnin' through the Needle are powerful strong, and unpredictable to boot. And just beneath the surface, countless jagged reefs."

The twins looked on in rapt attention as Mr. Anand sipped his lassi. Quint nursed his champagne flute, the story suddenly injected with a melancholy note for him. Uncle Jun's description of the Needle was nearly word-for-word the same as Pop's had been.

That was what made a memory, Quint thought. Not the events themselves so much as their recollection, recited and refined with each telling until it became a litany, the movements of the story as carefully choreographed as any dance. Like any entertainment, there was an art to it.

"...So there we were," Mr. Anand was saying as Quint's attention returned to the present. "The four of us in one skiff, smaller even than Thatch's old *Wisherman*. In the other Monty and three of his crew. We set off at the same time, a wind blowing in from the nor'east to drive us through the Needle's opening. Monty's vessel had the lead, but only by a hair, and we were fast behind."

"Your ma was in the prow," Jun chimed in, nodding at Lola Thatch as she continued to deftly weave her way through the partygoers, delivering drinks and clearing tables with practiced efficiency.

Quint felt a grin tugging at the corners of his mouth. For all her professed dislike of the *Wisherman*, Ma had always been an able hand on those occasions she'd joined in on their nautical outings.

"She's always had sharp eyes, but that day it was like the angels themselves were telling her where each shift in the current came, where every reef lurked just below the waves. By the time we were through, we were halfway convinced your pop's new lady friend was half an angel herself."

"I remember," Quint said, though of course these events had occurred well before his own birth. "He always said that was why he called Ma his angel."

This term of endearment had profoundly affected Quint's religious perceptions. Growing up, he'd always pictured angels not as ethereal, somewhat inscrutable beings unrestricted by such limited concepts as gender, mortality, and time, but as sturdy, practical women not much given to nonsense.

"Aye," Mr. Anand agreed. "She steered us true that day for certain. Your pop and I were both on the mainsail, tacking with the wind where we could and rowing where we couldn't."

"And Baba?" Tai asked. Her father did not meet her eyes.

"At the tiller, of course," Mr. Anand chuckled, giving Jun an affectionate pat on the shoulder. "Big man like him, of course he'd be our anchor. Steered us true according to every instruction Lola called out."

"Monty had the lead on us through most o' that mile of passage," Jun said, picking up the threads of the story. "But he an' his weren't so skilled, so gradually we closed the distance until we were neck an' neck, the mouth o' the Needle just ahead."

"At its narrowest," Mr. Anand said, setting his lassi on a table so he could bring his palms close together in demonstration, "the Needle's not more'n eight feet wide, right before it lets out into Ziltar Bay. We pulled ahead of the other skiff just as we reached it, passed 'em by close enough that I could've counted the hairs in ol' Monty's nose!"

"His face was the color of a tomato," Jun chuckled. "Livid, he was. I halfway thought he was going to draw a pistol on us then an' there, but fortunately it took everything he an' his crew had just to stay afloat."

Quint nodded, unbothered by this apparent overreaction. He'd known plenty of sailors who were liable to think with their trigger fingers first when angered, especially when it came to wagers of skill. Not all of those hotheads had been pirates, either.

"We pulled ahead," Mr. Anand continued, "past the other skiff and into the Needle's mouth. Twenty yards winnowing to a point hardly wider than our own little boat. We could've reached out and touched the cliff walls if we'd dared."

Uncle Jun shifted, his gaze restlessly roving about the Queen's Arms in search of something, anything, to distract himself from this conversation. His daughters leaned in, sensing their father's impending embarrassment as surely as sharks catching the scent of blood in the water.

"It was slow going by that point," Anand said, a grin spreading beneath his mustache. "The further we went, the narrower the passage. Your baba, he got it into his head that we weren't gonna make it through…"

"I never thought that," Jun mumbled, cheeks reddening.

"No?" Anand chuckled. "There was another reason you threw yourself off the stern end o' the boat, then?"

Ling let out a deep belly laugh as her father's cheeks turned a red that would have shamed the tomato-faced Monty. On Quint's other side Tai buried her face in her hands, broad shoulders shaking with barely suppressed laughter.

"I never—" Jun sputtered. "That is, I—"

"You should've seen him!" Mr. Anand was fighting to gasp out the words between his own howls of laughter. "Floundering around in the waves like a kid splashing in the shallows! By the heavens, I hadn't seen him that wet and embarrassed since—"

"*Manish*," Jun groaned. "These are my *kids*."

Mr. Anand's laughter stopped abruptly as he looked up at the two tall young women, as if seeing them for the first time.

"Right," he said, clearing his throat a little. "Erm. Anyway, we made it out of the Needle, well ahead of Monty and none the worse for wear. Exceptin' your baba's pride, of course."

Jun groaned and buried his face in his hands.

"Come on, Baba," Ling said, throwing an arm around her father's massive shoulders. Tai joined her on his other side. "Let's get you a drink from Auntie Lola, before Mr. Anand can tell us any more family secrets."

Tai giggled as they led their father away, still red-faced.

"What happened to him?" Quint asked Mr. Anand, his curiosity roused. "Monty, I mean."

Pop had always been vague about the other skiff's crew, other than assuring a concerned young Quint that Monty and his nameless cronies had made it out of the Needle alive, if somewhat the worse for wear.

"They made it out just behind us," Mr. Anand said, tugging at his mustache, "though their skiff had been smashed half to pieces. Good thing, too, since I don't think Jun was much exaggerating when he said Monty had murder in his eyes. We won fair an' square, of course, but I think Montcrief bore a grudge against your pop until—"

"Quentin!" Ma Thatch appeared at his side with a suddenness that was almost alarming. No longer encumbered by a tray of drinks, she looped her arm through Quint's. "Miss Rosa wants to hear all about the ports of call you've visited in the last year, and if you've met any young ladies who've struck your fancy. You don't mind if I borrow him, do you, Manish?"

Mr. Anand hardly had time to shake his head before Ma Thatch whisked Quint away, back into the flowing stream of half-remembered faces and near-forgotten stories of an almost mythical past.

10

Like all parties, Quint's homecoming fell into a tidal rhythm of ebb and flow. The initial festive atmosphere of surprise and welcome soon gave way to a more general merriment, as better than a hundred people had crammed themselves into the Queen's Arms, and Quint could only speak with so many at a time. Seeking a breather, he attempted to clear one of the tables of empty glasses, only for Ma to appear and pull him away.

"None of that," Lola Thatch chided.

"I feel bad not helping," Quint protested.

"Don't," Ma said, plucking an empty glass from his hands. "Won't have anyone saying I made the guest of honor bus tables at his own party."

Quint raised his hands in mock surrender, conceding the point.

"Enjoy yourself," Ma said, nodding over to the bar where Hari and Amara sat together on their stools, each sipping a sparkling cider. "Catch up with old friends. The dishes'll keep."

Quint ducked away to the bar, which was manned by a fresh-faced blond youth Quint didn't recognize who looked barely old enough to read the drink labels, let alone serve them.

Spending much of the day outdoors beneath the tropical sun had built up a powerful thirst in Quint, so he decided to ask for something nonalcoholic. He had scarcely opened his mouth when the youthful bartender slid a frothing mug of ginger beer to him, then moved on to the next customer without another word.

Bemused, Quint stared down at his drink, wondering if after years of fruitless attempts he had finally mastered the art of communicating his order without having to speak it aloud.

"That's Freddy Childs," Amara said, sidling onto the stool beside Quint, Hari on the one beside her. "Works evenings here. Your mom told him your drink of choice before you arrived."

"Much appreciated," Quint said, raising his glass in salute. It was halfway to his mouth before he stopped, frowning. "Wait. Childs? As in Andy Childs?"

"His son, if you'll believe it," Hari said. Andy had been one of their classmates, a lifetime ago. But Quint's memories were of a short, be-spectacled boy with a mournful countenance, little resembling the confident young man behind the bar.

Quint took a long pull of his ginger beer, its refreshing, clean taste washing over his tongue and warming the back of his throat. "I'm guessing Freddy takes after his mother, then?"

"Only his hair, actually," Amara said, taking a sip of water. "Andy Childs filled out after you left for the Navy, Quint. Practically doubled in height over the course of a year, started working in his grandma's lumberyard, and his face cleared up."

"You're kidding," Quint said, but now that he was looking he could see the faint resemblance to the boy he'd known in the lines of the younger man's face.

"Nope," Hari said, raising his glass in salute. "From about a year after you left until we were nineteen or so, every girl on the island was harboring some kind of feelings for Andy Childs, at least until he got hitched to Stacia Milliner."

"Not every girl," Amara said, leaning over and pecking Hari on the lips.

Hari absently brushed aside a loose curl from his wife's face before returning his attention to Quint. "Thank you for watching over Mani, by the way. I hope he won't be too much trouble."

"I'm sure he won't," Quint said. "He seems like a good lad."

"He is at that," Hari said fondly. "Gets it from his mother."

"Flatterer," Amara said, mock shoving Hari off his stool.

Something in their playful banter nagged at Quint. Not out of any lingering feelings for Amara, but because their easy affection reminded him with sudden sharpness of—

"Vanessa," he said, and only when Amara frowned at him did he realize he'd spoken her name aloud.

"Who?" Hari asked.

"No one," Quint said, shaking his head. *No one but a memory.*

"I never congratulated you two," he said, forcing a smile back onto his face as he raised his glass. "You make a lovely couple, and you have a beautiful family. Best wishes to you both."

Ginger beer in hand, he turned and dove back into the crowd of islanders. Strange, how a homecoming could dredge up memories unrelated to home at all. As if nostalgia for one place, one person, could bleed into a longing for a wholly different place, a wholly different person.

Tonight was not about Vanessa, he reminded himself as he made his way through the crowd. It was not even about him, though that had certainly been the pretense for this gathering.

It was about his father, of course, and his mother. Clarent and Lola Thatch had been pillars of the Ember Bay community for better than forty years, while Quint had run away from home as a young teen and returned only sporadically throughout his adult life. He had missed

Pop's funeral, but Quint would have wagered the *Bloody Angel* and the Imperial crown jewels both that not a soul in the Queen's Arms this night had not also been present for his father's burial.

He looked over to his mother and was only half-surprised to find she'd struck up a game of Ruff with Old Hawkins and several other of the more venerable townsfolk. Quint watched as she talked animatedly, waving her cards about to emphasize whatever point she was making without any regard for whether or not doing so showed her hand. A smile crept over his face. This was Ma Thatch in her element: surrounded by the people of the place she had made her home, the community that she'd found and fostered in her turn.

Another unexpected pang of longing pulled at him, one that was only slightly quieted by a swallow of lager. Was it nice, he wondered, to be surrounded by the same folk day in and day out? To wake each day to the view of Ember Bay out your window, to sleep soundly beneath the shadow of the island's great volcano?

He shook his head, bemused at his own melancholy. He had a ship—a fine ship, one he loved—and a crew who admired him, and for whom he held immeasurable affection in return.

Like all such vessels, the *Bloody Angel* was comprised of an odd and motley collection of individuals, each drawn to the uncertain and often precarious life of the buccaneer. They clashed and argued with one another with exasperating frequency—Fillbrick waged a continual one-man war against the general slovenliness of his shipmates, while the mates Vigo and Darby were in a perpetual cycle of either quarreling with or doting upon each other. But there was not a one among them Quint hadn't trusted with his life at some point or another, whether their backs were against the wall, the Navy hard on their stern, or (in one memorable instance) they'd been strung up as the main course by a cannibal clan. Not one he hadn't wrangled into some ill-advised scheme or been wrangled into in his turn. They were a gang of raucous, devious, opportunistic libertines, and Quint loved them with a possessive fierceness.

They were his crew, and they would sail the Eight Seas together for as long as there was breath in Quint's lungs.

His mood improved greatly with the arrival of dinner: fresh-caught tuna steaks marinated in a sesame ginger sauce, served with a side of sweetened rice and taro pudding for dessert. Quint found himself seated with the twins, Uncle Jun having excused himself to play a game of darts with some of the other old-timers. Despite their differences in age, Quint found he got on well with the girls, and soon the three were laughing uproariously at their fathers' shared stories. Quint was pleased and surprised to discover that, just as Uncle Jun had neglected to tell his daughters about his race through the Ziltar Needle, there were a handful of anecdotes his own parents had decided not to share with him. To his lasting astonishment, these stories tended to involve his parents either getting fantastically drunk, running afoul of the law, or otherwise making startlingly imprudent choices.

"You're joking!" he said, half-laughing and half-disbelieving as Tai finished a story about the time their parents had taken a countess's carriage for a joyride. "There's no way they made it all the way across the island before the constabulary caught on!"

"It's true!" Ling grinned, raising her left hand and crossing her heart. "Your ma was disguised as the coachman, powdered wig and all. Nobody thought to question it!"

"Not until Baba stuck his head out the carriage window," Tai said, a dreamy look on her face as if she could recall this incident that had occurred long before her birth. "Wind plucked the countess's wig right off his head!"

They all laughed, as much at their shared amusement over their parents' youthful antics as over their newfound friendship. Smiling, Quint shook his head and sipped at his drink, still trying to reconcile Jun's image of his mother and father as carefree young hooligans with the people who had raised him.

He supposed that all parents presented their children with the most respectable, sanitized versions of themselves. That they hid away those parts of themselves that did not align with the sort of role model they'd want their children to look up to, so that the dredging up of old shames and embarrassments would come as a surprise twenty, thirty years down the road.

Quint wondered what other secrets his parents had kept from him, and if there were any his father had taken to the grave rather than reveal to his only son.

"I wish we could have been there," Tai said, staring wistfully into her mug. "Out having adventures in the Jewel Isles or racing through the Ziltar Needle. Nothing ever happens on Ember Bay."

Quint almost laughed, thinking of how many times he'd expressed exactly the same sentiment himself when he was not much younger than they were.

"Why don't you leave?" he asked, genuinely curious. The twins were already a year or two older than he had been when he'd left home.

"We like it here," Ling said, shrugging. "I mean, sure, nothing happens, but it's nice, y'know? All our friends are here. So's our family."

"Not all," Tai pointed out. "There's our cousins back in Aiwa."

"Mom's family," Ling said, for Quint's benefit. "We visit them twice a year."

"We might stay for longer next visit," Tai confided. "Aiwa's a *lot* bigger than Ember Bay, and Aunt Su runs a calligraphy school there. She's talked with Baba before about taking us on as apprentices for a year or two."

Ling stifled a mock yawn. "If you think it's boring here, imagine being locked up in a room writing the same characters over and over for hours on end."

Sensing a fight about to break out, Quint stepped in. "There's lots to do in the big cities, sure. But big cities can mean big trouble, too."

"Ember Bay could stand a little trouble," Tai said, looking restlessly around the room. "Everyone here's just so...I don't know, *content*. Like this is the best possible place they could be, so why bother leaving?"

"There are worse places," Quint said before he could stop himself. He had traveled the length and breadth of the Archipelago, and in his voyages had witnessed both the heights of indulgent luxury and the appalling degradation of unrelenting poverty. Set against the decadent excess of the High Governor's manse and the starving children of the Port Fortune street gutters, Ember Bay seemed far preferable to either.

"Why'd you go, then?" Ling asked, raising an eyebrow as both twins turned their attention on Quint.

Quint scooped a spoonful of rice into his mouth, buying himself time to think over his answer while he chewed. The rice was thick, its natural starchiness offset by the sweetness of the sugar and coconut milk it had been boiled with.

Here, he reminded himself, he was not Captain Redbeard, infamous pirate, but merely a wayward son of the isle who'd sought his fortunes out in the wider world.

"I wanted to see what there was," he said at last, nodding toward a faded, much-tattered map of the known world hanging from one of the tavern walls. "Out there."

"So you joined the Navy?" Ling's tone was dubious.

Quint gave her a wan smile. "It seemed as good a way as any to get out of Ember Bay. Besides, I was only fifteen—"

"We're seventeen," both twins said, faintly indignant.

"And far wiser than I was at that age," Quint said, raising both hands in surrender. "I'm not proud to say that I was quite taken with all those boys' adventure novels about dashing captains and brave young midshipmen. Doubtless you're immune to such Imperial propaganda, but it had its intended effect upon me."

"Baba says the Empire's just a corporation disguised as a country," Tai said, though not with any real vehemence. "That it's the trading companies who are the real power in the Archipelago, and that the Navy's their enforcer."

"Your baba's not wrong," Quint admitted, glancing over toward the dart game. Uncle Jun was visibly red in the face, but if he was drunk it did nothing to impede his accuracy as dart after dart buried itself in the board's center. "The Empire likes to make a lot of noise about honor, chivalry, and patriotism, but at the end of the day its only real concern is putting as much coin into the Crown's coffers as possible and damn the consequences."

"Is that why you left?" Tai asked, leaning forward at the same time as her sister frowned and asked, "But you work for a merchantman now, don't you?"

Quint turned from one to the other, weighing which question to answer first, and with how much truth.

"I do," he said to Ling, inventing wildly. "But not for one of the big trading companies, y'see? The *Waterhouse* is a family operation. Elderly couple out of Sapphire own it and two other vessels. They've only ever dealt squarely with me, and as far as I know they've done the same for anyone else they're in business with."

All of this he'd invented wholly on the spot, emboldened by the memory of old injustices. Some quieter part of his mind was urging him to shut up, to not say anything about his cover that could be disproven later, but he could not stop himself. Words he had long thought but never voiced spilled from him, and it was only thanks to the renewed stamp of feet against the dance floor that kept the entire tavern from hearing them.

"Yes," he told Tai, sticking to the fiction he and Ophelia had created for themselves in the wake of their departure from the Navy. "Being in the Navy opened my eyes to the reality of the Empire, free of all the spit an' polish. No romance, just ugly truth. Whole nations beggared by unfair trade deals, unable to renegotiate terms they were forced to sign at the end of a cannon. Penal colonies no better than slave plantations, the workers brutalized and treated like chattel. Children ripped from their mothers' arms and forced into mission schools where they're beaten if they use their real names, speak their mother tongues, pray to their own gods."

He looked down at his hands, flat upon the table. Recalled for the first time in a long time how proud he'd been to don the Navy purple, his growing excitement at boarding ship for the first time. The sense of grand adventure as he'd stood in the prow of a ship flying the Imperial flag, the ocean growing broad and endless before him as Ember Bay sank into the distance behind.

How young he had been. How foolish.

Suddenly his anger drained away, replaced by a deep and abiding weariness.

"It was a mistake," he told the twins, and forced himself to smile. "My enlisting. One that I'd take back if I could. And after I realized I'd made it, I...was lost. For a long time."

"But not forever," Ling said, leaning forward. On his other side Tai patted his hand sympathetically. "You found your way home."

Quint looked from the twins to the crowd stomping and laughing their way across the dance floor, to the old-timers huddled over their drinks, to the dart game where Uncle Jun was howling with laughter at something Ma had just said.

"Aye," Quint said, raising his mug in silent toast to the Queen's Arms and everyone in it. "I suppose I have."

11

Long years of piracy had taught Quint that danger most often struck at a time when it was least expected, and the night of his homecoming party was no exception.

Later he would wonder whether it had been the pleasant weight of his full belly that had dulled his instincts, or if the familiar comforts of home had lured him into a sense of false security.

Or perhaps it was simply that no man, however cautious, expects to be attacked while answering nature's call.

Whatever the case, Quint had barely stepped out of the outhouse door before a dark figure came bursting out of the trees, charging him like an enraged bull. Quint's hand fell by long instinct to his side, searching for dagger, pistol, or cutlass, but came away empty.

The stocky figure plowed into his middle, driving the wind from Quint as strong arms wrapped about him and hoisted him into the air, spinning him around.

"Quentin Bloody Thatch!" his assailant crowed, still spinning them both about. "Come back home after years of adventure 'pon the high seas!"

Quint's struggles ceased as he relaxed, and in a moment his feet were set back upon solid ground, though the world about him continued to spin with irritating persistence. As soon as he'd heard the voice, he'd known he was in no real danger.

"Lex," he grunted by way of greeting. "Where's—"

Another pair of arms wrapped around his chest from behind, steadying and restraining him as the first of his assailants pummeled Quint's midsection. The punches were light, yet his stomach was so full that they forced a groan from him regardless.

"Turn out your pockets!" another familiar voice hissed in his ear, its attempt at menace undercut by a certain gentle dreaminess. "Let's see what ill-gotten gains you've plundered on your voyages!"

"No need to visit violence on my person, gentlefolk," Quint said, trying not to laugh as he turned out his pockets, scattering a few silver coins onto the dirt. "Ain't naught in my pockets but lint and a handful of reals, as you can see."

"A grave disappointment," the shorter assailant said, folding her beefy arms and glancing up at her taller companion. "What is it we do with those who disappoint us, Chuck?"

"Toss 'em in the harbor," Chuck replied, and though Quint's back was to him he could hear his grin. "Get his legs, Lex."

"Come on, mates," Quint complained, his stomach giving an uneasy lurch as Lex complied, tucking his legs under her thick arms. "This is no way to greet an old friend after an extended absence, is it?"

The patch of starlight filtering down through the palms was momentarily obscured by Chuck's silhouette, his long mane of curling hair bound back in a messy tail.

"Some friend, Quint," he said conversationally as he and Lex began to haul their human cargo downhill. "You never write."

"You can't read," Quint pointed out, swaying a little as they carried him downhill. The motion set his overfull belly to sloshing unpleasantly. Chuck Chambers and Lex Presley had been a few years above Quint in school, until they hadn't been.

"That's beside the point," Lex said, shaking her head. Even in their youth, she'd been shaped like a barrel, and the intervening years had not altered her physique. "It'd be nice if you *did* write us, was the point."

"Apologies," Quint said, swaying from side to side between them. Were it not for the way his stomach strained against his shirtfront, it would have been a surprisingly comfortable position in which to find oneself; Chuck and Lex had clearly had much practice hauling human cargo up and down the village hill. "But I wouldn't think a lapse in correspondence sufficient reason to take me for a swim."

"Nah, Quint." Chuck gave a mournful shake of his head. "We're giving you a toss since your pockets was empty."

"Oh," Quint said, as if that explained things. "So that was a shakedown?"

"Now you're getting it!" Chuck's tone was encouraging. "See, Lex? Told you ol' Quint was cleverer than he looks."

"Hey!" Quint said, struggling with real effort for the first time. But the hold Chuck had him in was surprisingly secure.

"By the nine hells," Lex grunted as they carried him downhill. "You've put on some weight, Quint."

"Ma cooks a mean tuna steak," Quint said, though from his suspended position he was beginning to regret having had a second helping. "How come neither of you were at the party, by the way?"

"Oh." Lex threw a guilty glance over her shoulder. "Your ma banned us from the Arms a few years back."

Somehow this did not come as a surprise. Devoted to caring for their elderly nana but both terminally unable to hold a steady job, Chuck Chambers and Lex Presley instead styled themselves as Ember Bay's criminal element; a two-person syndicate whose activities mainly involved lounging about the harbor or pulling the occasional shift at Jacques's Lumberyard when they found themselves short on beer money. Yet they were effectively harmless; real criminals would have knifed Quint before carrying him to the harbor.

"What'd she ban you for?" Quint asked.

"We tried robbing the place," Chuck said, sounding forlorn. "It didn't work out."

"You *robbed* my *parents*?" Quint demanded, indignant.

"We didn't use weapons or nothin'!" Lex objected, hoisting Quint's legs upward in a manner that suggested she'd been about to throw up her hands before recalling her human cargo. "Your ma and pop are nice folks. We weren't gonna hurt anybody."

"Your ma felt differently, though," Chuck said. "Whacked us black an' blue with a rolling pin 'til we dropped the keg and hightailed it outta there."

"Been banned ever since," Lex grunted.

"How'd your nana take it?" Quint asked. The cousins' grandmother had been a fixture in the Queen's Arms, yet he hadn't seen her this evening, either.

Both their shoulders slumped, lowering Quint until his backside nearly scraped the hill.

"Nana passed three years back," Chuck said quietly. Lex said nothing at all.

"Oh," Quint said, very softly. "I...angels above, mates, I'm sorry. I didn't know."

"'Course you didn't," Lex said. Then she sniffled. "She went peaceful, at least. Sleeping."

"That's..." Quint paused. "A mercy, I suppose."

"Guess so." Lex glanced over her shoulder at him again, just briefly enough that Quint caught the moonlight reflecting off her cheeks. "Sorry 'bout your pop, too."

"Thanks." Through the waving branches of a nearby tree Quint glimpsed the black stretch of the harbor, moonlight shining peacefully on the waves. "Seriously, you're not going to throw me in, are you?"

Lex cast a sympathetic glance over her shoulder but did not slow their downhill descent. "Sorry, Quint. You're an old pal, but we've got a reputation to maintain."

"Your reputation remains intact," he assured them, "but I still don't know what I did to get on your bad sides."

"You don't remember?" Again Lex craned her head around. "Last time you was here, years ago. You made us a promise, Quint."

"I did?" Quint asked, but even as the question left his mouth it was starting to come back to him. Another bungled shakedown, not unlike this one. Their faces staring at him over a pint, Chuck's sweetly honest, Lex's eyes narrowed and searching.

"We wanted to know why you'd left the Navy," Chuck said, helpfully attempting to jog Quint's memory. "You tried to offer up some excuse about working as a ship's clerk on a merchantman, remember?"

It was starting to come back to him, though the details admittedly remained somewhat hazy.

"You might've fooled most of the town with that story," Lex continued, not without admiration. "But you'd have to get up earlier than that to pull one over us, eh?"

The memory rose with a clarity that made Quint curse the sick sense of humor whichever angel watched over him undoubtedly possessed.

"Mates," Quint said, sudden alarm rising in his chest as he renewed his struggles. "Listen, Lex. Chuck. I told you last time, and I'm telling you again, *I am not a bloody pirate!*"

"Nice try," Lex said flatly. Ahead of them the broad dark shape of the harbor had come into view, the waves glimmering beneath the reflected light of the crescent moon. "You admitted you was, remember?"

"I—" Quint's mouth worked silently. He had, hadn't he? Had in fact been so amused by their envious speculations over his life of piracy that he'd played along, finding it easier than trying to bring them around to believing the meticulous lie he'd fooled the rest of Ember Bay with. It wasn't like he'd told them any of the details of his pirating life; just let them persist in their own assumptions, secure in the knowledge that no one else in Ember Bay would seriously credit the two's tall tales.

It had seemed funny at the time.

"Damn you, Past Quint," he muttered, but his mind was already racing, trying to find another way out of this. "Remind me the details of this promise, exactly?"

"You told us that next time you came home," Chuck said, reciting from memory, "you'd cut us in on any pirating business you might have."

"You've been home near a whole day," Lex continued. "Ain't come to see us once in all that time. So, we thought a little nighttime swim might jog your memory when it comes to keepin' promises."

A wild idea occurred to Quint, though like many such ideas only its outcome would determine whether it was mind-bogglingly brilliant or criminally stupid. *But I've already involved them...*

"Mates," he said, a hint of the cool, commanding captain's voice creeping into his tone. "Set me down."

They did, obeying almost instinctively. Just in time, too, Quint noted; they had just reached the pier. He stood, glad for the solid planking beneath his feet despite his stomach protesting at the sudden change in position.

"You're right," he admitted, fixing them with his most apologetic smile. "I made a promise, and may the angels curse me should I break it."

Chuck scratched his head. "Then why you ain't come to see us, Quint?"

"Discretion," Quint said, tapping the side of his nose. "How do you think it'd look if I docked after my dear pop's passing and came straight to you, mates? Mighty suspicious, yeah?"

Lex and Chuck looked at each other, then back to him.

"I s'pose it would," Lex admitted begrudgingly. "But there's been a lot of time 'twixt then and now."

"Had to lie low," Quint lied easily. "As it happened, I was planning on comin' to you after I used the outhouse anyhow. The party provides the perfect cover."

Lex still looked skeptical, but Chuck nudged her with an elbow. "Told you."

"Sure," she said, waving off her partner in crime. "Let's say you *was* planning to randy-voo with us right when we nabbed you. What's the job?"

"And when?" Chuck added, stifling a yawn. "We hadn't reckoned past throwing you in the harbor."

"Tomorrow night," Quint said. The task he had in mind would require several hours, and he had no intention of missing any more of his welcome home party.

"Mates," Quint said, grinning so widely that moonlight shone off his teeth. "How'd you like to help me bury a pirate's treasure?"

12

The older he grew, the less Quint found himself able to function the day following a night of little sleep and poor decisions. Having crawled back into his childhood bed in the Queen's Arms in the small hours of the morning, long after the party had wound down, he had fully expected his awakening to be an unpleasant affair.

It was a surprise to him, then, that he awoke a scant few hours later feeling as refreshed as though he'd gotten a full night's sleep. A glance out the window showed only the starless gray haze of the dying night, only an hour or so before dawn. The last of the nightfires from the other volcanoes in the Reach had just begun to die down, as if relieved of duty by the greater light of the sun.

Nor was he alone in the bed. A soft weight rested on his chest, small claws digging through sheet and shirt alike into his skin. Huge green eyes stared at him in the dark.

"Hey, Chum," Quint said, extending a hand to the cat. Chum sniffed it, his whiskers tickling Quint's fingers, then butted his head against Quint's palm, purring softly.

"Thanks, mate," Quint said, reciprocating by scratching the ancient cat under the chin.

According to his parents, Chum had appeared in the Queen's Arms one morning not long after Quint's departure to join the Navy. "Our other son," Pop had joked, once the sting of that departure had lessened. Lola had not been as taken with him, claiming that the last thing they needed was a stray clawing up the tavern's furniture. "We're not keeping him," she'd said.

She'd fallen asleep with Chum curled up in her lap that very night.

Like most siblings separated by a considerable age gap, Chum and Quint were not close. Chum viewed Quint as merely one of the inn's recurring guests, one who rudely slept in *his* bed. Quint, for his part, had on more than one occasion been forced to wrangle the cat away from making Jimmy into cutlets.

"You going to let me up?" Quint asked, ceasing his petting and propping himself up on his elbows. Chum answered with an annoyed yowl and hopped down, padding on silent paws across the bedroom and slipping out through the open door.

Quint rose, stretched, and was once again surprised to find he was not even sore. The benefit of sleeping in one's childhood bed, he supposed.

Not wanting to wake Ma across the hall, he tiptoed carefully about his room, old muscle memory reminding him which floorboards creaked and which were safe to step on. He dressed in silence and descended the stairs to the tavern's main room. The aftermath of the party was very much in evidence, most of the tables bearing piled dishes and half-full mugs. Several pairs of shoes were placed in a neat line near the door. Their owners, having had more than was good for them, had been carried upstairs by the other partygoers and deposited into one of the Arms' bedrooms to sleep off the worst of their excesses. Goodhearted soul that she was, Lola Thatch would not charge them for this unplanned stay at her inn. They would instead work off their debt by helping clean up the mess they'd contributed to, though not before Ma's famous eggs and hash had blunted the edge of their collective hangover.

For a moment Quint was tempted to stay himself. Ma would not object to another pair of hands to help with the washing up. But that obligation was outweighed by the promises he'd made to Mani, to Lurk, to Pop. Ma would understand, he told himself as he slipped behind the bar and into the kitchen. Besides, if the number of shoes lined up neatly by the door was any indication, she wouldn't be short on help.

The kitchen was unlit, but throwing together a breakfast for two in the dark wasn't nearly as difficult as he'd feared it would be, either. Quint had spent time in this room nearly every day of his first fifteen years, whether carried at Ma's hip while she prepared meals for the tavern's patrons, following at her elbow wanting to help her with her work, or simply loitering about as an aimless young teen while Pop washed up after meals. Quint had long joked with his crew that he could navigate the *Bloody Angel* blindfolded; as it turned out, the same applied to the kitchen of his family's tavern.

Strange how a heart could be so divided between two homes, he mused as he stuffed a picnic basket with his ma's banana muffins. One home smelled of salt and rum and wood, the other of flour and beer and fish sizzling on the skillet. One constantly rocking with the gentle swell of the waves beneath, the other as sturdy as the land on which she was built, excepting the occasional volcanic tremor.

Digging around in the kitchen, Quint added a few more items to the basket: bottles of chilled coconut milk, a loaf of bread, and a jar of pineapple jam. As an afterthought, he plucked a bottle of rum from one of the liquor crates, too.

A familiar fluttering of wings announced Jimmy's arrival as she descended from the rafters, where she'd spent the night, landing on Quint's shoulder and giving his ear an affectionate nibble.

"Hey, girl," Quint said softly, tickling her under the chin. "You want to stretch your wings?"

In answer, Jimmy let out a mercifully soft trilling sound, spreading both wings and shuffling from side to side on Quint's shoulder.

"Right, then," Quint said. "Off we go."

Parrot on his shoulder, Quint slunk out the back door of the Queen's Arms and into the brisk, chill air of an early island morning.

⚓

"And what's that one?" Lurk asked, pointing to Quint's forearm.

They lay in the shade of the *Wisherman*'s hull, enjoying the cool breeze blowing in from the cove. The empty picnic basket lay between them, and Lurk nursed the bottle of rum Quint had brought to wash down their meal.

"That one?" Quint looked down at the tattoo Lurk was pointing at. "It's a queen."

Lurk's dark eyes were drawn upward to Quint's face. "I have seen queens before. That is not a queen."

"Human queens?" Quint asked, his interest piqued. "Or mermaid ones?"

"Both," Lurk said, a ripple running down her dorsal fin. "Neither looked like...whatever *that* is."

"It's not a real queen," Quint explained. "It's a chess piece."

Lurk blinked her great eyes. "Chess?"

"It's a game." Quint gave her a quick rundown of the basics: the eight-by-eight grid, the different pieces and the ways each moved, the classic stratagems and a few of the more unorthodox ones.

"This game sounds very complex," Lurk said, sounding unimpressed.

"That's the point," Quint said, tapping a finger to his temple. "It requires the ability to plan ahead. Anticipate your opponent's moves and countermoves, while they're trying to think through yours at the same time."

Lurk pondered this, her tail swishing idly across the black sand of Cinder Cove. "So it's a game of cleverness."

"Exactly."

"Is that why you have a tattoo of the queen piece, then?" Lurk stared at him in that flat, expressionless way that still made Quint uncertain whether she was teasing him or being serious. "Because you think you're clever?"

"Hardly." Quint shook his head, then looked down at the tattoo on his forearm. Unlike Ophelia's extensive and impressive inkwork, Quint's tattoos were largely of simplistic design, and the queen was no exception. Just the silhouette of the piece, dark against his freckled skin. "I got it for a lady."

"A queen?"

Quint laughed, though his heart twinged a bit at the memory. "Not really. Queen of my heart, maybe."

"Ohh." Lurk nodded her head sagely. "She was your mate."

Quint rubbed his thumb along the tattoo. "Once."

"What happened?" Lurk asked, leaning forward with evident interest.

"We..." Quint frowned, trying to think how to put it in a way that would be comprehensible to Lurk. "Mermaids have clans, right? Groups of pods that are allied together?"

"It is more complex than that," Lurk said, frowning a little. "But yes."

"Well." Quint licked his lips. "Vanessa and I were from different clans. Enemy clans, at that."

"I see," Lurk said, leaning even closer. "We have stories like that. Lovers whose families keep them apart."

"I think everyone has stories like that," Quint said, smiling a little. It was comforting, somehow, how star-crossed love transcended the boundaries of species.

"Tell me yours, then."

Vanessa.

"I..." Again Quint looked down at the tattoo. "I can tell you how it started."

"Yes." Lurk swiftly coiled her tail around herself and rested her elbows atop it, settling in with a sip from the rum bottle.

"Well." Quint cleared his throat, gazing out at the waves. The soft sighing of the surf helped him think. "I was lying low at the time, after a big raid on a convoy outta Malachite. We were sheltering on Tourmaline, where Vanessa just happened to be on shore leave visiting her family."

"And the chess piece?"

"There was a chess tournament being held in town that very week," Quint said, smiling a little at the memory. "Players were coming from all over—not just the Jewel Isles, but across the Archipelago. I'd gotten pretty restless after a week of hiding out, so I forged some documents and entered myself as a competitor. Did pretty well, all things considered, until I got matched up with her."

He could still see her in his mind's eye: her dark hair tied back in a sensible plait, brow creased in concentration as her eyes roved the chessboard. How she had taken her time thinking over each move, yet each time she'd made her choice had committed to it fully, her hand darting out to seize a piece and place it decisively onto its square.

"She beat you?" Lurk asked, smiling her shark's smile.

"She destroyed me," Quint said, mopping his brow. Shade or not, it was still hot out. "I'd done alright until then, considering the caliber of opponent I was being matched to, but she was five moves ahead of me the whole game."

"Human ways are strange," Lurk said, her eyes narrowing, "but I do not think that performing poorly in a game of skill does much to recommend one as a mate."

"That's the thing," Quint said with a slight shrug. "I didn't do poorly. Bells, if I'd been matched against anyone else I might've lasted a few games more. She was just that much better."

Lurk made a thrumming sound in her throat that Quint supposed was the mermaid equivalent of a contemplative *hmm*. "I can see why you were impressed by her."

"To put it lightly," Quint said, raising his arm so that the sun shone on his tattoo. "In one move she captured my queen, and my heart."

"I see," Lurk said. "Did you ask her to mate with you then, or after?"

Quint's mouth worked soundlessly, before he weakly managed to croak out, "After."

Lurk let out a stream of hissing mermaid laughter.

"So," she asked once her mirth had subsided, dark eyes roving over Quint's arms, "when do *I* get a tattoo?"

13

Quint awoke to a faint sea breeze, someone hammering against his skull, and a snoring mermaid.

Wondering when his pillow had become slick and oddly scaly, he opened his bleary eyes, then immediately squinted against the bright sky and glittering waves. The sun peeking down between the palm fronds had shifted from the bright blaze of high morning to the lazy lowering of early afternoon. He and Lurk must have slept away three, maybe four hours after opening the bottle of rum.

The hammering continued, as did the snoring. Quint turned and saw Lurk stretched out on the sand perpendicular to him, cradling the empty bottle of rum against her chest, eyes closed and mouth slightly open. Her snore was high-pitched and whistling.

Part of her snakelike tail lay draped across Quint's shins, doubling back around to provide a pillow for his head. Between that and the cushion of the sand beneath them, it was a surprisingly comfortable position in which to fall asleep.

Not that they'd meant to, of course. Despite Quint's warnings to pace herself, Lurk had drained nearly the entire bottle herself, then promptly curled herself onto the sands to fall asleep. Quint had stretched himself out on the sand beside her, and the rhythmic pounding of waves and the kiss of sun on his skin had swiftly lulled him into dreams of his own.

Blinking as his eyes adjusted, Quint pushed himself up on his elbows, Lurk's snores continuing unabated. He felt a faint stirring of guilt; having never experienced one before, the mermaid's first hangover would make for an unpleasant surprise.

Water would help with that, and with Quint's own parched throat. Pop had always kept some waterskins in the *Wisherman*. With any luck there were still a few in the sailboat's cabin.

He rose, careful to disentangle his legs from Lurk's tail as gently as possible. The mermaid's snores were interrupted by a vague mumbling, but she didn't wake.

Quint stretched, yawned. The headache continued, as did the hammering.

He blinked. The sound was coming from the far side of the *Wisherman*. And there was something familiar about its erratic rhythm.

He walked around the broken bowsprit, the black sand shifting beneath his feet. The hammering continued.

"Up here, Captain Thatch!"

Quint craned his neck to see Mani sitting on the *Wisherman*'s deck, his legs dangling over the hull. He raised the hammer in both hands and brought it down, over and over again. Only one strike in ten landed on the nail he'd stuck into the center of one of the decking planks.

At least he's not hitting hard enough to do any permanent damage, Quint thought. He waved both arms over his head to get the boy's attention. "Belay those repairs, Mani!"

The effect was immediate.

"Aye, Captain Thatch!" Mani said, saluting—with the hand not holding the hammer, Quint was relieved to notice. That would've been hard to explain to Amara.

"What—" Quint massaged his temples with both hands, easing his headache a little. "What are you doing, lad?"

"Fixing up your ship, Captain!" Mani replied, still saluting. Now that he was looking, Quint noticed several nails sticking out of the *Wisherman*'s deck at odd angles, placed apparently at random. Mani had clearly been at it for a while prior to Quint's reluctant awakening.

"I see that," he said carefully, not wanting to dampen the boy's enthusiasm. He'd pull the wayward nails out himself later on. "And it's a boat, not a ship."

"*Hole in the boat!*" a familiar voice squawked as Jimmy landed on Quint's shoulder. He winced at the volume of the parrot's voice so close to his ear. "*Every man for himself!*"

"About time you showed up," Quint told her.

"She's right, Captain Thatch!" Mani piped up. He gestured wildly with the hammer at the far side of the boat. "There's a hole in the ship!"

"Boat," Quint corrected automatically, but Mani was still speaking.

"I wanted to fix it," he said, "but I couldn't figure out how." He stared down at the hammer, no doubt bewildered as to how his trusty tool had failed to solve a problem it hadn't been designed for.

"You could've asked me for help," Quint said, then frowned. "Actually, maybe you should've done that before starting repairs yourself. Er, not that I don't admire your initiative."

"I don't know what that means," Mani said brightly. "But I didn't want to wake you. Not while you and the mermaid were sleeping together."

"We weren't—" Quint felt himself redden in exactly the way that had so fascinated Lurk. "I mean, we were sleeping, and we were together, but—"

"*Winds be gusty, but the girl's lusty!*" Jimmy squawked in his ear. "*If the bunks are creakin', don't come a peekin'!*"

"Shush, you," Quint hissed at her. Ophelia had taught the parrot a veritable litany of bawdy jokes, each one filthier than the last.

Jimmy's response to this was to bite his ear harder than usual and shriek another filthy doggerel verse: "*Beware of ladies found ashore! For one in every ten's a—*"

Quint clapped both hands over the parrot's beak before she could utter the final syllable.

"What was she going to say?" Mani asked, leaning forward, his eyes bright with interest.

"Uh..." Quint cleared his throat, mind racing to think of an appropriate substitute rhyme, one that would not result in Amara using her pointier carpentry tools on him. "Bore. One in every ten's a bore, mate. But don't go repeating it to anyone, hear?"

"Aye-aye, Captain Thatch!" The hammer rose as Mani made to salute again. Quint released the struggling parrot and reached up with both hands, arresting the hammer's ascent toward Mani's forehead.

Jimmy flapped off, screeching her displeasure with Quint, the dirty rhyme mercifully forgotten in her indignity.

"Mani," Quint said, gently easing the hammer out of the boy's grip. "You've got to be more careful where you're swinging that thing."

"I know." Mani's face fell, his chipper demeanor giving way to resigned dejection. "Papa's always trying to get me to do the measurin' and draftin' in the shop instead of actually building things."

"Those are important tasks," Quint said, feeling the inadequacy of that attempt at comfort as soon as the words were out. He'd spent little time around children and had no idea how to console one. "I mean. If you make a house to the wrong dimensions, it's apt to fall down in a strong breeze, right?"

"I s'pose." Mani nodded, a little less gloomily. "I just wanna show my folks that I can pull my own weight."

There was something in the way he said these last words that tugged at Quint's heart. There was a subtle emphasis to "pull my own weight" that suggested the phrase was one Mani had not come up with himself, but rather overheard from his parents. Not directly, he assumed; Amara and Hari were too good of people for that. But Quint remembered being eight years old and eavesdropping on Ma and Pop, and could easily imagine young Mani listening in on his own parents discussing their concerns for their children.

"Why do you think they sent you to help me?" Quint asked, injecting a little bit of the gruffness he used to motivate his crew into his voice. "I can't fix this ship up myself, mate. And your folks told me I couldn't ask for better help than yours."

"Really?" Mani lifted his chin, his tone dubious but his expression hopeful. "They said that?"

Useless at repairs, Hari had actually said, *but he'll do great on the boat, once you get her seaworthy. He's almost as obsessed with ships as he is with record-keeping.*

"Aye," Quint lied, giving Mani what he hoped was an encouraging grin. "I'm a bit short on coin at the moment..."

This was another lie, even discounting the treasure stashed in his sea chest, but Quint didn't want to advertise his piratically acquired wealth more than necessary. The wages of a ship's clerk were enough to make a decent enough living, but Quint was wary of spending too much out of pocket, lest doing so attract unwanted questions. Nor did he trust Mani's discretion.

"...but your folks and I struck up a deal," he continued. "In exchange for your help fixing up the *Wisherman*, I'm to give you sailing lessons once she's seaworthy again. How's that sound?"

"Truly?" Mani's eyes grew huge.

"Cross me heart," Quint said, drawing an X over his chest with his finger. "Have we a deal, then?"

Mani whooped and leapt from the rail, all four limbs outspread. Compelled by a vision of Amara running at him with a hammer for letting her son break his legs, Quint caught Mani, wrapping his arms about the boy's back as he came crashing down. Unprepared for the impact of even a reedy eight-year-old crashing into his chest, Quint went sprawling across the black sand.

"Thank you, Captain!" Mani said, saluting as he clambered to his feet. Quint was momentarily grateful that the hammer, having fallen from his grasp, lay in the sand several feet away.

"First rule of nautical terminology," Quint grunted, pushing himself up on his elbows. "Drop the 't' in 'captain.' Only landsmen say it like that. Any sailor addresses his commander as Cap'n."

"Cappen," Mani repeated.

"Cap'n. Shorter space between the syllables."

"Cap'n," Mani said, and his face glowed at Quint's approving nod. "Aye, Cap'n!"

"Second rule," Quint said, climbing to his feet and brushing sand from his sides. He rapped the *Wisherman*'s hull with his knuckles. "This ain't a ship, mate. It's a boat."

Mani's brows drew together. "What's the difference?"

"Ship's bigger," Quint said. Mani's frown deepened, prompting him to explain further. "That is, a ship's large enough to carry a boat. See?"

Manny scratched his head. "So that makes *Wisherman* a boat?"

"Right." Quint nodded, glad the boy was getting it.

"What if we built a very small boat and put it on the *Wisherman*?" Mani asked, eyes alighting with the possibility. He turned this way and that, doubtless searching for his hammer. "Would that make her a ship?"

"No," Quint said, moving to stand between the boy and his dropped hammer. "It doesn't work like that."

"Why not?"

"I..." Quint rubbed his chin, once again surprising himself with the absence of beard there. "It just doesn't, alright? Now, are you ready to start work on the repairs?"

All quibbling over the difference between boat and ship vanished as Mani sprang to attention. "Aye, Cap'n!"

"Very good," Quint said, returning the boy's (surprisingly correct) salute. "Now, the first order of business. Have you got a ledger and pen?"

Mani reached into the pouch sewn into the leather toolbelt he wore and produced both of the requested items. "Here, sir!"

"Excellent." Quint glanced at the *Wisherman*'s chipped and faded paint. "The first thing we'll need to do is make a list of the damage. An inventory, if you will."

"An inventory?" Mani whispered wonderingly, his tone as quietly reverent as most boys' would have been had Quint declared they needed to dig up Captain Wolf's legendary buried treasure.

"That's what I said, isn't it?" Quint grinned. *What an odd child.* But then, any boy whose life's ambition was to become a ship's clerk would have to be. "After that, I'll need you to start making a second list of supplies and tools we might need—"

He found himself talking to empty air. Mani had already sprinted around to the starboard side of the boat, doubtless intending to begin his log of her necessary repairs with the hole in the hull. Quint smiled after him, recalling a distant era when he too had been full of the unflagging energy of youth.

"Not bad, huh, Pop?" he murmured to himself, resting his hand against the *Wisherman*'s hull. He had been younger even than Mani when Pop Thatch had first set him to the task of repairing their vessel. Like all their time aboard the boat, it was an opportunity for father and son to bond over a shared passion.

In Quint's experience, the piratical lifestyle was not compatible with good parenting, and he had no wish to bring any children into the world who would not be loved and provided for as well as he himself had been. But here, at least, was one small way he might pass along his pop's legacy to a younger generation.

"We'll get the old girl fixed up soon," he promised his Pop, running his hand affectionately along the *Wisherman*'s rail.

A scream rang out along the beach.

14

Heart dropping into his stomach, Quint dashed around the *Wisherman*'s bow, wishing that he'd brought any sort of weapon to this secluded cove.

Lurk was awake, the long dark coil of her tail wrapped around Mani's skinny frame, pinning his arms against his sides. Quint was reminded again of the mermaid's resemblance to the deadly anacondas, who strangled their prey before devouring them whole.

"STOP THAT!!" he thundered.

At the same time Mani called out, "Cap'n, help!!"

"Quit *yelling*," Lurk said, twisting around to face him, hands clapped over her ears. She squinted at Quint, her enormous eyes narrowed to slits. "That drink was *poison*."

"It's an acquired taste," Quint said, striding forward until they stood face to face. "Let the boy go, Lurk."

She looked at him as if he'd just asked her to dance a jig, legs or no legs. "Why?"

"You're crushing him."

"Only a little, sir," Mani chimed in, putting on a brave face for his Cap'n. "I reckon I might be able to slip free!"

"No, you can't," Quint and Lurk said in unison, not looking at him.

"I told you to let him go," Quint said.

"But I'm *drowning* him," the mermaid protested, gnashing her shark's teeth.

"You're not," Quint said firmly. "Remember the terms of our deal? You don't drown me, or anyone who comes here with me. That was the agreement."

"But he didn't come here with you," Lurk insisted, wincing. "We both fell asleep, after we had too much of...whatever was in that bottle."

"Rum," Quint said automatically. "He's here to help me fix the boat, Lurk. That makes him..."

He searched about for the proper term, settled on a concept he was certain the mermaid would understand. "That makes him part of my pod, alright?"

Lurk's coils stopped moving, and her slitted eyes widened fractionally. "You have a pod?"

"Aye." Quint nodded. Like whales and dolphins, mermaids traveled the open seas in small family groups. "He's part of it. A lot of the people on this island are, for that matter. So please, let the boy go."

Lurk's frown was surprisingly human. Her coils relaxed, and Mani clambered out from them, none the worse for wear.

"You alright, mate?" Quint asked, fighting to keep his tone nonchalant, as if attempted drownings by mermaids were a daily hazard in the life of a ship's clerk. Showing his own worry would only frighten Mani.

"Fine, Cap'n!" Mani reported. Then, to Quint's surprise, he reached out and patted Lurk's tail, as he would a horse's flank. "She didn't squeeze too tight."

"Glad to hear it," Quint said, hoping Lurk wouldn't be too offended by the gesture. "Got another task for you, though. Run into the *Wisherman*'s cabin. There should be a few waterskins stowed under the portside berth. Refill three of them from the stream a little way into the jungle, just past the rock shaped like a ship's prow. You know the one?"

"Aye-aye!" Mani dashed off, his recent peril already forgotten.

"As for you," Quint said, returning his attention to Lurk. But she spoke first.

"Quint," she said. "I'm sorry."

That had been the last thing he'd expected. He opened his mouth, closed it.

"If I'd known he was part of your pod I never would have tried..." Lurk wrung her hands, an impressive gesture for someone with webbed fingers. "I lost mine, you see."

Quint's anger grew muted, though it did not disappear entirely. The peril she'd put Mani in was real. But this display of vulnerability was as sudden as it was unexpected, and it softened his heart. "You lost your pod?"

"Or they lost me." Lurk turned her serpentine body, peering out at the cerulean crescent of Cinder Cove, and at the darker blue of the open ocean that lay beyond. "Last wet season, when the storms came. We were separated."

"Oh." Quint wasn't sure what else to say. Mermaids seldom spoke openly about their own society. Those few scholars who'd devoted time to studying the elusive race speculated that there was some species-wide taboo against revealing too much to humanity. Considering the Empire's often-bloody, seldom-peaceful colonization of the Archipelago, Quint could not fault the mermaids for their reticence.

"I tried to stay with them," Lurk continued, still gazing out to sea, lost in her memories of loss. "I swam as hard as I could, for as long as I could, but the waves pulled me away, until I couldn't even hear them sing anymore. Even then I kept swimming, kept trying, but..."

"Your strength gave out before you did," murmured Quint, who was no stranger himself to the body's fragility relative to the spirit's fortitude.

"Yes." In Lurk's mouth the single syllable became a mournful whistle. "I fell into the black, into the Deep. I thought I was going to drown."

Mermaids, Quint reflected, *must not possess much sense of irony.*

"Instead, I washed up here," Lurk said, spreading her arms wide to take in Cinder Cove. "In this place."

"Did you..." Quint nearly asked whether she had seen his pop—surely the storm that had beached Lurk on Ember Bay must have been the same one that had damaged the *Wisherman*? But this was not the time for him to indulge in such questions. "Have you seen your pod again? Or...heard from them?"

Lurk shook her head, her tail lashing in agitation across the sand. "For three turns of the moon I have not heard their song, not even from far off. Not even when I try to swim into the Deep, as far as my body can carry me before I grow too weary. They are gone, and I am alone."

Instinctively, Quint rested his hand on the mermaid's shoulder. Her scaly skin was smooth, slick, but not unpleasant. Lurk glanced down at it curiously, but made no attempt to wave him off.

"Maybe they'll come back this way," Quint said. Mermaids were migratory, save for maroons like Lurk, or the even rarer outcasts who'd been exiled for unfathomable transgressions.

"Maybe," Lurk said, but she did not sound as though she believed it.

"They will," Quint said, projecting a confidence he did not feel. Sometimes, he knew, it was better to cling to whatever hope you could, even if it was false. The alternative was despair, and that was a drowning death. "You can be part of my pod 'til then, if you'd like."

He'd meant it half-jokingly, but Lurk turned to him with alarming speed, her great dark eyes opening nearly as wide as they'd been at their first meeting.

"Truly?" she asked, and there was a plaintive note to her melodic voice that tugged at his heart.

"Truly," Quint said, putting his other hand on her other shoulder. "I've spent most of my life collecting those who are lost, or forgotten, or plain don't fit in. Gatherin' them to me until we've made a cre—I mean, a pod of our own. I'd be glad to count you as part of it."

"I..." She looked down at the sand, suddenly shy. "...would like that. I think."

"And we've got a ship," Quint said, glancing over his shoulder at the *Wisherman*. "Bigger'n this one. A real oceangoing triple-master."

"I've seen such ships," Lurk said, lifting her head. Was that a flicker of interest in those black eyes? It was difficult to be sure. "Out in the Deep. You could...I mean, do you think we...?"

"We could," Quint said slowly, his caution finally winning out against his compassion. Best not to commit himself to a promise he couldn't deliver, especially when the Imperial navy was still trawling the Eight Seas in search of Captain Redbeard's *Bloody Angel* and the stolen Imperial crown jewels. "Maybe not right away. But it's possible."

"Especially with a ship!" Mani piped up. Quint turned to see the boy standing on the *Wisherman*'s deck, leaning over the rail. The trio of waterskins hung from his leather belt. "I thought you were just a boat captain, Cap'n!"

"I am," Quint lied automatically. Lurk frowned.

"That is," Quint amended, silently cursing, "I have *access* to a ship. The ship that I'm ship's clerk on. *Waterhouse.*"

"That's a silly name for a ship," Lurk said. "It's like calling an island *Landreef*."

"*I* didn't name it," Quint lied.

"Your skin's changing color again," Lurk observed.

"Is it because you're in love?" Mani asked, leaning over the rail for a better look. "That's what Papa says makes Mama turn red—"

"*No,*" Quint said, emphatic. He rubbed his chin in frustration. "Mani, how'd you get back here so fast? Did you run all the way to the stream and back?"

"Aye-aye, Cap'n!" Mani said, pulling two of the waterskins from his belt and tossing them down. Quint caught them both and handed one to Lurk, who looked at it, puzzled.

"Like this." Quint popped the cap, took a long drink.

Lurk followed his example, sputtering a little. "There's no salt!"

"Nope," Quint said, wiping his mouth with the back of his wrist. "Lurk, I need to get Mani home to his parents. But we'll be back tomorrow morning. Alright?"

"Alright," she agreed, giving him a sharky smile. "I'm glad I didn't drown you, Quint."

"That makes two of us."

That awful smile widened. Then she turned and slithered back down the beach, her motions startlingly quick. When she reached the shoreline she dove in, disappearing beneath the waves with hardly a splash.

"You ready to go home, Mani?" Quint said, turning to see the boy slipping from the *Wisherman*'s rail onto the sands.

"Aye, Cap'n!" Mani reached for Quint's fishing rod, but Quint shook his head.

"Leave it," he said. "For tomorrow. I have a feeling we'll have worked up an appetite. Until then, let's go home."

He clapped Mani on the shoulder and strode into the trees, only to realize a moment later that Mani was not following but staring instead into the jungle behind them.

"I met a mermaid today," the boy said, marveling. He turned back to Quint, his awestruck expression giving way to a grin that was not without mischief. "Wait until I tell Mama!"

"Don't," Quint said, panicked, then realized that was too tall an order for such an irrepressible child. "I mean. Don't tell her about the drowning part, eh? Wouldn't want her to forbid you from coming here again."

"She won't," Mani said breezily, hurrying past Quint to charge head-long through the jungle. "They like having me out of the house and not bothering anyone at the shop."

"Slow down!" Quint called, jogging after him. To his surprise, Mani did, turning around as a pensive frown came over his face.

"I did have a question though, Cap'n."

Quint raised an eyebrow. "About the mermaid?"

"Not her." Mani shook his head, as if the mermaid were already old news. "About something Jimmy said, while you were sleeping."

Oh no, Quint thought, but the question was already tumbling from Mani's mouth.

"Cap'n, what's a prosti—"

15

By the time they returned to Ember Bay, the sun had already sunk beneath the long slope of the volcano, its long rays climbing up toward the sky. The first of the distant nightfires had just begun to bloom like a flower on the horizon, like earthbound harbingers of the coming stars.

Quint halted as he crested the top of the trail, taking in the broad sweep of the glittering bay, the narrow cluster of buildings climbing up the hill beneath them. Over all, the dark shadow of the volcano loomed, but in the tranquil light of late afternoon it seemed more like some towering guardian spirit than a herald of impending doom.

"Wait a minute," he called down to Mani, who was already heading down the trail.

The boy turned around, frowning a little. "What for?"

"I'm taking in the view."

This answer only seemed to perplex Mani further. He hiked the short distance back up to where Quint stood, looking out at the panorama displayed before them.

"What view?" Mani asked, his eyes roaming over the boats bobbing upon the waves, the stately palms waving in the breeze, the picturesque houses and storefronts lining the main street, the majestic volcano. "You mean the town?"

"Aye." Quint nodded, wondering if he too had been blind to the beauty of Ember Bay when he was that young. Or perhaps one's home was like those paintings he'd glimpsed in the High Governor's manse, which could only be properly appreciated from a certain distance. Perhaps distance too was required before one could accurately assess the merits of the place they were from without bias. Too close, and the reality of home became too entangled with one's memories of it.

"You ever just stop to look at it?" he asked Mani. "Just...take it in?"

"What for?" Mani's expression was scornful as only an eight-year-old's could be. "There's too much to *do*."

Having reached the limit of his patience, he turned and raced downhill toward town. Quint spared one last wistful look, then hurried after.

He left Mani at his parents' carpentry shop, though not without first extracting a solemn promise from the boy to be at Cinder Cove no later than an hour after sunup the following morning. Mani saluted his understanding, before turning and running into the shop, loudly shouting to his brothers and Hari that he'd seen a mermaid. Not wanting to stick around and explain that incident, Quint muttered something about helping Ma at the Queen's Arms and excused himself.

He did not head straight to the Queen's Arms, though. Instead Quint skirted around the edge of town until the familiar smells of sawdust and pine filled his nostrils as he approached the tall fence of Jacques's Lumberyard. As he'd expected, two familiar figures were lounging against the fence.

"Heads," Chuck called, tossing a coin into the air. Lex's eyes followed it as it flipped end over end, landing on Chuck's outstretched palm.

"Eighty-five in a row!" he grinned, looking down at the unsmiling face of the late Dowager Empress.

"There's got to be some sort of trick to it," Lex said, taking the coin from his hand and examining it carefully. "You're sure it's not weighted—oh. Hullo, Quint."

"Mates." Quint nodded to them. "Making wagers against fate?"

"Something like that," Chuck said, offering Quint the coin. "Care for a toss?"

"Actually," Quint said, sticking his hands in his pockets and grinning at them, "I've got plans for this evening. Plans that involve you, mates, if you'll recall."

Chuck and Lex exchanged excited glances.

"Already?" Lex asked, eyes shining as she turned her attention back to Quint. "We're not going to wait until it's fully dark?"

"It'll be night before you know it," Quint replied, laying a finger alongside his nose. "Tonight, mates, you two become proper pirates."

⚓

"Harps and bells," Lex swore as she and Chuck dragged Quint's sea chest through the jungle. "What'd you pack in this thing, cannonballs?"

"Doubloons," Quint called back to her, a little way ahead of them. They were on the same trail as he'd taken to Cinder Cove, Quint leading with a torch in hand while the two aspiring pirates carried his sea chest between them, just as they'd hauled Quint to the harbor the night before. Each of the three held a shovel in their spare hands.

"Must be an awful lot of them," Lex grunted. "How many are ours?"

"Depends," Quint said, brushing aside a strand of trailing vines. Up ahead was a fork in the jungle trail, marked by the standing stone carved with the face of an Ikai nature god by some long-forgotten mason. "I haven't brought you on yet. Depends on how well you do tonight, and the rest of the time I'm here."

"Like an audition," Chuck said, smiling his guileless smile. "We do a good job at this, and you take us on as part of your crew."

"That was the agreement." Quint nodded. He felt a small pang of guilt at how easily he'd convinced them to assist him in burying his sea chest. He'd only had to hint at the offer of acceptance into his crew before Lex and Chuck were falling over themselves to be of use. It felt almost manipulative, but he *did* need help, for the chest was heavy, and the cousins were strong.

Besides, Quint reassured himself, hiring the pair wasn't the *worst* idea. Lex and Chuck were earnest in their desire to prove themselves, and had already hauled the chest across acres of jungle with little complaint. And without their nana, there was little tying them to Ember Bay any longer. Perhaps he was even doing them a favor by offering them a place amongst his crew.

Angels knew he'd recruited the *Bloody Angel*'s crewmembers under stranger circumstances than these. They'd found Fillbrick stranded on a scanty island little more than a sandbar, having been marooned by his previous vessel after he'd stumbled across evidence that the captain was embezzling from the crew's wages—a crime the honest boatswain could not countenance ignoring. On the opposite end of the moral spectrum, Rustbucket had been one of several crew brought aboard during a jailbreak as Quint and his mates fled the vengeful Governor of Sanmarra. And though Ophelia had voiced her reservations about bringing a man imprisoned for arson aboard a wooden ship, Rustbucket's particular skillset had proven useful on more than one occasion.

No, Quint realized, glancing over his shoulder at Chuck and Lex as they dutifully carried the sea chest between them. Offering these two the chance to join on felt so strange because he'd kept the two halves of his life separate for so long. No one else on Ember Bay knew that Quint Thatch was the fearsome Captain Redbeard, just as none of the *Bloody Angel*'s crew had ever set foot on Quint's island home. To bring these two from one life into the other felt like a blurring of lines.

Moreover, Lex and Chuck had never even been off Ember Bay, as far as Quint was aware. As much as they might aspire to become true marauders, the actual life of a pirate was one fraught with danger and hardship—a reality Quint doubted either of them was prepared to face.

But the least he could do was give them a chance to prove themselves.

"Which way?" Lex asked, halting as they stood before the Ikai stone. In daylight the stylized lines of the forgotten god's face were odd but unthreatening; almost humorous when viewed from the right angle. But now, deep in the night and lit only by Quint's torch, the flickering shadows made the strange face seem to dance and move, lending it an air of quiet, forlorn menace.

"Left," Quint said, striding further inland, the path growing gradually steeper beneath his feet as they headed deeper into the jungle.

"We're doing good so far, ain't we, Quint?" Chuck asked, his blatant eagerness tugging at Quint's guilty conscience once again. "I mean, we got the chest out of your room without being spotted. That's good, right?"

"Very good." Quint nodded.

He'd snuck them in through the back door at the height of the dinnertime rush. They'd made their way up to his room and back out without being caught, the sea chest containing the Imperial regalia carried between the two while Quint led the way.

"Stop here," he said, halting as a familiar tree loomed along the trail ahead of them.

"Why?" Chuck asked, but complied.

In response, Quint nudged the nearest of the upraised tree roots with the toe of his boot. There was a rustling sound, followed by a deeper rumble.

Suddenly the trail in front of them crumbled away, revealing a deep, steep-sided pit. Lex yelped and backed away, but, failing to drop Quint's sea chest, didn't get far.

"That's one of the old Ikai traps!" she exclaimed, her voice uncharacteristically shrill. "I thought they'd all fallen to pieces by now!"

"Nah," Quint said, peering over the edge. In the adventure novels he'd devoured as a kid, pits like these would have been lined with poison-tipped spikes, or at the very least contained a hungry tiger. The real version was decidedly less dramatic; just a deep fissure in the ground, its sides too steep to climb.

"But the Ikai haven't been to the island in..." Chuck scratched his head, trying to think precisely how long it had been since Ember Bay's original inhabitants had paid their old home a visit. "...a long time."

"Right," Quint said, taking a careful step around the open pit. "Pretty much all their old traps either fell to pieces or were dismantled after the village was founded."

"Then who did this?" Lex half-whispered, staring at the lip of the pit with wide eyes, as if she expected angry Ikai ghosts to come roiling up from it like fog at any moment. "Was it...?"

"Not ghosts," Quint said, shaking his head as he beckoned for the others to follow. "My pop did it."

"Old Clarent?" Chuck sounded even more confused than usual as he and Lex resumed hauling the chest, skirting as wide around the pit as possible. "What for?"

"You remember about two years back when some fool trader brought a shipment of Helven plums to Ember Bay?" Quint asked. He had not been there at the time, of course, but Pop had written of the incident at length. "Turns out that he also brought stowaways. Helven rats."

"I remember that," Lex nodded, frowning. "Real damned nuisances they were. Ate everything they could see and a fair number o' things they couldn't."

"But those plums were their favorites," Chuck said. "I remember Rosa had to put 'em under lock and key to keep the rats from 'em."

Quint frowned, not wanting to imagine the petite, aged shopkeeper confronted by ravenous Helven rats. "You remember how the town got rid of them?"

"Your pop came to the town council with a plan to trap 'em," Lex said. "They bought all the Helven plums the town's budget could supply as bait for the rats..."

Quint halted and turned, so that he could see the exact moment she put two and two together. He was not disappointed.

"Oh!" Lex's face, scrunched in concentration, widened into a picture of dawning understanding. "These were the traps!"

"Exactly." Quint nodded, then pointed. "Watch that root, there. That's another one."

Pop, angels rest his soul, had always been a visual sort. Quint had been raised on bedtime stories of the exploits of the Archipelago's most famous pirates, more often than not accompanied by illustrations. Sometimes, depending on how busy Pop had been that day, these were little more than rough sketches detailing the action of some pitched sea battle between notorious pirates like Captain Montcrief and Black Betty, or the vague outline of whichever island Captain Wolf had elected to bury his treasure on. But on days when business at the tavern had been slow or the wet season had kept the *Wisherman* in her berth, Pop's stories were accompanied by elaborately detailed visuals: portraits of the various pirate captains and their infamous crews, treasure maps

carefully stained and tattered to make them look aged, and breathtak-
ingly vivid scenes of desperate sword fights and narrow escapes from
the patrolling Navy.

Thus, it had come as little surprise to Quint when Pop's lengthy letter
about the rat problem and his solution to it had included a detailed
map of the area. The old man had been extremely proud of both the
plan itself and the map, judging by the evident care with which he had
plotted out the location of each trap, and all of the various hidden levers
and triggers that activated them.

Or at least, Quint hoped it had been all of them.

Lex cut a wide circle around the pit he'd indicated, trailing Chuck
behind her. "But that was years back. Why'd they leave the traps up,
then?"

"In case of another rat invasion," Quint said. "Mrs. Cavendish got a
lot choosier about which ships she'd allow to dock from which ports o'
call after that, but it opened Pop's eyes to the danger of the same thing
happening again. So, he took steps. Here we are."

He halted, lifting the torch so that the others could see the broad,
squat edifice that loomed up suddenly before them from the jungle
depths.

No one knew quite why the Ikai had erected a fort in the depths of the
jungle. For defense seemed unlikely. They had not been a warlike people, and none of the resources that could be found upon the island later
settlers would call Ember Bay were rare enough to require fortification.
Some locals speculated it was a burial ground, others a temple to those
same gods whose statues dotted the island. Regardless, most of Ember
Bay's folk gave the place a wide berth, not wanting to anger the spirits
of those their own ancestors had displaced.

Quint lifted his torch higher, watching its light illuminate the carved
blocks of unmortared stone that made up the structure. These were of

basalt and coral, carved by the same unknown masons who had erected the standing stones about the island.

"Forgive us our trespass," he muttered, and stepped into the fort.

"In there?" Lex called after him, naked fear in her voice.

"There might be more traps," Chuck added, his own tone dubious.

"There certainly are." Quint half-turned, grinning. "Good thing you're with me, then."

Inside was a maze of looming rock and narrow corridors leading to what Quint supposed had once been rooms. The fort was open to the jungle canopy above, but Pop had speculated in his letters that the fort had once sported a roof of thatched palms, which had naturally crumbled away long before the stones would even begin to show signs of weathering. Its floor was made of broad tiles of the same stone as the walls, though grass grew between most of them and the roots of trees had snaked up to crack and twist others. It was a place of ruined dignity, made all the statelier by its crumbling majesty.

They moved slowly, Quint counting each turn and the number of paces in his head. Occasionally he would call a halt so that they could edge around one of the hidden pit traps his pop's map had indicated, Lex growing visibly more nervous with each one.

"You're sure your pop marked them all?" she asked, eyes on the path directly ahead of her, searching for any clue to a hidden pitfall.

"Absolutely," Quint said, ducking under a low-hanging vine that had fallen across the corridor. "Pop was a meticulous soul, 'specially when it came to diagrams and plans. I'd bet all the gold in that chest that he didn't leave out a single trap from his map."

"You keep talking 'bout this map," Chuck observed, "but you've got a torch in one hand and a shovel in the other. Where's the map, then?"

"My head, o' course," Quint said, striding confidently ahead of them. The actual map, like all his correspondence with his parents, was securely in his cabin desk aboard the *Angel*.

"So we're trusting in your memory not to fall into a hole," Lex said, her steps slowing as she glanced fearfully about at the tall stones to either hand. "Or for the walls to start shooting darts, or—"

"Mates," Quint said, turning around and walking backwards with his arms outstretched, a cavalier grin on his face. "There's naught to worry about in here. I've a mind like a steel—"

One of the stones beneath his feet sank, and a loud *click* echoed through the night.

"Trap?" Chuck's eyes widened, just as the ground gave way beneath Quint.

Quint threw himself forward, propelled less by conscious thought and more by an instinct for self-preservation that had been honed over years of near-death experiences. But the familiar comfort of being home must have dulled his reflexes, for his foot slipped as the pit opened up behind him.

For a moment he stood there, teetering on the edge of a long fall, arms windmilling helplessly. He managed to keep hold of his torch, but the shovel slipped from his fingers. It seemed to take a very long time before he heard it crash against the floor of the pit.

"Here!" Strong hands wrapped about his free arm, pulling him forward. Quint collapsed against Chuck's towering form, steadied by Lex's firm hand on his back.

"You alright?" she asked, patting him between his shoulders.

Quint tried to answer but found he could only nod. His heart was beating faster than it had since he'd first received the black letter, the fear that had pushed him away from the hidden trap not yet abated.

Chuck leaned over the pit, staring down into the blackness. "Deep one."

"Yeah," Quint said, the word coming out in a hysterical laugh. "Pop *really* didn't want those rats getting out, I guess."

Lex frowned as she bent to retrieve the shovels she and Chuck had thrown down in order to save Quint. "Thought you said your pop mapped all these. He leave this one out?"

"Nope," Quint lied automatically. In truth, he couldn't remember. He gave them both a guilty grin. "Guess that'll teach me to look where I'm going, eh?"

Lex grunted and seized the chest by one of its handles, Chuck obligingly taking the other. Quint had to hand it to them both: they had acted decisively in a moment of danger and had risked themselves to save him without a second thought.

Perhaps they might be cut out for the pirating life, after all.

"Right," he said, clearing his throat in an attempt to resume his air of dignified captaincy. "Let's backtrack a bit, shall we?"

They retreated back down the corridor, all three stepping more carefully now despite Quint's assurances that no more surprises awaited them. The tiled floors beneath them grew increasingly uneven, until near to what Quint estimated to be the fort's northern wall, they gave way entirely to loose tropical soil.

"This is the place," Quint decided as they entered what must have once been a storeroom of some sort, judging by its size. He rested his torch against the wall, held out his hand expectantly. "Borrow one of your spades, mates?"

Chuck handed his over. Quint hefted the shovel, feeling its weight, then dug its tip into the ground. The loose dirt, specked here and there with hardened bits of fossilized coral and gnarled roots, nonetheless gave way easily beneath his weight.

"You ready to be pirates, mates?" he asked, tossing the first shovelful of dirt over his shoulder.

"Aye," they said in unison, heads bobbing.

Quint drove his shovel into the ground again, putting his boot on top of it as he grinned at them. "Then let's start diggin'."

16

The next morning Quint arrived to find Mani already at the beach, ready and eager to begin the day's labors. Quint was somewhat relieved to see that, while the carpenter's son had indeed brought his leather tool belt, Mani had thoughtfully refrained from hammering any more nails into the *Wisherman* without Quint's express permission.

"Morning, Cap'n!" Mani said, saluting. The first rays of the sun had just begun to creep above the eastern end of Cinder Cove, yet Mani was as irrepressibly chipper as ever. "Crewman Mani, reporting for duty!"

"At ease," Quint said, returning the salute. "My compliments on being on time, Crewman. Timeliness is very important aboard a vessel."

"*First aboard, last ashore!*" Jimmy squawked, fluttering down from the trees overhead.

"I know," Mani said seriously, fishing a pocket watch from his belt and checking it. "This didn't say sunup, but I figured six was a good start."

"You've been here half an hour already?" Quint asked, a pang of guilt tugging at his conscience. He made a silent vow to give Mani a more exact time than "sunup" for tomorrow.

"Yessir!" Mani pointed over his shoulder to the *Wisherman*, her prow jutting out from the thick jungle. "I got started as soon as I got here but Lurk told me to stop."

"Little landman was being loud." A rustling of leaves as Lurk's serpentine body slid out from the trees behind the *Wisherman*'s stern, her arms held tight against her sides. She halted a few feet from where the two humans stood, raising herself up to Quint's eye level. "Woke me from my sleep with all that *banging*."

She held up Mani's hammer in one webbed hand, pointing it at him accusingly.

"I see," Quint said, schooling his face into a stern countenance. "Mani, what'd we discuss yesterday?"

Mani chewed his lip, looking about for some clue before his gaze settled on Jimmy. "Not to ask my parents what anything your bird says means, Cap'n!"

"Very good," Quint said, the urge to laugh growing with every passing moment. "But I meant about repairing the *Wisherman*."

"Not to—" Mani trailed off, a guilty look coming into his eyes as he cleared his throat. "Ah, not to start without you. Cap'n."

"That's right." Quint nodded, shrugging the canvas bag he'd grabbed from the shed behind the Arms off his shoulders. Before he opened it, a thought occurred to him. "Lurk?"

She blinked her huge eyes. "Me?"

Right, she's not used to her new name. "What were you doing behind the *Wisherman*? I...were you *sleeping* in there?"

"No!" Lurk said, entirely too quickly. "I was just closing my eyes!"

"For how long?" Quint pressed.

She glowered, showing those sharklike front teeth. "For none of your business!"

"She was snoring, Cap'n!" Mani piped up. Lurk turned her glare on him.

"I see," Quint said. He did, actually. As an aquatic airbreather, Lurk would want to spend her nights ashore rather than in the ocean, where most of the mermaids' few natural predators dwelt. And the *Wisherman*'s small cabin would make the ideal spot: above the tideline, dry, and secluded from any terrestrial predators that might come looking for a nighttime snack.

Pretty sure Chum is the largest predator on the island, Quint reflected, thinking of the family cat, but of course Lurk wouldn't know that. All she'd know is that, alone in a strange world and separated from her family and friends, the *Wisherman* had made her feel safe.

Quint could empathize.

"Lurk," he said, very seriously. "While you were in the *Wisherman*'s cabin—"

She cocked her head. "The what?"

"Inside," Quint said, nodding at the boat. "Did you see anything unusual in there?"

"All landfolk things are unusual," Lurk said flatly, then furrowed her brow in concentration. "But...there *was* a strange object in there. Shaped sort of like this—"

She pressed her elbows together, making a sharp angle of her arms. "But when I touch it, it moves like this, or like this." Keeping her elbows pressed against each other, she widened and then closed the angle between them. "It's hard, and very shiny. Is it...important?"

Quint nodded. "It's a sextant."

"Cap'n!" Mani's face paled. "My folks say you shouldn't talk about—"

Quint clapped a hand over Mani's mouth.

"Belay that talk, sailor," he told him, then returned his attention to Lurk. "That sextant is very important, Lurk. We can't sail the *Wisherman* without it."

"Really?" The mermaid's mellifluous voice was dubious. "It's not even attached to the boat."

"Which is why I need you to keep an eye on it," Quint said. "Especially at night when I can't be here. Can I trust you to do that?"

"You're my pod," Lurk said, puffing out her chest. Evidently that was answer enough.

"Very good," Quint said. "Come here, Mani."

Mani stepped forward obediently as Quint knelt and opened the canvas bag he'd brought with him, producing a cloth of the same material. He spread it across the sand, then laid the rest of the bag's contents atop it. They were a collection of his pop's tools, well-maintained despite constantly being used to repair either the *Wisherman* or the Queen's Arms.

"There's more tools than just the hammer," he said. "Your folks taught you that, right?"

"They have." Mani nodded, his face falling a little. "Or tried to. I just...get distracted, sometimes."

"How come?" Quint asked. Hari and Amara were good parents, he knew, but sometimes parents were too close to their children to see where they fell short with them.

"Numbers," Mani said, brightening. He reached into his belt and produced his little leather-bound log. He flipped it open and leaned in conspiratorially. "I like doing math."

Quint glanced down at the log, saw equations scrawled across its pages in a surprisingly tidy hand. Quint was a fair hand at mathematics; any Imperial Navy officer had to be in order to serve, since so much of their duties revolved around plotting a course between two distant points with only the stars as guides. Yet the equations here were a level beyond any Quint was familiar with; the sort he suspected university scholars might value.

"Where did you learn all this, Mani?" he asked. Ember Bay's one-room schoolhouse certainly did not teach mathematics at this level, unless things had drastically changed on the island in the quarter century or so since he'd been Mani's age.

"Books," Mani said, as if that were obvious. "It's important for a ship's clerk to know math, so I learned all the math I could."

"You certainly did," Quint agreed. "Er...what is it about being a ship's clerk that so fascinates you, exactly? If you don't mind my asking."

"Well." Again, uncertainty crept into Mani's voice. "I'm...not great with my hands. I mean I *try* to be, but my mind always wanders, unless it's something I'm already interested in. Like math, or sailing."

"And being a ship's clerk combines those two," Quint said, starting to get it. "It's a way for you to serve aboard a vessel that doesn't ask as much of you, physically."

Mani looked self-conscious but nodded. "Aye, Cap'n."

"Well." Quint looked down at the tools. "If we're going to fix up the *Wisherman*, I'm going to need you focused, and that requires using tools. Do you think you can try and learn how to use each of them, if it's for the boat?"

Mani's face took on the air of unselfconscious seriousness only eight-year-olds were capable of. "I'll try. Cap'n."

"Good. Your first lesson starts now." Quint reached down and plucked a tool at random from the cloth. "This one's an awl."

"*All ashore that's going ashore!*" Jimmy squawked, flapping out across the beach. The sun peeked above the horizon at last, painting the sky purple and gold as Quint began to teach Mani how they were going to repair the *Wisherman*.

17

Part of Quint had feared that, after so long aboard the *Bloody Angel*, he would come back to Ember Bay a stranger, having forgotten all he'd once known of his hometown. But like all such places, time moved slowly on Ember Bay, and the island had changed far less in the intervening years than Quint himself had.

He fell into a daily routine with startling ease. Each morning he'd rise early and head to Cinder Cove, Pop's tools under one arm and a picnic lunch for himself, Mani, and Lurk in the other, Jimmy flying overhead.

"Why's your parrot have a boy's name?" Mani asked one morning, a few days later. They were perched in the *Wisherman*'s prow, sanding down a plank that had become splintery after too long exposed to direct sun.

"Pop thought she was a boy when he got her." Quint glanced at Jimmy, who stood perched on the broken bowsprit, her bright beady eyes peering with interest at their work. "Didn't realize otherwise 'til she laid a clutch of eggs."

"*Cabin boy an' the captain's daughter!*" Jimmy crowed, flapping her wings for balance and taking a few wobbling steps closer to them. "*Both get wet when tossed in the water!*"

"So, she was your papa's?" Mani asked, oblivious to Quint's frantic signaling to Jimmy not to continue the rhyme.

"Nah." Quint shook his head, sending beads of sweat scattering across the *Wisherman*'s deck. "He got her for me. A going-away present, for when I joined the Navy."

"Didn't you say he didn't want you to, though?"

"He didn't," Quint allowed. "Made his feelings on the subject very well known, in fact. But he never tried to forbid me from joining."

"Why not?" Mani asked, frowning.

"Maybe 'cause he knew it wouldn't work," Quint said, shrugging. "Headstrong an' foolish lad that I was, I probably would've gone anyway if he had."

Mani was quiet for a moment, digesting this.

"I'm not sure if I could," he said, his frown deepening. "Do something even if my parents told me I shouldn't."

"That's because you're a better son than I was, mate." Quint clapped Mani on the back. "In any case, I don't think that was my pop's real reason for letting me go. I think he knew that it was something I had to do for myself. Mistakes I had to make to become the person I ended up being. You understand?"

"No," Mani said, shaking his head.

"You might, once you're older."

Mani groaned. "Grown-ups *always* say that about stuff like this."

"That's because it's trite but true." Quint leaned in conspiratorially. "There's only one real difference between you and the grown-ups, mate. You wanna know what it is?"

"They're..." Mani looked askance at Quint, wary of some trick question. "...older?"

"Got it in one!" Quint sat up, his back protesting after so long bent double to sand the deck. He certainly *felt* older. "It's just time, mate. Time and experience. And my pop, he knew that I needed both."

"Even though he didn't like you joining the Navy," Mani said. "Why give you Jimmy, then?"

"As a reminder." Quint stretched out his hand, beckoning. Jimmy fluttered onto it, the sharp points of her talons digging into his wrist as she balanced herself. "Of where I came from, and who was waiting for me if I ever chose to come back."

The repairs to the *Wisherman* came along with remarkable speed. The superficial damage was easily fixed. It took no more than a day's work to repair the rail, for instance, and the bowsprit was easily replaced with a long spar of wood from Jacques's Lumberyard, hauled to Cinder Cove courtesy of Lex and Chuck. Eager to prove themselves suitable pirates, they'd returned the following day with more planks, and by the week's end the hole in the *Wisherman*'s hull had been plugged.

Quint had dreaded inspecting the jammed wheel—if the lines had been damaged it'd be a far trickier business to fix them. To his immense relief, the source of the jam turned out not to be any mechanical problem, but a natural one.

"It's a bird's nest!" Mani protested, close to tears as Quint dug out clumped handfuls of sticks and brown pine needles that had stopped up the boat's rudder stock. "You can't just throw it away!"

"Mani," Quint said, more patiently than he would have been able to a few weeks previously. "The boat won't steer if we just leave it in there."

"But it's someone's *home*," he protested, folding his arms in a motion that was uncannily similar to Lurk's posture of protest. Currently the mermaid was on the deck, holding Quint's compass in both her webbed hands, angling it this way and that in an ongoing effort to see if she could make the needle point in any direction other than north. "Would you get rid of Jimmy's home?"

"Jimmy's home is my home," Quint said, reaching in and pulling out another handful of thatch. His hand closed around something hard but delicate. "Besides. Take a look."

He handed the bundle of twigs and pine needles to Mani, who took it gingerly before looking down to see the speckled white shards within. "Eggshells?"

"Aye," Quint said, picking one up for a better look. "This was a fairy tern, I think. You've probably seen plenty of 'em—all white except a black spot on their heads, like they've got hair. Notice how they're just shells, though, not eggs?"

Mani nodded. "So...they're gone?"

"Right." Quint looked out across the cove, where a flight of terns was even now swooping low across the water. "Birds like that only nest for as long as they need for their eggs to hatch. Once they do, they're gone."

Mani watched the terns, but was not so easily convinced. "What if they want to come back?"

"They don't nest in the same place twice," Quint said, rubbing at his shoulder. "Makes it too easy for predators to find them."

Mani looked up at Quint. "So, they don't have a home?"

Quint watched the terns swooping across the sky, the lowest of them nearly touching the water. They flew with perfect coordination, moving as a unit with every turn and swoop, each acting in perfect harmony with its fellows.

"I wouldn't say that," he said.

⚓

"You're sure about this?" Quint asked Lurk one morning, a few weeks after his arrival on Ember Bay.

She lay stretched out along the sand beside him, her tail idly swishing back and forth. She turned her head, her dorsal fin flaring a little as she peered up at him with those great black eyes. "I'm sure."

"It's going to hurt," Quint said, glancing up and down the beach. Mani wasn't there today, since Amara had needed his help around the shop with work his brothers were too young to help with. Mani had been disappointed, of course, but Quint and Lurk had been waiting for a day like this.

"Been hurt before." Lurk's voice was flat. "Besides. You said all of your crew have them."

Not all of them, Quint wanted to protest, but realized it wasn't true. "Yes, but...it's not a requirement."

"Quint." Lurk's voice was calmer than he'd ever heard it. "You *promised.*"

Quint knew he'd lost the argument.

"Alright," he said, pressing the needle against Lurk's shoulder. The mermaid did not so much as flinch, only took a swig from the bottle of rum Quint had provided her for the occasion. "But hold still. This is going to take a while."

"What is *that*?" a wide-eyed Mani demanded the next morning, mere moments after Lurk had emerged from the *Wisherman*'s cabin.

Lurk preened, her dorsal fin lifting as high from her neck as it could as she pointed a webbed finger at her shoulder. "Do you like it?"

"Cap'n," Mani said, staring at Quint. "You gave Lurk a *tattoo*."

"I did," Quint admitted wearily, surveying his handiwork. All things considered, he was fairly proud of himself. The image inked on Lurk's shoulder was not an exact replica of that on his own. The linework was a bit rougher, and the face was less detailed. *But still not a bad job,* he congratulated himself.

"It's a mermaid," Lurk told Mani proudly, pointing at the fish-tailed woman inked on her shoulder. "See?"

Mani peered closer. "That doesn't look like you."

"It does not," Lurk agreed, laughing. She darted toward Quint, tugging down the shoulder of his shirt so that more of his own tattoos were exposed. "It's like Quint's!"

"Huh." Mani chewed his lip. "They've got hair hanging over their—"

"Tails," Quint said hastily. Knowing that Mani would see Lurk's tattoo, he'd elected to censor it in the same manner as his own. "But we're wasting daylight, mate. Look."

He fished a pair of broad-bristled brushes from the canvas bag of tools and handed one to Mani before popping the lid on one of the heavy buckets he'd hauled to the cove that morning.

"Repairs are all finished," he said, slapping the *Wisherman*'s refurbished hull affectionately. "Last thing she needs is a fresh coat. I say we give her one, eh, lad?"

"Aye, Cap'n," Mani said, saluting with the brush (Quint had confiscated the hammer some time ago). "Except..."

Oh no, Quint thought, as Mani asked the question he'd been afraid he would.

"When do *I* get a tattoo?"

18

Time might have passed slowly on Ember Bay, but it passed nonetheless. The next bright morning dawned to find Quint and Mani surveying their handiwork, repairs completed at long last.

The *Wisherman* looked as fine a vessel as Quint had ever seen. Her hull was patched, the fresh coat of paint making it so that the place where it had been punctured was indistinguishable from the rest of the wood. The new bowsprit held sturdy, the rail had been straightened, the rudder system cleared of any bird's nests. Jimmy flapped overhead, as if eager to set sail.

"We've done a fine job, mate," Quint said, clapping Mani lightly on the back. "She looks as fresh as she did the day my pop purchased her."

"Aye, Cap'n." Mani nodded, glancing up at him. "I'm sorry he's not here to see it."

"Who says he ain't?" Quint said, taking a step forward to rest his hand on the hull. They'd restored her paint scheme to what it had been before weather and time had chipped and cracked it: whitewashed deck and hull, with red edging along the trim. The name *WISHERMAN* was painted in bold black capital letters along the prow, just as it had been before their repairs had begun. Quint had traced over his father's lettering with his own, taking great care to replicate it exactly. It was still his pop's boat, after all.

"We sail now?" Lurk's voice asked. Quint looked up to see her serpentine body draped over the rail, her great black eyes peering down at them. She held a compass in one webbed hand, the sextant in the other.

"Soon," Quint reassured her. "We've got to get her into the water first."

Lurk made a disconsolate noise and slithered down from the prow, joining the two humans on the sand. Mani looked doubtfully up at the *Wisherman*, the difficulty of hauling her down the beach having no doubt just occurred to him. "She's awfully heavy, Cap'n."

"Not as much as some," Quint said. "Besides, I've brought help."

He nodded toward the jungle, where two figures were struggling their way out of the undergrowth.

"Midshipman Presley reportin' for duty, Cap'n," Lex said, giving Quint a surprisingly passable salute.

"You ain't a man, Lex," Chuck objected, stumbling out after her.

Lex elbowed him in the ribs. "Midshipman's a rank, ya oaf."

"Ah." Chuck nodded sagely. He cocked his head to one side, eyes widening with interest. "Say, Cap'n. Is that a mermaid?"

Quint glanced in the direction indicated, where Lurk had abruptly halted her slither across the beach toward the newcomers. She'd been out in the lagoon hunting for eels when they'd dropped off the planks the other day. "Lurk?"

"Yes?" She looked at him, webbed hands clasped behind her back. Out of the corner of his eye Quint saw Mani bend over to retrieve the sextant and compass where she'd dropped them in the sand.

"Were you trying to drown them?"

Lex sputtered, her face going white. Chuck merely gave Lurk an appraising look, as though weighing her odds when it came to drowning him.

"No," Lurk said, though the quiver that ran down her dorsal fin gave her away.

"*Lurk.* No drowning anyone who comes here with me, remember?"

"You never let me drown *anyone*," Lurk moaned, baring her shark's teeth. Lex shrank behind Chuck, who cracked his knuckles.

"Nope," Quint agreed. "They're here to help us pull the *Wisherman* into the water. You, me, an' Mani can't do it by ourselves."

Lurk considered this, then looked at Lex and Chuck. "Does this mean they're part of your crew, then?"

Nor was she the only one who wanted to know. Lex peeked out from behind Chuck, who glanced over at Quint while keeping his posture facing Lurk.

Quint still felt a tug of reluctance, but he knew it was unfair. They'd done well at burying the treasure, and he'd enlisted them in a few other minor tasks about town over the past few weeks. Neither would ever be considered the brightest stars in the sky, but they'd proven themselves dependable, and they deserved a chance.

"Yes," Quint said, sighing. "They're part of my crew."

Lex let out a whoop, seizing Chuck around his middle and hoisting him into the air, his long legs kicking as she spun him 'round, just as she'd done to Quint on his first night back in Ember Bay. "Y'hear that, Chuck?! We're pi—"

"Piloting the *Wisherman*," Quint finished, cutting them off before Mani could hear the word "pirates." "Aye, mates, but not 'til after I've had a pass."

He turned and strode back to the *Wisherman*, seizing hold of one of the long ropes that had been fastened to her prow. "Now, are we gonna stand about jawin' all morning, or are we gonna take this beauty on the water?"

Quint had timed the *Wisherman*'s launch well. The tide was so high that they only needed to haul the boat a dozen yards down the beach before she was bobbing in the water. Lurk slithered around to the prow, still pulling as her powerful tail lashed back and forth in the surf. Quint stood waist-deep in the swelling waves, pulling with her, while Lex and Chuck pushed from the stern, Mani assisting them as much as his slight frame allowed.

A wave rose, lifting the sailboat with it. The tide ebbed, drawing the *Wisherman* into the cove, waves lapping against her prow. Quint let drop the line he'd been holding and threw himself aside, the hull passing by him as the boat's prow cut smoothly through the water.

He swam around to her stern, to find Mani clinging to one of the lines trailing from her aft.

"All aboard, mate," Quint said, seizing Mani by the back of his shirt and hauling him onto the boat's stern. He lifted himself up after the lad, then turned and began hauling in the trailing line Mani had been clinging to.

"Come on, mates!" he hollered to Chuck and Lex, who stood in the shallows, the tide lapping at their knees.

"Can't swim!" Chuck called back, his curls bouncing as he shook his head.

"We'll meet you back ashore tonight!" Lex shouted, cupping her hands to her mouth.

Quint nodded his understanding. He coiled the rope he'd been hauling and tossed it to the deck behind him.

"Treat yourself to lunch at the Arms!" he shouted to them.

Lex's face scrunched up in consternation. "But we ain't allowed!"

"Tell Ma it's a favor to me!" Quint yelled, the waves nearly drowning out his voice as the *Wisherman* slipped toward the deep end of the cove. "Just mind you behave yourselves!"

"Aye, Cap'n!" Chuck saluted, and with that the pair of them turned and began to trudge back up the beach.

Quint turned his back on land, the breeze blowing his hair from his face as he looked out at the broad blue horizon beyond the protective jetties of Cinder Cove.

"Crewman Mani!" he called, stepping easily across the rolling deck, marveling at how swiftly his sea-legs had returned after weeks spent ashore.

"Aye, Cap'n!" Mani called, and to Quint's immense approval he was already hauling away on the mainsail rope. Quint joined him, and together they pulled until the great white triangle of the *Wisherman*'s sail rose above them, rippling and billowing in the breeze.

The deck lurched beneath them, sending Mani's arms windmilling as he struggled to keep his balance.

"Easy, lad!" Quint said, clapping a hand on his shoulder to steady him. With his other hand he grabbed the wheel, steering the *Wisherman* out between the jetties and into the sea beyond the cove. "Where's Lurk?"

In answer, the mermaid shot up from the water at the boat's prow, rocketing into the air as swiftly as if she'd been launched from a cannon. Water glistened off her scales as she arced over the *Wisherman*'s prow, arms pressed tight against her sides. Her head turned as she reached the apex of her leap, grinning her shark's smile at Quint and Mani.

"Cap'n!" Mani said, tugging at his sleeve as Lurk arced downward, back toward the waves. "Lurk's *beautiful!*"

Quint could not help but agree, black eyes and shark's teeth included.

Cinder Cove sank into the distance behind them with startling rapidity. Quint tacked a course that took them east toward the morning sun, making sure to keep land on their port bow all the while. The *Wisherman* was a sturdy vessel and could easily sail to the neighboring islands on the Reach, but for her maiden voyage following her repair Quint had set his sights closer to home.

They cruised along, the wind filling her sails, the deck rolling gently beneath them with every swell of the ocean waves. At first Mani was uneasy, not trusting his constantly shifting footing, which did nothing to ease his natural clumsiness. Quint showed him how to secure himself by always keeping a hand on one of the ship's lines, the two of them walking the length of the *Wisherman* from prow to stern and back with their hands on the lines. Within an hour Mani had forgotten his trepidation and was racing across the deck like an old hand.

Jimmy soared alongside them, her green wings flapping hard as she circled the mast, landing on the rail or Quint's shoulder whenever she grew tired. At times she would cling to the long forestay cable running from the bowsprit to the top of the mast, which was festooned with a variety of detachable semaphore flags fluttering in the breeze.

Lurk too kept pace with them, occasionally hauling herself onto the low stern to ride along. When the wind really caught them, she slithered up to the prow, resting her webbed hands upon the rail, head thrust forward as her great black eyes scanned the horizon. Searching, Quint knew, for any trace of her pod.

He steered them a bit further from land and let Mani try his hand at the wheel. As he'd expected, Mani took to it quickly, though his overeager excitement nearly capsized them when he tried to turn too sharply into the wind.

"*Abandon ship!*" Jimmy screeched, flapping madly about Quint's head. "*Every man for himself!*"

"BELAY THAT!" Quint hollered back, his muscles straining as he pulled at the wheel with all the strength he possessed, Mani clinging to his side to keep from slipping overboard.

Jimmy squawked and landed on his shoulder, her talons tearing into his shirt and the skin beneath. In the prow Lurk decided to heed Jimmy's warning, slithering beneath the portside rail and disappearing into the blue.

Quint gave a titanic heave on the wheel. Slowly, inch by inch, the *Wisherman* righted itself until they were once more sailing along as smoothly as if they hadn't nearly capsized.

"Right," Quint said, panting a little as he wiped sweat from his brow. "That's enough learnin' to sail for one morning, I think."

19

B ut that was not the end of their adventures aboard the *Wisherman* that day.

Though Ember Bay was the largest island on this end of the Reach, it was surrounded by several neighboring islets, many of them little more than sandbars, the tall palms sticking up from them like ship's sails. Quint charted a course for one of the nearest of these, Little Buster. They dropped anchor offshore. The water beneath them was a sparkling, startlingly bright azure, broken in spaces by the darker shapes of submerged reefs.

"Reefs are good fishing," Quint explained, handing Mani one of the rods he'd brought for just such a purpose. "They're like little underwater towns. All manner o' fish congregate around them, so all you gotta do is drop a line and wait until one gets curious enough to come give it a nibble."

He showed Mani how to bait his hook, using one of the brightly colored lures his pop had hand-carved and stowed aboard the *Wisherman*.

They cast their lines, the corks that served as floaters bobbing above the waves, then settled in to await a nibble, legs dangling over the rail.

"This is a very stupid way to catch fish," Lurk observed, arms folded across her chest.

"Not stupid if it works," Quint said, grinning as his cork bobbed beneath the water, his line going suddenly taut. His fingers cranked the reel at a slow, even pace, occasionally letting out a little line whenever the line strained beneath the fish's attempts to flee. Mani watched in rapt fascination.

"Got 'im!" Quint crowed, hauling up the still-struggling fish. Quint set his rod down and lifted the line, from which the flopping, gasping catch dangled. It had a broad mouth that opened and closed rhythmically along with its gills, and a slightly humped head, behind which it had a dorsal fin not unlike Lurk's. Its scales were a spotted rusty red above and a paler color below.

"Wow," Mani said. "It's *ugly*."

"It's a grouper," Quint said, deftly unhooking the fish's mouth from his lure. He held it out to Mani, keeping a firm grip on the flopping fish. "You want to touch it?"

Mani plucked up his courage and extended two fingers, pressed them against the glistening scales, then jerked them away as if he'd been burned. "It's slimy!"

"Rude," Lurk said, watching these proceedings from her place in the prow, unimpressed.

"Not slimy," Quint corrected, "just slick." He held up the grouper to the sunlight, admiring the way its scales glistened and shimmered.

"Are we gonna eat it?" Mani asked, his revulsion evidently not extending to the prospect of a meal.

"Grouper are good eating," Quint said, then shook his head. "But nah. You never eat the first one. It's bad luck."

Mani frowned. "Says who?"

"Everyone," Quint said, though in truth this was one of the countless lessons Pop had taught him. "You always throw the first one back. It's a...gesture of faith, I guess. That the first catch of the day won't be the only one."

Mani considered this. "But we can keep the others, right? And eat them?"

Quint laughed. "Once we get back ashore, sure. 'Less you wanna eat 'em raw."

Mani made a face.

"Raw is tasty," Lurk chimed in. She cast another dubious glance at Mani's float, still bobbing over the reef. "I'm hungry."

"I brought lunch," Quint said, nodding to the cabin. "But if you want to catch your own, go ahead. Just stay on the far side of the islet. I don't want you scaring any of the fish away."

"Fine." Lurk made a face. "But I bet I catch more than you with your little sticks." She slipped off the starboard rail, becoming no more than a dark serpentine shape gliding away beneath the waves.

The grouper still in Quint's hand had slowed its struggles, its tail tapping feebly against his wrist. Quint lifted it to his face and pressed his lips to its flank, tasting salt and the greasy feel of scales.

"Ew!" Mani blanched as Quint tossed it back into the water. "Why'd you do that?"

"Luck," Quint said. Another thing he'd learned from his pop.

The grouper floated in the water, stunned. Then it flopped beneath the surface, righting itself with a little shake like a dog that had just experienced a bad dream. It swam downward, disappearing from view.

"Now," Quint said, readying his rod for another cast, "let's see who can catch the biggest one, yeah?"

Mani gave him a gap-toothed grin. "You're on, Cap'n."

⚓

It had been a nearly perfect day, one that Quint knew even as he set a course for home he would treasure for the rest of his life. The wind had filled the *Wisherman*'s sails, giving her new life. He and Mani had fished together, and he'd taught the boy a bit about how to sail, even if Mani had nearly capsized the boat. Quint knew he'd be getting an earful about that from Amara and Hari at some point down the road, but he could hardly bring himself to care. No one had gotten hurt, after all, and Mani would not forget his first adventure aboard the *Wisherman*.

"Are we going back to Cinder Cove?" Mani asked, glancing starboard as they approached the long stone jetties that marked the cove's entrance.

"Why bother?" Quint asked, grinning. "Might as well roll into town in style now that the boat's fixed, eh?"

"The ship already rolled once," Lurk pointed out, jabbing an accusing finger at Mani. "When he was steering."

"That's not—" Quint stopped himself. Lurk spoke Imperial fluently, but metaphor and certain turns of phrase tended to be a challenge for her. "Never mind. Lurk, do you want us to let you off at the cove?"

She swayed a little on her serpentine lower half, in what Quint recognized as a mermaid's posture of indecision. "If the boat is fixed...will you still..."

"Come and visit?" Quint guessed. Lurk nodded, as if not trusting herself to say more.

"Of course we will," Mani said, wrapping the mermaid in a hug.

Lurk wriggled uncomfortably, then stiffly returned the hug. Her shoulders slumped in evident relief when Mani released her. She looked at Quint, who nodded his confirmation of Mani's assertion.

"See you tomorrow, then," she said, and slipped over the rail and beneath the waves.

They passed by Cinder Cove, around the southwest side of the island, into the setting sun before turning north, then doubling back eastward toward the harbor of Ember Bay. The sky was streaked orange and purple behind them, the lamps of the town already lit, guiding them home like an earthbound constellation.

As they cruised into the bay, Quint was surprised to find a ship anchored in the harbor. Not a boat, but a *ship*; triple-masted, with a hull of dark wood and an angelic bronze figurehead.

A dizzying sense of vertigo seized Quint, as if the waves beneath him had suddenly disappeared, leaving him to crash into a dry seabed. He knew that figurehead.

He knew that *ship*.

Her sails were furled, and the black flag was nowhere in evidence, but Quint would recognize his *Bloody Angel* anywhere.

"Wow," Mani said, staring openmouthed at it. "Is that a Navy ship?"

"No," Quint said, his own mouth dry. He was about to adjust course to pull alongside the *Bloody Angel*, which should not, *could not*, be here in Ember Bay, when movement along the pier caught his attention.

Dread knotted in his stomach as he turned his head. There, standing on the edge of his hometown's docks, stood his crew of pirates.

20

Not his *whole* crew, of course. It was a foolish captain who left his vessel entirely unmanned and unguarded while anchored at port, and Quint had been the victim of more than one shipjacking in the early days of his career. But even from this distance he could recognize those lined along the docks.

Ophelia stood in the lead, her heavily inked arms bared to the world as she waved the *Wisherman* forward. Fillbrick stood behind her, a burly mountain of a man beneath whom the dock's timber planks looked as fragile as matchsticks. Beside him, looking something like a matchstick himself, was the tall, stork-like figure of Darby, the second mate, polishing his glasses against his waistcoat. Lingering behind the other three was Bonnie Kate, her mane of black locs held back by a bright orange head wrap that circled her brow like a crown. True to form, she clutched a ledger tight against her chest, as though fearing if she loosened her grip, it might go plummeting into the bay.

Rustbucket stood a few feet from the other four, flanked on either side by a pair of men Quint thought looked vaguely familiar, but were decidedly *not* members of the *Bloody Angel*'s crew. Rustbucket himself was not waving, instead tugging repeatedly at the coiled orange fuse of his beard, an agitated tic that surfaced whenever Rustbucket knew an admonishment from his captain was imminent.

This was not, Quint surmised, going to be a pleasant reunion.

"Are they friends of yours?" Mani asked, peering intently at them, his eyes brightly eager with interest.

"Aye," Quint said, his mouth dry. "Though what they're doing here—"

He found himself speaking to empty air as Mani darted forward to the prow, waving and hollering out across the bay to the motley collection of pirates on the dock. "Ahoy, mateys!"

"*Ahoy!*" Fillbrick's basso baritone bellowed back across the water, answering Mani's own clear piping voice. Gritting his teeth, Quint raised a hand from the wheel and returned their waves, hoping the curtness of the gesture conveyed his displeasure at...whatever this was.

The *Wisherman* cruised smoothly across the sunset-sparkled waves, pulling up alongside the wooden pier. Quint called Mani's attention back to the task at hand, ordering the lad to toss out the coiled rope fenders that kept the dock from damaging the boat's hull. As Mani worked, Quint fixed the wheel in place and began to haul in the sail, furling the great sheet and storing it away in its canvas sheathing.

Whatever the circumstances of their arrival in Ember Bay, Quint's crew fell to aiding the *Wisherman*'s docking by silent assent, seizing hold of the ropes Quint and Mani tossed them and fastening the sailboat tight against the pier's upraised pylons. Only once she was secure did Quint step from ship to pier, the wood feeling less sturdy beneath his boots than it had on his first arrival.

"Fancy seeing you lot here," he said, keeping his tone light even as his jaw tightened. "What a surprise."

"These are your crewmates?" Mani asked from behind him, balancing precariously on the *Wisherman*'s rail, arms wheeling.

"Aye, mate!" Grinning, Ophelia leaned forward and caught Mani before he could fall, depositing him easily on the pier. "You a new recruit, then?"

Mani looked up at Quint, his dark eyes huge and shining. Quint avoided his gaze, looking instead at Ophelia. "I'd say that's your decision, *Captain*."

"Ah." Ophelia's grin faded at the reminder that they could not speak openly here. Squaring her shoulders, she cleared her throat, speaking with a slower, more careful diction as she glanced at Mani. "You're a bit on the young side, lad."

"That's all right!" Mani said, undeterred. "Cap'n Quint taught me everything I need to know!"

Ophelia's questioning glance at Quint was mirrored by the rest of the crew.

"Only Cap'n of the sailboat, Mani," Quint said, shifting his weight uncomfortably. "The *Bloo*—I mean. The *Waterhouse* is a lot bigger, Mani."

"She is!" Mani agreed, turning for another look at the great dark ship anchored behind them. "Biggest I've ever seen in the harbor!"

Quint stepped as surreptitiously as he could between Mani and the ship, trying to keep the *Bloody Angel*'s prow out of Mani's sight. He sent a silent prayer of thanks to his angel that they'd painted the ship's name in red lettering against black; this late in the evening it would be difficult to make out.

"She's got a full complement," Quint told Mani, searching for some passable lie. "And at any rate you'd have to get your folks' permission first—"

"I'll go ask them!" Mani said, sprinting through the assembled pirates up the dock. Rustbucket yelped as the boy darted past, nearly knocking him into the bay.

"Cute kid," Fillbrick rumbled, watching him go.

"Aye," Quint agreed, folding his arms across his chest. "Now, mates. Anyone want to explain what in the nine hells you're all doing here?"

To his chagrin, they immediately fell to shouting at once, each trying to convey their version of events to the captain.

"I did like you said," Ophelia started, her posture still stiff from pretending to be the *Angel*'s captain. "Resupplied in Solace, then struck course for the outlying isles—"

"Weren't there two weeks before a storm blew up—" Fillbrick cut in. "Tore the foresail to tatters afore we could strike it—"

"That's not the worst of it," Bonnie Kate interrupted, stepping forward from between Fillbrick and Darby. "Some o' the foodstuffs stowed on deck hadn't been properly secured, so we lost better'n a fortnight's provisions overboard—"

"If you're going to cast blame, Kate," Darby objected, his face reddening, "at least say who you mean! I know you think me 'n' Vigo—"

The argument grew to a cacophonous crescendo as each of them vied to explain what had gone wrong, and whose fault it was. Only Rustbucket and his two unknown companions, Quint noticed, refrained from joining in.

"Quiet," Quint said to no effect. He cupped his hands to his mouth and tried again. "OI! STOW THAT CHATTER, LADS AND LASSES!"

They fell silent immediately, backs straightening in instinctive response to their leader's instant shift from humble Quint Thatch to Captain Redbeard, scourge of the Eight Seas.

"Now," Quint said, sparing a brief glance shoreward to check that no one had heard them. "We need to get you lot back to the ship before anyone notices—"

"Respectfully, Cap'n," Darby spoke up, clearing his throat, "the town's already noticed. Ship's a bit hard to hide."

"And it'd be more suspect if we just anchored there without *anyone* coming ashore," the ever-sensible Bonnie Kate pointed out. "And seeing as we're already here..."

"Fine," Quint said, grinding his teeth. He glanced up at the sky, swiftly fading to dusk. "Let's head someplace you won't be noticed, then. You can explain on the way."

His crew parted before him as he strode down the dock, heartbeat lurching with every groan of the wooden planks beneath him. They could not be here, in his home, the one place untouched by the piratical side of his life. Just the sight of them trooping along behind him struck him again with that weird sense of unreality, as if the two halves of his life had exchanged places without consulting him. Quint could not have been more bewildered if his Ma had appeared on the deck of the *Bloody Angel* one day, a cutlass in one hand and a pistol in the other, a tricorn hat upon her head.

"Evenin', Mrs. Cavendish," he said as the ragtag group approached the harbormaster's office at the foot of the pier. "The day treat you right?"

"Passably," she allowed, lowering the yellowed newspaper she'd been perusing to squint through her spectacles first at Quint, then at the odd assortment of characters behind him. "Where'd all these come from?"

Quint opened his mouth to spin some lie, but Ophelia interposed herself before he could.

"A fine evening to you, miss," she said, pressing her hands against her heart and giving Mrs. Cavendish a courteous bow. Quint watched the old harbormistress's eyes roam over Ophelia's multitudinous tattoos, taking some sort of mental inventory. "Ophelia Price, cap'n of the good ship *Waterhouse* anchored in yon harbor."

She gestured grandly toward the aforementioned vessel, now just a dark silhouette against the lowering sun. Quint's shoulders relaxed, just a little. No one would be able to read the name painted on the ship's prow in this light unless they rowed up alongside her.

"*Waterhouse,*" Cavendish said, adjusting her glasses. "You'd be young Thatch's commanding officer, then?"

"Aye." Ophelia grinned—a little too widely, in Quint's estimation. "Come to retrieve our wayward clerk afore we set out 'pon our next voyage."

"Thought you were going to be here a few weeks more," Cavendish said, squinting harder at Quint. "Your ma know you're leaving again?"

Out of the corner of his eye Quint noticed the other pirates visibly perk up at the mention of his mother. He'd told them enough tales of his upbringing on Ember Bay that the name of Lola Thatch was familiar to them all. The possibility of actually encountering their captain's ma had clearly piqued their collective interest.

"I'm on my way to tell her now," Quint lied, a bead of sweat crawling down his spine. He'd been so shocked at his crew's sudden arrival that he'd hardly paused to consider how he'd explain away their presence to Ma, let alone the rest of Ember Bay.

One problem at a time, he told himself.

"Best get to it, then," Cavendish said, returning her attention to the yellowed newspaper she'd been browsing when they'd arrived.

Dismissed, Quint began striding up the hill toward the Arms as quickly as his feet could carry him without breaking into a run, his crew following doggedly along. With the sun at his back sinking toward the ocean, it was only a matter of time before the townsfolk began lighting their lamps, and he wanted to hurry his crew out of sight before anyone thought to wonder at their presence in the village.

"Ophelia," he said, beckoning her forward as the rest trotted a little ways behind. "Now that we're a little less flustered, let's try again. We were supposed to rendezvous in Sweetharbor three weeks from now. What happened?"

"Short answer," she said, throwing a significant glance over her shoulder at Rustbucket and his two associates, "we've had a string o' bad luck, complicated by individual negligence."

"And the long answer?"

"It's like I was tryin' to tell you, Quint," she said, lowering her voice to head off further interruptions and embellishments. "After Solace we spent a fortnight cruisin' the outer isles, never anchored in the same cove two nights running."

"Until the storm," Quint said, having gleaned that much at least from their overlapping chatter.

"Until the storm," Ophelia agreed, nodding grimly. "Happened like Kate an' Fillbrick said—blew up so fast it shredded the foresail and washed a fair amount o' rations overboard."

"Darby seemed to take some exception to that," Quint observed, glancing back over his shoulder. Sure enough, the quartermaster and the second mate were pointedly ignoring one another, keeping Fillbrick's considerable bulk between them while Rustbucket and the other two followed along behind.

"That's 'cause it's Vigo who was in charge of securing the aforementioned supplies," Ophelia said, lowering her voice even further. "They're in a bit of a spat over it, as you might imagine, but Darby's still taking ill to anyone else pointing out where his partner's fallen short."

That explained both Darby's sour disposition and why Vigo was presumably still aboard the ship.

They crested the top of the hill, the familiar shape of the Queen's Arms looming over it, wooden sign swaying gently in the tropical breeze. For the first time in weeks, the sight of his childhood home brought Quint no comfort.

"In here," he said, beckoning the group to follow as he ducked into the narrow alleyway formed by the space between the tavern and the neighboring storehouse. He had no intention of further upending his peaceful stay on Ember Bay by introducing his crew of pirates to his mother. One of them would let the truth of his occupation slip sooner or later, and then everything would fall apart. The storehouse wall had no windows, and there were only a handful near the roof of the Arms, which made this as private a spot as Quint could expect to find in town.

The alleyway's narrow confines were made all the more cramped by a scattering of crates and barrels. Fillbrick took up a post at the alley's mouth, keeping an eye out in case any passersby should overhear them.

"Right," Quint said to his assembled crewmen and crewwomen once they had seated themselves atop barrels and crates. "So, a storm blew up and you lot had to head back to civilization for resupply and repair. That I can apprehend."

He rubbed his chin, the lack of bristles feeling strange for the first time in weeks. "What I *cannot* fathom is how that led you here, against my explicit orders to leave this place be—"

"Beggin' your pardon, Cap'n," Ophelia said, interrupting, "but we ain't got an abundance of time. The Navy's on its way."

A chill that had nothing to do with the tropical breeze crept down Quint's spine.

The Navy. The Imperial Navy he had fled eighteen years ago. The Navy that had dominated the Archipelago with coin and cutlass for longer than he'd been alive, the Navy he'd dedicated his life to robbing, harassing, and otherwise troubling. That Navy was coming here. To Ember Bay, his quiet, peaceful little hometown.

He looked at his crew, none of whom would meet his eyes, and knew that it was their doing.

"Then you'd better explain quickly," he said, frost creeping into his voice.

"Aye." Ophelia nodded, sounding chastened but also relieved to finally have it out. "As it happened, the nearest port was Sweetharbor..."

Quint massaged his temples, suddenly feeling very tired. "Of course it was."

"Not her fault, Cap'n," Darby piped up. "It *was* the closest, and we couldn't get far with the foresail in the condition it was in."

"We were there two days," Bonnie Kate chimed in, her and Darby's animosity set aside. "Long enough for *someone* to run into his cousins."

All heads turned toward Rustbucket and his two associates. Upon closer inspection, Quint realized they did bear a passing resemblance to one another, though Rustbucket was shorter than either. "Care to make introductions, Rusty?"

"Aye," Rustbucket said, nodding first to one cousin, then the other. "This is Berk, and that's Bert."

The cousins nodded at Quint, unsmiling. Despite the sameness of their names, they were clearly not twins—Berk was nearly as scrawny as Darby, though there was a certain wolfishness to his frame that the second mate lacked. Bert, on the other hand, was broad-shouldered and thick in the belly, with a grayish collection of whiskers that was scarcely more deserving of being called a beard than Rustbucket's twisting braid.

"Gentlemen," Quint said, inclining his head slightly before returning his attention to their cousin. "What'd you do to get the Navy on our tail, Rusty?"

"Nothing!" Rustbucket protested, glowering. The others drew in a breath to argue this point but were silenced by Quint's upraised hand.

"Try again, mate," he told Rustbucket. "And keep in mind that I ain't too pleased with you for bringin' your cousins aboard without my leave, on top of luring the Navy *here*."

"Weren't my fault," Rustbucket muttered, his face reddening. "I was just playin' a round o' cards with the lads while we was docked. There was a real pretty moll at the table, and she wouldn't believe me when I told her that I was one o' Captain Redbeard's crew. I told 'er I could prove it, only the Cap'n weren't aboard right now, 'e was paying a visit to—"

"To Ember Bay," Quint finished, his voice tight. "That's what you told her, aye?"

Rustbucket's face turned scarlet as he nodded tersely.

"Only she wasn't a moll," Ophelia said, picking up the tale's threads. "Or if she were, she was in the Navy's employ, 'cause next thing we knew every patrol in the port was lookin' for the *Angel*'s crew. We barely made it out o' the harbor afore one o' the Navy's frigates crested the horn—"

"How far behind?" Quint asked. His anger had given way to sudden, suffocating fear; a vise gripped tight around his heart. "How many days, Ophelia?"

"Two," she said, faltering. "Three, maybe. We managed to blow a hole in that frigate's foremast, so that bought us some time. Besides which, the *Angel*'s fast, and the wind was with us. But Quint, we have to go—"

She was right. Every moment they lingered in Ember Bay was a moment the Navy drew closer. Better for his crew and his town both that they be far over the horizon by then.

These last few weeks had been a respite, one he hadn't realized how badly he'd needed until it had all come crashing down around him. But they were merely a dream, because he wasn't only Quint Thatch, he was Captain Redbeard, the most wanted pirate in the Archipelago—and that was *before* the Fort Amell raid. With the theft of the crown jewels,

Quint wouldn't be surprised if the price on his head had doubled or even tripled.

"We'll go," he said, cutting off Ophelia's repeated urgings to do the same. "Just...there's some things I need to do. Affairs to set in order."

Ophelia looked ready to argue, then decided against it. "How long?"

"Not long," Quint assured her. He'd fulfilled his promise to his pop. The *Wisherman* was fixed, and he'd taken her for one last voyage. Regret tugged at his heart at the prospect of leaving without bidding farewell to Mani, but if that was how it had to be, that was how it had to be.

Quint closed his eyes and took in a deep breath. The last time he'd left Ember Bay, he'd had two parents. He had not known—could not have known—it would be the last time he and Pop laid eyes upon each other.

What had they said at that final parting, the one neither party knew would be their last? Quint would have given every doubloon he'd ever stolen to know, yet whatever words they'd exchanged were lost to the fog of memory. Had he told his pop that he was his hero; that every choice he'd made trying to right the Navy's wrongs was guided by the example his father had set? That he treasured the hours they'd spent aboard the *Wisherman* above all wealth, and that he would trade the Imperial crown jewels for just one more minute of the same?

Had Pop told Quint that he was proud of him? That no matter the choices Quint had made in his life, the man he'd grown into was one Clarent Thatch could speak of with pride in his voice?

They had not, of course, for they had made the mistake of fathers and sons everywhere. They had assumed they would have more time—time in which to tell one another the things they'd left unsaid across a lifetime. As if anyone under the heavens were promised any time beyond the present moment.

It was a mistake Quint would not repeat, not if it meant he would spend the rest of his life rotting in an Imperial cell.

"Not long," he said again, and if his crew noticed his voice quavering, they said nothing of it. "Just let me say goodbye to me—"

"Quentin?"

Dread pricked the back of Quint's back as the last voice he'd wanted to hear at this exact moment drifted down from the open window above. He'd wanted to speak to her alone, not be found skulking in an alleyway with a motley gang of reprobates. Yet fate, it seemed, had other plans in store for the family Thatch.

This must be how a fish feels when it's caught on the line, he thought, feeling his gaze drawn irresistibly upward.

"Aye?" he asked, staring up into his ma's quizzical face as her eyes roved over the odd assortment of folk gathered beneath her window: tattooed Ophelia, hulking Fillbrick, gorgeous Bonnie Kate, reedy Darby, shifty Rustbucket and his shiftier cousins. "I mean, yes?"

"Who're all these, then?" she asked, learning further out the window for a better look. "Friends o' yours?"

Quint desperately wracked his brain for any kind of lie, however implausible, that might prop up the crumbling wall between the two halves of his life.

Instead, it was shattered by Fillbrick, who called up in his deep basso voice: "Are you Lola Thatch, then?"

Ma's brows scrunched together. "I am, though I'm afraid you've got me at a disadva—"

The rest of the word was drowned out by a deafening chorus of delighted pirates shouting out as one:

"*MA!!!*"

21

This is a dream, Quint told himself as the crew emerged from the alleyway like a group of malcontent teens who'd just been caught loitering. *A terrible, surreal dream I'll be waking up from in three, two, one...*

He squeezed his eyes shut, opened them. Instead of the ceiling of his cabin aboard the *Bloody Angel*, he saw Ma Thatch standing there beneath the Queen's Arms signboard, hands on her hips as she beamed at the scraggly gang of pirates.

"So this is the crew of the *Waterhouse*, then?" she asked, eyes roving over them. Quint couldn't help but notice how her gaze lingered on Ophelia's copious tattoos. "Not...exactly how I'd pictured you'd look."

Quint opened his mouth to reply but found there was nothing he could say. His crew looked unmistakably, undeniably piratical. Quint suspected that between the seven of them—eight, counting himself—they boasted more piercings and tattoos than the rest of Ember Bay's population combined. At least Ophelia had possessed the foresight not to bring any visible weapons ashore. The sight of openly worn pistols or cutlasses in the sleepy town would have raised both alarm and questions. Though knowing Ophelia, there was probably an entire arsenal of small knives hidden somewhere on her person.

"Sailors are sailors," Ophelia said, stepping into the conversational void left by Quint's disorientation, "no matter the flag they fly under.

'Fraid a merchantman's crew ain't a great deal more presentable than a roving band of cutthroats, at least to look at."

"I suppose that's true," Ma said, pursing her lips. "Are you Quentin's—"

"Captain," Quint cut in, recovering the power of speech. "This is my *captain*, Ma."

"Cap'n Ophelia Price," she supplied, doffing an imaginary hat and sketching a courteous half-bow in Ma's direction. "Apologies for our unannounced arrival, Missus Thatch. Me an' my crew place ourselves entirely at your service."

To Quint's chagrin, Ma's pursed lips curled into an approving smile. "You've nothing to apologize for, dear. I just...hadn't expected you."

"That makes two of us," Quint muttered, but Ma either didn't hear him or chose to pretend not to.

"Well, don't just stand there in the dark," she said, reaching behind her to open wide the front doors of the Queen's Arms. "Come on in! Drinks and dinner on the house, lads and lasses."

If there was a single trait universal to all pirates, it was the inability to refuse the offer of free booze. Any remaining hope Quint had of maintaining the divide between the two halves of his life was dashed to pieces as his crewmates jostled past him, crowding through the doors of his childhood home and into the life he'd been rediscovering there.

Half an hour later they were seated around one of the tavern's largest tables, each with a steaming scarlet lobster plated in front of them and a generous mug of frothing ale beside it, along with a serving of steamed corn. Fillbrick, Darby, and Bonnie Kate had all dug into the meal with gusto, while Rustbucket and his cousins were already on their third round of drink. Specks of shell flew everywhere as they cracked their lobsters' claws and tails to get at the succulent flesh within, liberally seasoning it with squeezes from lemon wedges or the enormous crock of melted butter at the table's center.

Quint, however, had no appetite. Once again, he tried to convince himself that this was a dream, but the sharp pinprick of pain that shot through his finger when he pricked himself with a lobster fork under the table dissuaded him of the notion.

If there was any consolation to be found, it was that the Arms was nearly empty. Besides his crew and Ma, there were only three other patrons. Hawkins sat in his usual booth, nursing what for all Quint knew might have been the same mug he always had. Chuck and Lex leaned over the bar, one or the other of them occasionally glancing around at the tavern's interior, as if struggling to believe they were really inside the Arms again after their yearslong probation. Quint surmised they'd spent the entire day here, afraid that Ma Thatch would rescind the amnesty her son had granted them the moment they departed the tavern.

Catching him looking, Lex lifted her mug in salute, while beside her Chuck's eyes roamed over the pirates, taking their measure. Yet despite their evident interest, neither approached his table—something Quint attributed to lingering fear of Ma rather than any social anxiety over meeting his crew.

A crew they'd soon be joining, he remembered, feeling again an echo of that odd vertigo that came of his lives colliding. He'd promised them, after all, and they'd upheld their end of the bargain with surprising dependability. Besides, it couldn't be too hard to teach them how to swim...

"Quentin?"

Quint started guiltily and turned, realizing his mother had been addressing him. "Sorry?"

"I was saying to your captain," Ma began, turning to Ophelia. "Now, Cap'n Price—"

Ophelia waved her off.

"Please, Missus Thatch," she said, giving Ma a wink. "I'm only Cap'n to these jackanapeses. You can call me Ophelia."

"Only if you'll call me Ma," she replied. "I won't have any friend of Quentin's calling me anything else."

Across the table, Rustbucket caught Quint's eye and mouthed *Quentin?* Quint shrugged.

"Aye," Ophelia said, grinning and raising her mug in salute. "What's it you wanted to ask, now?"

"Ophelia," Ma said, trying the name out. She shot a sidelong glance at Quint. "Are you spoken for?"

Quint groaned. Ophelia's grin widened. "Can't say as I am, Miss—Ma."

"I see," Ma replied, trying to catch Quint's gaze as he determinedly looked anywhere but at his mother. "In that case, are you and my son—"

"*Ma,*" Quint groaned, sounding less like the fearsome pirate captain he was and more like the gawky teenager he'd been, once upon a time. "She's my f—"

Ophelia nudged him hard in the ribs, still grinning at Ma. Quint gasped, then course corrected. "Ophelia's my commanding officer—"

"I'll bet she is," Hawkins muttered, clearly audible from across the room.

Not for the first time, Quint mourned the loss of his beard, which would have covered a decent proportion of the flush creeping up his neck and cheeks.

Ma pursed her lips, one eyebrow raised. "You were going to say something else, dear. That Ophelia's your f—"

"Friend," Ophelia cut in, taking pity on him at last. "I'm his captain, aye, but we're also friends. That's what your son was trying to say, Ma."

"Hmm." Ma tapped a finger against her chin, redirecting her attention back to her furiously blushing son. "You know, your father and I were friends, before…"

"This must be hell," Quint muttered into his beer. "I'm dead, and this is some previously undiscovered tenth hell where your mother tries to set you up with your shipmates—"

"Don't knock it 'til you try it," Darby observed, raising his glass to toast his absent better half.

"You should be so lucky," Ophelia said, her grin wide enough to rival Lurk's. She threw an arm around Quint's shoulders and gave him a companionable kiss on the cheek before turning her attention back to Ma. "Alas, Ma Thatch, I'm afraid that I prefer my bedfellows to be of the feminine persuasion."

"That's something you and Quint have in common, then," Ma said, undeterred. She looked slowly around the table at Fillbrick, Darby, Rustbucket, and the cousins, and added, "Unless that's changed…?"

Darby snorted and shook his head. "Nahhh, not our Quint."

"'Fraid it'll never work, Ma," Ophelia said, patting Quint's shoulder. "With me or any o' the lads, alas. Hope that doesn't dampen this festive mood. I must say, I ain't had an ale this fine in more years than I care to count."

"If you're trying to flatter me, it's working," Ma said with a wink before turning her attention to Bonnie Kate, who was busily trying to fit nearly an entire lobster tail into her mouth. "What about you, then?"

"Mmm?" Kate mumbled through the lobster.

"Yes, dear, you," Ma said encouragingly, throwing a significant glance at Quint. "Are *you* spoken for? Or do you only fancy lasses as well?"

Kate chewed her lobster slowly, which Quint assumed was as much to buy herself time as because of the enormous mouthful.

"Don't fancy anybody," Kate said at last, once she'd swallowed. "All it takes to make me happy is a full purse and an inventory list."

If Ma Thatch was disappointed, she didn't show it.

"I do love a good shopping trip, myself," she nodded, raising her mug, only to find it empty. "'Scuse me, but all this talk has given me a powerful thirst. Who's up for another round?"

An affirmative chorus answered her. Lola Thatch stood from the table, collecting empty mugs from the others out of habit before she retreated to the bar. Quint watched her go, vaguely noticing how Lex and Chuck shrank away from her as she passed them by.

"Right," he said once she'd begun pouring rounds from the tap. He leaned in, beckoning the rest of them to do likewise, and spoke in a lowered voice. "So, here's what we're going to do. We'll have another round, then dessert if Ma's made some—"

"Dessert?" Fillbrick, who'd been busily devouring his lobster, looked up hopefully.

"Aye, dessert," Quint said, waving an impatient hand. "After which we're going to spend the night here at the Arms—"

"Hold up," Ophelia said, frowning. "Did you forget the whole 'Navy frigate only a few days behind us' bit?"

"Like you said," Quint shook his head, "we've got a three-day lead. We can spare one night."

"He's right," Rustbucket said, speaking up for the first time since they'd set foot in the Arms. "We can't just run out tonight, not unless we feel like leaving the crown jewels for the Navy to stumble over."

"Keep your voice down," Quint said, glancing around to make sure they hadn't been overheard. At the bar Ma was arguing with Lex and Chuck over their tab. "The treasure's safe as can be. I hid it someplace the Navy won't ever find it. Also, I hired us a few more pairs of hands."

Rustbucket followed his gaze, frowning. "Not those two yahoos at the bar?"

"There's also a mermaid," Quint said, thinking back on his promise to Lurk that she was now a part of his crew.

Rustbucket blanched. "A *mermaid*?"

"You're one to talk, Rusty," Ophelia said, giving his cousins a significant look. "Hiring new recruits is the captain's prerogative, remember?"

Rustbucket jutted his chin at her, which would have been more defiant if it hadn't set his knotted little beard to swaying like a dropped rope. "It was that or leave me kin high and dry for the Navy—"

"We can argue about this later," Quint said. "Captain's also got prerogative to issue orders, so here're mine: we stay the night here. At first light we say our goodbyes, then take the *Angel* around to the cove south of here. Treasure's buried not too far from there. After that, we head out towards open water, and by this time tomorrow we'll be on the high seas—"

"Tomorrow?"

Quint nearly jumped out of his seat at his ma's return, a tray full of frothing mugs balanced expertly on her upraised hand. She frowned down at her son, and Quint frantically wondered how much she'd overheard.

"You can't be leaving just yet," Ma said, lowering the tray to the tabletop. To Quint's muted relief, she glanced at Ophelia rather than him. "My Quentin told me just the other night that he'd be in the Bay at least another week before heading off to meet you back in Sapphire."

"I wish it were so," Ophelia said, glancing at Quint. He was surprised (and a little touched) to see genuine regret in her eyes. "But we've had an emergency come up, and we need all hands on deck. Er, so to speak."

Ma's gaze flickered between them, as though trying to discern what they weren't saying. "An emergency."

"Afraid so." Quint nodded, his mouth going dry. Sticking to a preestablished cover identity was one thing; improvising a lie to his mother was something else entirely.

Ma Thatch quirked an eyebrow. "An emergency that necessitated you sailing all the way out here just to retrieve your ship's clerk?"

Quint looked to Ophelia, who was regrettably not much better at thinking on her feet than he was.

"It's a clerking emergency," she said.

Ma Thatch looked between them, her eyes appraising. Quint steeled himself for the inevitable questions to follow, knowing that the house of cards would come tumbling down the moment she pressed them for further details. That all the lies would be uncovered, and he'd have to confess to her how he'd really spent most of the last two decades.

"Well," Ma said, settling into her seat beside Ophelia, "I suppose when duty calls, one must answer, whether it's convenient or not."

She began sliding mugs of ale across the table, with perhaps more force than was strictly necessary. Quite a bit of ale sloshed onto Fill-brick's front. Quint nearly missed his mug as it came sliding toward him, and only Ophelia's sharp reflexes saved him from having his lap soaked. Ma was accepting their story at face value, as improbable and flimsy as it was. Maybe his life was not about to fall apart after all.

Yet like any son who gets away with lying to his mother, Quint felt at once relieved and wretched.

"I'll try and get back as soon as I'm able," he heard himself promise. But that was a problem for Future Quint. "Spend more time in the Arms, next time around. It...I was away too long since last visit."

There was so much unsaid in that fragmentary sentence, yet it seemed to mollify Ma somewhat. She nodded, reaching across Ophelia to pat her son's hand. "You've always got a place here, Quentin. Don't you forget that."

She raised her head, looking around at the rest of the table as they silently watched this exchange. Quint wondered if any of them had dared breathe since Ma had interrupted their scheming.

"That goes for all of you," Ma Thatch said, her broad smile returning. "Spend the night in a proper bed tonight; the Arms has plenty of open rooms. We usually get a strong southwester blowing through around sundown, as you may have noticed. If you head out that time tomorrow you'll have a swifter time getting across the Reach than if you set sail in the morning."

The crew's heads turned as one toward Quint. Time was of the essence, as Ophelia had reminded him, but Ma's assessment of the weather patterns around Ember Bay was accurate. They could afford to wait one more day. One more day to say goodbye: to Mani, to Hari and Amara, to Uncle Jun and Tai and Ling. To the *Wisherman*, to Ma. To Pop.

One more day.

Or so Quint hoped.

"Sure," he said, raising his mug in salute. "We set sail tomorrow at dusk. Until then, let's enjoy ourselves, eh?"

The others raised their own mugs in toast, though no one spoke. Quint tossed back his own, hoping that the choice he'd just made would not be one he'd later have cause to regret. After all, it was only one more day; plenty of time before the Navy caught up to them.

Where was the harm in that?

22

"Right," Quint said, first thing the next morning once they'd reconvened around the same table. "Everyone sleep well?"

"Like a log," Fillbrick confirmed. Beside him Kate and Darby nodded their agreement.

"Took me a bit to drift off," Ophelia admitted, stretching like a cat waking from a nap. "Felt strange not to have the deck rolling 'neath me. But I didn't wake once, neither, after I'd drifted off."

"Lucky you," Rustbucket muttered. As they had last night, he and his cousins sat in a cluster on one side of the table. All three had dark circles beneath their eyes. "Ain't nobody else get woken up at the stroke of two by a rooster screaming his bloody head off?"

"Ah," Quint said, nodding sagely toward the front door. "That'd be Remy."

"Remy the rooster?" Ophelia snorted, brushing hair from her eyes. "I thought they're supposed to cry at dawn."

"Remy's got a loose grip on the concept of time," Quint said. "You get used to 'im."

"Hope we're not stuck here long enough that we have to," Rustbucket muttered, glaring down at the empty table. "What's a fella gotta do to get served around here, anyway?"

"Ask nicely," Ma Thatch said, emerging from behind the bar with a tray piled with breakfast foods: sliced mangoes, fresh-baked toast with orange marmalade, heaps of scrambled eggs, and still-sizzling rashers of bacon accompanied by steaming mugs of hot coffee. Quint's crew murmured in delight as she passed the plates around the table, pointedly serving Rustbucket and his cousins only once the others had already begun to dig in.

"So, Cap'n," Ma said, settling into the open seat beside Ophelia. "What's the plan for today?"

The question fell on deaf ears. Ophelia had begun shoveling eggs into her mouth the moment her plate had hit the table, her eyes closed in silent bliss as she chewed.

"*Cap'n,*" Quint said loudly, nudging her in the ribs. Ophelia's eyes flew open, head snapping toward Quint. "Ma wants to know our plan for the day."

Ophelia's eyes widened, first in understanding, then in panic. She turned back to Ma, still chewing furiously, and gesticulated toward Quint.

"Er..." Quint found himself suddenly wishing he had the excuse of a mouthful of breakfast to buy himself time. "I'll tell you, then?"

Ophelia nodded fervently.

"Right," Quint said, wondering if his crew would be able to keep up the ruse of being merchant sailors for the entire day they were due to stay in town. "First thing, we've got to procure some timbers in case we need to do more repairs afore our next landfall."

"Jacques's Lumberyard's got plenty stored up," Ma interjected. "Last typhoon season didn't do near as much damage to the town as we'd anticipated, so they've got plenty of extra stock on hand."

"Good," Quint said, glancing around at his assembled mates. "Darby, you take Rustbucket and the cousins to the lumberyard, pick up some timbers and take 'em to the *An*—"

This time it was Ophelia's turn to elbow Quint's ribs.

"—to the *end* of the pier," Quint rephrased, wincing. Fortunately, Ma had been busy refilling her coffee from the silver carafe in the middle of the table and didn't seem to have noticed. "Load the cargo onto the dinghy and take it back to the, er, ship."

"That'll take a few trips," Darby said, frowning a little.

"Yeah!" Rustbucket nodded his agreement. "You can't expect us to carry all that between the four of us?"

"Nah," Quint said, glancing across the room. "You'll have help."

Chuck and Lex were both collapsed against the bar, gently snoring, pillows beneath their heads.

"Been here since yesterday lunch," Ma said with a shrug. "Seemed scared I'd kick 'em out again if they left."

"Thoughtful of you to give them pillows," Kate observed, crunching noisily on her toast.

"Ain't a soul stayed at the Queen's Arms yet who's had cause to complain about the bedding," Ma said.

"What about the rooster?" Rustbucket said. Quint shot him a warning glance.

"Remy's not sleeping in your bed, is he?" Ma pointed out, rising from her place at the table with mug in hand. "Though speaking of fowl, I've got to stop by the coop out back for more eggs. If there are any, who wants a second help—"

The chorus of "aye!" drowned out the last word. Ma grinned and strode across the room, stepping gingerly around Chuck and Lex before disappearing through the kitchen doors.

"Right," Quint said, leaning toward his crew, elbows pressed against the table. The others mirrored him, forming a conspiratorial huddle. "Like I was saying. Take those two—"

He jerked a thumb over his shoulder, indicating Chuck's and Lex's snoring forms. "—and let 'em help you load up the ship with spare timbers. After that, take the crew that're ashore and sail around the island. You lot got in late enough last night that no one's looked too closely at the name on that prow, but all it'll take is some fisherman getting curious to see that it's the *Bloody Angel* out there and not the *Waterhouse*."

"Where to, then?" Fillbrick asked.

"There's a cove well to the south," Quint said, "bordered by a pair of stone jetties, one o' which has a dock. Keep sailing until you're well past it, then lay anchor somewhere offshore. That should be far enough that no one from town's gonna happen across you. Then, wait until the rest of us get to the ship before setting sail."

"Hold yer own sails, Cap'n." Rustbucket scowled, glancing over at the pair of toughs slouched over the bar. "What about the treasure? We can't be leavin' without the crown j—"

Fillbrick reached across the table and clamped a huge hand across Rustbucket's mouth. His cousins scooted hastily away; Fillbrick weighed as much as the three of them combined.

"Leave *that* to me," Quint said, eyes scanning the Arms. Fortunately, Ma's departure had left them alone, save for the sleeping pair at the bar and old Hawkins stationed at his usual booth, glowering into his mug without giving any indication that he'd overheard. "And don't you mention it again while you're on this island, hear me?"

Rustbucket glowered at him over Fillbrick's hand, but he nodded.

"That goes for everyone," Quint said, still scanning the Arms in case any townsfolk were seized with a sudden craving for Ma Thatch's breakfast service. "Until the wind's in our sails and that volcano's sunk below the horizon, you an' me an' everyone aboard the *Angel* are respectable, upstanding Imperial citizens, crew o' the fine merchantman *Waterhouse.* Hear me?"

"Aye," the others murmured in chorus. The mood was subdued as they dug into their breakfast, though it promised to pick up again once Ma Thatch returned with a second helping of eggs.

In the time it took for Ma Thatch to check the chicken coop and return, Quint had outlined the plan for the day. In addition to the timbers from Jacques's Lumberyard, the *Bloody Angel* would also need fresh supplies for the voyage across the Reach. Bonnie Kate was quick to explain that they'd not yet replenished all the stores that had been washed overboard before the Navy had set off after them, and that unless Quint wanted his crew sailing on half rations, they'd better restock.

"You'll want Rosa's Mercantile for general supplies," Quint told her. "And Avon's Grocery for foodstuffs and perishables. Don't take Rosa's prices at face value; the woman loves to haggle and has everything listed for twice what it's worth."

"And the grocer?" Kate asked, furiously jotting notes in her ledger as she bit into her third slice of toast.

"Avon's prices are fair," Quint said, "but you'll have to remind him to give us the wholesale rate, since we're buying bulk. Now—"

"I suppose you'll want us hauling that stuff to the dock as well?" Rustbucket objected, glancing at the bar. "Us and those two—"

"Stow whatever you're about to say," Quint said mildly. "It's been relayed to me that if you'd been able to keep a hold of your big gob, Rusty, we wouldn't be in this particular predicament. Seems to me that the least you can do in repentance is move some cargo."

That shut him up, though the admonishment evidently did not extend to his cousins.

"What about you?" the scrawnier, more wolfish-looking of the two asked. Berk, Quint was fairly certain. "What'll the captain be getting up to while the rest of his crew slaves away?"

"The *captain*," Ophelia cut in, jabbing a thumb at her own sternum, "will be here, assisting our inimical hostess in washing up from the fine repast she's prepared us."

"Inimitable, you mean," Quint said, glancing toward the kitchen doors as Ma Thatch emerged with a single massive plate of freshly scrambled eggs. "Look unthreatening, mates o' the good ship *Waterhouse*."

"Here we are!" Ma said brightly, clearing a space in the table's center to set down the eggs. "Now, I know we said last night that you were going to get underway this evening, but I got to thinking…"

Quint paused, a forkful of eggs halfway to his mouth.

"Seeing as it's been so long," Ma continued, "and that you've been so busy working on the *Wisherman*—"

"My pop's boat," Quint explained to the crew.

"—I was thinking," Ma said as if he hadn't interrupted, "the least we could do is throw you a farewell party. Send you and your crew off in proper fashion."

Everyone seated at the table perked up at this, their gazes darting between Quint and his ma, returning hastily to Ophelia as they recalled who the captain of the alleged *Waterhouse* was supposed to be.

"We're on a tight timetable, Ma Thatch," Ophelia said, but her eyes were fixed on Quint, not wanting to answer for him.

"I know you are," Ma acknowledged. "But seeing as you're not leaving until sundown, my thought was we could have a great big fish fry this afternoon."

"Fish fry?" Fillbrick's bushy brows rose. Beside him, Kate licked her lips.

"Aye," Ma nodded, grinning. "With all the traditional dishes. Sweet potato, poi, fresh fish and fresher fruit…"

One look around the table was enough to show that the *Bloody Angel*'s crew was practically salivating. Ophelia glanced at Quint, who gave her the slightest nod.

"I don't see why not," Ophelia said, shrugging before turning her attention back to Ma. "Of course we'd love to stay for Quint's farewell. Do you need another hand in the kitchen?"

"Always," Ma said, her smile widening. Quint stared at his first mate in muted shock. The few times Ophelia had attempted to fix a meal in the *Angel*'s galley had been uniformly disastrous. Quint prayed to his own angel that Ma's expertise would mitigate Ophelia's lack thereof, or they'd have to find dinner elsewhere.

"Since when did you volunteer for galley duty?" he hissed at Ophelia as Ma busied herself refilling Bonnie Kate's cup. "You *hate* cooking."

"Who said anything about cooking?" Ophelia said, and winked. "I'm hoping for a peek at Amara."

"She's happily married," Quint pointed out. "And very pregnant."

"A challenge, then." Ophelia grinned. But before Quint could argue her out of seducing his childhood friend, Ma Thatch clapped her hands together, recalling their attention.

"It's decided, then!" Ma said, beaming at them all. "One big shindig of a sendoff, in this very spot. That's as long as I'll keep you. By nightfall you'll be sailing eastward, and we'll be over the horizon. Give you my word as Quentin's ma. And in the meantime, all the victuals you could want!"

The crew broke into a chorus of whoops and hollers, too excited over the prospect of a meal which promised to be even grander than the one they were enjoying now. With the smell of fresh coffee in their noses and bellies full of eggs, bacon, and toast, none of them could find it in themselves to worry much over the specter of the pursuant Navy vessel, which in the bright light of morning felt less like a looming threat and more like some nighttime phantom banished with the coming of dawn.

Only a few more hours, Quint told himself again, and hoped they could keep the *Waterhouse* ruse going for that long.

23

I t proved to be more of a challenge than he'd expected.

The crimes of the *Bloody Angel*'s crew were many and varied, ranging from the typical (piracy, public drunkenness, shipjacking) to the slightly more unusual (arson, conspiracy, possession of stolen goods) to the completely unexpected (smuggling of exotic animals, impersonation of a cleric, tax evasion). Surely, Quint assumed, with such an impressive list of felonies under their collective belts, they'd be capable of sticking to a simple cover story.

Yet he'd overlooked one simple detail: for all their roguish exploits, none of those who'd come ashore were any good at lying.

The problem first reared its head not long after breakfast. Quint and Ophelia were helping Ma tidy up from the night before, clearing away dishes and wiping down tables with wet rags, while Ma regaled Ophelia with a series of increasingly embarrassing anecdotes from Quint's childhood.

"...and then Quentin," Ma was saying as she bussed plates off a table and into a wooden basin, "who couldn't have been older than three or four, insists that he can go all the way down to Cinder Cove himself because 'I know the way, Ma...'"

Ophelia laughed and tossed a look over her shoulder at Quint, who was busily scrubbing down the bar with a bucket of soapy water and a thick-bristled brush. "Precocious little lad, weren't you, Quint?"

"Aye, he *was*," Ma said, her back turned so that she could not catch the exasperated look Quint shot his first mate. "Especially once he started fixating on joining the Navy. You should've seen this skinny little redheaded child, striding around shouting at folks to hoist the sails and swab the decks, demanding everyone address him by rank—"

The doors to the Arms were thrown open as Bonnie Kate came bustling in, hands balled in her long skirts. "Cap'n!"

"Aye?" Quint answered in chorus with Ophelia, momentarily forgetting himself. Catching his mother's questioning gaze, he hastily amended: "Aye, Kate, the cap'n's here."

"Oh." Kate's head swiveled between them, clearly uncertain how to proceed. Quint jerked his head, motioning her over.

"Right," Kate said, clearing her head. "Actually, Cap'n, I was coming to find C—I mean, to find Quint. Need the clerk's help on some, er, clerking business."

"Of course, dear," Ma Thatch said, hefting the basin full of soiled dishes onto her hip and looking appraisingly around the tavern. "I think the place looks presentable enough for now. Ophelia, love, will you help me rinse off all these platters...?"

They bustled past Quint and into the kitchen to the accompaniment of clattering dishware, leaving him alone with Kate. He wiped his hands on the front of the apron he'd donned for the task. "Well?"

Kate took a deep breath. "What kind of shipping is it we do, Quint? The *Waterhouse*, I mean."

"I..." Quint stopped himself, realizing he had no satisfactory answer at hand. "Who wants to know?"

"Miss Rosa," Kate said, her dark locs swinging as she glanced over her shoulder, as if afraid the elderly shopkeeper had pursued her up the high street into the tavern. "We got to talking down at her store, and I asked how she was able to maintain such a varied inventory when Ember Bay's so far off any o' the major trade routes..."

"And naturally she wanted to know what manner o' cargo the *Waterhouse* ships," Quint realized, inwardly cursing himself. Why hadn't he thought of that before sending Kate to haggle with Miss Rosa?

The answer, of course, was that Quint Thatch, ship's clerk, was a passable cover identity for him alone. But by involving the rest of his crew in the deception, the ruse had by necessity grown more complex. Kate could not simply deflect a direct question that she, as quartermaster, should have been able to answer sufficiently.

"Sugar," he said, seizing at last on a trade good the *Angel* would have a reasonable supply of aboard. "Sapphiric sugar, shipped between the Jewel Isles and the rest of the Archipelago."

One of Kate's dark eyebrows rose toward her headscarf. "Permission to offer up a few sacks from the *Angel*'s galley in the negotiations?"

"Granted." Quint nodded. If the crew had to drink their tea and coffee unsweetened for a few weeks, it would be the least of their worries. "Now get back there and remember: we trade in sugar. Aye?"

"Aye, Ca—" Kate's hand was halfway to a salute when Ma Thatch came bustling out of the kitchen, humming to herself. Kate hastily turned the salute into an awkward pat on Quint's arm. "—I mean, aye, Quint. Sugar."

She turned and hurried from the tavern without another word.

"You sure she's not sweet on you?" Ma asked, frowning. "I thought I just heard her call you sugar..."

⚓

Ma Thatch left not long after Bonnie Kate's departure, heading to Avon's Grocery to purchase food for the fish fry. On the way out she passed Amara, who'd come to aid in the morning's chores at the Arms.

Amara's arrival was not a source of relief for the beleaguered Quint. To his lasting chagrin, she and Ophelia struck up an immediate friendship as the three of them washed dishes together, instantly finding common ground in stories of Quint's less-admirable moments.

"...in front of the whole island?" Ophelia asked, her shoulders shaking with suppressed mirth. "A *serenade*?"

"I know!" Amara giggled, cupping one hand over her mouth. "I don't know what he was thinking."

"No guts, no glory," Quint muttered, his face as red as the lobster shell he plucked from the plate he was washing and tossed over his shoulder. "Or something along those lines."

Chum twined about his feet, sniffing intently at the dropped bit of shell.

"Aye, that's my Quint," Ophelia said, reaching over and ruffling his hair with a soapy hand. "Wouldn't be the first time he leaped without looking, would it, mate?"

"I don't know what you mean," Quint lied, staunchly ignoring Amara's look of intense interest.

"Sure you do," Ophelia said, her grin widening. "Or are you forgetting that time we got into an argument with ol' Margherita an' her crew—"

The plate slipped from Quint's grip, clattering noisily into the sink. At his feet Chum yowled and sprinted away for safer quarters. But Amara was less easily deterred.

"*Captain* Margherita?" she asked, eyes going wide. "The pirate queen?"

"I wouldn't call her *queen*, exactly—" Ophelia started, oblivious. Quint whipped a sodden dishrag at her, causing to turn around. "Wha—"

"We didn't *know* she was a pirate at the time," Quint told Amara, hoping that Ophelia would get the hint. "Else I never would've challenged her to an arm-wrestling contest."

Amara barked out a short, surprised laugh. "Did you win?"

"Of course not." Ophelia snorted. "And a good thing, too, otherwise Margherita might've started cutting pieces off 'im."

"Your confidence in me is inspiring," Quint muttered, though inwardly he was relieved that the conversation seemed to have returned to safer waters.

"Tell me, Amara," Ophelia said, throwing an arm over the other woman's shoulders and leaning in with a faux-conspiratorial whisper. "Has our dear Quentin always had noodles for arms, or is it the clerking life that's made him such a wimp?"

She lifted her other arm and flexed, displaying a prominent bicep that was half-covered by the inked tentacles of an octopus tattoo.

"Nah," Amara said, grinning wolfishly at Quint. "He's always been this way. Let me tell you about the time young *Quentin* locked himself in the outhouse for two days..."

Sighing, Quint turned his attention back to the stack of dishes waiting beside the sink. It was going to be a very long wait between now and the fish fry.

⚓

Once the tavern had been cleared out and the dishes cleaned, they broke for an early lunch, after which Amara took her leave, so that she could join Hari and her boys for the lunch her husband had prepared.

"I like her," Ophelia said as the tavern door swung shut in the wake of her departure. "Shame you let her get away, eh?"

"Nah," Quint said, wiping his hand on a napkin. "It wouldn't have worked out. 'Sides, she's got a lovely family. Cute kids."

"And you got me," Ophelia said, throwing her arms around his neck and pulling him in for a sloppy kiss on the cheek.

"Angels above," Quint groaned, disentangling himself from his best friend's embrace. "Do that again and my ma's gonna sneak a wedding ceremony into the fish fry."

The tavern door swung open again. Fillbrick and Darby trooped inside, followed by Rustbucket and his cousins, with Chuck and Lex taking up the rear. The latter two kept casting nervous glances about the Arms, as if they expected Ma Thatch to appear at any moment to expel them, rolling pin in hand. All seven of them were flushed and sweaty after a morning spent hauling goods from shore to ship.

"Let me fill your glasses, mates," Quint said, rising from the table to duck behind the bar. To his surprise, Fillbrick followed, the burly boatswain leaning against the bar as Quint poured.

"Everything alright?" Quint asked, him, glancing over to Rustbucket and the cousins, who sat on the opposite side of the table from Lex and Chuck. "That lot give you any trouble?"

Fillbrick grunted. "Rusty and the other two moaned at first, so I gave 'em the heavier loads until they shut their mouths. Chuck and Lex worked hard."

"Glad to hear it," Quint said, handing Fillbrick a frothing glass of pale ale. "You look a bit put out, though."

"Darby talks too much," Fillbrick said, grimacing. "Usually to Vigo, but when Vigo's not around..."

"He'll bend the ear of whoever's closest," Quint said, looking over Fillbrick's shoulder toward Hawkins, sitting alone in his solitary booth. "Tell you what, mate. You head on over to that seat there. Old Hawkins don't mind the occasional drinking companion, and he'll talk as little as you'd like. Sound good?"

Fillbrick considered for a moment, then gave a ponderous nod. "Thanks, Quint."

He turned and trundled across the tavern to Hawkins's booth. The old man gave him a grunt of acknowledgment and a nod as Fillbrick slid his bulk into the seat opposite him. They began to drink in silence.

Quint returned to the main table with a drink-laden tray, passing them out to his crewmates. With Hawkins being the only non-pirate in the tavern, they could talk freely so long as they kept their voices down.

"Right," Quint said, settling back into his seat between Ophelia and Chuck. "How'd we do out there, mates? Everything go smoothly?"

"Aye," the others chorused, with varying degrees of enthusiasm. Though they were as grimy and smelly as anyone else, Lex and Chuck practically shone with eagerness.

"We hauled quite a fair bit o' timber, Cap'n!" Chuck grinned, saluting with the wrong hand.

"Fantastic," Quint said, taking Chuck's wrist and gently putting his hand back by his side. "But remember, I'm just Quint until we're on the open sea, aye?"

"Aye, Just Quint," Lex said, and Quint honestly could not tell whether or not she was poking fun at him.

"Speaking of," Quint continued, taking a sip of his beer, "Darby. Any slipups I might need to know about?"

"None worth reporting on," Darby said, peering through his spectacles at Quint and Chuck. "Everyone we met seemed rather surprised that these two have signed on with your crew. Er, Ophelia's crew, that is."

"It's 'coz they don't know we're pirates," Lex said, leaning in conspiratorially. "I told everyone we ran into that we convinced you to let us sign on with the ship *Housewater.*"

"*Waterhouse,*" Quint corrected, but this slipup bothered him little, as the good folk of Ember Bay were too used to Lex and Chuck to pay anything they said much mind. "You two staying around for the party, then?"

"Party?" Chuck asked, exchanging glances with his partner in petty crime. "There's a party?"

"There's gonna be a fish fry for my farewell," Quint said, recalling how the two of them had been draped over the bar during breakfast. "And your farewell too, I suppose—"

"No," Lex said, standing so abruptly that her chair nearly toppled to the floor. "Nope, absolutely not. Last thing I want is everyone blubberin' and wailin' over how much they're going to miss us while we're off having adventures. I'm ready to board that vessel as soon as you'll permit, Ca—"

"Quint," Quint and Chuck corrected at the same time.

"Ain't no one saying their farewells yet," Chuck said, tugging at his cousin's sleeve. "Finish your beer."

Lex reluctantly allowed herself to be seated. Chuck leaned over and said to Quint in a conspiratorial tone that was nonetheless the same volume as his usual speaking voice: "She don't like goodbyes, Lex. Gets all weepy."

"Do not," Lex sniffed, but sipped her beer as Chuck advised.

"All right then," Quint said slowly, digesting this. "How about you two board the *Waterhouse* once we're done here, then? Vigo'd certainly be glad to have an extra pair of hands aboard to sail her 'round the isle."

"I outrank Vigo," Darby said, wiping his wrist across his upper lip. "And he's still a little sensitive about the whole 'supplies overboard' thing, Ca—er, Quint. Better that I take command, eh?"

"Suppose so." Quint nodded. "Right. Darby, once we're finished up here, you take these two back to the ship, then set off for the southern end of the island."

"What about the—" Rustbucket shut his mouth, glancing furtively about the Arms before leaning toward Quint. "You *know*. The K-R-O—"

"Starts with a C," Quint corrected. "And don't you worry. Those are a brisk hike inland from that cove I mentioned. Actually..." He returned his attention to Darby. "Tell Vigo I'm not upset with him about the supplies; these things happen. But if it'll help ease his conscience an' restore his confidence, I've got a task he can do."

Darby's expression brightened. "Name it."

"The sailboat I was on last night," Quint said. "The *Wisherman*. Used to be my pop's."

The others exchanged uneasy glances, still uncertain how to cope with a grieving captain. Quint ignored them and pressed on: "Tell Vigo to sail it to that cove I mentioned; there's a dock you can tie it to. There'll be a mermaid there, name o' Lurk."

"You mentioned a mermaid before," Darby said warily. Mermaids' propensity for drowning was known across the species.

"Aye," Quint said. "Have Vigo tell her he's part o' my crew, and that she's not to drown him. Oh, and give her this."

He reached across the table and plucked one of the mangoes sitting in a bowl at its center. "After Vigo's dropped off the boat, pick him up in the dinghy, and tell Lurk to follow along beside. Take the *Wisherman* to the far south end of the island, where there's inlets and islets you can hide out in, then the rest of us will be along before the night grows cold."

"Don't you worry, Quint," Darby said, raising his glass in salute. "Vigo will see it done."

"I've no doubt about it," Quint said, returning the salute. "As for the rest of you..."

He looked around at their shining faces, eagerly awaiting their captain's next words. Quint raised his glass, grinning.

"Who's ready for a fish fry?"

24

Quint had expected his farewell celebration to be a modest affair. It was the middle of the day, after all, and the stores and businesses of Ember Bay were not due to close until near sundown. He had assumed that the fish fry's attendees would be mostly those who'd managed to sneak away from the day's business, and in that he was not disappointed.

What he had not expected was that seemingly almost *everyone* on Ember Bay had put away their work to attend the festivities. By the time Uncle Jun had fired up the old fryer behind the Arms, better than a hundred people had already crowded into the tavern, with more mingling around out front or in the back. Amara and Ma weaved deftly through the little knots of gathered townsfolk, passing out beverages and small bowls of poi as appetizers before the main feast began.

"Need a hand with anything?" Quint asked, sidling up between Uncle Jun and his daughters. The twins were busily cleaning and dressing the fish, knives flashing expertly in their big hands as their baba manned the fryer.

"*Catch o' the day!*" Jimmy squawked, fluttering down from where she'd been circling the party to land on Quint's shoulder, her head bobbing as she peered at the fish.

"What, and have everyone see the subject o' celebration laboring away over his own feast?" Jun chuckled as he squeezed a lemon over a pair of cod fillets. "Nah, lad. Your ma wouldn't let me hear the end of it, for one."

"You're probably right," Quint acknowledged, glancing over to where his mother was hustling Bonnie Kate and Ophelia back inside, loudly scolding them for attempting to help her and Amara pass out the appetizers. "Thank you, by the way."

Uncle Jun's smile faded a little as he unscrewed the lid of a spice jar and seasoned each cod fillet with a generous heaping of the jar's contents. "For what, lad?"

"Taking care of Ma," Quint said, scratching Jimmy under the chin. "After...after Pop, I mean. When I first heard I was worried about her being here, all alone."

"Ah, lad." Jun clapped a big hand on Quint's shoulder. "You should know better'n that by now. Your ma misses Clarent—hells, we all do—but she ain't the type to sit and stew in her own sadness. Not when there's a tavern to run, folk to serve, merriment to make."

"Aye," Quint said, feeling a lump growing in his throat. "I know. But...still. Thank you."

Jun nodded as he took a fillet and dipped it in a bowl full of cornmeal, coating the fish first on one side, then the other. "It ain't nothing, lad. Your ma's family, and so're you."

"Likewise," Quint said, a smile tugging up at the corners of his mouth. "It's been nice, being home like this. I didn't know how much I missed the Bay until I'd come back."

"We missed you too, lad," Jun said, tossing the cod fillet into the fryer with a satisfying sizzle. "So make sure you don't spend so long between visits again, hear?"

"Aye." Quint grinned. On his shoulder Jimmy preened, her feathers tickling his ear.

"Quint," Tai said, nudging him with her elbow. Quint turned his attention to the twins, arguing over who'd contributed more of the day's catch to the feast.

"Help us settle a bet," Ling said to him, holding up a flat-bodied flounder demonstratively. "What counts as the better contribution to this fry, a halibut or a tuna?"

"Tuna's bigger," Tai objected, lifting a truly massive specimen by the tail for Quint's inspection.

"But halibut tastes better," Ling objected.

Grinning, Quint stooped to retrieve a beer from the bucket of cool water at Jun's feet. He popped the cap of a bottle and sipped at it, contentedly listening to the twins' arguments weaving into the tapestry of the sounds of home.

Ember Bay was an easy place to love.

Quint had discovered this sometime over the course of the last several weeks, or perhaps it was more accurate to say that he'd rediscovered it. The close-knit island community his younger self had once regarded as smothering had become a welcome respite from the vagaries of fortune that swirled and eddied like an undertow, hidden just out of sight. The smallness of the place itself no longer seemed confining but comforting—a safe harbor from the tumultuous winds that blew him from one side of the Archipelago to the other. A place untouched by time or trouble, as so much of the wider world was.

Had he been asked, Quint would have been unable to precisely identify just when this change in his disposition had occurred. Perhaps it was in the nightly revels at the Queen's Arms, when half the town turned out to sing, drink, and be merry in one another's company. Or perhaps it was during the long mornings spent laboring over the *Wisherman*, sweat streaming down his back under the hot tropic sun, the gentle lapping of waves against shore performing a melody with the beat of the hammer in his hand. Or—and Quint found this the likeliest answer—perhaps it was in the way everyone had accepted his return after a yearslong absence without question or complaint, merely delighting in his renewed presence among them rather than scorning him for his abandonment.

It was not as though he'd never left—his pop's absence made that abundantly clear. It was simply that Quint's leaving had not created an empty space to be filled in, as he'd expected. Instead, the townsfolk had reserved the place he'd occupied in their hearts, keeping faith in the eventual return of their prodigal son. Every smiling face, every friendly hug, assured him that he would always have a place on Ember Bay, no matter how far he roamed.

Nor was he surprised to see his crew fall in love with the place, a little at a time. He saw it in the way Bonnie Kate stood throwing darts with Miss Rosa and Beauregard, animatedly discussing the finer points of maritime trade. He saw it in how Ophelia had gathered a crowd of admirers as she sat perched on the bar, gesticulating demonstratively as she told stories of her adventures on the high seas, the details changed just enough to avoid any allusions to piracy or other criminality. He saw it in the way Fillbrick sat with Hawkins at the old man's usual booth, the two of them sipping the enormous fruity cocktails Ma had served them in companionable silence.

What surprised Quint was that Ember Bay seemed to love his crew right back.

By the time the main feast of fried fish served with crispy potato wedges and garnished with lemon was served, each had formed new relationships with the townsfolk. Kate had struck up a trade deal with Rosa's Mercantile, Ophelia had several pretty young townswomen actively vying for her affections, and Fillbrick and Hawkins had stumbled from their booth to stagger about the tavern floor, sloshing their absurd cocktails as they bellowed out an off-key rendition of that classic sea shanty, "Don't Forget Your Old Shipmate."

"*Safe an' sound at home again!*" Fillbrick boomed, Hawkins's creaky voice joining in. "*Now we're safe ashore, Jack!*"

"*Long we've tossed on the rolling main!*" Ophelia crowed, disentangling herself from her gaggle of admirers to seize Quint under the arm. "*Now we're safe ashore, Jack!*"

She squeezed, and he found himself singing along. "*Don't forget your old shipmate!*"

"*Folly rolly rolly rolly ry-di-dol!*" Hari appearing to pull Quint into a half hug as the three of them sang the chorus together, off-key and uncaring. "*Long we've tossed on the rolling main!*"

"*NOW WE'RE SAFE ASHORE, JACK!*" the whole tavern shouted back, and soon the walls of the Arms were shaking with the old shanty.

By the time the final verse was finished Quint found himself panting and out of breath, red-faced and grinning. The crowd, shouting and stomping, called out for more, and before his mind could catch up Quint found himself calling out the opening lines to another favorite.

"*When I was just a little lad,*" he began, his clear baritone cutting through the whoops and laughter of the crowd. His eye found Ma amongst them, laughing and nodding along with the rest, "*or so my ma, she told me...*"

"*Away haul away!*" the crowd roared back, stomping in time to the shanty. "*We'll haul away Joe!*"

And another, and another, through the whole catalogue of shanties Quint had ever learned. The patrons of the Arms knew most of them, from "Drunken Sailor" to "Leave Her Johnny" and "Roll the Old Chariot Along."

Others chimed in, leading the crowd with strange lyrics to familiar tunes, which Quint clapped and stamped along to with the best of them, his crew's voices mingling with those of the people who'd raised him. He closed his eyes, and in the bellowing call-and-response of the shanty he could almost imagine he was back aboard the *Angel*, the rum he'd drunk doing a passable imitation of the deck rolling beneath his feet.

Soon, he told himself. Soon he'd be back to the life he'd chosen, to the open sea and the endless sky.

But not yet.

For now, Quint Thatch was content to be exactly where he was.

Exhausted and grinning, he collapsed into a chair at the main table, which had remained reserved for himself and his crew, though at the moment only Rustbucket and his cousins occupied it. Fillbrick was still drunkenly leading the chorus of "Blow the Man Down," while Kate, having learned of Mani's interest in becoming a ship's clerk, had cornered his parents to enthusiastically regale them with the minutiae of such work.

"Having fun, lads?" Quint asked as Ophelia sank into the chair beside him, flushed with drink and good humor.

"Food's good," Bert acknowledged, earning a dirty look from his diminutive cousin.

"It is," Rustbucket grudgingly admitted, glancing about furtively before leaning in conspiratorially. "Lissen, Quint. It's getting near sundown. When are we planning to retrieve the you-know-what?"

Quint raised his mug to his lips, taking his time before answering. Toward the back of the room someone struck up a lively tune on the dust-covered harpsichord that graced the Arms' low stage. Quint was both surprised and amused to see the musician was none other than Mrs. Cavendish, her expression dour as ever despite the cheerful melody she played. Encouraged by the music, Rosa and Beauregard Deveraux struck up a jig, the elderly couple dancing arm in arm with a sprightliness that belied their years. Others joined in, shoving tables and chairs to the sides to clear space for an impromptu dance floor.

"Well?" Rustbucket snapped his fingers, calling Quint's attention back to himself. "I know you're having fun with your little visit home, but—"

"Lay off him, Rusty," Ophelia said, and though her easy grin had not faded something dangerous glinted in her eyes. "There's good food and free beer. Loosen up a tad, why don't you?"

"I'll loosen when I know that we've got the treasure safe in the *Angel*'s hold," Rustbucket hissed. "Food an' drink's well and good, but it's coin I signed on for, not a free meal."

"Belay that talk," Ophelia said, her smile disappearing entirely. "Less you want to spend the rest o' the voyage across the ship in the brig—"

"We're not taking the treasure with us," Quint said.

All four of their heads turned toward him, their expressions varying shades of shocked.

"We're *what*?" Rustbucket asked, his voice strangled.

"Treasure stays here," Quint said, shaking his head. "I've thought about it and it's just too hot for us to pawn right now, Rusty. Navy's gonna be chasing us for a while, now, and it's safer for us to have stowed it someplace—"

"Here, though?" Rustbucket glanced about the Arms dubiously, as if he thought Quint had buried the crown jewels beneath the floorboards.

"'Course not," Quint said. "It's well into the jungle. Navy ain't finding it without my help."

"So we're just…" Rustbucket's mouth worked soundlessly like a fish gasping for air as he tried to find suitable words for his astonishment. "Just *leaving* the bloody treasure here. Gonna set back out on the open seas empty-handed."

"I wouldn't say that," Quint said, looking around at the celebration engulfing the tavern, at both halves of his family coming together at last.

But Rustbucket was not so moved.

"Aw, *hang* this!" he snarled, kicking out from his chair. It clattered against the floor as Rustbucket leapt onto the tabletop, reached into his coat, and pulled out a pair of pistols.

25

Q uint lunged forward, only to be pulled back against his seat by
Ophelia. Their eyes met, Quint's wild with hot anger and confusion, hers desperate, pleading. Ophelia's swoop of blonde hair swayed
from side to side as she shook her head and shot a frantic warning
glance across the table.

Quint followed her gaze to see that Rustbucket's two cousins had
followed his lead, each producing his own short, wide-barreled pistol.
Bert's was aimed straight at Quint's heart, while Berk held his at an
angle, in case any of the tavern's other patrons got ideas.

"*Oi!*" Rustbucket shouted over the din, and when that failed to gar-
ner him the crowd's attention he raised one pistol toward the ceiling
and squeezed the trigger. The tang of gunpowder filled Quint's nose
and mouth even as the *bang* of the shot reverberated off the wooden
walls. A moment later it was echoed by a dull *thwump* as the lead shot
fell back onto the table, smoke rising from it.

I'll be damned, some distant part of Quint that was not watching
his life fall apart thought. *Pop always said the Arms had timbers like an
ironside.*

The gunshot had the desired effect. Mrs. Cavendish's harpsichord
faltered, then died away completely as every face in the Arms turned toward Rustbucket. To Quint's surprise, no one screamed. The townsfolk
of Ember Bay merely looked at the wild-eyed little man standing atop

the tavern's largest table and waving his guns around as if he were a curiosity; the most interesting thing to happen on their island in weeks. Which, Quint supposed, was accurate.

"Right," Rustbucket said into the ensuing silence. He cleared his throat, as if uncertain how to proceed now that he had their full attention. "Listen up, you lot. We're taking this town hostage. Cooperate and there won't be anybody hurt, unnerstand?"

"Ain't you one o' young Thatch's mates?" Hawkins asked, leaning against Fillbrick and squinting hard at Rustbucket.

"Not if he doesn't put the guns away and sit hisself down right now," Quint said. He leaned forward but was arrested by the click of Bert thumbing back his gun's hammer. Quint held out his empty palms and resumed his seat, glaring up at Rustbucket. "Only chance I'm giving you, Rusty."

"Stow it," Rustbucket growled. His eyes swept the tavern, taking in the faces of those assembled, the knickknacks lining the walls. "You've let this place turn you soft, Cap'n."

A rustle of murmurs swept around the tavern, too soft to catch. To Quint they felt like spiders crawling across his neck.

"It's a mutiny, then," Quint said, ignoring other patrons, the cousins, even Ophelia. There was no one in the world at this moment save himself and Rustbucket. If he could just talk him down, there might be some way to salvage the situation yet. Somehow.

"Aye." Rustbucket nodded, undiscouraged.

"Slow down," Amara said, her high voice calling clear from across the bar. "Why'd you call Quint 'captain'? I thought it was her—"

"It ain't," Rustbucket snapped. "'Fraid this town's wayward son ain't exactly been truthful 'bout what he's been up to all these years. Have you, Quint?"

"Rustbucket," Quint warned, but it was too late. From a few tables over the twins were peering intently at him, Uncle Jun's arms wrapped protectively about his daughters' broad shoulders.

Nor were they the only ones. Quint felt a flush creep up his neck as he realized that the attentions of the entire tavern were fixed squarely on him.

"What's he talking about, Quentin?" Miss Rosa asked, leaning toward him from her table.

"Your *Quentin*," Rustbucket sneered, drawing out Quint's given name several syllables longer than it warranted. "Ain't no 'umble ship's clerk, no. I dunno what *he's* told you—"

Quint found himself staring down the impossibly large barrel of the pistol as Rustbucket jabbed it toward him for emphasis.

"—but *Cap'n* Redbeard and all his crew are the bloodthirstiest, schemingest, most villainous gang of pirates to sail the Eight Seas!"

"Oh," Rosa said, leaning back in her chair. She almost sounded disappointed. "That."

Quint blinked. Above him, Rustbucket echoed his thought aloud. "What?"

The crash of breaking glass turned Quint's head. Hawkins staggered forward, the neck of a beer bottle in one hand, pale yellow drink still dripping from the jagged edges where he'd smashed it against a table.

"Best put that thing down, son," the ancient mariner growled, pointing the broken bottle across the room at Rustbucket. "Else someone's liable to get hurt."

Rustbucket was not so easily cowed, however.

"Looks like you brought a bottle to a gunfight," he sneered, but all around the Queen's Arms the folk of Ember Bay were suddenly armed.

Uncle Jun reached up and, almost casually, plucked an ancient pair of crossed cutlasses from the wooden shield they'd been mounted on. The twins each took one as their baba stood and pulled down an enormous stuffed tuna from the wall. Nearer at hand, Rosa and Beauregard each drew a matching pair of ivory-handled pistols from beneath their jackets, while on the stage Mrs. Cavendish had produced a multiple-barreled musket nearly as large as she was from the harpsi-chordist's bench.

In the space of seconds, the townsfolk of Ember Bay—the ordinary, provincial neighbors Quint Thatch had grown up with—had somehow armed themselves to the teeth with a startling array of weaponry.

But the moment that truly, irrevocably shattered Quint's world was when Lola Thatch stepped up behind Rustbucket, the long harpoon that had hung above the tavern's bar since time out of mind gripped tight in both her calloused hands, and pressed its point against Rust-bucket's back.

"I don't take kindly to troublemakers in my establishment," Ma said. "Why don't you put the guns down, now?"

On either side of her Bert and Berk had swiveled in their chairs, their own pistols aimed at Ma in a moment that made Quint's heart falter.

"Wouldn't do that, lads," Uncle Jun said, raising the enormous stuffed tuna at them in a way that somehow managed to remain threat-ening. "It ain't easy to hang a man from a palm tree, but I'm confident we can manage it."

Rustbucket's cousins looked around, realizing just how badly they were outgunned. Berk swiveled so that he was once more aiming at the crowd, the pistol wavering from one townsperson to the next.

"What in the blazes is happening?" Rustbucket said, again echoing Quint's own thought.

"A reverse mutiny," Ma said, driving the harpoon's tip a little harder between Rustbucket's shoulders. "You ain't the only pirates in this tav-ern."

"What?" Quint heard himself say, but even as the word escaped him, he felt his gaze being drawn toward the bar, to the snarling brass dog's head adorning it. But if he squinted, it looked a bit more like a wolf...

"Angels above," Ophelia breathed, coming to the same conclusion only a moment later. "You're Captain Wolf's crew? The Sea Dogs?"

"Some of us, anyway," Uncle Jun said, hefting the enormous stuffed tuna onto his broad shoulders. "Lola, how you want to play this?"

"Slow an' easy," Ma replied. "Lower the guns, dear."

"And let you run me through like that sailfish?" Rustbucket sneered, nodding toward the gamefish mounted over the bar. "No thanks."

"Ma?" Quint asked. Impossibly, the gun pointed at his head was no longer his main concern. "You and Uncle Jun, and...and Pop...?"

"Aye, dear." Ma Thatch nodded, giving him a sad smile over Rustbucket's shoulder. "We were pirates, once."

"Not just any pirates," Ophelia murmured reverently beside Quint, her stage whisper carrying across the room. "The Sea Dogs! Crew of the fearsome ship *Howler*, sworn mates of the notorious Captain Wolf—"

She trailed off, realization overcoming her excitement. She turned to Quint, an apology on her lips, but in that moment her captain had eyes only for his ma.

"Pop?" he asked her, trying to reconcile his memories of the kind, patient, gregarious man who'd raised him with the daring adventures and perilous escapades of the greatest pirate the Archipelago had ever known. Tales Pop had told him as bedtime stories for as far back as Quint could remember...

"He wanted to tell you," Ma said, her smile growing sadder. "When you were ready."

"I..." Quint cleared his throat, looking past Rustbucket's gun at Uncle Jun and the twins. "You knew it, too?"

The twins looked at one another, then at the cutlasses their baba had thrown them.

"Knew what?" Ling asked.

Beside her, Tai wore an expression of identical confusion. "We were just ready to fight."

"They didn't know," Jun said, shaking his head. "I...your folks and I, and the rest of us old-timers."

He nodded at each of the armed elders of Ember Bay: Hawkins, Manish Anand, Rosa and Beauregard, Mrs. Cavendish, and dozens of others.

"When we first settled here, we all made a vow," Mrs. Cavendish said in her creaking old voice, adjusting her spectacles even as the many-barreled musket remained fixed on Berk's head. "That we'd leave the past in the past."

"No telling any of the kids," Hawkins growled.

"Though some of us were better at keeping it a secret than others," Rosa remarked mildly, glancing at Beauregard, who suddenly became very interested in something on the floor.

"Right." Rustbucket audibly ground his teeth. "Anyone else in on this big secret, then?"

After a moment Hari raised his hand tentatively. "My pa let it slip. More'n once, actually."

There was a chorus of groans.

"And Hari told me," Amara added from where she half-crouched behind the bar, shielding her pregnancy from any wayward bullets. The groans redoubled.

Yet all of this was occurring in the periphery of Quint's attention, which remained squarely fixed on Lola Thatch.

"You could have told me," Quint said to his mother.

"We wanted to, dear." A muscle worked in her jaw. "But you were so enamored with running off to join the Navy, soon as you were able to.

Seemed unwise to reveal to our teenage son that we were some o' the most wanted pirates in history when he slept with a Navy eagle flag as a blanket most nights."

Ophelia's jaw dropped. Quint's mouth too fell open, trying to find a rejoinder, but unable to think of anything that might reassure his mother that his younger self had been worthy of her trust.

Rustbucket loudly cleared his throat and thumbed back the hammers of both his pistols, sending a menacing *click-click* echoing through the Arms. "Right. All this family drama and revelation is very compelling, but if Quentin here doesn't tell me where on this miserable island he buried the Imperial bloody crown bloody jewels, I'm going to start pulling triggers in three, two..."

A *bang* reverberated through the tavern—not from the guns in Rustbucket's hands but coming from the entrance. Shock moved Quint to swivel around in his chair, momentarily forgetful of the danger at his back as he saw the door to the Arms flung open, creaking on its hinges.

"Wow!" Mani said brightly, eyes shining as he looked around at half of Ember Bay's populace crammed into the tavern, more of them holding weapons than not. "No one told me we're having a sword party!"

Quint looked over his shoulder, but Rustbucket seemed to be as perplexed at the intrusion of a young boy onto his attempted mutiny as Quint had been at the sudden armament of the town.

"Sweetheart," Amara said, moving swiftly across the tavern to crouch in front of Mani, placing herself squarely between him and Rustbucket. Without a word Hari moved beside them, shielding his pregnant wife and his son with his own body. "This is—you shouldn't be here, Mani."

"Because I don't have sword?" Mani asked, undeterred. "That's all right! I can go and get my hammer—"

"*No*," Amara snapped, her voice startlingly loud in the silence. She pulled Mani close, running a hand through his wavy dark hair. "No, sweetheart, it's an adult party, that's all. You run along now—"

"But Mama," Mani said, excitement rising in his voice, "there's a ship!"

Cold fear wrapped its icy hands around Quint's spine. He rose from the table, no longer concerned with whether or not Rustbucket would fulfill the threat of the pistols in his hands, and walked over to Mani.

"Mani," he said, and the hoarseness in his voice had nothing to do with song or drink. "What kind of ship?"

"A big one!" Mani said, spreading his arms demonstratively wide. "Bigger than the *Waterhouse* even, with square sails an' three masts—"

"Sweetheart," Amara said, placing both hands on her son's shoulders and looking him firmly in the eye. "What did her flag look like? Please, think about it for me. Okay?"

Mani's brow furrowed in concentration as he shut his eyes, trying to recall. The attention of every soul in the room was fixed on him, holding their collective breaths.

"It was purple," he said at last. "With a white bird on it. An eagle, I think."

A chorus of indrawn breaths greeted this. Amara looked at Quint, a frown creasing her brow.

"It's the Navy," she said.

26

"They found me at last!" Hawkins croaked, stumbling toward the door with his broken bottle in hand. "Well, if it's a fight those bilge-drinking sea-rats are after, it's a fight they'll—"

"Belay that," Quint said, rising and turning around. His voice was clear and surprisingly steady—no longer the voice of Quentin Thatch, son of Ember Bay, but that of Captain Redbeard, leader of the fiercest buccaneers ever to ply the Eight Seas. "We're not fighting them. But we're not getting arrested, neither."

Something in his tone straightened the spines of the townsfolk, causing them to look at him with renewed respect. Fleetingly, Quint wondered if the old-timers saw something of their own Captain Wolf in the set of his shoulders, in the steady timbre of his voice.

He swallowed, shunting those thoughts aside until there was time for such introspection.

"Rustbucket," Quint said, his gaze cutting across the tavern to his mutinous crewmate, still standing atop the table with drawn pistols. "Back in Sweetharbor, when you let slip that I—that Captain Redbeard was on Ember Bay. What is it you said, exactly?"

"Nothing!" Rustbucket lied automatically. Ma prodded him with the harpoon. "I mean, I were boastin' of bein' on the *Angel*'s crew, and about the Amell raid. Only the moll don't believe me. Asks where the crown jewels was, if I didn't have 'em with me or on the *Angel*. So I says to her that Cap'n Redbeard his own self had taken them to be buried on Ember Bay."

"You bleeding idiot," Ophelia muttered, to the general agreement of everyone else in the Arms, Bert and Berk included.

"But that's all you said?" Quint pressed. "Nothing about the rest of the crew, or that my family lives here?"

"I'm not a *complete* idiot," Rustbucket muttered, having enough self-awareness to look abashed. "Said Cap'n Redbeard had come here to bury the treasure, an' that's all."

A murmuring swept through the tavern, but Quint hardly noticed, his mind racing. The prevailing winds and the currents surrounding Ember Bay meant the Navy vessel would have rounded the island on its north side. With the *Bloody Angel* anchored well to the south, they wouldn't have even noticed the pirate ship's presence. And if the Navy was only searching for Captain Redbeard and the jewels, if they had no idea that either his crew or the incognito Sea Dogs were here...there might be a way out of this yet.

"Mani," he said, turning back to the boy. "How far off was this ship?"

"It'd just anchored in the harbor," Mani said. Like the *Angel*, any Navy ship of sufficient size would be far too large to dock at the pier.

"Meaning they'd be sending a party ashore in a dinghy," Amara said to Quint, still holding Mani protectively against her. She turned him round, tilting his chin so that he was looking up at her. "Mani, sweetheart, I need you to listen hard and do exactly as I say. All right?"

Mani nodded, the gravity of the situation clearly sinking in even if he did not understand the details. "Aye, Mama."

"Run home and lock the doors," she said. "Take your brothers and go into the bedroom. Keep all the lights off and don't talk, and don't answer the door for anybody but your papa or myself. Understood?"

Mani nodded. Amara kissed him on his cheeks, on the top of his head, then gently pushed him toward the door and out of it.

"You should go with him, too," Hari said, moving toward his wife, but stopped as one of Rustbucket's guns turned on him.

"No one's going anywhere," Rustbucket said.

"Rusty," Quint said, still in his calm, collected captain's voice. "What do you think the Navy's going to do if they walk in and find *this*?"

He gestured at the ongoing standoff, the dozens of weapons the townsfolk had conjured seemingly from nowhere. Rustbucket frowned, and the guns in his hands wavered, just a little.

"Here's how it's going to be," Quint said, speaking to the room as a whole. "The Navy's probably rowing ashore as we speak, but they're only after one man. Me. So I'm going to head down there—"

"Like hells!" Ophelia snarled and would have risen from her chair had Berk not trained his gun on her. "This ain't the time for martyrdom, Quint—"

"Nobody's getting martyred," he said, raising his voice over hers. "I'm not turning myself in. But having been in Her Imperial Majesty's service, I know how the Navy operates. So I'm going to go down to the pier before they can dock to try and head them off."

"But they're looking for you," Ma objected over Rustbucket's shoulder.

"Nah," Quint said, rubbing his smooth and hairless chin. "They're looking for Captain Redbeard."

"And the jewels—" Rustbucket objected, but Quint cut him off.

"Let's table that argument," he said. "Rustbucket, I'm walking out those doors. Up to you whether you put a bullet in my back on the way out. But if you're smart, you and everyone else in here is going to play it cool."

He nodded to the Sea Dogs, and to the bemused townsfolk caught up in the unfolding drama, most of whom also had just discovered that their older relations were infamous pirates. "Everyone act normal. You're at a party having a grand old time. Mates—"

Quint caught the eyes of each of his crew in turn: Ophelia, Fillbrick, Bonnie Kate, and even Rustbucket. "Each of you pair up with a local or two. They'll show you how to stay inconspicuous while I'm down there smooth-talking the Navy. Aye?"

"Aye," Ophelia said. Fillbrick nodded, as did Bonnie Kate, and—to Quint's surprise and relief—so did Rustbucket. He and his cousins slowly lowered their guns, though they did not holster them. In response the rest of the tavern lowered their own weapons, though Quint noticed Ma Thatch still held her harpoon poised to run Rustbucket through.

"Right," Quint said, supposing this was as close to peaceable as things were going to get. He turned and placed his hand on the tavern door. "I'll, ah...I'll be going, then. Angels watch over you all."

"Me, too," Miss Rosa said, rising from her chair and hurrying over to the door. "There's some, ah, *inventory* in the shop I'd prefer the Navy not inspect too closely."

"Best we were off, then," Quint said, and threw open the door.

It was easy to become used to how glorious the evenings on Ember Bay were, Quint reflected as he headed downhill toward the pier, Rosa veering off toward her shop. When every nightfall presented a sky painted orange and purple, gold glittering off the waves, it was easy to take paradise for granted.

But if there was one thing Quint had learned in his weeks at home, it was to treat each day like the rare miracle it was. Now, marching downhill toward the great ship anchored in the harbor, its furled sails like the folded wings of some great bird, Quint felt every beat of his hammering heart was a precious gift, each breath of cool tropical air a priceless treasure.

He shook his head to clear it of its melancholy. *No one's dying tonight. All I gotta do is convince the Navy they're wasting their time here, and they'll be on their way without a clue.*

As he reached the bottom of the hill, he could make out the dark blotch of a dinghy being rowed toward the pier by a squadron of Imperial Marines, their deep purple jackets looking black against the sparkling waves. Quint ducked into the harbormaster's office to await their arrival, carefully closing the door behind him before seating himself on Mrs. Cavendish's stool and doing his best to affect her bored, dismissive manner.

Once again, he was glad that he'd maintained his clean-shaven appearance during his weeks at home. Common Imperial sentiment held that pirates were notoriously vain, and the prospect of Captain Redbeard shearing himself of his namesake would likely not even have occurred to the average Navy commander.

The dinghy docked at the far end of the pier, several purple-coated Navy officers hopping from the little boat to tie it to the dock's moorings. Quint watched from his post in the harbormaster's little shack, the thatched roof of which was low enough that he was shadowed from view.

There was, he supposed as the officers came trooping out of the dinghy and onto the dock in two neat rows, some slight chance that someone in this shore party would recognize him from his own days in the service. But Quint had not been a Navy man for near on twenty years now, and the skinny, freckled young man he'd been bore little resemblance to the tall, svelte pirate captain he'd grown into. No one in the Imperial Navy would recognize the beardless Quint Thatch as he was now.

"Commander ashore!" one of the officers shouted. The harbor echoed with the sound of booted feet clacking together as the two rows stood to attention, the muskets hanging from their shoulders turning them into a small forest of bayonets.

A tall, elegant woman stepped easily from dinghy to dock. Like all the soldiers ashore, she wore the purple jacket of the Imperial Navy, though hers boasted braided golden epaulets at the shoulders, as befitting the rank of commander. Her dark brown curls were pulled back from her face, the fading sunlight painting her mahogany features golden.

"Vanessa," he breathed, and ducked low behind the wall of the harbormaster's office, out of sight.

Vanessa.

Whatever angels guided his fate and hers must have been possessed of some keen sense of dramatic irony, for the commander of the forces sent to his hometown to be none other than his former lover. Even that one brief glimpse of her had unlocked a tidal wave of feelings Quint had taken and buried away in a distant corner of his heart. Some cruel admixture of longing and regret and desire mingled together and blended into a bitter cocktail.

His heartbeat roared like the ocean in his ears, and Quint was seized by conflicting urges: to run out onto the dock, soldiers bedamned, and take her into his arms and beg her forgiveness. Or—and this seemed the likelier course—to sink as deeply beneath the window of the harbormaster's office as possible and stay out of sight until she had gone somewhere, anywhere, other than here.

Instead of giving in to either of these wild urges, Quint peeked his head above the lip of the office wall, hoping that the shadows were sufficient to hide him from sight.

"Troops," Vanessa said, her clear, husky alto carrying across the water to him. Her boots clacked solidly against the wooden dock as she paced slowly between the two rows of Marines, hands clasped behind her back. "We come to these shores by the grace of Her Imperial Majesty for two purposes. Firstly, to recover the Imperial crown jewels."

She reached the end of the rows, turned on her heel and began marching the other way, still addressing her soldiers.

"Secondly," Vanessa continued, "to apprehend the perpetrator of the theft, the pirate styling himself Captain Redbeard. He stands a hair over six feet, weighs some thirteen and a half stone..."

Rude, Quint thought, pressing a hand against his middle.

"...and, as I'm sure you've surmised, is possessed of a red-hued beard."

A chuckle rippled through her troops. Vanessa's back was still to him, but Quint could envision the little half-smile she permitted herself in moments of levity with heart-twisting clarity.

"He also goes by a number of aliases," Vanessa continued. "Including but not limited to the following: Eliphas Blackburn, Red Roger, Jack Jackson, the Scourge of Santianno, and so forth."

Quint breathed a sigh of relief. Though she was one of the few living souls not of his crew or Ember Bay that knew his true name, Vanessa had not listed it among his aliases. Perhaps she assumed he would not be so stupid as to use his real name while allegedly incognito on this out-of-the-way island for the sole purpose of stashing the crown jewels.

Or maybe there's another reason, the hopeful part of him that had wanted to rush out onto the dock insisted, before Quint firmly quashed any such notion.

"Our intelligence puts Redbeard here as little as a week ago," Vanessa said, turning to stride down the line of soldiers once more. "Given the size of this island, our best bet is to find and apprehend Redbeard, and coerce him into revealing the jewels' location. To that end, we'll be conducting a house-to-house search, questioning the locals as to whether they've seen anyone of Redbeard's description in recent weeks. Are there any questions?"

One soldier, a blonde-haired young officer at the end of the row nearest town, raised her hand. Vanessa nodded to her. "Midshipman Forester?"

"How *strenuous* should our questioning be, Commander?"

The question was asked in a neutral, respectful tone, but the slight emphasis the midshipman placed on the second word sent a shiver down Quint's spine.

"Very lightly," Vanessa replied, and there was a frost to her voice Quint instantly recognized. "These are good, hardworking citizens of the Empire, Midshipman, and due all the protections and respect such citizenship entails. Likely they've no idea whatsoever of Redbeard's true identity or purpose in coming to their island."

That part's actually true, Quint thought.

"Finding out where he's been will be easy," Vanessa said, her tone less chiding as she strode up the dock. "This isn't the sort of place to receive many visitors, I'd warrant. Likely the arrival of an enigmatic traveler has been the talk of the town for weeks. We'll discover Redbeard's whereabouts soon enough. Now, move out."

Marching feet echoed across the water as the Imperial Marines marched down the pier toward town. Quint ducked fully out of sight, pressing his back against the office wall, directly under Cavendish's window. The rhythmic tramping came closer, closer. Now it was just outside his door. Now it was past it...

"Hold on," Vanessa's voice came from directly over his head. "I need to report in with the harbormaster."

The door shook in its frame as she rapped smartly on it. Quint stared at the handle, trying to recall whether he'd locked it before stepping inside.

Vanessa knocked again. Quint's breathing seemed very loud in his ears, and he shrank further against the wall.

"No one home," Vanessa said to her troops. Quint could hear her frowning.

"Shall we proceed, Commander?" someone asked.

"Go ahead," Vanessa said. "Patrols of three, one house at a time. Treat the locals kindly but search thoroughly. I'll stay here and write out a report myself."

A smile crept across Quint's lips. The Vanessa he'd known was always a stickler for doing things by the book. It was good to know that the years had not changed her beyond recognition.

"Company, move out!" shouted someone Quint presumed to be Vanessa's lieutenant. The order was swiftly obeyed, marching feet heading up the hill to the nearest of Ember Bay's houses.

The doorknob rattled, causing Quint to jump so badly that he nearly banged his head on the overhanging lip of Mrs. Cavendish's window ledge. The rattling came again, and this time it was accompanied by Vanessa muttering to herself. "Is it locked, or..."

Quint stood, careful to keep himself out of sight, and placed his hand on the doorknob. His plan to fast-talk the Navy out of investigating Ember Bay was dead in the water, but there was still one way out of this that would leave both his family and his crew unharmed.

The doorknob rattled again, and Quint flung it open.

Vanessa stumbled into the cramped office, one hand still on the doorknob. Quint grabbed at her, but the years had not dulled her reflexes, and he nearly caught a fist to the eye.

A brief but furious grapple ensued. Vanessa would have cried out to her troops if Quint had not immediately clapped his hand over her mouth, using his slight advantage in height to keep his face out of reach of her clawing hands as she tried to scratch at him. Finally, he managed to turn her around, letting the last rays of the setting sun shine full upon his face.

Above his hand, Vanessa's eyes went wide. "*Quint?*" she managed.

He nodded, then removed his hand from her mouth, a finger pressed against his lips. He sent a silent prayer to his angel that, for the sake of what they'd once shared, she would not cry out.

"Quint," she said again, looking almost as surprised to see him as he was to see her. "I...where's your *beard?*"

"Shaved it," he said automatically. This was not how he'd pictured their reunion going.

"What..." Vanessa blinked. "How...what are you *doing?*"

Quint took a deep breath, then thrust both hands toward her, wrists upward. "Offering you my surrender."

27

The words had hardly left Quint's mouth before Vanessa had pulled a pair of iron manacles from her belt and clapped them over one wrist.

"Hey!" Quint yelped, jerking his other hand away and raising it protectively above his head, out of her reach. "I didn't mean *right now*!"

Vanessa's eyes narrowed. "Why'd you offer up your hands, then?"

"I was making a gesture." Quint shook his manacled hand for emphasis, the loose cuff dangling from it jangling dully. Vanessa's eyes flickered to the chess piece tattooed on his forearm, then widened slightly. "Nice to see you too, by the way."

"You know why I'm here, then," Vanessa said, her tone more guarded than accusatory. Quint took that as a good sign.

"Knew ever since that frigate sailed into harbor," he said, nodding out the window. "Though I figured we still had a day's lead on you. You got here quick."

"We were in the Reach on patrol," Vanessa said. "Got word direct from Navy Intelligence that Captain Redbeard had absconded with the crown jewels and was reputed to be hiding on Ember Bay."

"So that wasn't the frigate the *Angel* ran afoul of off Sweetharbor," Quint said, nodding to the vessel anchored offshore.

"No," Vanessa said, the curls framing her face bouncing as she shook her head. "My patrols are never anywhere near Sweetharbor."

Small wonder, that. For as much as the Empire professed itself the source of law and order in the Archipelago, those in charge had never troubled themselves overmuch about the islands' most notorious den of vice. As Rustbucket's slipup had proven, there was more profit to be had in seeding Sweetharbor with informants and spies than stamping out the place entirely.

Not that Vanessa would ever tolerate anything less than the direct approach to such lawless debauchery, which Quint surmised was the reason her superiors kept her well away from the place.

"You volunteered to be the one to capture me, then?" Quint asked.

"No!" Vanessa shook her head, then amended, "I mean, yes. But I wasn't expecting to actually *find* you. I assumed you'd come to this nowhere island to bury the jewels, then hightail it out of here on the next boat heading back across the Reach."

"Reasonable assumption," Quint said, grimacing. "Save for the fact that this nowhere island's my hometown."

"...Oh." A frown crinkled Vanessa's features, calling Quint's attention to the way the wrinkles around her eyes had deepened since they'd last been together. "So...your family?"

"Here." Quint nodded, fighting to keep his voice steady. This wasn't the time to bring up his father's passing. "Thought I'd spend some time visiting before setting off again."

It was a sentiment he knew would rouse Vanessa's sympathies. They had met in her own hometown, neither knowing the other's profession until they'd already begun to fall for one another. He'd met her fathers and her sister, but things had fallen apart before he could bring her to Ember Bay to meet Lola and Clarent.

"You're putting me in a bind, Quint," Vanessa said, running her hand through her curls in a familiar gesture of agitation. "I've found you, so now I'm obligated to take you into custody."

"You're already halfway there." Quint shook his manacled wrist demonstratively. "But I'm not turning myself in without terms."

Vanessa put her hands on her hips and leaned against the door. "Let's hear them, then."

Quint took a deep breath, knowing he was about to put not only his own fate, but that of his crew and his town, in Vanessa's hands. The outcome of that choice rested squarely upon a simple question: whether Vanessa's affections were stronger than her sense of duty or her ambition.

"My crew's here, too," he said. Her eyes widened in surprise. "Only a few of 'em ashore, but the *Bloody Angel*'s anchored off the south side of the island."

"They came to rescue you," Vanessa said, catching on quickly. "After they let slip that you were here."

"Aye." Quint nodded, quirking a smile. "They're a good bunch, warts an' all. Which is why I'm offering myself up in their place."

Vanessa's frown deepened, but Quint held up a hand to forestall any objection, the loose manacle still swinging from it. "Your orders are to capture Captain Redbeard and retrieve the crown jewels, aye?"

"Aye," Vanessa said, inclining her head. "And what exactly is stopping me from arresting you now, then finding the crown jewels myself, *and* arresting your crew of pirates into the bargain?"

"I grew up here," Quint pointed out. "There's a thousand places I could have hidden that treasure. You're not finding it without my help, not if you search this place for a hundred years."

Vanessa chewed her lip, considering. "So, you want me to let your crew go in exchange for turning yourself in and giving up the jewels?"

"Not only my crew," Quint said. "The people of this island, too."

"What about them?" Vanessa asked, confused.

"Leave them be," Quint said. "Call off your troops. You and I both know that, as careful as you might try and be, the Navy's presence here is gonna put the whole town on edge. Most of them ain't ever *seen* a Navy officer in the flesh, as far out in the Reach as we are."

"They're not under any suspicion—"

"Ness, *please*." The nickname slipped from his lips without consulting his brain. Vanessa's expression turned wistful, but Quint pressed on. "Look. You've got your people knocking on doors and searching homes, and you can't tell me that won't scare and disrupt these people's lives. Right now, there's a party going on at my...at the tavern my parents run. Please, let's not ruin it."

Vanessa considered, her fingers drumming a rhythm on her hips.

"This is a good place," Quint said. "Full of good people. I'm giving you what you want, and all I ask is that you not disturb my home. That strikes me as more than fair."

An agonizing minute passed.

"Alright," Vanessa said at last, and Quint let out a breath he hadn't realized he'd been holding. "I accept your conditions. Your surrender and the jewels, in exchange for amnesty of your crew, and to leave Ember Bay and its citizens unmolested."

"Fantastic," Quint said, holding out his cuffed hand. "Now, get this off my wrist—"

"Absolutely not," Vanessa said, shaking her head. "You're still my prisoner. Now take me to the jewels."

"Can't," Quint said, raising both hands to forestall her objections. "They're pretty deep in the jungle. Hard enough to find in daylight, and even if we left now it'd be full dark by the time we reached them."

"Convenient," Vanessa said, tucking a stray curl out of her eyes. "What, then? We just hole up in this shack until morning?"

"Or we part ways amicably," Quint suggested. "You go sleep in your cabin, while I head back to the little shindig my town's throwing—"

"As if you won't go running for your ship the moment you're out of my sight," she said. "No deal."

"It's not like that," Quint protested, though the thought *had* occurred to him. "I just...want one more night with everyone. That's all."

Something softened in Vanessa's gaze. She bit her lip, considering.

"I'll go with you," she said.

Quint blinked, glanced down at the commander's epaulets on her shoulders. "Dressed like that? Ness, I can't bring home a Naval commander."

"I can take the jacket off," she said with a shrug. "We'll pretend I'm someone else so we don't spook your crew or the town. Besides, there's got to be *someplace* in this town that sells clothes."

"All right," Quint said slowly. They'd have to come up with a reason for Vanessa to have suddenly appeared at his side after he'd talked the Navy away, but it was hardly the worst idea. And at this point, he'd take whatever he could get.

"All right," he said again. "Now can you unshackle me?"

"Afraid not," Vanessa said. "Consider it a reminder that you're still my prisoner."

"How am I gonna explain this to folks?" Quint demanded, trying and failing to pull the iron manacle off his wrist. "I'm not exactly the bracelet-wearing type."

"Pull your sleeve down," Vanessa suggested, opening the door. "Let's go."

She strode from the pier onto the bricks of Ember Bay's waterfront. Her troops had not yet dispersed to conduct their house-to-house search. Judging by the snatches of overheard conversation as Quint and Vanessa approached, they were arguing over how to divvy up their patrol groups.

"Don't wanna go with Forester," a midshipman with pale skin and wiry brown hair was complaining. "She's like a human icicle—"

"Maybe this tropic heat'll melt her," one of the others suggested, to a general chorus of snickering.

"Commander ashore!" a thin man wearing lieutenant's stripes called, catching sight of Vanessa's approach.

All scuttlebutt ceased immediately as the troops came stiffly to attention, though Quint caught more than a few curious glances cast in his direction.

"Change of plans," Vanessa announced, hands clasped behind her back once more, her authoritative voice carrying across the waterfront. "Belay previous orders."

"New orders, ma'am?" the lieutenant asked, his gaze flickering briefly to Quint.

"This is our local informant," Vanessa said, patting Quint's arm. "He tells me we've arrived in the middle of a town celebration at the tavern at the top of the hill, and that if we go door-to-door as we planned, Redbeard's going to catch wind and flee."

A current of restrained excitement rippled through the Navy officers at the confirmation that their prey was indeed present on this small, backwater island. Quint could practically see them fantasizing about the promotions they'd receive for their part in capturing the Archipelago's most infamous pirate.

"I'm going there undercover," Vanessa continued. "I'll apprehend Redbeard myself. You'll stay here at the harbor, make sure no one tries to leave by boat."

"For how long, ma'am?" the thin lieutenant asked.

"High noon tomorrow," Vanessa said, to Quint's relief. That was plenty of time to bid his crew and family farewell, and to retrieve the crown jewels from their hiding place. She glanced at him. "Is there someplace they can quarter themselves without disturbing the town?"

"There's the barracks, there," Quint said, nodding toward a dilapidated stone building a stone's throw from the harbor.

By Imperial law, all settlements large enough for a town charter were required to have a barracks, which served as both lodging for visiting soldiers and a jail for local troublemakers. Until today, no one from the Navy had set foot on Ember Bay in decades, while the worst troublemakers on the island were the effectively harmless Lex and Chuck. As far back as Quint could remember, the barracks had mainly been used for storing fishing supplies.

There was no need to trouble Vanessa's troops with that detail, though. They'd find out for themselves soon enough.

"Right," Vanessa said, nodding to her troops. "Divide up the watches and make sure no one leaves the island. The rest of you, make yourselves comfortable in those barracks. Angels willing, I'll be back here by tomorrow noon with Redbeard and the jewels."

"Aye-aye, ma'am!" the lieutenant called, saluting, and was echoed by a chorus from the other officers. "*Aye-aye!*"

Vanessa gave them a curt nod, then strode uphill, Quint easily keeping pace alongside her.

"Thank you," he murmured to her, once he was sure they were out of earshot. "For going along with this."

"It's the least I could do," Vanessa said, a hint of bitterness tinging her tone. "Seeing as you're about to hand me the biggest success of my career on a platter."

"Still no chance of letting me out of the cuffs?"

"None." Vanessa glanced up at him, frowning. "Where's Jimmy?"

The non sequitur startled a laugh from Quint. "She's around. Most nights she sleeps at the tavern, but since there's a party going on she probably wouldn't find that too restful."

"You're not worried she'll wander off?"

"Nah." Quint shook his head. "Don't matter how far I let her fly. She always comes back to me, sooner or later."

They continued up the hill without speaking, until the first strains of music from the Queen's Arms were carried down to them on the tropical night air.

"Wait," Quint said, putting out a hand.

Vanessa halted, giving him a questioning look. Quint felt an echo of that same vertigo he'd felt upon his crew's arrival, seeing her standing beside him here on Ember Bay, the deep purple of her Navy jacket in stark contrast with the bright pastels of the village houses.

"Before we go in," Quint said, "we're going to have to get you out of those clothes."

28

"I have to admit," Vanessa said a short while later as they stood beneath the wooden signboard of the Queen's Arms, "this isn't how I'd originally pictured meeting your family."

"That makes two of us," Quint said, glancing down at her under the lanternlight. "You look lovely, by the way."

"Thanks." The ghost of a smile graced Vanessa's lips as she looked down at herself, smoothing down the front of her bodice. "It's been a while since I wore a gown."

They'd bundled up her Navy commander's jacket and stashed it in an alleyway, then detoured briefly to Rosa's Mercantile, where Rosa had been busily lugging several crates into a crawlspace beneath a display mannequin. It had taken some persuading, but Quint had convinced her to sell Vanessa a crimson gown in exchange for Vanessa turning a blind eye to whatever it was Rosa was trying to hide. Once Vanessa had changed clothes, they'd bid Rosa farewell and continued up the hill.

"You ready?" Quint asked, putting a hand on the door of the Arms. They'd discussed her cover story on the way up, but now was the time to put it into action. From inside came the muted sounds of music, the rhythmic stomp of dancing feet.

"Aye." Vanessa nodded, taking a deep breath. "Into the breach, mate."

She's always been good at startling a laugh from me, Quint observed as he threw open the door to his home.

Within, the tense standoff between Rustbucket's crew and the rest of the tavern had been replaced by a more solemn atmosphere. It was certainly not the raucous, casual island party Quint had departed not half an hour earlier.

Instead, he felt as if he'd stumbled into an evening salon held by some Imperial marchioness. The music was not the jaunty, fast-paced jig the folk of Ember Bay preferred to dance to. Instead, Mrs. Cavendish was plucking out a slow, mournful tune, one whose energy was matched by the doleful steps of the couples dancing before the stage in two somber lines. Quint could pick out Fillbrick's huge form among the dancers, making an exaggerated bow to his partner before stepping into a restrained turn.

As his eyes swept the room, Quint saw that this affected formality had infected the entire rest of the party. The free-flowing liquor had been replaced by silver trays piled high with enamel teapots and teacups, only a few sets of which actually matched. The partygoers sat about these, each in an unnaturally straight posture, pinkies outthrust as they conversed.

"So I said to the comtesse," Quint heard Ophelia saying in a high, affected accent, "why, my dear Desdemona, whatever is the *point* of all those pearls if you're not going to wear them?"

A chorus of laughter greeted that proclamation, as hollow and false as Ophelia's strained accent. Quint looked over and saw that his first mate had somehow procured one of the towering, beehive-shaped powdered wigs that had been the height of fashion in the Imperial court some twenty years back, though the swoop of her blonde hair still protruded from underneath it. Bonnie Kate sat beside her, though she'd dressed herself up in a men's frockcoat and a tricorn hat.

Vanessa, who had gotten to know Ophelia rather well before she and the crew had discovered their irreconcilable differences in vocation, gave Quint a questioning look. "What is *happening*?"

"I told them to act normal," he said, massaging his forehead. "I suppose they all assumed this was what you hoity-toity Imperial types found normal."

"This really is a backwater," Vanessa murmured, but Quint saw the humor glimmering in her eyes. "Go ahead, Quint. Put them at ease."

"Oi!" Quint said, cupping his hands to his mouth. "I'm back!"

A discordant note from the harpsichord rang out as the music abruptly stopped. So did the dancing. Every head in the tavern turned toward Quint and Vanessa standing in the doorway, and the affected air of gentrified conversation died away altogether as the incognito pirates awaited news of their fate.

"Coast is clear, mates!" Quint called, plastering a grin across his face. "Navy's done poking around on Ember Bay."

Bonnie Kate looked up from under her tricorn hat. "So, we don't need to leave tonight?"

"Nope!"

A murmuration of relief swept through the crowd, but before it could spread far Hawkins pointed a gnarled finger at Vanessa.

"All well and good," he said, squinting at her, "but where'd you find *this* beauty?"

Right. Quint's grin stayed frozen to his face. "This is—"

"*Vanessa!!*"

Ophelia's wig tottered and fell from her head as she barreled through the crowd, straight for them. Beside him Quint felt Vanessa tense, but before either of them could move Ophelia had thrown her arms around the other woman, pulling her tight into a bony hug.

"I missed you," he heard her murmur in Vanessa's ear.

Vanessa's hands rose to just beneath Ophelia's shoulder blades, pulling her in tight. "Well, aren't you a sight for sore eyes. I missed you, too."

Ophelia pulled away, putting her hands on Vanessa's shoulders. "Angels above, love. You look amazing. How's your sister?"

"Estelle's doing well," Vanessa said, smiling. "She's working on her dissertation."

Ophelia let out an impressed whistle. "Always knew she was smart. She seeing anyone these days?"

Vanessa snorted. "Wouldn't you like to know?"

As the two of them fell into a pattern of familiar banter, Quint looked around at the tavern. Many of the crowd hastily averted their eyes as he caught them looking, no doubt wondering how Quint had managed to both drive away the Navy and return with a beautiful woman at his side. The less curious among them were already returning the party to its previous incarnation, producing liquor bottles hidden away inside coat pockets or under petticoats, teacups cast unceremoniously aside. On the stage Mrs. Cavendish struck up a fast-paced tango, which the dancers picked up with visible enthusiasm.

"Step lively," Quint said to Ophelia, spotting Ma weaving through the crowd toward him.

Ophelia followed his gaze, then looked pointedly between Quint and Vanessa. "Ah."

She squeezed Vanessa's hand tightly. "We'll talk again soon, love. In the meantime, best of luck."

"With what?" Vanessa asked, but Ophelia had already slipped away into the crowd, somehow acquiring a bottle of beer before she'd gone three paces.

"Quentin!" Ma Thatch stood before them, looking at Vanessa with an expression of intense interest. "How'd it go with the Navy? And who is this *ethereal* creature?"

Quint felt a flush climb his neck and spread across his cheeks, the sight of which only intensified his mother's interest.

"Ma," he said, clearing his throat. "This is my—ah, this is..."

"Vanessa Delacort," Vanessa said, holding out her hand. "A pleasure to meet you, Mrs. Thatch."

Ma took the proffered hand and pumped it twice.

"Strong grip," she said approvingly, then looked to Quint. "And how did Miss Vanessa come to be in our company, dear?"

"She came with the Navy," Quint said, which was true.

Lola Thatch raised an eyebrow. "Wasn't aware the Navy was in the business of transporting passengers."

"Not usually," Vanessa agreed, "but occasionally they'll make an exception."

She leaned in and whispered conspiratorially. "It's gauche to say so, but I'm very rich."

Ma barked out a laugh. "Beautiful *and* wealthy? Why have you been hiding this one from me, Quentin?"

"I wanted her to be a surprise," Quint said—also not a lie. "I, ah. We're—"

"We're engaged," Vanessa said.

"*Engaged?*" Ma Thatch clapped her hands to her mouth. Quint's face turned nearly as red as his hair as every head in the tavern turned toward them, just in time to see Ma Thatch envelop Vanessa in an enormous hug. Vanessa let out a startled gasp but returned the hug as best she could with her arms pinned to her sides.

"Welcome to the family, dear," Ma said, and there was a tremor in her voice that nearly broke Quint's heart. How easily his ma accepted, and how easily she loved.

How could he tell her the truth about Vanessa's purpose here, when even now tears glistened at the corners of her eyes?

"I'm so glad to meet you," Vanessa said back, and Quint was surprised to hear a tremor in her voice as well.

They broke apart, and to Quint's surprise Vanessa looped her hand through his arm and leaned against him, sending a thrill running through his whole being.

She's just selling the illusion, he told himself, but it was hard to think straight when his nose was filled with the coconut and jasmine smell of her hair.

"Everyone!" Ma Thatch called, raising her voice so that the crowd fell silent. "My son's engaged!"

Shocked silence greeted this, until Hawkins, of all people, lifted his mug and toasted: "About damned time!"

Laughter shook the walls of the Queen's Arms, and then the party *really* began.

Had their engagement been real and Vanessa not planning to arrest him within the next day, it would have ranked among the best nights of Quint's life.

To celebrate, Ma declared another round of drinks on the house, prompting an answering round of cheers. She hustled Vanessa and Quint into a booth near the center of the tavern, then hurried away to pour them drinks—gin and lime juice for Vanessa, coconut rum for Quint.

"To the happy couple!" Ma cried out, raising her own bottle. The rest of the tavern followed suit, cheering and calling out good-natured jokes at Quint's expense.

This must be what the Empress feels like, Quint thought as an impromptu line of well-wishers formed to offer their sincere congratulations, like courtiers waiting to pay their respects. Each had some piece of advice to impart to them, whether it be about the nuances of married life, the trials of raising a family, or any other bit of wisdom they saw fit to impart.

Ma stuck close by for a bit, asking everything she possibly could about their history, the circumstances of Quint's proposal, and their wedding plans. Still reeling from the night's revelations, Quint found himself struggling to produce satisfactory answers, but fortunately Vanessa was able to pick up his slack. Ma listened, enraptured, as Vanessa gave her a sanitized version of the whirlwind romance that had blossomed between them during a visit to her own hometown on Tourmaline. Tactfully, she left out the disastrous incident that had revealed each of their professions to one another, as well as the ensuing carriage chase and rooftop swordfight.

To Quint's relief, Ma was called away by the demands of running a tavern that had just offered up free drinks before she could inquire further about the details of their wholly fictitious proposal. She promised to return soon for the full story but had scarcely departed before Uncle Jun burst through the crowd, introducing himself as Vanessa's new honorary uncle and inquiring after her own family at length.

"Mind if I borrow your better half?" Ophelia cut in, sliding into the booth beside them as Jun asked another question about Vanessa's sister's dissertation, which it turned out had to do with the sexual dimorphism present among the various sea serpent species.

Vanessa gave them an appraising glance, one brow raised. "So long as you don't go far."

"Never out of sight," Quint promised her.

Ophelia slid out from the booth, Quint close on her heels. A few moments later they were seated in a booth on the far side of the tavern, one of the few with a window boasting a view of the rest of town.

"Navy's not totally scarpered, then," Ophelia said, nodding through the glass at where Vanessa's frigate lay anchored in the harbor.

"'Fraid not," Quint admitted, shaking his head. "Best I could do was forestall them."

"Talk to me, Quint," Ophelia said, looking sidelong at him. "Vanessa's the one the Navy sent to capture you?"

"More or less," he said with a shrug. "She didn't think I'd be here."

"But you *are*." She studied his face intently, then groaned, running a hand through her hair. "Hells, mate. You did something stupid, didn't you?"

"You'd think so." Quint hesitated, not wanting to tell her. But out of every soul in the Archipelago, Ophelia was the only one he'd never kept any secrets from, and he would not start doing so now. "Vanessa's here after Redbeard and the jewels, and that's it."

Ophelia considered this, then slapped him.

"Ow!" Quint pressed a hand to his cheek, more surprised than hurt. She hadn't hit him hard.

"Quentin Thatch, you bleeding noble idiot," Ophelia said, her voice a blend of exasperation, irritation, and fondness. "You did exactly what I told you not to do, didn't you? You turned yourself in."

"In exchange for her letting you go free and leaving Ember Bay alone," Quint protested, rubbing at his cheek. "It was that or let the

Navy go kicking in doors until they found us. Fine disguise, by the way. Where'd you get the wig?"

"Your ma had it in a box somewhere," Ophelia said, refusing to be diverted. "Quint, you're our *captain*. You can't turn yourself in."

"Wouldn't be much of a captain if the whole crew's inside of a cell," Quint countered, then frowned. "Speaking of which, where're Rustbucket and his lot? I haven't seen them since I got back."

"Somewhere in the jungle getting eaten alive by mosquitoes, if the angels have any sense of justice," Ophelia said. "After you left, he had no more reason to be threatening anyone, since you're the only one who knows where the jewels are hidden. So we all put our weapons away and started the little high society production you saw. He and the other two made like they were taking part, then slipped away when no one was watching."

Quint blinked. "You all just...let them go?"

"Mate," Ophelia said, punching him lightly in the arm, "we've all been drinking for *hours*. I told Fillbrick to watch 'em, but he thought I was talking to Bonnie Kate since she was standing nearby, and..."

"I get the idea." Quint nodded, frowning. The idea of Rustbucket and the others loose on the island did not sit well with him, but he doubted they'd try anything overt while the Navy was still anchored in the harbor. Still, he made a mental note to make sure Ma locked the Arms up tight once the party was over.

"Come on," he said, throwing an arm around Ophelia's shoulders. "It's gonna work out alright, mate. I've escaped from an Imperial prison before, haven't I?"

Ophelia did not quite smile. "Not without the help of your loyal crew, need I remind you."

"Then it's a good thing that they'll be home free while I'm cooling my heels," Quint said, "and with you at the helm. C'mon, Ophelia. Let's just enjoy the party while we can."

"Aye," Ophelia agreed, looking around the tavern until her eyes alighted on Bonnie Kate, who was balanced precariously upon the back of her chair, tricorn hat askew as she gesticulated wildly. "Speaking of, I'd better rescue Kate."

"Good luck," Quint said, glancing over to where he'd left Vanessa. Ma had returned to their booth and was busily regaling Vanessa with some tale of Quint's childhood. Figuring that would buy him a few minutes, he detoured to the bar, where Hari sat nursing a beer, Amara sipping a glass of water beside him.

"Congratulations," he said, raising his bottle in salute. "Welcome to the ranks of the happily shackled."

"About that…" Quint said, glancing around to make sure no one was paying them any mind. He reached down and surreptitiously tugged up his sleeve, revealing the iron manacle clasped around one wrist, its mate dangling from it.

Amara gave him a knowing look. "That have something to do with your lady? Nice to see you haven't changed, Quint."

"What?" her husband asked, spinning around in his stool so fast he nearly fell off.

"Nothing, dear," Amara said, kissing him on the cheek.

"It's not—" Quint shook his head, realizing that anything he said would only make things worse. "Listen, Hari. Is there any way you could remove this? Vanessa, ah, lost the key."

Hari didn't answer at first, instead taking a slow pull on his bottle before setting it down on the bar. He looked across the tavern to Vanessa, then back to Quint.

"Nope," he said, shaking his head. "Sorry, mate. I'm too drunk."

"That's your second beer," Amara said.

"Like I said, can't do it." Hari grinned and looked Quint right in the eye, then leaned in and whispered conspiratorially. "Bit of advice from one married man to one about to be. Whatever makes the lady happy in the bedroom, you go along with it."

Quint groaned.

What had begun as a fish fry lasted well into the night, prolonged by a combination of relief at the Navy having been diverted, Quint's alleged impending nuptials, and (most of all) because the good folk of Ember Bay would take any and every excuse to party the night away. Moreover, the townsfolk's initial acceptance of Quint's shipmates had transformed into a deeper camaraderie, as the *Bloody Angel*'s crew and the grizzled Sea Dogs swapped tales of piratical adventure upon the high seas. Ophelia remained as awestruck as Quint had ever seen her, hanging on every word as Uncle Jun told stories Quint had thought he'd known from childhood, now given new context by the revelation that his pop was the famed Captain Wolf. Bonnie Kate, now as deeply in her cups as Quint had ever seen her, had cajoled an entire table of Sea Dogs, including Manish Anand and Mrs. Cavendish, into a game of "On Me Life I Never." And Fillbrick, sweaty and tuckered out from all the dancing, had collapsed into Hawkins's booth, the two of them loudly snoring on each other's shoulders.

By the time things finally began winding down midnight had already come and gone, and more than a few of those in attendance had been bundled into the Arms' guestrooms. Fillbrick, Uncle Jun, and Bonnie Kate were included among these.

"Now," Ma said, heaving herself into the booth beside Vanessa with a contented sigh. "You'll be staying in Quint's room, of course."

"Ma," Quint said, his cheeks coloring, "she doesn't—"

"Nonsense." Lola Thatch waved his protests aside. "You're grown adults, not Callinist nuns. There ain't no shame in sharing a bed, 'specially since you'll be married soon."

Quint shot a pleading, panicked look at Vanessa, who merely smiled and said, "That would be lovely, Mrs. Thatch."

"Call me Ma," Ma said.

"Ma," Quint said, clearing his throat, "surely there's an extra room—"

"Look about you, dear," Ma said, waving a weathered hand in a gesture that encompassed the whole of the tavern's interior. Despite the steady stream of inebriated patrons being carried up to the guestrooms, many more remained scattered about the room in various states of semiconsciousness, draped across booths or snoring softly atop tables.

"We're full up," Ma reiterated, pursing her lips. "Frankly, dear," she said to Vanessa, "I wouldn't even let Quint sleep in his own room tonight, were it not for your big news."

"That's very kind of you," Vanessa said, giving her a genuine smile. She leaned her head against Quint's shoulder and looked up at him, dark eyes glittering in the lamplight. "I just can't stand to let him out of my sight."

"It's cute how sweet on each other you two are," Ma said, patting her hand. "Just keep in mind that I'm sleepin' across the hall."

29

"Wow," Vanessa said, once Ma's footsteps had retreated down the stairs to the tavern's main room. "So, this is it. The bedchambers of the dastardly Captain Redbeard."

"I prefer notorious,'" Quint said, stepping inside behind her. He left the door open a crack; the plan they'd agreed upon required an early rising, and the doorjamb tended to stick. "'Dastardly' makes me sound like I twirl my mustache and cackle while menacing young maidens."

"Like this bloke?" Vanessa asked, holding up one of the battered, dogeared novels he'd devoured as a youth, which lay open to the title page on his dresser. Sure enough, the woodblock print on the page featured a villainous-looking pirate with truly impressive black mustaches looming over a young blonde woman in a nightgown several sizes too small, who looked like she was either screaming in terror or yawning.

"Give me that," Quint said, grabbing for it, but Vanessa snatched it deftly out of his reach, reading the title aloud.

"*The Mad Passions of Captain Claw*," she said, glancing down at the cover again. Both the pirate's hands ended in curving hooks. "Maybe not so much with the mustache-twirling, then. You really read this?"

"Probably a hundred times," Quint admitted, coming over to sit on the bed. "Are you quite done making fun of my teenage self?"

"Not even close," Vanessa said, slowly looking about the room as she took in the various nautical memorabilia. "There never was the slightest chance of you being a landsman, was there?"

"None," Quint said, patting the spot on the bed beside him. "We should talk, though. About tomorrow."

Vanessa's teasing grin vanished. She carefully set *The Mad Passions of Captain Claw* down on the dresser, still open to the ridiculous title image, and leaned against the dresser with her arms folded. "Aye. You ready to tell me where the treasure's hid?"

Quint rolled up his sleeve, revealing the manacle dangling from his wrist "You ready to let me out of this?"

Vanessa's eyes lingered on the chess queen tattooed on his forearm, just above the manacle. "That's new."

"I got it after we..." Quint shook his head. This was not the time to dwell on the past. "Answer the question."

Vanessa's expression softened, but she still shook her head. "Nope."

"There's your answer, then," Quint said. "Here's what I'm thinking. We wake early, afore dawn. Sneak out and head to where I've buried the jewels."

"Buried treasure," Vanessa said, glancing down at the novel on the dresser. "You take all your cues from the pirates in books, then?"

"Truth in fiction," Quint said with a shrug. "Anyway. We sneak out and dig it up. I've got a sailboat not too far from where it's buried. We load the chest aboard and sail back to the harbor to that ship o' yours."

"Uh-huh," Vanessa said, sounding unconvinced. "And how do I know you're not planning to overpower me and steer this boat of yours back to *your* ship?"

Quint gave her a lopsided smile. "My sense of honor?"

"Funny."

His smile faded. "I guess we'll just have to trust each other."

"Guess so," Vanessa said, glancing out the window at the black night outside. "We'd better turn in, then. Early morning and all that."

"Aye." Quint stretched, the very prospect of rising before the sun wearying him further after an already-long day. He started to stand. "You can have the bed, Ness. I'll take the floor—"

"Absolutely not," Vanessa said, coming over and pushing him back onto the bed. For a moment Quint's heart raced as he recalled similar moments from their past. He reached for her—

Vanessa grabbed his hand and clapped the other manacle around her own wrist, then sat on the bed beside him. Quint blinked down at her dark brown wrist handcuffed beside his freckled one.

"What the hell?" he managed.

"Security," Vanessa said, reaching down and easing her boots off with one hand—a task that presented some difficulty. "Can't have you sneaking out to unbury the jewels once I've drifted off."

"So much for trusting each other," Quint muttered. "Where's the key?"

"Here," Vanessa said, reaching down the front of her gown's bodice and producing a brass key. "And that's where it'll stay—"

"Absolutely not," Quint said, shaking his head. "For all I know you could wait until *I* fall asleep, then head down to your Navy friends and enlist their help searching the island for the jewels."

"You know I wouldn't do that," Vanessa said. "We made a deal. Besides, they're not as bad as you make out—"

"No?" Quint snorted. "Including Midshipman 'How Strenuously Can We Interrogate Them' Forester?"

Vanessa blinked, not realizing he'd overheard that part, but swiftly recovered. "She's a bit overzealous, I'll admit—"

"Overzealous?" Quint hissed, struggling to keep his voice down. "She was talking about *torturing* the townsfolk, Ness. All those people you just met down there. You think they deserve that?"

"Of course not," Vanessa said, her voice a furious whisper. "I'd *never* permit that, Quint, you know that—"

"I know you wouldn't," he said, shaking his head. "But your precious Navy would."

Vanessa shifted uncomfortably. "Navy policy *does* allow for certain enhanced interrogation methods," she admitted, "but no honorable officer—"

Quint snorted. "I'm sure it's a relief to everyone who's ever been put to the screws by Forester and her ilk that there are other officers who'd refrain from doing so."

Vanessa had no answer to that.

"That's that thing about the Empire, Ness," Quint said, suddenly feeling unspeakably tired. "It was founded on violence, and it's maintained by violence. Doesn't matter how honorably you conduct yourself, or those under your command. It's not enough to wash the blood away."

"Bold words from a pirate," Vanessa said. "You think your hands are clean, just because you've washed them of the Navy?"

"I never said that," Quint said, shaking his head. "I just..."

He rubbed his chin, feeling the faintest bristling of stubble that had arisen since he'd last shaved that morning. Funny how quickly they'd fallen back into the same argument that had doomed their relationship.

"Look," he said, striving to keep his tone even. "I'm not going to justify myself to you, and I don't expect you to do the same for me. I'm just trying to make it clear why I don't want any of your purple jackets in my town."

"Good thing we settled on this plan, then," Vanessa said, gesturing to her gown. "What's that they say about compromises? The good ones leave nobody happy."

"Aye," Quint said. "So here we are, still cuffed together."

"Right." Vanessa chewed her lip, thinking. She held up the key, examining it in the dim light of the lamp on Quint's bedside.

He reached for it, only for Vanessa to toss it away with an underhanded throw. It landed with a clatter on the dresser on the other side of the room, directly atop the open pages of *The Mad Passions of Captain Claw.*

"There," she said, reaching down and continuing to remove her boots. "Now neither of us can get up without waking the other. Happy?"

"Jubilant," Quint said, reaching down to untie his own laces.

An uncomfortable silence ensued as they struggled to remove their boots one-handed. Vanessa had shackled her right hand to Quint's left, which at least left them each with their dominant hands free.

"Here," Vanessa said after half a minute had passed without either of them successfully managing to free their feet. She reached down and helped Quint ease off first one boot, then the other.

"Thanks," he said, then returned the favor.

Some of the tension eased out of the room once they were done. Or perhaps, Quint reflected, it was simply hard to actively mistrust someone when you could both see each other's socks.

"You, uh..." Quint cleared his throat, looking down at the narrow bed. "You still prefer the side nearer the door?"

"If you don't mind," Vanessa said. Funny how quickly they'd gone from argument to this exaggerated politeness. Quint suspected he wasn't the only one thinking of their previous experiences in a shared bed.

"I don't," he said, leaning so that his back was against the wall and swinging his legs up onto the bed.

It took some maneuvering, but in a minute they were both lying side-by-side, heads resting next to each other on the pillows as they stared up at the ceiling of Quint's childhood bedroom. Vanessa reached over with her free hand and turned off the lamp, leaving them in the dark.

Quint could hear the soft sigh of Vanessa's every breath, and his nose was full of the coconut and jasmine scent of her. Though they were both careful not to touch any more than was strictly necessary, the bed was narrow, so they lay pressed side against side. Heat radiated from her.

How long had it been since they'd last lain together like this? Years, Quint knew, yet the reality of this moment made that intervening time seem like a waking dream.

"Quint?" Vanessa whispered.

"Hm?"

"You awake?"

"Aye." He glanced over, could just make out the faint moonlight shining in through the window reflecting in her eyes. "Do you need me to adjust, or...?"

"No," she said quickly. "Just...wanted to make sure I wasn't keeping you up."

"You're not," he assured her. Another silence, somehow comfortable and awkward at the same time.

"This was nice," Vanessa said into the dark. "Tonight, I mean. Meeting everyone."

"It *was* nice," Quint agreed. "Ma liked you a lot, I think."

"The feeling's mutual," Vanessa said, and he did not need to see her to hear her frown. "Where's your pop? I was so caught up in it all that I didn't think to ask after him."

Quint closed his eyes, though it hardly made a difference. His breathing must have grown shallower, because the bed creaked as Vanessa shifted toward him.

"He's gone," Quint said. Two words, beneath which lay an ocean of feeling.

"Oh," Vanessa said after a moment, very softly. "Oh, Quint."

Then she was pressed up against him, her head nestled into his shoulder, her soft curls tickling his cheeks, which were suddenly damp. Their shackled arms still lay between them, but Vanessa wrapped her free arm across Quint's chest and pulled him tight against her. Quint reached up his own free hand, curling his fingers around the smooth circle of her forearm.

"Quint," she said murmured, her breath warm against his neck. "I'm so sorry."

"Thanks," he said. Another word too small for its meaning.

They lay there like that, holding each other close. Everything that had transpired between them—their whirlwind romance, their falling out, even the matter of the crown jewels—seemed suddenly far away and unimportant.

"I..." Quint cleared his throat. "This is why I came back. To Ember Bay."

"The funeral?"

"Too late for that," he murmured. "But...to mourn. And to reconnect. He really loved this place."

"It's an easy place to love," Vanessa said, smiling in the dark. "I saw that tonight. You come from good people, Quint."

He breathed out a shallow laugh, thinking of the night's revelations. Would she still think the same if she knew the roof she slept beneath owed its timbers to Captain Wolf's *Howler*, or that the woman who'd accepted her so freely into her home and family was one of the Sea Dogs?

Perhaps she would, at that. She'd fallen for him, after all.

"Yeah," Quint said, inhaling a shallow breath. "I...I miss him."

His voice broke, just a little. Vanessa squeezed so hard that his ribs hurt, but he did not mind. That was a good pain, the pain of someone loving him even as their rough edges pressed against each other. The pain in his chest was the ache of an unfillable absence.

"I'm sorry," Quint said, once he could trust himself to speak again.

"Tell me about him," Vanessa said.

Four simple words, yet they spoke volumes. That her interest was not in how his pop had died, but how he had lived.

Quint drew in a shuddering breath, but when he spoke he was relieved to hear his voice come out steady and even.

"He was..." Angels above, how could he describe him with something as paltry as mere words?

"Start simple," Vanessa murmured, as if she guessed where the difficulty lay. "Did he look like you?"

"Everyone always said so," Quint said, smiling a little. "For as far back as I can remember. 'Cept for the hair—Ma was the ginger one. Other than that and maybe our noses, everyone said I looked just like him."

"He must have been very handsome, then."

"Flatterer," Quint said, laughing a little. "I suppose he was. He was taller than I turned out to be, and broader, too. He had a big brown beard, though it went gray with the rest of his hair. Deep wrinkles around his eyes. From laughing so much, Ma always said, which I figure was true."

"So he's to blame for your awful sense of humor?"

"Completely," Quint agreed. "No matter the situation, he always had a joke ready."

"I'm sure he'd find something amusing in this, then," Vanessa said, jiggling their shackled hands.

"Doubtless," Quint agreed. "But he was never cruel with his humor. Always made you feel like you were in on the joke, not the butt of it. I loved that about him."

Vanessa's thumb traced an absent circle on his shoulder. "Tell me what else you love about him."

"He was patient," Quint said, the words beginning to spill from him as a thousand memories of his pop came rising to the surface. "More than the father of any teenage son had a right to be. Kind, too. When you were down he always knew how to pick you back up, whether with a joke or offering a hand. If he saw someone on the street struggling under a heavy load, he'd stop and help them take it to where they were going, even if he'd been headed in the opposite direction. He was that sort of person."

"A good man," Vanessa said quietly.

"The best man," Quint said. "He was...angels above, he was everything. Everything I wanted to be as a person. Hardworking but humble, wise but funny, principled and kind. He knew what I needed even when I didn't, understood me when I didn't understand myself. He...he was my hero, Ness."

A tear slipped down his cheek. Vanessa gently wiped it away. "I wish I could have met him."

"So do I."

They lay there in silence, Quint drawing comfort from the warmth of her pressed so close against him.

"Quint?" Her voice was soft in the quiet night.

"Hm?"

"Why didn't you tell me your pop was Captain Wolf?"

Quint bolted upright, then turned to stare down at Vanessa. "Who told you?"

Just enough moonlight filled the room to illuminate Vanessa's triumphant smile. "You just did."

"How...what..." Quint swallowed, mind racing. "How'd you figure it out so quickly?"

"Half the older folks downstairs match the Sea Dogs' description, allowing for the passage of forty years," Vanessa pointed out. "And that one gentleman, Manish, kept making cryptic references to the trouble he and your parents got up to when they were younger. And the wolf figurehead at the bar..."

Quint hoped the room was dark enough that she wouldn't see his grimace. "I thought it was a dog."

Vanessa snorted.

"I didn't know," he said, in answer to her original question. "They didn't tell me when I was growing up. Who they'd been. They've run this tavern for longer than I've been alive."

"When *did* you find out, then?"

"Today."

Vanessa clapped her free hand over her mouth, shoulders shaking with suppressed laughter.

"It's not funny!" Quint groaned in protest, burying his face in his pillow. But now that he'd recovered somewhat from the shock, a knot was growing in the pit of his stomach.

"Ness," he said, raising his head from the pillow. "You promised me that if I cooperated, you'd leave the townsfolk alone—"

"I did," she said, her voice soothing. Her fingers found his. "I was sent here to find Captain Redbeard and the crown jewels, not the Sea Dogs.

No one's getting arrested for crimes they committed before either of us were born."

"Thank you," Quint said, the knot in his stomach dissipating. Quiet lapsed between them, Vanessa's breath tickling his ear.

"Quint?" she said again, almost shyly.

"Ness?"

"Tell me a bedtime story?" she asked. "One about you and your pop."

The corners of Quint's eyes crinkled into a smile.

"Alright," he said, shifting so that he was facing her. In the dim moonlight Vanessa's eyes were huge and dark, and he could not have stopped himself from falling into them if he had tried. Nor did he want to.

"When I was about eleven years old," he began, "Pop and I took the *Wisherman*—that's his sailboat—out to go spearfishing on the reefs off Little Redcoral. Now, this was only my second time spearfishing, and I hadn't quite gotten the hang of it..."

Vanessa closed her eyes and snuggled up against him, so close he could hear her heart beating against his chest. He could not say when either of them fell asleep, as she listened to him tell first one story about his pop, then another, each tale weaving into the next as they did what only stories could do. For in stories, the dead live again.

30

It was still fully dark outside when Quint found himself awoken by a faint scratching sound.

He had been dreaming a strange and confusing dream about a subaquatic tea party, which numbered among its attendees his parents, Vanessa, Lurk, and the grouper they'd caught the other day. Jimmy was also present, wearing Ophelia's tall powdered wig and speaking in a posh accent.

The scratching came again, more insistent, rousing Quint from the nonsensical dream into confused waking. His sluggish thoughts took a moment to connect the presence of another person pressed up against him to the events of the night before.

"Wassat?" Vanessa mumbled as the scratching sound repeated.

Quint blinked, clearing his eyes of sleep. The bedroom was lighter than it had been when they'd retired, though the deep gray of the sky outside the window hinted that sunrise was still more than an hour away. The faint illumination was just enough to make out a furry shadow squatting atop the dresser on the far side of the room.

"Chum," Quint grunted as the black cat continued pawing at something on the dresser.

"Huh?"

"Cat," Quint said, as Chum knocked whatever he'd been pawing at off the dresser. It landed against the floorboards with a surprisingly heavy *thunk*.

"Quint," Vanessa said, sitting up hurriedly. "The *key*."

"Huh—" he started, but she was already swinging her legs over the edge of the bed as Chum leapt from the dresser after his new toy. Vanessa tried to grab for it, only for her motion to be arrested by the manacles binding their wrists together. Quint let out a strangled yelp of pain as his arm twisted uncomfortably.

Chum let out a triumphant trill, followed by the soft *clink* of the brass key being grasped between feline teeth. The full magnitude of what was transpiring struck Quint then, and he scrambled madly out of the bed after Vanessa.

The result was the opposite of what he'd intended. In their mad scramble, he and Vanessa somehow wound up tangled up in both one another and the bedsheets, sending them both crashing to the floor. Quint stifled a groan as pain shot up his elbow from where he'd landed wrong.

"Gimme that!" Vanessa hissed, grabbing for Chum with her free hand. Delighted by this new game, Chum sprang out of her reach and disappeared through the cracked-open door, the bronze key glinting between his teeth.

"After him!" Vanessa hissed, but Quint grabbed her free hand with his own before she could give chase.

"It's no good," he whispered with a shake of his head. "Hiding toys is Chum's favorite game."

Vanessa turned to him, the predawn light just enough for him to see the disbelief in her eyes. "You're kidding."

"Nope." Quint stifled a yawn. "One time he got into Ma's jewelry box. We're *still* finding necklaces and bracelets in odd corners of the tavern all these years later."

"Fantastic," Vanessa sighed, frowning down at their manacled hands. "I've got a spare key, but it's aboard my cabin—*why are you laughing?*"

"Sorry," Quint said, covering his grin with a fist. "It's just...you didn't want me out of your sight, aye?"

"Trust me," Vanessa said, "the irony is not lost on me."

"Well." His grin widened as he reached down to pull on his boots one-handed. "Looks like we're stuck together."

There was no sign of Chum in the hall, and theirs was the only bedroom door that was open. Descending the narrow staircase proved a challenge, but they managed to reach the tavern's main floor without awakening any of those who'd overnighted at the Arms. Most had been lodged in the guestrooms, but the party had been such a smashing success that a greater than usual number had passed out in the main room, though Ma had thoughtfully placed pillows between their heads and the tables before retiring to her own room.

"Here, kitty kitty," Vanessa whispered, crouching and holding out her free hand. But Chum declined to appear.

"Come on," Quint said, shaking his head. There were a thousand little nooks and crannies in the Arms the black cat might have hidden himself in, and by the time they'd searched them all the rest of the partygoers would have awakened.

He and Vanessa tiptoed through the kitchen and into the cool morning air, the sky scarcely lighter than it had been upon their rude awakening. From their vantage point at the top of the hill, Quint could make out the distant torches of the nightfires still shining on the horizon.

He and Vanessa stopped at the shed out back, the door's rusted hinges protesting as Quint threw it open.

"Your ma doesn't lock it?" Vanessa asked, brows lifting in surprise.

"No one locks anything on the Bay," Quint said, retrieving a pair of shovels. "It's that kind of a place."

Vanessa smiled, then glanced down at the shovels.

"You really did bury the jewels, then," Vanessa said, shaking her head. "Such a romantic."

"If it works, it works." Quint shrugged, handing her one of the shovels.

Vanessa took it, hefting its weight. "Gonna be difficult to dig one-handed."

"We'll manage," Quint said, with a confidence he didn't feel. He turned, facing them toward the darkened trees that marked the boundary line between town and jungle. Though the stars had disappeared from the sky overhead, night still hung heavy beneath those branches.

"Let's go," Vanessa said, setting off. Quint kept pace alongside her. Only once they were beneath the eaves of the trees did he allow himself a backwards glance.

The Queen's Arms stood framed against the gray sky, the square blocks of Ember Bay's other buildings little more than dim shapes behind it, leading down to the great black mass of the ocean. The only light in all the world was that of the lighthouse at the far end of the harbor, looking lonelier than ever.

Quint's heart gave an unpleasant lurch inside his chest. In that moment he wanted nothing more than to turn back, to head inside the warmth and comfort of the Arms and tell his ma how much he loved her. How much her gentle, constant support meant, no matter how far he'd roamed from home or how long it had taken him to return. To tell her that her approval meant more than any amount of wealth or treasure—all the things he had wanted to tell his pop, only for it to be too late for him to do so.

"Quint?" Vanessa's voice was gentle, and when he turned back to her there was an expression on her face he couldn't quite place. "You alright?"

"Fine," he said, swallowing down those feelings in favor of focusing on the task at hand. He strode forward, spade over his shoulder, into the darkened jungle. "Let's go dig up the treasure."

It was so dark beneath the jungle canopy that they nearly doubled back for a lantern, only for them both to think better of it. With dawn not far off, Ma would be rising soon, and explaining to her why they were heading into the jungle with a pair of shovels while handcuffed together this early in the morning was a prospect neither Quint nor Vanessa much wanted to face.

Thankfully, Quint had trodden this path on his way down to Cinder Cove so many times over the intervening weeks that he suspected he could walk it in his sleep, a theory which was put to the test with the addition of a shackled partner. Vanessa was forced to rely on his guidance as he picked his way carefully along the ancient Ikai trail, their boots squelching heavily against dirt that had been softened to mud by the predawn mist. They'd not gone more than twenty minutes before the hem of Vanessa's gown had become irreparably dirtied.

"Doubt you'll be able to sell it back to Miss Rosa like that," Quint remarked. The branches overhead still cast them in deep shadow, turning the world around them oddly drab and colorless, but there was enough light in the hidden sky that they could see each other properly. Dawn was not far off now.

"Too bad," Vanessa said, as the two of them stepped over a jutting tree root at the same time. They were becoming quite adept at this tandem walk by now. "Especially considering her original asking price."

"She's an old swindler," Quint said fondly. "I remember when I was a kid, she used to—"

His words were cut short by a startled cry from Vanessa as something came swooping toward them out of the darkness. She raised her shovel, ready to club whatever it was as it flapped around their heads.

"*Cap'n on deck!*" a familiar voice squawked.

"Ahoy, Jimmy!" Quint grinned as Jimmy landed on the shoulder opposite Vanessa, her sharp talons digging through the shirt he'd slept in.

"*Jimmy good bird,*" Jimmy cooed, peering past Quint's jaw at Vanessa. Quint supposed he might have been projecting, but he thought there was a distinctly cool look in the parrot's beady black eyes.

"Oh," Vanessa said, lowering the shovel and looking abashed. "Sorry, Jimmy."

Jimmy did not deign to answer, only preened and adjusted her balance on Quint's shoulder.

"Told you she'd be back," he said, setting off further down the trail, Vanessa keeping pace beside him. Ahead of them a tall shape loomed, their approach swiftly revealing it to be one of the standing stones dotting the trail.

"Handsome fellow," Vanessa said, frowning a little as she surveyed the carven face, its huge and exaggerated features eerie in the low light.

"That's Natl," Quint said, taking a closer look. "The Ikai god of rain and storm."

"The Ikai lived here?" Vanessa asked, looking around as if she half-expected those ancient people to emerge from the trees at any moment.

"Not year-round," Quint said, shaking his head. "Wasn't their way to settle in any one place. But they used the island as a stopover on their voyages, or to ride out the rainy season someplace high and dry."

"What happened to them?"

"The Empire," Quint said, continuing before Vanessa could object. "That's not me casting blame, it's just history. Few hundred years back, the Navy would move in and lay claim to any of the Ikai's stopover islands almost as soon as their catamarans had crossed the horizon. Being a nomadic lot, the Ikai would come back months or years later and find undeveloped jungle cut down for grazing livestock or growing sugarcane, and Imperial Navy frigates patrolling the waters."

"You're saying we stole it from them," Vanessa said quietly.

"We did," Quint agreed, his eyes on the ancient stone carving. "This whole Archipelago's stolen, when it comes down to it. There ain't never been a spot of good land in these islands that someone wasn't already living on when the Empire moved in."

"But you were born here," Vanessa pressed. "And I've seen how much you love this town, Quint. This island. Would you rather the Empire hadn't settled here?"

"Not about what I want," Quint said. "And I wouldn't have traded my upbringing here for anything, Ness. But there's some Ikai kid out there somewhere who's never seen this place, even though maybe he should have."

Before Vanessa could answer, the *crack* of a breaking branch filled the early morning air. Jimmy squawked and flapped off, disappearing into the branches above them.

Instinctively, Vanessa and Quint pressed themselves back to back, each hefting their shovel as best they could with one hand.

"Really wish your cat hadn't made off with the key," Vanessa muttered, her gaze scanning the deep shadows beneath the trees.

"Really wish you hadn't handcuffed us together," Quint shot back.

They waited in tense silence, their hearts racing. Somewhere in the distance a rooster crowed.

"Huh," Quint said, more to himself than Vanessa. "Remy finally got it right."

Another *crack*, this one far closer. Quint and Vanessa turned to see a figure emerge from the trees, both his guns trained on them.

"I hate that bloody bird," Rustbucket said.

31

Quint moved to shield Vanessa from Rustbucket's aim, only for another snapping branch to draw his attention. He turned to see Bert emerging from the undergrowth with his own gun raised, while from the opposite side Berk appeared from behind a thick tree, lacing up the front of his britches with one hand and aiming his pistol at Quint and Vanessa with the other.

"We've got you surrounded," Rustbucket said, unnecessarily. His gaze shifted to Vanessa, who looked ready to charge him with her shovel, had the manacle shackling her and Quint together not impeded her. Rustbucket's lips twisted into an amused sneer. "Well, well. Look who the Navy sent to bring in her own sweetheart. Nice to see you again, Vanessa."

"Wish I could say the same, Rusty." She bared her teeth. "Speaking of sweethearts, how's your sister?"

"I never—" Rustbucket composed himself with an obvious effort and gestured with both pistols. "Real smart, tryin' to piss off the man with the guns."

"All right, Rustbucket," Quint said, drawing his attention away from Vanessa. "You've captured us. Well done. So, what happens now?"

"Same thing as you were already plannin' on doing," Rustbucket said, nodding to the shovels they carried. "You lead us to wherever you stashed the jewels and dig 'em up. Then we set sail and leave this miserable island in our wake, find someplace to pawn the goods, and live like kings for the rest of our days."

"I'm guessing Quint and I aren't included in that last part," Vanessa said.

"Nope." Rustbucket shook his head. "But long as you cooperate, we'll let you live."

"Very fair," Quint said. "But seeing as you don't have a way off Ember Bay—"

"*Don't* argue with me, Quint," Rustbucket said, his voice dropping into a growl. "I've had a helluva night out here, dodging snakes and spiders the size o' me fist and angels only know what else. It weren't exactly restful."

Truth be told, Rusty did look rather the worse for wear. Deep circles ringed his eyes, and the vest he wore sported several new holes. Shallow cuts and scratches marred the smooth dome of his scalp, and a glance at his cousins revealed a veritable bird's nest worth of twigs and leaves sticking out of their hair.

"Besides," the little mutineer said, mastering himself with a visible effort, "you told Darby to have Vigo steer that boat of yours to a cove near here, didn't you? So I'm thinking we haul the treasure onboard, then make our getaway in that."

Somehow the thought of Rustbucket absconding with his pop's beloved *Wisherman* chilled Quint in a way that the guns leveled at his heart could not.

His alarm must have shown on his face, because Rustbucket's lips split into a crooked-toothed grin. "Seems we've come to an understanding then, *Cap'n*. Now, lead the way to the treasure, or I put a bullet in your lady love."

Quint looked to Vanessa, who looked ready to try her chances against Rustbucket, manacled or not. He caught her eye, gave a slight shake of his head. *Not yet.* She nodded.

"Follow me, then," Quint said, setting off down the Ikai trail.

He had not gone more than thirty paces when wings fluttered over their heads, accompanied by Jimmy's screeching voice: "*Storm a-brewin'! Batten the hatches!*"

"If anyone's following us, that stupid bird'll lead them right to us," Bert grumbled, raising his pistol toward the canopy and thumbing back the hammer.

"*Don't—*" Quint said, panicked, but Bert was already squeezing the pistol's trigger.

Vanessa reacted faster than he did, swinging her shovel upward to knock aside the pistol's barrel as Bert fired. The gunshot rang out through the foliage, a plume of blue smoke rising into the branches.

"*Fire the cannons!*" Jimmy squawked, and to Quint's relief she sounded angry rather than hurt. A flutter of wings as she swooped over their heads, winging her way back toward Ember Bay. "*All hands on deck! All hands on deck!*"

"Good riddance," Rustbucket spat after her. Turning back, he gestured for Quint and Vanessa to continue along the trail.

"Not much help, was she?" Vanessa murmured to him, too low for the others to hear.

"Don't be so sure," Quint murmured back. "'All hands on deck' is Jimmy-speak for 'get help.' With any luck she'll fetch Ophelia and the others."

"Great." Vanessa grimaced. "More pirates."

The Ikai fort was unchanged since Quint's last visit in the company of Chuck and Lex. On first approach, Quint was tempted to try and lead Rustbucket and his cousins into one of the traps he'd managed to avoid tripping previously, but it soon proved to be enough of a challenge just for him and Vanessa to navigate the fort without setting them off themselves.

Conjoined as they were, digging up the chest he'd buried the crown jewels in proved an even bigger challenge, but after several trial-and-error attempts they managed to make it work. After a laborious half hour of digging, they were rewarded with the jarring *thwunk* of shovel hitting chest.

Maneuvering it out of the loose dirt in which it'd been buried was an added difficulty, so that by the time they heaved it onto the broken stones of the Ikai fort both Quint and Vanessa were panting and flushed, sweat running down their brows and backs.

"Open it," Rustbucket ordered, gesturing with the pistol.

Quint obliged, reaching down and opening the chest. Gold glittered in the early morning, seeming to illuminate the stones of the long-abandoned fort.

"Harps and bells," Vanessa breathed, staring down at the treasured regalia of the Imperial Crown. The short, curving blade of the Pearl Knife, the glimmering silver and fiery opals of the late Emperor's Carcanet, the Queen Mother's Rings, and more.

"Harps and bells," Rusty agreed, sounding as close to reverent as Quint had ever heard him. "Forget living like kings, mates. Hoard like this, we could *be* kings."

Quint prayed to whatever angel might be listening that the day never came when Rustbucket's bald head was graced with a crown.

"We should get going, Rusty," Bert muttered, glancing at the treetops. "Sun's up, and folk'll start wondering where these two got to."

Rustbucket did not answer at first, only continued staring at the crown jewels with an avaricious longing. Quint watched as he shook himself from the golden reverie, jerking his head in a sharp nod.

"Aye," he said shortly. "Best we be on our way. Shut it."

Quint and Vanessa closed the chest's lid and latched it, hiding the Archipelago's greatest treasures from the newly risen sun.

Carrying the treasure chest was not nearly as hard as digging it up had been. Vanessa seized its handle in her free hand, Quint in his, and together they were able to support its weight on the hands that remained shackled together.

"Hurry up," Rustbucket growled as they picked their way carefully among the ruined paving stones of the Ikai fort. Now that the dawn had cleared the unseen horizon, he'd grown noticeably more agitated, Bert's warning that Vanessa's and Quint's disappearance would not go unremarked for much longer having clearly rattled him.

"We're going as fast as we can, Rusty," Bert snapped, his patience with his cousin's browbeating reaching its end. He prodded Quint's side with his pistol. "You remember what this one said about this place being chock-full of booby traps? Treasure ain't worth nothin' to a man with a broken neck."

"Or poked full of holes," Quint suggested, unable to help himself. "Some o' these pits are full of spikes."

That was a lie. Pop's campaign of eradication against the invasive rats had been more practical than dramatic, but the sight of Bert's face turning the color of curdled milk was too amusing to resist. In point of fact, one of the flagstones lying a little way ahead of Quint and his captors was a trigger plate for one of the pit traps Pop had renovated during his campaign to eradicate the invasive rats. If he could just get close enough to activate it, he might be able to send all three tumbling into the hole—

"See?" Bert demanded, rounding on his cousin. "One false step, and your ol' mates are the least of our worries."

Rustbucket opened his mouth to respond, only for the ground to give a sudden, violent heave beneath their feet.

"What in the hells?" Rustbucket yelped, all his bravado draining away as he swayed where he stood. Quint tried to take a step nearer the pressure plate, but Vanessa stumbled against him, forcing him to devote his attention to keeping them upright and the treasure from spilling across the paving stones.

"Look," Berk said, pointing a thin finger upward. Bert and Rustbucket followed it to a gap in the canopy, through which the dark cone of Ember Bay's volcano was plainly visible.

Black smoke billowed from its peak into the bright morning sky.

"Harps and bells!" Bert swore. "This whole island's about to blow!"

He turned, pirouetting with surprising alacrity for a man of his girth, and took off running for the fort's exit. Berk and Rustbucket were slower to react, their gazes still fixed on the volcano spewing plumes of dark ash over the island.

Quint stuck out a foot, grateful for his long legs, and pressed the toe of his boot down on the pressure plate.

Another tremor shook the earth, this one smaller in magnitude but far closer to hand. Bert's startled cry echoed off the fort's walls as the flagstones beneath him suddenly gave way, opening up to a yawning black chasm.

"What in the blazes—" Rustbucket snarled, whirling about, but despite the violence in his voice naked fear was written plain across his face. He looked down at the pit that had swallowed his cousin, then back to his prisoners. Both pistols rose to the level of Quint's heart.

"What did you *do*?" he demanded. Behind him Berk was still watching the eruption, an uneasy expression curling his lips.

"I didn't set the volcano off, if that's what you're implying," Quint said, calmer than he felt. He hoisted the chest a little higher, shielding his own chest behind it.

"You did *something*—" Rustbucket insisted, but by this point Vanessa had taken all she could stand.

"Oh, *can it*, Rusty," she said in a snarl nearly as guttural as Rustbucket's own. "Your mate was just saying that this place was full of traps. It's his own fault if he ran headlong into one of them. It'd serve him right if he broke his neck on the way down."

"Hrm," Rustbucket grunted, which Quint supposed was as close to having her point acknowledged as Vanessa was likely to get from him. Guns still trained on his captives, Rustbucket glanced to the pit that had opened up beside them. "Bert? You still alive?"

The silence that ensued was just enough to tug at Quint's sense of guilt. Despite the situation, he had hoped to avoid killing Rustbucket or his cousins if at all possible.

"...hurts," Bert's voice came drifting feebly up a moment later, to Quint's relief. "Angels above, Rusty, it *hurts*—"

"What hurts, you great oaf?" Rustbucket snapped, though there was relief in his voice as well.

"Leg," Bert grunted a moment later. "Bleeding angels, my *leg*, it's...it's bent wrong, I think it's broken—"

Holstering one pistol, Rustbucket tugged furiously at his beard, thinking. He leaned over the edge of the pit and whistled. "Bollocks, mate. How deep this is, you're lucky you didn't break your neck."

Quint and Vanessa exchanged glances, wondering if now was their moment. All it would take was one good shove to send Rustbucket tumbling into the pit alongside his cousin, and then they would only have one more captor to deal with...

Behind them, Berk clucked his tongue, echoed by the sound of his pistol's hammer being thumbed back. Quint and Vanessa turned, seeing a wolfish smirk tug at one corner of Berk's mouth as he gave them a shake of the head, clearly having guessed what they were thinking.

"Rusty?" Bert's voice, high and tight with pain. "Rusty, the walls are awful steep. I don't think I can climb up, you'll have to find some way to lift me out—"

"We haven't time," Berk growled. Rustbucket leaned away from the pit's edge. Beneath them the ground trembled again.

"Either that mountain's gonna blow and take this island with it," Berk continued, "or the tattooed wench and the rest o' your mates are gonna find us afore we can slip away. Or both."

"You'd leave your own brother?" Vanessa asked, nose wrinkling in disgust. Her moral outrage outweighed even her contempt for the unfortunate Bert.

"He's only me half-brother," Berk corrected with a dismissive shrug. He looked past her to Rustbucket. "Besides, this means we've only got to split the booty two ways."

That decided the issue as far as Rustbucket was concerned.

"You're right." He nodded, looking again at the gap in the canopy where the volcano had spouted another plume of ash. "Much as I want to get off this island, I'd prefer not to do it by being launched sky-high. You two, take the lead."

Urged on by Rustbucket's pistols, Quint and Vanessa stepped carefully around the pit Bert had fallen into, giving it as wide a berth as the confines of the fort permitted, lest the lip crumble and send them falling in, too. For a moment Quint was tempted to heave the treasure chest in after Bert but was unwilling to risk either Vanessa or himself being shot in retaliation.

"Rusty?" Bert's voice came up to them, faint and hopeful. "Rusty, give me a hand..."

"Sorry, mate," Rustbucket said, but his grimace was not one of a man filled with deep regret. Instead, it was the determined, somewhat disgusted expression of one tasked with delivering bad news, having resolved to do so as quickly as possible before making a swift exit. "Can't spare the time."

"*Rustbucket!*" Bert yelped, his voice echoing off the walls. "Damn you, Rusty, you can't just leave me here!"

"Can't be helped," Rustbucket muttered, looking anywhere but at the pit.

Bert's pleas did not cease once they were past the pit, instead growing higher and more desperate the further Quint and the others got from him. By the time the Ikai fort's exit loomed before them all that could be heard was a keening, wheedling voice echoing dimly off the ancient stones, as if the ghosts of the long-ago voyagers had finally been given voice.

"Come on," Rustbucket said, setting out ahead of them down the path leading toward Cinder Cove. Quint and Vanessa followed, chest in hand, Berk's pistol trained on their backs. Behind them a mournful, ghostly wail echoed from the fort.

"Let's go," Rustbucket snarled. "I've had enough of this island for one lifetime."

32

"Fine display of leadership you showed back there," Quint remarked to Rustbucket as they tramped through the jungle alongside him.

Rustbucket refused to dignify that with so much as a glance. "Shut it, Quint."

"I'm just saying," Quint pressed. "Real inspiring, how you abandoned your cousin to be covered in lava."

"Like you're one to talk," Rustbucket snorted. "Captain's supposed to watch out for their crew, right?"

Now it was Quint's turn to bristle. "I've never left any of my own behind, and you know it."

"What do you call this, then?" Rustbucket demanded, gesturing with his guns at the jungle around them. "You dump the hottest plunder we've ever scored in our laps, then run off to vacation in your hometown? Real captainly of you."

"The way I hear it," Vanessa cut in, "it would have gone fine if you'd been able to hold your tongue, Rustbucket."

"Like I need any of this from the enemy," Rustbucket said, ducking beneath a particularly low-hanging vine. "All that talk about captain's duty to his crew sounds mighty fine, Quint, but he's also got a duty to his crew's purse."

"Rusty," Quint sighed, genuine regret weighing down his steps, "if you truly think that, then I really have failed as your cap'n."

Rustbucket came to a sudden halt and pressed the barrel of his pistol to Quint's cheek. Quint tensed, expecting at any moment for the thundering gunshot to be the last thing he heard.

"Look at this," Rustbucket scoffed instead, running the cold metal circle of the barrel along Quint's jaw. "Smooth as a babe's bottom. Hells, even I make a better Captain Redbeard than you."

From behind them Berk laughed, low and ugly.

To Quint's mingled disappointment and relief, by the time the trees thinned and the glimmering blue waves of Cinder Cove grew visible through the leaves, the quakes had mostly subsided. Relief, because the volcano's return to slumber meant that Ember Bay was not about to be wiped from the ash in torrents of fire and smoke. Disappointment, because the threat of imminent eruption had been their best and only chance at distracting Rustbucket before they could reach Cinder Cove.

"That's it?" Rustbucket asked, peering through the trees at the glittering blue waters under the bright morning sun between the two encircling jetties of tumbled rock. The *Wisherman* lay moored alongside the wooden pier thrust into the cove from the northern jetty, bobbing gently in the low tide. Quint had a moment to admire the crisp red and white of her fresh paint before he was being prodded forward at gunpoint.

"No funny business, now," Rustbucket reminded them as they stepped from the jungle foliage onto the long sweep of black sand. "Either one of you so much as steps funny or whistles a shanty, and I'll send your brains as sky-high as that volcano was blowin'."

They took their first trudging steps onto the loosely packed sand, which shifted beneath them so that every footfall left deep furrows in the beach.

At least we'll leave an easy trail to follow, Quint thought, *so long as anyone looking for us comes here before high tide washes it all away.*

He kept his eyes on the glittering blue waves, wishing desperately that he hadn't ordered Lurk to follow after the *Bloody Angel* when he'd dismissed his ship and those still aboard it to safety. If only she were still here, she might be able to help.

"Step lively, now," Rustbucket said as they reached the pier, motioning them forward with a wave of a gun. Behind him Berk looked about, eyes scanning the beach for any pursuers. None produced themselves.

Quint and Vanessa stepped from sand to pier, the solidity of the aged wooden planks beneath their feet a welcome change from the beach. As Quint's eyes scanned the cove, he wondered if Lurk was nearby, skulking somewhere out of sight.

"Quint," Vanessa said, nudging him with her elbow as they walked down the length of the pier toward the *Wisherman*, still carrying the treasure chest between them. "Look."

He followed her gaze upward, to the top of the *Wisherman*'s mast. A small bird perched there, her plumage a vivid green.

"Jimmy?" Quint breathed, hardly daring to hope.

No answering squawk drifted down from the mast, but she preened in a familiar self-satisfied manner that tugged at Quint's heartstrings. That was Jimmy, alright.

"All hands on deck," Quint murmured, his gaze drifting down to the *Wisherman*'s deck. Behind him Rustbucket and Berk had followed them onto the pier. If Ophelia and the others were lying in wait, now was the time to spring their ambush.

From the waters beneath the pier there came a splash, not loud but startlingly close.

"What you stopping for?" Rustbucket asked as Quint and Vanessa came to a halt mere yards away from the *Wisherman.* "Load her up, you—"

"All hands on deck!" Quint shouted, his voice carrying across the cove. "Stand by to repel boarders!"

He and Vanessa turned, maneuvering themselves so that the chest blocked most of their torsos from Berk's and Rustbucket's guns. At any moment Ophelia and the others would come leaping up from their hiding place aboard the *Wisherman*, weapons drawn. Even Rustbucket, for all his bluster, would surrender in the face of such overwhelming firepower.

"Aye, Cap'n!" a high, piping voice answered. Not Ophelia's.

Oh no, Quint thought.

"What in the hells is this, Quint?" Rustbucket asked, eyebrows rising as he peered over Quint's shoulder. "You hirin' kids, now?"

Dread gnawed a hole in Quint's stomach as he glanced behind him. Mani had emerged from the *Wisherman*'s cabin, his trusty hammer held high in both hands.

"Jimmy told me you were in trouble, Cap'n!" he shouted as he hopped onto the wooden pier, striding up to stand beside Quint and Vanessa. "So I came to help!"

"*All hands on deck!*" Jimmy crowed from somewhere overhead.

"Mani," Quint said, his heart racing in his chest. "Listen closely. You need to get out of here—"

He was interrupted by Rustbucket's laugh, low and cruel. "Oh, well *done*, Quint. I should've known you'd send the bird to get help."

"And he brought this brat?" Berk asked, frowning at Mani.

"Leave him be—" Quint said, moving to place himself between Mani and the mutineers.

"Hey!" Mani glowered at Berk with all the withering scorn an eight-year-old could muster. He stepped forward and pointed his hammer threateningly at Berk. "Jimmy's a girl!"

Quint grabbed for Mani, but Rustbucket clucked his tongue and raised his gun at Quint's head. As Quint froze, movement in the water below caught his eye. Something dark and sinuous was winding its way just below the surface under the pier, too long and large to be an eel.

He looked back to the pier just in time to see Berk step forward and club Mani with the butt of his pistol. Mani let out a startled cry and dropped to the wooden planks, the hammer clattering from his hand as he moaned and clutched at his shoulder.

"Brat," Berk spat.

"OI!" Quint bellowed, his voice ringing out across the cove. He stepped forward, standing protectively over Mani, pulling Vanessa and the treasure along with him. "NO MAN OF MY CREW LAYS HIS HAND ON A CHILD!"

Water rippled beneath the dock. Berk turned from Mani, who lay softly groaning atop the wooden planks, and pressed his pistol against Quint's heart.

"Berk—" Rustbucket started, alarm in his eyes, but his cousin was no longer listening.

"Good thing I ain't one of your crew, am I?" Berk sneered. There was a cold gleam in his eye Quint had seen many times before; the cruel thrill of a man about to kill.

"No," Quint said, with a cold smile twice as vicious as Berk's own. "You're no crew of mine."

Berk's finger tightened on the trigger.

Water roiled and erupted into a foaming geyser beside the dock. All four of those still standing turned as a dark, scaly shape rose with it like an avenging sea goddess, the morning sun reflected in her huge dark eyes.

Rustbucket screamed. Vanessa gaped, openmouthed, the treasure chest slipping from her numb hands to clatter onto the wooden pier. Quint grabbed her with his free hand, pulling them out of the line of fire as Berk's pistol turned from them to the mermaid diving toward him, webbed fingers outstretched. His own finger squeezed the trigger, but the shot went wide, and before he could so much as scream, scaly arms had wrapped him in their cold embrace.

"*DROWN!*" Lurk sang, the word a paroxysm of delight as she barreled toward the water, a frantically struggling Berk held tight against her chest.

Then they were gone, the cool blue waters of Cinder Cove closing in over the mermaid's tail as she dove beneath the surface, swiftly becoming no more than a graceful black shape gliding along the seabed.

"What in the hells—" Rusty started, but Vanessa and Quint were already in motion. Before the mutineer could even raise his guns they charged him, their manacled hands clasped together as they each darted to one side of Rustbucket—Quint to his left, Vanessa to his right—using their joined arms to bind Rustbucket's arms tightly to his sides, rendering him unable to point his pistols anywhere but at his own feet.

"Repelling boarders, Cap'n!" Mani shouted, having recovered his wits, his feet, and his hammer in short order. Before Quint could so much as shout "Belay," Mani was whacking Rustbucket cheerfully about the region of his waist with the hammer, causing him to groan and writhe in Quint's and Vanessa's conjoined hold.

One of Mani's blows must have connected with Rustbucket's hand, for he let out a high yelp and the gun clattered from his grip. The second followed a moment later.

"Mani!" Quint managed to yell, his breathing coming in fits as he struggled against both the resisting Rustbucket and the urge to laugh. "Mani, are you alright?!"

"Aye, Cap'n!" Mani said, saluting with his free hand as he stepped back a pace, hammer raised threateningly toward Rustbucket. Relief flooded through Quint as he saw that Mani could lift the hammer normally—Berk hadn't done the boy any lasting damage.

"You ready to surrender yet?" Vanessa hissed in Rustbucket's ear.

A loud splash cut off Rustbucket's answer. A moment later Lurk was heaving her coiling upper half onto the pier, wrapping her snakelike body protectively about Mani even as her tail and lower half remained submerged beneath the pier. Of Berk, there was no sign.

"Is he one of your crew?" she asked, huge dark eyes peering intently at Rustbucket.

"Well, Rusty?" Quint asked, holding on stubbornly against Rustbucket's renewed panic as he struggled to free himself. "You in my crew, or out of it?"

Lurk grinned, revealing her shark's teeth. What little color remained in Rustbucket's face drained away completely.

"Aye," he said, his struggles ceasing at last. He turned to look up at Quint, and gave his captain a short, bitter nod. "I'm one o' your crew."

33

The morning sun shone bright upon them as they steered the *Wisherman* away from Cinder Cove. Vanessa and Quint stood at the helm, each with a hand on the ship's wheel as they shouted orders for Mani to adjust the trim on the sail.

Rustbucket sat sulkily in the prow, bound hand and foot with a spare length of rope. He'd complained mightily at first, alternately cursing them and pleading for mercy, until Quint had stuffed a balled-up rag in his mouth for all their sakes.

Now Lurk sat on the prow beside him, the length of her tail coiled beneath her so that she looked more snakelike than ever. Anytime Rustbucket's gaze drifted to the treasure chest lying secured against the mast, the mermaid would give him one of her wide and toothy smiles.

"See you're still making interesting friends wherever you go," Vanessa remarked, watching Rustbucket lean as far away from Lurk as his bonds would permit.

"Suppose I am," Quint agreed, his hand steady on the helm as Cinder Cove shrank rapidly into the distance behind them. Their course out of the cove took them due south, toward open ocean.

"Heading, Cap'n?" Mani called from his place by the *Wisherman*'s boom.

Quint hesitated, considering. If they turned west and followed the coast northward, they would soon come into sight of Ember Bay itself, and Vanessa's waiting frigate. Within the hour the crown jewels would be returned to Imperial custody, and Quint would find not one but both his hands clapped in irons before he was thrown into the vessel's brig. After that, an unpleasant voyage across the Reach, culminating in imprisonment and trial.

Or.

Or he could turn the wheel the other way, making eastward toward where he'd ordered his crew to hide the *Bloody Angel* out of sight. She was there even now, hiding somewhere among the numerous inlets and islets that dotted the south side of the island. Once they reached her, Quint could anchor the *Wisherman* somewhere near shore, leaving Mani in Lurk's care while he and his crew sailed for the horizon and the freedom it promised. Vanessa would resist, of course, but with Lurk's help he could probably restrain her long enough for them to reach the *Angel.*

"Quint?" Vanessa asked, a frown creasing her brow. He wondered how much of his thoughts she had guessed. But looking into her soft brown eyes, he knew he could no more do violence to her than he could to anyone else he cared for.

Or.

A third possibility seized him, wild and unlikely though it might be. Or they could simply keep sailing south, into the wide horizon. The four of them—five, he supposed, counting Rustbucket—setting off into the great unknown, in search of new adventures and untamed islands. Together.

"Quint," Vanessa said again, softer this time. "It's time to head out."

And just like that, the fantasy evaporated. Even if Vanessa somehow agreed to run away with him, he could not whisk Mani away from his family, from his home. And even Rustbucket, mutinous malcontent that he was, deserved better than to be dragged along on a voyage he hadn't agreed to.

"Aye," Quint said, shaking his head and breathing in deeply of the fresh salt air. "Just thinking."

Vanessa nodded, her own expression thoughtful. Quint wondered if perhaps he was not the only one contemplating sailing south, away from all the troubles and responsibilities their positions saddled them with.

They had struck a bargain, he and Vanessa. Quint's pop had long ago taught him that, pirate or not, a man was only as good as his word.

And if the price of his family's safety and his crew's freedom was his own imprisonment, well. A captain's chief duty was his crew's well-being. That was what leadership meant. Pop had taught him that, too, every day of his life. It was a trade Quint had agreed to willingly, and would make a hundred times over, if it were offered to him again.

"Lurk," he said, and found he had to fight to keep his tone light. "It's time you were off."

She slithered around to face him, to Rustbucket's visible relief. "Off?"

Quint nodded portside. "The *Angel*'s somewhere in that direction. I need you to head that way and tell Vigo what's happened."

Lurk's expression was flat, but her voice trembled. "You don't want me with you?"

"'Course I do," Quint said. "But someone needs to tell them about the mutiny, and that the rest of the crew will be there soon. Can you do that for me?"

"Yes," Lurk said, reluctantly. She slithered up to the prow, draping her serpentine body along the portside rail, then turned to look back at Quint. "Do you think they'll like me?"

Quint's eyebrows lifted. "Who?"

"Your crew." Lurk's dorsal fin was pressed almost flat against her skull. "I...I haven't been in a pod in a long time."

"Lurk," Quint said, wishing he were not cuffed to Vanessa, that he could take his hand from the rail and go to the mermaid. "They're going to love you. I promise."

Lurk's huge dark eyes stared at him for a long moment. Then her mouth split into a smile that, despite her sharp teeth, was not remotely sharklike.

"Does this mean we're not going to see each other again?" Mani asked, stepping past Rustbucket to join Lurk at the prow.

"I'm sure we will," Lurk said, glancing at Quint. Vanessa too was watching him, frowning just a little.

Quint's heart gave an unpleasant twist, but once again he forced cheer into his voice. "Aye," he said, jerking his head toward the island behind them. "The *Bloody Angel* will be weighing anchor at Ember Bay more frequently now, I think. Plenty o' time to swap tales of the adventures we've had while apart."

Mani grinned his gap-toothed grin, then turned and threw his arms around Lurk's shoulders. She stiffened, then relaxed as he clung to her like a barnacle. Slowly she raised her own arms and wrapped him in a scaly hug.

"Be good, little landman," she murmured in his ear. "And careful where you swing that hammer."

Mani nodded, his lip quivering. Lurk gently extricated herself from his embrace, then turned her attention back to Quint.

"I'll see you soon," she promised, "Cap'n."

Then she slipped over the prow and, with hardly a splash, she was gone.

Mani sniffled, just a little. Rustbucket let out a long breath, his shoulders relaxing for the first time since he'd been brought aboard. Quint found he had to swallow hard before he could speak again.

"Catch a westward wind, Mani," he called, and smiled at his youngest crewmate. "Let's get you home."

They sailed in a companionable silence around the westward face of the island, keeping its green jungle and golden beaches on their starboard side as they tacked northward.

"Thank you, by the way," Quint said to Vanessa as they rounded a bend in the land. Beyond lay the broad sheltering stretch of Ember Bay, the distant pastel-colored buildings bright and cheerful against the green trees in the late morning light.

Vanessa cocked an eyebrow. "For what?"

"For leaving my crew be," he said. "For honoring our agreement."

"I could still betray you," she said with a weak smile. "Clap you in irons, then set off after your crew with the first tide."

"You won't," Quint said, shaking his head. "You're too good of a person for that."

"I thought I was just another heartless enforcer of the Empress's will," Vanessa said, her smile turning bitter. "Remember? Just a soldier for an evil empire."

"You're not," Quint said, his gaze shifting to the purple flag fluttering above the Navy frigate, the eagle upon it growing more distinct as they drew closer. "Institutions and systems are evil, Ness. But people aren't, mostly."

"Not even Rusty?" Vanessa asked, nodding toward the prow where Rustbucket sat glaring.

"Greedy and selfish," Quint admitted, "which is close. But not the same thing."

Vanessa frowned, and they did not speak again as they sailed into Ember Bay, into the shadow of the great Navy frigate that had first darkened the waters of Quint's hometown not a day earlier.

Their commander's return prompted much confusion amongst the crew of the Imperial frigate *Valiant*, particularly as she came aboard covered in a tattered, mud-splattered gown, shackled to an unknown civilian, accompanied by a trussed-up pirate and a young boy who was practically bouncing with glee at being aboard an actual Navy vessel. Their consternation swiftly gave way to awestruck anticipation as Vanessa ordered the treasure chest brought aboard.

"Crew," Vanessa said, clearing her throat. "Before I and most of the other officers departed for the island, you might have heard scuttlebutt that we weren't sent here only to capture the pirate Captain Redbeard. We were also dispatched to retrieve the Imperial crown jewels, lately stolen by that same Captain Redbeard from the vaults of Fort Amell."

An excited buzz rippled through the assembled sailors, confirming Vanessa's assumption that the confidential orders dispatched to her and her officers had nonetheless made their way down to the ranks of the noncommissioned. Despite both his impending incarceration and dislike of the Navy, Quint could not help but smile, seeing in Vanessa's leadership a reflection of his own relationship with his crew.

"It is my distinct pleasure to inform you all," Vanessa said, clasping her free hand behind her back and looking every inch the commander despite still being clothed in a tattered and mud-splattered red gown, "that we have succeeded in both of these objectives."

The rustling whispers through the crew were shocked into silence. Vanessa glanced at Quint. "Give me a hand?"

"Couldn't refuse if I wanted to," Quint said, and as one they bent and heaved the treasure chest open.

The shocked silence lasted a moment longer, and then was replaced by a roaring cheer as every crewman and woman aboard the *Valiant* tossed their hats into the air at the sight of the priceless treasures shining brightly in the morning sun.

"Three cheers for Commander Delacort!" someone shouted, but Vanessa raised her free hand for quiet.

"The recovery of the Empire's greatest treasure couldn't have been accomplished without the assistance of the good folk of this island," she said, nodding toward the pastel-colored houses ashore. "Nor the capture of Captain Redbeard."

She turned—not to Quint, but toward Rustbucket, whose eyes widened over the gag stuffed into his mouth.

"Take Captain Redbeard to the brig," Vanessa ordered, and before Quint could fully register what was happening two brawny crewmen had seized Rustbucket by the upper arms. He shook his head frantically, the braided orange length of hair dangling from his chin waggling like a fishing line that had just caught a bite.

"Not much of a beard," Quint heard a nearby Navy crewwoman mutter to one of her mates. "Thought it'd be more impressive than that."

The two hulking crewmen half-carried, half-dragged Rustbucket away, his protests muffled by the gag stuffed in his mouth.

"You…" Quint said, turning his attention back to Vanessa. "Did you…"

Vanessa winked, so swiftly and subtly that Quint almost thought he'd imagined it.

"Commander?" A portly man in a lieutenant's uniform stepped up to them, clearing his throat. "Good to have you aboard, and congratulations on the mission. But, er…"

Vanessa nodded to him. "Speak plain, Desmond."

"Who's this, then?" Lieutenant Desmond asked, his gaze darting to Quint.

Vanessa glanced at him, a softness in her dark eyes Quint had glimpsed only on a handful of occasions previously.

"Just an islander," she said.

"Right." Desmond glanced over his shoulder at the aforementioned island. "Speaking of, ma'am. Shall I send a jollyboat for those still ashore?"

"Aye," Vanessa said, "but not right away. That young boy—"

She nodded at Mani, who stood at the foot of the mast with his head craned, trying to see up to the crow's nest at its top. "—has been promised a tour of the ship. See to it he gets one, will you?"

"Aye-aye," the lieutenant said, saluting.

"And," Vanessa added, "there's an old Ikai fort in the jungle ashore, dotted with pit traps. One of them has a man inside. An accomplice of Ru—"

Quint coughed.

"Of Redbeard's," Vanessa corrected swiftly. "He'll have a broken leg. Have a local guide you around the traps, then apprehend him and bring him aboard."

"Aye-aye." The lieutenant saluted again, but before he could hurry away Vanessa had another task for him.

"Oh," she said, holding up her wrist and Quint's. "And get the spare key from my cabin, will you?"

⚓

"There," she said several minutes later, as the key turned in the lock with a satisfying *click*. The shackle Quint had worn for the better part of a day fell away, leaving his wrist suddenly bare. "You're free of me now."

"I don't think I'll ever be that," Quint said before he could stop himself.

Vanessa looked away, but not before Quint caught the hint of a flush creeping across her cheeks—or the smile on her lips. "You do know how to keep a girl interested, Quentin Thatch, I'll give you that."

Quint grinned, but before he could say anything else Lieutenant Desmond had reappeared at Vanessa's elbow.

"Jollyboat's ready, ma'am," he said, looking over the rail at where the rowboat bobbed alongside the *Valiant*. "I presume this gentleman and the lad are going ashore as well?"

"Aye." Vanessa nodded. "Go fetch him, will you?"

Desmond saluted, then hurried over to where Mani was attempting to scale the rigging, waving and shouting to get the boy's attention. Quint and Vanessa were alone at the rail once more, for perhaps the last time.

"Will I see you again?" Quint asked.

Vanessa smiled at him. "Depends on how much trouble you get into."

Quint returned her smile with his own broad grin. He reached down and took her hand in his, intertwining their fingers. Vanessa allowed him to, not bothering to hide her bemused smile.

Quint bent and kissed the back of her hand, then looked up at her and winked. "I'll see you soon, then."

"Fine ship you've got here," Ma Thatch said a week later, looking around approvingly as Quint helped her up onto the *Bloody Angel*'s deck.

"I thought you weren't much for sailing," Quint teased, watching appreciatively as his ma turned her head, taking in the *Angel*'s rigging, her furled sails. "Or was all that just part of your charade?"

"Wasn't a charade, dear," Lola Thatch said, putting her hands on her hips. "Ships like this one or your Pop's *Howler* are all well and good. It's boats I'm not overfond of. They're too small."

Quint laughed and offered her his arm, which she gamely took. They strode about the *Bloody Angel*'s deck, Ma inspecting her son's vessel with a keen eye as Quint pointed out scars in the ship's rail from old battles and narrow escapes. The sight of Ma aboard his pirate's vessel sent that strange sense of vertigo through him, but now that both knew the secret of the other's piracy, he was eager to share all the stories he'd hidden from her for so long.

They were not the only ones aboard, of course. As Quint and Lola paced along the starboard bow, they passed Chuck and Lex practicing loading and firing the *Angel*'s cannons under Fillbrick's patient instruction. Quint was relieved to see that the dependable boatswain had possessed the foresight not to conduct this training exercise with live powder, a decision which had limited the collateral damage to bruised toes, courtesy of Chuck dropping a cannonball on Lex's foot. She rounded on her partner in crime, but whatever curse she'd been about to utter died on her lips as Lola and Quint passed them. Whether out of respect for their new captain or his mother, Quint couldn't say.

"Hope those two aren't too disappointed you're staying on awhile," Ma commented once they were safely out of earshot. "I know they were looking forward to putting Ember Bay behind them."

In the week following the *Valiant*'s departure, the crew of the *Bloody Angel* had held a vote to determine whether they would take to the high seas again, now that the danger of capture had passed, or spend some well-earned shore leave on Ember Bay.

The vote had been unanimous.

"They were," Quint agreed, glancing over his shoulder at where Fill-brick was instructing the two cousins on which end of the ramrod to hold. "'Least, until they got on board and realized neither of them had the faintest clue how to sail a ship."

"Why haven't they come back ashore, then?" Ma asked, frowning.

Quint grinned. "They're afraid that if they leave the ship they won't be allowed back aboard."

"Ha!" Ma's laugh rang out across the bay. "You can take the tiger out of the jungle, but you can't make it change its stripes."

"Something like that," Quint agreed.

The rest of his crew had proven less reticent to exercise their privileges of shore leave. Even now, Ophelia and Bonnie Kate were somewhere on the rocky eastern coast of the island, learning to surf under the expert tutelage of Uncle Jun and his daughters.

Nor was the exchange one-way. As Ember Bay suddenly found itself playing host to dozens of ill-mannered but well-intentioned pirates, more than a few curious townsfolk had decided to come aboard the *Bloody Angel*. Nearly all the Sea Dogs had made an appearance, even old

Hawkins, who had taken one look about the deck, grunted, and asked to be shown to the galley. The other veteran pirates, more gregarious than Hawkins, had swiftly formed friendships with Quint's crewmates, swapping tales of adventure on the high seas and comparing old scars. At that very moment Manish Anand was playing a game of shuffleboard on the forecastle with Vigo and Darby, the three of them trash-talking one another with the easy familiarity of those who had known one another for years, rather than mere days.

Closer at hand, Manish's grandson leaned over the *Angel*'s rail, an old brass pocket watch dangling from his hands above the lapping waves.

"Ready?" Mani called down. Quint and his ma halted to see Lurk bobbing in the water below, her dark eyes peering up at Mani.

"This is a stupid game," she said flatly.

Mani gave the mermaid a gap-toothed grin. "Bet you're just saying that because you know I'll win."

"This harbor isn't even that deep," Lurk insisted, but Quint did not miss the way her head turned to follow the watch as Mani let it dangle back and forth on its chain.

"Then you won't have any problem finding it, then," Mani said, and threw the watch as hard as he could. Quint watched as it arced into the air, flashing in the sunlight. It hit the water with a faint *plop*, then swiftly disappeared beneath the waves. A splash of Lurk's tail followed as she dove, giving chase.

Ma turned to Quint, quirking an eyebrow. "Was that your watch?"

"I have others." Quint shrugged, looking as Mani leaned even further over the rail, waiting to see if his friend could find the sunken bauble. "Besides, there's more important things than treasure."

"Speaking of..." Lola grimaced. "I'm sorry you had to give up the crown jewels. That was a treasure your pop would have been proud of you for claiming, and no mistake."

"That's alright," Quint said around the sudden lump in his throat, and found as he spoke the words that it was. "It all worked out in the end. Besides, we stole them once. How hard could it be to steal them again?"

As if to emphasize his point, the pocket watch came hurtling through the air to land with a clatter on the deck, now thoroughly wet and tangled with seaweed. Mani let out a triumphant whoop and ran off in search of something else for Lurk to retrieve.

Quint leaned against the rail, staring out at the glittering waters of Ember Bay, at the colorful houses and the towering cone of the volcano behind them, once again sleeping peacefully.

"I'm sorry I didn't tell you," he said after a moment. The words came hard, but they'd been gnawing at him ever since Rustbucket had outed him as Captain Redbeard that night a week ago.

No, longer. It had been eating at him ever since he'd left the Navy in the first place. The yearslong deception, which was at least partly the reason his visits home had been so few and far between.

"Tell me what, dear?" Ma asked, leaning against the rail beside him.

"You and Pop," Quint said, faltering. He gestured helplessly at the deck around them. "This."

Ma patted his arm. "Take your time."

Quint nodded, taking in a deep breath as he marshaled his thoughts.

"I'm sorry I didn't tell you that I was—that I am—Captain Redbeard."

"Oh," Ma said sympathetically. "That's alright, dear."

"It's not," Quint said, shaking his head with sudden vehemence. "I mean, I wanted to tell you, I just...I didn't know how. Didn't know what you'd think or say. And now Pop..."

His throat felt suddenly constricted, but Quint forced the words out anyway. "I'll never get the chance to tell him now."

"Quentin Thatch," Ma said, reaching up and wiping away his tears in that kindly yet brusque way only mothers seemed capable of. "Your pop knew exactly who you were."

Quint turned to her, hardly daring to believe what he heard. "He...you both knew?"

"We both did." Ma gave him a fond smile. "Neither of us ever believed much in coincidence. So, when a bold new red-headed pirate captain started giving the Navy hell right around the time your letters home grew suspiciously vague, it didn't take long for us to put two and two together."

A laugh worked its way free of Quint's throat, and somewhere between one breath and another it became a sob.

"Oh, Quentin," Ma sighed, pulling him close. Quint rested his head against hers, letting his mother's strong arms comfort him as they had all the days of his youth.

"Your pop knew all along who you were," she murmured in his ear. "He was so damned proud of you, son."

A sob shuddered through Quint, but Lola Thatch held her boy tight. "And so am I."

They stayed that way for a long while, swaying a little with the rocking of the ship in the gentle surf. Only once Quint had his breathing under control did they separate.

"So," Ma asked, nudging Quint with an elbow, "what's next for the fearsome Captain Redbeard and his loyal band of cutthroats? Another daring raid on an Imperial fort? Or tracking down that mysterious beauty who disappeared right around the same time the Navy turned tail out of here?"

This time there were no tears to interrupt Quint's laughter. Ma had asked the questions jokingly, but there was a gleam in her eyes that made it easier to imagine her as the bold and fearsome Sea Dog she must have been before retiring to raise a son and run a tavern.

"Eventually," Quint said, his grin returning. He glanced down at Lurk, her head and shoulders bobbing in the surf as Mani struggled to lift a cannonball over the rail. "Lurk's pod—her family, I mean—is somewhere out there in the great blue. Might be we go looking for them."

A loud splash split the air as Mani finally succeeded in tossing the cannonball overboard. Quint and Ma turned just in time to see Lurk's tail disappearing beneath the waves in pursuit.

"Doesn't look like she's in any hurry," Ma remarked.

"Nah." Quint shook his head, smiling. "Besides, I think the crew deserves a little more shore leave after all our troubles. Know any good places in town to grab a bite and a beer?"

"I've been around enough hungry pirates," Ma snorted. "You'll devour the whole island's store of provisions within the week, if left to run amok."

But she said it with a smile.

Quint nodded. They would not linger on Ember Bay overlong; neither he nor any of his crew could resist the call of the waves, nor the promise of the distant horizon. Adventure beckoned, and they would follow its siren call wherever it led. But it was a comfort knowing that Ember Bay lay behind them—a safe harbor for him and his to return to once more when the world beyond grew stormy and unwelcoming.

They would be back upon the high seas soon enough, sailing into unknown peril in search of fame and fortune. But not yet.

Quint Thatch rested one hand on the *Angel*'s rail, feeling the familiar woodgrain beneath his palms, gazing out across the waters at the brightly painted houses of town.

For now, it was good to be home.

PRISONERS OF A PIRATE QUEEN

Read on for a preview.

Available December 19, 2023

PRISONERS OF A PIRATE QUEEN: Chapter 1

"Have I ever told you how much I love the theatre, Cap'n?" Ophelia Price, first mate of the pirate ship *Bloody Angel,* asked as she touched two fingers gingerly against the false nose she wore.

"You have a time or two," acknowledged Quint Thatch, better known across the Archipelago as Captain Redbeard. This was in fact a significant understatement; he'd lost track of the number of times Ophelia had dragged him along to some terribly-staged melodrama whenever they were in port for more than a day. "Didn't the makeup artist tell you the prosthetic's going to fall off if you keep on touching it?"

"Right," Ophelia said, jerking her hand away from the bulbous fake nose. "Sorry. It's just *fun,* pretending you're someone else."

"It is odd to see you like this," her captain admitted, eyeing her. Like him, Ophelia was dressed in the purple uniform jacket of the Imperial Navy, her thin stripe of loose blonde hair covered up beneath the double layer of a bicorn hat and a brown wig. A foundation of makeup concealed the tattoos that ordinarily would have peeked out of her collar and sleeves, making her already-fair complexion look unnaturally pale beneath the tropical sun overhead. "You look...blank."

"Aye," Ophelia agreed, and winked at him. "But at least I ain't wearing two beards in this heat, mate."

Quint's hand was halfway to the fake beard he wore over his real one before he recalled the makeup artist's warnings about touching their prosthetics. He lowered his hand self-consciously, avoiding Ophelia's knowing smirk as they marched towards the wooden stage.

It was a broad wooden platform of the sort used by theatrical productions who had no need of a backstage and were comfortable performing outdoors, exposed to the elements. Behind it the cool blue waters of Amell Bay glittered with reflected sunlight. From where they stood Quint could just see the ships docked in the harbor below, directly behind the steep, straight slope of the hill upon which the stage stood.

He tried not to look at the ranks of uniformed Navy officers they marched past, each dressed in their purple jackets and standing at attention in neat rows before the stage. Guards stood stationed all around the periphery of the open square, muskets resting conspicuously against their shoulders. This was not the largest gathering of Imperial Navy officers he'd ever encountered at once, but it certainly merited placement in the top three.

"So far so good," Ophelia breathed, glancing over her shoulder at the towering ramparts of Fort Amell looming behind them. "At least, nobody's come running outta the fort yet shouting about how we ain't actually Commodore Goosegrow and Admiral Merryfeather."

"So far," Quint agreed. He resisted the urge to fidget with his stolen uniform, disliking the unfamiliar weight of the commodore's golden epaulettes at his shoulders or the numerous medals pinned to his chest. "Assuming neither of us gives the game away."

"You just gotta get more into character, Cap'n," Ophelia reassured him out of the corner of her mouth. "Remember, you're a stuffed waistcoat here to hobnob with your equally stuffy peers. Walk like you've just made a mess in your breeches."

Quint stifled his laugh with a fist pressed against his mouth, passing it off as a coughing fit instead.

"Vigo in place?" he asked once he'd recovered himself.

"Aye," Ophelia said as they mounted the steps onto the stage, where a dozen chairs had been erected for the highest-ranking officers attending the day's ceremonies. "Assuming that stagehand's spare keys are any good, he should be ready and waiting for the signal."

"The coins we slipped her were good enough," Quint remarked as they took their seats. No one else wearing an admiral's or commodore's uniform had arrived yet, so for the moment they were alone onstage, staring out at a sea of purple jackets. "And I doubt her production company pays her well enough anyway."

"And they call us the thieves," Ophelia grinned ruefully.

Other men and women began to filter onto the stage, each of their uniforms bearing rank insignias of captain or higher. The youngest of them looked to still have a good two decades on Quint and Ophelia, but none paid the two newcomers any mind beyond polite greetings as they took their seats.

"Game ain't given away yet," Ophelia whispered.

Quint nodded his agreement. Their scheme had relied upon the fact that, of the dozen or so high officers invited to the day's ceremonies, all were from different fleets flung across the vast reaches of the Empire. Odds had been good that many of them had never met in person before. Yet the Empire prized good breeding in its ranking officers—so much so that Quint had elected to wager his whole plan on the assumption that none of the admirals, captains, or commodores would dare be so boorish as to admit to not knowing who they were.

He allowed himself a slight smile, imagining the confusion of the *real* Commodore Goosegrow and Admiral Merryfeather when they awoke from the drunken stupor he and Ophelia had left them in. By which point they would, of course, be leagues and leagues away, with a strong breeze in their sails and the Crown Jewels safely stowed away in their hull.

Quint's gaze drifted upwards, towards the towering shadow that was Fort Amell. He and his crew had already stolen the Crown Jewels from the stronghold's supposedly impenetrable vaults months ago, before circumstance had forced them to relinquish them into the Navy's custody. It was a truly daring pirate who managed to pull off such a successful heist the one time. But twice?

That was the stuff from which legends were made.

A band near the back of the square struck up a drumbeat, a rapid martial rhythm that snapped every sailor and soldier in attendance into an upright posture. Quint and Ophelia did their best to straighten themselves from the slouches they had sunk into.

The drumbeat echoed off the walls of the fort above. Soon it was joined by the first bombastic chords of the Imperial anthem. Quint found himself holding his breath as a troop of Navy officers came marching down from Fort Amell's gates, down the center of the aisle formed by the soldiers standing at attention and towards the stage.

Quint's own attention was fixed on the woman striding proudly at the head of the procession. She was tall and long-limbed, her curling dark brown hair pulled back from her face and bound in a high bun. Her purple uniform and golden epaulettes were a pleasing contrast to her mahogany features, and though her face was schooled into a model of military dignity, Quint recognized the slight twist to her lip that meant she was fighting down the urge to smile.

Vanessa, he thought, a pang of longing piercing him. He forced his lingering feelings down, knowing she would not be similarly pleased to see him here today.

The opposite, really.

"Hey, loverboy," Ophelia said, nudging him with her elbow and pointing. "There's Rusty."

Quint looked where she pointed. A few paces behind Vanessa marched a shorter, considerably more bedraggled figure in threadbare clothes, flanked on either side by a pair of intimidatingly broad-shouldered Navy guards.

Rusty "Rustbucket" Russell, formerly a member of Quint's crew turned mutineer, had certainly seen better days. His ordinarily scrawny features had turned alarmingly gaunt, while his beard—typically tied into a tight orange braid—hung wild and scraggly from his chin. The bright sun reflected angrily off the shiny dome of his scalp. A pair of iron manacles bound his wrists together, and someone had tied a cotton gag across his mouth.

"Looks a little worse for wear," Ophelia observed. Quint nodded his agreement, a guilty twist in his gut at the thought that he was at least partially responsible for Rustbucket's current state. True, Rustbucket's mutiny against Quint had led him directly to the predicament he now found himself in, but still. He was part of Quint's crew.

Not anymore, Quint reminded himself, forcing his gaze away from Rustbucket. On Vanessa's other side marched another pair of Navy guards, these ones flanking not a prisoner but a prize: a heavy wooden chest bearing an impressive number of locks. Within lay the Imperial Crown Jewels.

Soon, Quint promised himself, that chest and all its contents would be in his possession once more. And this time neither Vanessa nor Rustbucket would be able to foul things up.

The procession reached the stage and mounted it, Vanessa in the lead. Quint shrank back into his chair as she passed, and for a moment he swore her eyes passed over him, then darted back. A cold thrill crept along his spine at the possibility that she'd seen through the disguise. How would she react—

At the far end of the stage, someone cleared their throat. Vanessa's momentary gaze left Quint, fixing instead upon an elderly, bewhiskered admiral. The man's uniform bore so many medals that he'd probably sink any vessel he stepped aboard smaller than a frigate. Vanessa's heels clicked together as she gave an exactingly precise salute.

"Rear Admiral Stetson," she said, her back straight enough to put a flagpole to shame. "Commander Vanessa Delacort of Her Imperial Majesty's ship *Valiant*, reporting."

"At ease, Commander," the aged admiral squeaked, his voice high and reedy as he returned the salute. Vanessa lowered her hand but remained at attention.

"You were dispatched to seek out the renegade pirate styling himself Captain Redbeard," Rear Admiral Stetson continued, raising his voice loud enough to carry across the assembled onlookers, "and to recover the Imperial Crown Jewels which he stole from this very fort."

From where he sat onstage, Quint could actually see the murmur of consternation rippling through the assembled sailors and their officers. The Navy had expended what Quint considered a gratifyingly significant effort to hush up his theft of the Crown Jewels, rightfully fearing the damage to their Empire's reputation that such a scandal might cause. That Rear Admiral Stetson had just confirmed the inevitable scuttlebutt surrounding the manhunt for Captain Redbeard sent a ripple of shock through the watching crowd.

"I have, sir," Vanessa said, saluting once more. There was a slight crinkling about her eyes. It was an expression he knew well—not a smile, exactly, but the satisfied look from across the chessboard she got just before pronouncing checkmate.

"Show me," Rear Admiral Stetson ordered.

Vanessa obeyed, producing a ring of keys from her jacket and meticulously unlocking the chest's locks, a process which stretched on for nearly a minute. Quint supposed that, considering the trouble she'd gone through in order to retrieve them from him in the first place, he couldn't fault her for the increased security.

Not that it would do her any good.

Finally, the last tumbler clicked into place and the final latch opened. Vanessa glanced to Stetson, who nodded, and threw open the chest.

This time an audible gasp echoed through the crowd as the Imperial Crown Jewels lay exposed and glittering beneath the bright tropical sun: the Pearl Knife, the Emperor's Carcanet, the Queen Mother's Rings, and countless other official regalia belonging to the Empire's head of state. The gemstones each were inset with were mined from across the islands, representing the tribute the Empire enacted upon its subject isles. Each of the Crown Jewels was priceless in its own right, but together they formed a potent symbol of the Empress's dominion over the Archipelago.

And Quint Thatch was going to steal them all.

"Rear Admiral," Vanessa said, coming to her feet with another salute. "I present to you the Imperial Crown Jewels, and commit them to the safekeeping of Fort Amell."

"As I commend you for your valiant actions in retrieving them," Stetson said, smiling thinly. "I understand you have apprehended the criminal responsible for their theft?"

"I have," Vanessa said after a brief hesitation. She turned to the bulky guards flanking Rustbucket and gestured them forward. Rustbucket offered no resistance, though he frantically shook his head from side to side and did his best to protest around the gag in his mouth.

"This is the pirate styling himself Captain Redbeard?" Stetson asked, squinting at Rustbucket, whose beard was little more than a wild tuft of orange sprouting from his chin.

Vanessa hesitated again, then gave a curt nod. "Aye, sir."

"Thought he'd have a bigger beard," Stetson muttered, barely loud enough for Quint to hear. He turned back to the waiting crowd, gesturing as he did so for Vanessa to shut the lid of the chest and locked it. There was an audible sigh of disappointment from the spectators as the glittering Crown Jewels were hidden from sight once again.

"Captain Redbeard," Stetson said, allegedly to Rustbucket but clearly intending for his words to be heard by every soul present. He unfurled a parchment scroll and began to read in his high, quavering voice. "For your many and sundry crimes against Her Majesty the Empress and the Empire she controls, including but not limited to the following: Piracy, Conspiracy, Rebellion, Shipjacking, Impersonation of a Cleric, Theft, Fraud, Smuggling..."

Quint tuned out the list of his crimes, which was long and not remotely close to comprehensive. Instead his gaze was fixed on where Rustbucket and Vanessa stood center stage, the chest containing the Crown Jewels beside them.

"They couldn't have found their mark better if they were professional actors," he murmured approvingly to Ophelia. "You ready to ditch this shindig?"

"Aye, Cap'n," Ophelia nodded, grinning.

They stood in unison. The heads of the other high-ranking officers turned to stare curiously up at them, as did many of those still in the audience.

"...Evasion of Taxes," Stetson droned on before them, oblivious. "Gross Indecency, Petty Theft—"

"Begging your pardon," Quint said, loudly clearing his throat. "But I object to that last. Weren't nothing petty about it."

Every eye in the square was on him now. And, though he was no actor, Quint Thatch found himself enjoying the spotlight.

Out of the corner of his eye he saw the faces of those assembled upon the stage craning towards him, their expressions shocked and disbelieving—none more so than Rustbucket, who looked up at Quint as if his former captain were the Angel of Justice in all his terrible glory. Or Vanessa, who was staring at Quint with a mixture of recognition and the dawning horror of someone who'd just come home to find their family dog had made a mess on the carpet. Her mouth shaped his name.

"I *beg* your pardon, sailor," Stetson said, his high voice growing positively shrill as he recovered the power of speech. "Who exactly do you think you are, that you can interrupt official Imperial matters of state—"

"Ain't it obvious?" Quint grinned as he tossed the bicorn hat from his head and yanked off the fake beard, eliciting a gasp from somewhere in the audience. He sketched a courtly bow and said, in a voice that resounded off the walls of the fort above: "I'm Captain Redbeard, mate."

Someone in the crowd screamed. Nearer at hand, one of the admirals muttered to a commodore, "that's hardly more of a beard than the bald one's got."

Quint ignored them both. He'd only been growing it a few months, after all.

What he couldn't ignore were the unfriendly gazes of the guards stationed nearest the stage as they lowered their muskets from their shoulders.

"None of that!" Ophelia called to them, her hands flying to her coat and pulling out a pair of matchlock pistols, which she levelled at the guards. "Let's let the man say his piece, eh?"

The guards hesitated, though Quint suspected their resolve wouldn't waver for long. Nor did he need them to.

He took a step closer, Ophelia moving beside him as carefully as if this were a dance long rehearsed, until the two of them occupied the same eight-foot square in the center of the stage as Rustbucket and the Crown Jewels.

"If you're *really* Captain Redbeard," Rear Admiral Stetson said scornfully, though he could not quite conceal the faint tremor in his voice, "than you surely must know that you're hopelessly outnumbered and outgunned. What exactly is your plan, here?"

"Thought that was obvious, too," Quint replied cheerfully. "I'm here to retrieve what I rightfully stole from you."

With that, he lifted his foot and stomped down twice upon the stage, sending a hollow *thwunk-thwunk* echoing across the square.

Nothing happened.

"Redbeard," Vanessa said, her voice low and disbelieving. Quint was briefly thankful she had not used his given name, which she alone of the gathered Imperials knew. "What are you—"

"Hold on," he said, and stomped twice more. Again, nothing.

"Guards!" Stetson shouted, waving both hands over his head. "Don't just *stand* there! Apprehend them!"

"Cap'n," Ophelia said, her face going white even under her makeup as the guards obeyed, levelling their rifles at the two pirates onstage.

"Just give me a—" Quint started to say, as beside him Rustbucket whimpered something unintelligible through his gag. Quint raised his foot to stomp a third time, only to hear a groan of ancient timbers creaking. Suddenly the stage shifted beneath Quint's feet, lurching like a ship caught in a gale, then fell away entirely, sending them tumbling down into darkness.

Acknowledgements

The first and biggest thank you is to my wonderful wife, Megan. This book would not have been possible without her encouragement, support, and love. I doubt I could have written it as quickly if she hadn't wanted to read a new chapter daily. Thank you, my love, for being the wind in my sails.

Thank you also to my mom, to whom Quint's own Ma owes a great deal. Both of these women have persevered through grief to become the centers of the community they build around themselves. Mom, you're the strongest person I know—thank you for everything.

And a special thank you to my beta readers, who were instrumental in shaping this book into what it has become. To Cameron, without whom I would not have even one novel published, let alone four. To Emily, Natalia, and Rebecca for turning a TikTok connection into an actual friendship and community. And to Chase and Adelyn, for always reading anything I send you without fail.

I love you all and I am so very grateful.

About the Author

Marshall J. Moore is a writer, traveler, and martial artist who was born and raised on Kwajalein, a tiny Pacific island. He is the author of the Rites of Resurrection trilogy, a fantasy series about a necromancer soldier who investigates murders within his city. Marshall has trained a professional mercenary in unarmed combat, once sold a thousand dollars' worth of teapots to Jackie Chan, and on one occasion was tracked down by a bounty hunter for owing $300 in overdue fees to the Los Angeles Public Library. He lives in Atlanta, Georgia, with his wife Megan and their two cats Delilah and Furiosa.

marshalljmoore.com